KING SOLOMON'S MINES
and
ALLAN QUATERMAIN

King Solomon's Mines

AND

Allan Quatermain

H. RIDER HAGGARD

WORDSWORTH CLASSICS

For my husband
ANTHONY JOHN RANSON
with love from your wife, the publisher.
Eternally grateful for your unconditional love,
not just for me but for our children,
Simon, Andrew and Nichola Trayler

Readers who are interested in other titles from
Wordsworth Editions are invited to visit our website at
www.wordsworth-editions.com

For our latest list and a full mail-order service, contact
Bibliophile Books, 5 Datapoint, South Crescent, London E16 4TL
TEL: +44 (0)20 7474 2474 FAX: +44 (0)20 7474 8589
ORDERS: orders@bibliophilebooks.com
WEBSITE: www.bibliophilebooks.com

This edition of *King Solomon's Mines* first published in 1998 by
Wordsworth Editions Limited
8B East Street, Ware, Hertfordshire SG12 9HJ
Allan Quatermain added in 2009

ISBN 978 1 84022 628 7

Text © Wordsworth Editions Limited 1998 and 2009

Wordsworth® is a registered trademark of
Wordsworth Editions Limited,
the company founded by Michael Trayler in 1987

Typeset in Great Britain by Antony Gray
Printed and bound by Clays Ltd, St Ives plc

Contents

KING SOLOMON'S MINES

ALLAN QUATERMAIN

King Solomon's Mines

INTRODUCTION

Now that this book is printed, and about to be given to the world, a sense of its shortcomings, both in style and contents, weighs very heavily upon me. As regards the latter, I can only say that it does not pretend to be a full account of everything we did and saw. There are many things connected with our journey into Kuku-analand that I should have liked to dwell upon at length, to which, as it is, I have scarcely alluded. Amongst these are the curious legends which I collected about the chain armour that saved us from destruction in the great battle of Loo, and also as to the 'Silent Ones' or Colossi at the mouth of the stalactite cave. Again, if I had given way to my own impulses, I should have wished to go into the differences, some of which are to my mind very suggestive, between the Zulu and Kukuana dialects. Also a few pages might have been devoted profitably to the consideration of the indigenous flora and fauna of Kukuanaland.* Then there remains the most interesting subject – that, as it is, has only been touched on incidentally – of the magnificent system of military organisation in force in that country, which, in my opinion, is much superior to that inaugurated by Chaka in Zululand, inasmuch as it permits of even more rapid mobilisation, and does not necessitate the employment of the pernicious system of forced celibacy. Lastly, I have scarcely spoken of the domestic and

---

* I discovered eight varieties of antelope, with which I was previously totally unacquainted, and many new species of plants, for the most part of the bulbous tribe. A.Q.

family customs of the Kukuanas, many of which are exceedingly quaint, or of their proficiency in the art of smelting and welding metals. This science they carry to considerable perfection, of which a good example is to be seen in their *tollas*, or heavy throwing knives, the backs of these weapons being made of hammered iron and the edges of beautiful steel, welded with great skill on to the iron frames.

The fact of the matter is, I thought, with Sir Henry Curtis and Captain Good, that the best plan would be to tell my story in a plain, straightforward manner, and to leave these matters to be dealt with subsequently in whatever way ultimately may appear to be desirable. In the meanwhile I shall, of course, be delighted to give all information in my power to anybody interested in such things.

And now it only remains for me to offer apologies for my blunt way of writing. I can but say in excuse of it that I am more accustomed to handle a rifle than a pen, and cannot make any pretence to the grand literary flights and flourishes which I see in novels – for sometimes I like to read a novel. I suppose they – the flights and flourishes – are desirable, and I regret not being able to supply them. At the same time I cannot help thinking that simple things are always the most impressive, and that books are easier to understand when – like the Bible – they are written in plain language, though perhaps I have no right to set up an opinion on such a matter. 'A sharp spear', runs the Kukuana saying, 'needs no polish;' and on the same principle I venture to hope that a true story, however strange it may be, does not require to be decked out in fine words.

ALLAN QUATERMAIN

CHAPTER I

I Meet Sir Henry Curtis

It is a curious thing that at my age – I shall never see sixty again – I should find myself taking up a pen to try to write a history. I wonder what sort of a history it will be when I have finished it, if ever I come to the end of the trip! I have done a good many things in my life, which seems a long one to me, owing to my having begun work so young, perhaps. At an age when other boys are at school I was earning my living in the old colony and Natal. I have been trading, hunting, fighting or exploring ever since. And yet it is only eight months ago that I made my pile. It is a big pile now that I have got it – I don't yet know how big – but I do not think I would go through the last fifteen or sixteen months again for it; no, not if I knew that I should come out safe at the end, pile and all. But then I am a timid man, and dislike violence; moreover, I am almost sick of adventure. I wonder why I am going to write this book; it is not in my line. I am not a literary man, though very devoted to the Old Testament and also to the *Ingoldsby Legends*. Let me try to set down my reasons, just to see if I have any.

First reason: Because Sir Henry Curtis and Captain John Good asked me.

Second reason: Because I am laid up here at Durban with the pain in my left leg. Ever since that confounded lion got hold of me I have been liable to this trouble, and being rather bad just now, it makes me limp more than ever. There must be some poison in a lion's teeth, otherwise how is it that when your wounds are healed they break out again, generally, mark you, at the same time of year that you got your mauling? It is a hard thing when one has shot sixty-five lions or more, as I have in the course of my life, that the sixty-sixth should chew your leg like a quid of tobacco. It breaks the routine of the thing and, putting other considerations aside, I am an orderly man and don't like that. This is by the way.

Third reason: Because I want my boy Harry, who is over there at the hospital in London studying to become a doctor, to have something to amuse him and keep him out of mischief for a week or so. Hospital work must sometimes pall and grow rather dull, for even of cutting up dead bodies there may come satiety, and as this history will not be dull, whatever else it may be, it will put a little life into things for a day or two while Harry is reading of our adventures.

Fourth reason and last: Because I am going to tell the strangest story that I remember. It may seem a queer thing to say, especially considering that there is no woman in it – except Foulata. Stop though! There is Gagaoola, if she was a woman and not a fiend. But she was a hundred at least, and therefore not marriageable, so I don't count her. At any rate, I can safely say that there is not a *petticoat* in the whole history.

Well, I had better come to the yoke. It is a stiff place, and I feel as though I were bogged up to the axle. But *sutjes, sutjes* – as the Boers say – I am sure I don't know how they spell it – softly does it. A strong team will come through at last, that is if they are not too poor. You can never do anything with poor oxen. Now to make a start.

I, Allan Quatermain, of Durban, Natal, Gentleman, make oath and say – That's how I headed my deposition before the magistrate about poor Khiva's and Ventvögel's sad deaths; but somehow it doesn't seem quite the right way to begin a book. And, besides, am I a gentleman? What is a gentleman? I don't quite know, and yet I have had to do with niggers – no, I will scratch out that word 'niggers', for I do not like it: I've known natives who *are*, and so you will say, Harry, my boy, before you have done with this tale, and I have known mean whites with lots of money and fresh out from home, too, who *are not*.

At any rate, I was born a gentleman, though I have been nothing but a poor travelling trader and hunter all my life. Whether I have remained so I know not, you must judge of that. Heaven knows

I've tried. I have killed many men in my time, yet I have never slain wantonly or stained my hand in innocent blood, but only in self-defence. The Almighty gave us our lives, and I suppose He meant us to defend them, at least I have always acted on that, and I hope it will not be brought up against me when my clock strikes. There, there, it is a cruel and wicked world, and for a timid man I have been mixed up in a deal of fighting. I cannot tell the rights of it, but at any rate I have never stolen, though once I cheated a Kafir out of a herd of cattle. But then he had done me a dirty turn, and it has troubled me ever since into the bargain.

Well, it is eighteen months or so ago since first I met Sir Henry Curtis and Captain Good. It was in this way. I had been up elephant hunting beyond Bamangwato, and had met with bad luck. Everything went wrong that trip, and to top up with I got the fever badly. So soon as I was well enough I trekked down to the Diamond Fields, sold such ivory as I had, together with my wagon and oxen, discharged my hunters, and took the postcart to the Cape. After spending a week in Cape Town finding that they overcharged me at the hotel, and having seen everything there was to see, including the botanical gardens, which seem to me likely to confer a great benefit on the country, and the new Houses of Parliament, which I expect will do nothing of the sort, I determined to go back to Natal by the *Dunkeld*, then lying at the docks waiting for the *Edinburgh Castle* due in from England. I took my berth and went aboard, and that afternoon the Natal passengers from the *Edinburgh Castle* transhipped, and we weighed and put out to sea.

Among these passengers who came on board were two who excited my curiosity. One, a gentleman of about thirty, was perhaps the biggest-chested and longest-armed man I ever saw. He had yellow hair, a thick yellow beard, clear-cut features, and large grey eyes set deep in his head. I never saw a finer-looking man, and somehow he reminded me of an ancient Dane. Not that I know much of ancient Danes, though I knew a modern Dane who did me out of ten pounds; but I remember once seeing a picture of some of those gentry, who, I take it, were a kind of

white Zulus. They were drinking out of big horns, and their long
hair hung down their backs. As I looked at my friend standing
there by the companion-ladder, I thought that if he only let his
grow a little, put one of those chain shirts on to his great
shoulders, and took hold of a battle-axe and a horn mug, he
might have sat as a model for that picture By the way it is a
curious thing, and just shows how the blood will out, I
discovered afterwards that Sir Henry Curtis, for that was the big
man's name, is of Danish blood.* Also he reminded me strongly
of somebody else, but at the time I could not remember who it
was.

The other man, who stood talking to Sir Henry, was stout and
dark, and of quite a different cut. I suspected at once that he was a
naval officer; I don't know why, but it is difficult to mistake a navy
man. I have gone on shooting trips with several of them in the
course of my life, and they have always proved themselves the best
and bravest and nicest fellows I ever met, though sadly given,
some of them, to the use of profane language. I asked a page or
two back, what is a gentleman? I'll answer the question now: a
Royal Naval officer is, in a general sort of way, though of course
there may be a black sheep among them here and there. I fancy it
is just the wide seas and the breath of God's winds that wash their
hearts and blow the bitterness out of their minds and make them
what men ought to be.

Well, to return, I proved right again; I ascertained that the dark
man was a naval officer, a lieutenant of thirty-one, who, after
seventeen years' service, had been turned out of her majesty's
employ with the barren honour of a commander's rank, because it
was impossible that he should be promoted. This is what people
who serve the queen have to expect: to be shot out into the cold
world to find a living just when they are beginning really to
understand their work, and to reach the prime of life. I suppose
they don't mind it, but for my own part I had rather earn my bread

* Mr Quatermain's ideas about ancient Danes seem to be rather confused;
we have always understood that they were dark-haired people. Probably he
was thinking of Saxons. ED.

as a hunter. One's halfpence are as scarce perhaps, but you do not get so many kicks.

The officer's name I found out – by referring to the passengers' list – was Good – Captain John Good. He was broad, of medium height, dark, stout, and rather a curious man to look at. He was so very neat and so very clean-shaved, and he always wore an eyeglass in his right eye. It seemed to grow there, for it had no string, and he never took it out except to wipe it. At first I thought he used to sleep in it, but afterwards I found that this was a mistake. He put it in his trousers pocket when he went to bed, together with his false teeth, of which he had two beautiful sets that, my own being none of the best, have often caused me to break the tenth commandment. But I am anticipating.

Soon after we had got under way evening closed in, and brought with it very dirty weather. A keen breeze sprung up off land, and a kind of aggravated Scotch mist soon drove everybody from the deck. As for the *Dunkeld*, she is a flat-bottomed punt, and going up light as she was, she rolled very heavily. It almost seemed as though she would go right over, but she never did. It was quite impossible to walk about, so I stood near the engines where it was warm, and amused myself with watching the pendulum, which was fixed opposite to me, swinging backwards and forwards as the vessel rolled, and marking the angle she touched at each lurch.

'That pendulum's wrong; it is not properly weighted,' suddenly said a somewhat testy voice at my shoulder. Looking round I saw the naval officer whom I had noticed when the passengers came aboard.

'Indeed, now what makes you think so?' I asked.

'Think so. I don't think at all. Why there – ' as she righted herself after a roll, 'if the ship had really rolled to the degree that thing pointed to, then she would never have rolled again, that's all. But it is just like these merchant skippers, they always are so confoundedly careless.'

Just then the dinner-bell rang, and I was not sorry, for it is a dreadful thing to have to listen to an officer of the Royal Navy when he gets on to that subject. I only know one worse thing, and it is to hear a merchant skipper express his candid opinion of officers of the Royal Navy.

Captain Good and I went down to dinner together, and there we found Sir Henry Curtis already seated. He and Captain Good were placed together, and I sat opposite to them. The captain and I soon fell into talk about shooting and what not; he asking me many questions, for he is very inquisitive about all sorts of things, and I answering them as well as I could. Presently he got on to elephants.

'Ah, sir,' called out somebody who was sitting near me, 'you've reached the right man for that; Hunter Quatermain should be able to tell you about elephants if anybody can.'

Sir Henry, who had been sitting quite quiet listening to our talk, started visibly.

'Excuse me, sir,' he said, leaning forward across the table, and speaking in a low deep voice, a very suitable voice, it seemed to me, to come out of those great lungs. 'Excuse me, sir, but is your name Allan Quatermain?'

I said that it was.

The big man made no further remark, but I heard him mutter 'fortunate' into his beard.

Presently dinner came to an end, and as we were leaving the saloon Sir Henry strolled up and asked me if we would come into his cabin to smoke a pipe. We accepted, and he led the way to the *Dunkeld* deck cabin, and a very good cabin it is. It had been two cabins, but when Sir Garnet Wolseley or one of those big swells went down the coast in the *Dunkeld*, they knocked away the partition and have never put it up again. There was a sofa in the cabin, and a little table in front of it. Sir Henry sent the steward for a bottle of whisky, and the three of us sat down and lit our pipes.

'Mr Quatermain,' said Sir Henry Curtis, when the man had brought the whisky and lit the lamp, 'the year before last about this time, you were, I believe, at a place called Bamangwato, to the north of the Transvaal.'

'I was,' I answered, rather surprised that this gentleman should be so well acquainted with my movements, which were not, so far as I was aware, considered of general interest.

'You were trading there, were you not?' put in Captain Good, in his quick way.

'I was. I took up a wagonload of goods, made a camp outside the settlement, and stopped till I had sold them.'

Sir Henry was sitting opposite to me in a Madeira chair, his arms leaning on the table. He now looked up, fixing his large grey eyes full upon my face. There was a curious anxiety in them, I thought.

'Did you happen to meet a man called Neville there?'

'Oh, yes; he outspanned alongside of me for a fortnight to rest his oxen before going on to the interior. I had a letter from a lawyer a few months back, asking me if I knew what had become of him, which I answered to the best of my ability at the time.'

'Yes,' said Sir Henry, 'your letter was forwarded to me. You said in it that the gentleman called Neville left Bamangwato at the beginning of May in a wagon with a driver, a *voorlooper*, and a Kafir hunter called Jim, announcing his intention of trekking if possible as far as Inyati, the extreme trading post in the Matabele country, where he would sell his wagon and proceed on foot. You also said that he did sell his wagon, for six months afterwards you saw the wagon in the possession of a Portuguese trader, who told you that he had bought it at Inyati from a white man whose name he had forgotten, and that he believed the white man with the native servant had started off for the interior on a shooting trip.'

'Yes.'

Then came a pause.

'Mr Quatermain,' said Sir Henry suddenly, 'I suppose you know or can guess nothing more of the reasons of my – of Mr Neville's journey to the northward, or as to what point that journey was directed?'

'I heard something,' I answered, and stopped. The subject was one which I did not care to discuss.

Sir Henry and Captain Good looked at each other, and Captain Good nodded.

'Mr Quatermain,' went on the former, 'I am going to tell you a story, and ask your advice, and perhaps your assistance. The agent who forwarded me your letter told me that I might rely upon it implicitly, as you were, he said, well known and universally respected in Natal, and especially noted for your discretion.'

I bowed and drank some whisky and water to hide my confusion, for I am a modest man – and Sir Henry went on.

'Mr Neville was my brother.'

'Oh,' I said, starting, for now I knew of whom Sir Henry had reminded me when first I saw him. His brother was a much smaller man and had a dark beard, but now that I thought of it, he possessed eyes of the same shade of grey and with the same keen look in them: the features too were not unlike.

'He was,' went on Sir Henry, 'my only and younger brother, and till five years ago I do not suppose that we were ever a month away from each other. But just about five years ago a misfortune befell us, as sometimes does happen in families. We quarrelled bitterly, and I behaved unjustly to my brother in my anger.'

Here Captain Good nodded his head vigorously to himself. The ship gave a big roll just then, so that the looking-glass, which was fixed opposite us to starboard, was for a moment nearly over our heads, and as I was sitting with my hands in my pockets and staring upwards, I could see him nodding like anything.

'As I dare say you know,' went on Sir Henry, 'if a man dies intestate, and has no property but land, real property it is called in England, it all descends to his eldest son. It so happened that just at the time when we quarrelled our father died intestate. He had put off making his will until it was too late. The result was that my brother, who had not been brought up to any profession, was left without a penny. Of course it would have been my duty to provide for him, but at the time the quarrel between us was so bitter that I did not – to my shame I say it (and he sighed deeply) – offer to do anything. It was not that I grudged him justice, but I waited for him to make advances and he made none. I am sorry to trouble you with all this, Mr Quatermain, but I must to make things clear, eh, Good?'

'Quite so, quite so,' said the captain. 'Mr Quatermain will, I am sure, keep this history to himself.'

'Of course,' said I, for I rather pride myself on my discretion, for which, as Sir Henry had heard, I have some repute.

'Well,' went on Sir Henry, 'my brother had a few hundred pounds to his account at the time. Without saying anything to me he drew out this paltry sum, and, having adopted the name of Neville, started off for South Africa in the wild hope of making a fortune. This I learnt afterwards. Some three years passed, and I heard nothing of my brother, though I wrote several times. Doubtless the letters never reached him. But as time went on I grew more and more troubled about him. I found out, Mr Quatermain, that blood is thicker than water.'

'That's true,' said I, thinking of my boy Harry.

'I found out, Mr Quatermain, that I would have given half my fortune to know that my brother George, the only relation I possess, was safe and well, and that I should see him again.'

'But you never did, Curtis,' jerked out Captain Good, glancing at the big man's face.

'Well, Mr Quatermain, as time went on I became more and more anxious to find out if my brother was alive or dead, and if alive to get him home again. I set enquiries on foot, and your letter was one of the results. So far as it went it was satisfactory, for it showed that till lately George was alive, but it did not go far enough. So, to cut a long story short, I made up my mind to come out and look for him myself, and Captain Good was so kind as to come with me.'

'Yes,' said the captain; 'nothing else to do, you see. Turned out by my Lords of the Admiralty to starve on half pay. And now perhaps, sir, you will tell us what you know of the gentleman called Neville.'

CHAPTER 2

The Legend of Solomon's Mines

'What was it that you heard about my brother's journey at Bamangwato?' asked Sir Henry, as I paused to fill my pipe before replying to Captain Good.

'I heard this,' I answered, 'and I have never mentioned it to a soul till today. I heard that he was starting for Solomon's Mines.'

'Solomon's Mines!' ejaculated both my hearers at once. 'Where are they?'

'I don't know,' I said; 'I know where they are said to be. Once I saw the peaks of the mountains that border them, but there were a hundred and thirty miles of desert between me and them, and I am not aware that any white man ever got across it save one. But perhaps the best thing I can do is to tell you the legend of Solomon's Mines, as I know it, you passing your word not to reveal anything I tell you without my permission. Do you agree to that? I have my reasons for asking.'

Sir Henry nodded, and Captain Good replied 'Certainly, certainly.'

'Well,' I began, 'as you may guess, generally speaking, elephant hunters are a rough set of men, who do not trouble themselves with much beyond the facts of life and the ways of Kafirs. But here and there you meet a man who takes the trouble to collect traditions from the natives, and tries to make out a little piece of the history of this dark land. It was such a one as this who first told me the legend of Solomon's Mines, now a matter of nearly thirty years ago. That was when I was on my first elephant hunt in the Matabele country. His name was Evans, and he was killed the following year, poor fellow, by a wounded buffalo, and lies buried near the Zambesi Falls. I was telling Evans one night, I remember, of some wonderful workings I had found whilst hunting koodoo and eland in what is now the Lydenburg district of the Transvaal. I see they have come across these workings again lately in prospecting for gold, but I knew of them years ago. There is a great wide wagon road cut out of the solid rock, and leading to the mouth of the working or gallery. Inside the mouth of this gallery are stacks of gold quartz piled up ready for roasting, which shows that the workers, whoever they were, must have left in a hurry. Also, about twenty paces in, the gallery is built across, and a beautiful bit of masonry it is.

' "Aye," said Evans, "but I will spin you a queerer yarn than that;" and he went on to tell me how he had found in the far interior a ruined city, which he believed to be the Ophir of the Bible, and, by the way, other more learned men have said the same long since poor Evans's time. I was, I remember, listening open-eared to all these wonders, for I was young at the time, and this story of an ancient civilisation and of the treasures which those old Jewish or Phoenician adventurers used to extract from a country long since lapsed into the darkest barbarism took a great hold upon my imagination, when suddenly he said to me, "Lad, did you ever hear of the Suliman Mountains up to the northwest of the Mashukulumbwe country?" I told him I never had. "Ah, well," he said, "that is where Solomon really had his mines, his diamond mines, I mean."

' "How do you know that?" I asked.

' "Know it! why, what is 'Suliman' but a corruption of Solomon?* Besides, an old Isanusi or witch doctress up in the Manica country told me all about it. She said that the people who lived across those mountains were a 'branch' of the Zulus, speaking a dialect of Zulu, but finer and bigger men even; that there lived among them great wizards, who had learnt their art from white men when 'all the world was dark', and who had the secret of a wonderful mine of 'bright stones'."

'Well, I laughed at this story at the time, though it interested

* Suliman is the Arabic form of Solomon. ED.

me, for the Diamond Fields were not discovered then, but poor Evans went off and was killed, and for twenty years I never thought any more of the matter. However, just twenty years afterwards – and that is a long time, gentlemen; an elephant hunter does not often live for twenty years at his business – I heard something more definite about Suliman's Mountains and the country which lies behind them. I was up beyond the Manica country, at a place called Sitanda's Kraal, and a miserable place it was, for a man could get nothing to eat, and there was but little game about. I had an attack of fever, and was in a bad way generally, when one day a Portugee arrived with a single companion – a half-breed. Now I know your low-class Delagoa Portugee well. There is no greater devil unhung in a general way, battening as he does upon human agony and flesh in the shape of slaves. But this was quite a different type of man to the mean fellows whom I had been accustomed to meet; indeed, in appearance he reminded me more of the polite doms I have read about for he was tall and thin, with large dark eyes, and curling grey mustachios. We talked together a little, for he could speak broken English, and I understood a little Portugee, and he told me that his name was José Silvestre, and that he had a place near Delagoa Bay. When he went on next day with his half-breed companion, he said goodbye, taking off his hat quite in the old style. "Goodbye, señor," he said; "if ever we meet again I shall be the richest man in the world, and I will remember you." I laughed a little – I was too weak to laugh much – and watched him strike out for the great desert to the west, wondering if he were mad, or what he thought he was going to find there.

'A week passed, and I got the better of my fever. One evening I was sitting on the ground in front of the little tent I had with me, chewing the last leg of a miserable fowl I had bought from a native for a bit of cloth worth twenty fowls, and staring at the hot red sun sinking down over the desert, when suddenly I saw a figure, apparently that of a European, for it wore a coat, on the slope of the rising ground opposite to me, about three hundred yards away. The figure crept along on its hands and knees, then it got up and staggered forward a few yards on its legs, only to fall and crawl again. Seeing that it must be somebody in distress, I sent one of my hunters to help him, and presently he arrived, and who do you suppose it turned out to be?'

'José Silvestre, of course,' said Captain Good.

'Yes, José Silvestre, or rather his skeleton and a little skin. His face was bright yellow with bilious fever, and his large dark eyes stood nearly out of his head, for all the flesh had gone. There was nothing but yellow parchment-like skin, white hair, and the gaunt bones sticking up beneath.

' "Water! for the sake of Christ, water!" he moaned and I saw that his lips were cracked, and his tongue, which protruded between them, was swollen and blackish.

'I gave him water with a little milk in it, and he drank it in great gulps, two quarts or so, without stopping. I would not let him have any more. Then the fever took him again, and he fell down and began to rave about Suliman's Mountains, and the diamonds, and the desert. I carried him into the tent and did what I could for him, which was little enough; but I saw how it must end. About eleven o'clock he grew quieter, and I lay down for a little rest and went to sleep. At dawn I woke again, and in the half light saw Silvestre sitting up, a strange, gaunt form, and gazing out towards the desert. Presently the first ray of the sun shot right across the wide plain before us till it reached the faraway crest of one of the tallest of the Suliman Mountains more than a hundred miles away.

' "There it is!" cried the dying man in Portuguese, and pointing with his long, thin arm, "but I shall never reach it, never. No one will ever reach it!"

'Suddenly he paused, and seemed to take a resolution. "Friend," he said, turning towards me, "are you there? My eyes grow dark."

' "Yes," I said; "yes, lie down now, and rest."

' "Aye," he answered, "I shall rest soon, I have time to rest – all eternity. Listen, I am dying! You have been good to me. I will give you the writing. Perhaps you will get there if you can live to pass the desert, which has killed my poor servant and me."

'Then he groped in his shirt and brought out what I thought was a Boer tobacco pouch made of the skin of the *swart-vet-pens* or sable antelope. It was fastened with a little strip of hide, what we call a *rimpi*, and this he tried to loose, but could not. He handed it to me. "Untie it," he said. I did so, and extracted a bit of torn yellow linen, on which something was written in rusty letters. Inside this rag was a paper.

'Then he went on feebly, for he was growing weak: "The paper has all that is on the linen. It took me years to read. Listen: my ancestor, a political refugee from Lisbon, and one of the first Portuguese who landed on these shores, wrote that when he was dying on those mountains which no white foot ever pressed before or since. His name was José da Silvestra, and he lived three hundred years ago. His slave, who waited for him on this side of the mountains, found him dead, and brought the writing home to Delagoa. It has been in the family ever since, but none have cared to read it, till at last I did. And I have lost my life over it, but another may succeed, and become the richest man in the world – the richest man in the world. Only give it to no one, señor; go yourself!"

'Then he began to wander again, and in an hour it was all over.

'God rest him! he died very quietly, and I buried him deep, with big boulders on his breast; so I do not think that the jackals can have dug him up. Then I came away.'

'Aye, but the document?' said Sir Henry, in a tone of deep interest.

'Yes, the document; what was in it?' added the captain.

'Well, gentlemen, if you like I will tell you. I have never shown it to anybody yet except to a drunken old Portuguese trader who translated it for me, and had forgotten all about it by the next morning. The original rag is at my home in Durban, together with poor Dom José's translation, but I have the English rendering in my pocketbook, and a facsimile of the map, if it can be called a map. Here it is.'

I, José da Silvestra, who am now dying of hunger in the little cave where no snow is, on the north side of the nipple of the southernmost of the two mountains I have named Sheba's Breasts, write this in the year 1590 with a cleft bone upon a remnant of my raiment, my blood being the ink. If my slave should find it when he comes, and should bring it to Delagoa, let my friend [name illegible] bring the matter to the knowledge of the king, that he may send an army which, if they live through the desert and the mountains, and can overcome the brave Kukuanas and their devilish arts, to which end many priests should be brought, will make him the richest king since Solomon. With my own eyes have I seen the countless diamonds stored in Solomon's treasure chamber behind the White Death; but through the treachery of Gagool the witch-finder I could bring nought away, scarcely my life. Let him who comes follow the map and climb the snow of Sheba's left breast till he reaches the nipple, on the north side of which is the great road Solomon made, from whence three days' journey to the king's palace. Let him kill Gagool. Pray for my soul. Farewell.

JOSÉ DA SILVESTRA*

When I had finished reading the above, and shown the copy of the map, drawn by the dying hand of the old dom with his blood for ink, there followed a silence of astonishment.

'Well,' said Captain Good, 'I have been round the world twice, and put in at most ports, but may I be hung for a mutineer if ever I heard a yarn like this out of a story book, or in it either, for the matter of that.'

---

* Eu Josê da Silvestra que estou morrendo de fome ná pequena cova onde não ha neve ao lado norte do bico mais ao sul das duas montanhas que chamei seio de Sheba; escrevo isto no anno 1590; escrevo isto com um pedaço d'ôsso n' um farrapo de minha roupa e com sangue meu por tinta; se o meu escravo dér com isto quando venha ao levar para Lourenzo Marquez, que o meu amigo – leve a cousa ao conhecimento d'El Rei, para que possa mandar um exercito que, se desfiler pelo deserto e pelas montanhas e mesmo sobrepujar os bravos Kukuanas e suas artes diabolicas, pelo que se deviam trazer muitos padres Fara o Rei mais rico depois de Salomão. Com meus proprios olhos vé os di amantes sem conto guardados nas camaras do thesouro de Salomão a traz da morte branca, mas pela traição de Gagoal a feiticeira achadora, nada poderia levar, e apenas a minha vida. Quem vier siga o mappa e trepe pela neve de Sheba peito à esquerda até chegar ao bica, do lado norte do qual està a grande estrada do Salomão por elle feita, donde ha tres dias de jornada até ao Palacio do Rei. Mate Gagoal. Reze por minha alma. Adeos.

JOSÉ DA SILVESTRA

The sketchmap of the route to King Solomon's Mines

'It's a queer tale, Mr Quatermain,' said Sir Henry. 'I suppose you are not hoaxing us? It is, I know, sometimes thought allowable to take in a greenhorn.'

'If you think that, Sir Henry,' I said, much put out, and pocketing my paper – for I do not like to be thought one of those silly fellows who consider it witty to tell lies, and who are forever boasting to newcomers of extraordinary hunting adventures which never happened – 'if you think that, why, there is an end to the matter,' and I rose to go.

Sir Henry laid his large hand on my shoulder. 'Sit down, Mr Quatermain,' he said, 'I beg your pardon; I see very well you do not wish to deceive us, but the story sounded so strange that I could hardly believe it.'

'You shall see the original map and writing when we reach Durban,' I answered, somewhat mollified, for really when I came to consider the question it was scarcely wonderful that he should doubt my good faith.

'But,' I went on, 'I have not told you about your brother. I knew the man Jim who was with him. He was a Bechuana by birth, a good hunter, and for a native a very clever man. That morning on which Mr Neville was starting I saw Jim standing by my wagon and cutting up tobacco on the *disselboom*.

' "Jim," said I, "where are you off to this trip? Is it elephants?"

' "No, baas," he answered, "we are after something worth much more than ivory."

' "And what might that be?" I said, for I was curious. "Is it gold?"

' "No, baas, something worth more than gold," and he grinned.

'I asked no more questions, for I did not like to lower my dignity by seeming inquisitive, but I was puzzled. Presently Jim finished cutting his tobacco.

' "Baas," said he.

'I took no notice.

' "Baas," said he again.

' "Eh, boy, what is it?" I asked.

' "Baas, we are going after diamonds."

'Diamonds! why, then, you are steering in the wrong direction; you should head for the Fields.'

' "Baas, have you ever heard of Suliman's Berge?" – that is, Solomon's Mountains, Sir Henry.

' "Aye!"

' "Have you ever heard of the diamonds there?"

' "I have heard a foolish story. Jim."

' "It is no story, baas. Once I knew a woman who came from there, and reached Natal with her child, she told me. She is dead now."

' "Your master will feed the *aasvögels*" – that is, vultures – "Jim, if he tries to reach Suliman's country, and so will you if they can get any pickings off your worthless old carcass," said I.

'He grinned. "Mayhap, baas. Man must die; I'd rather like to try a new country myself; the elephants are getting worked out about here."

' "Ah! my boy," I said, "you wait till the 'pale old man' gets a grip of your yellow throat, and then we shall hear what sort of a tune you sing."

'Half an hour after that I saw Neville's wagon move off. Presently Jim came back running. "Goodbye, baas," he said. "I didn't like to start without bidding you goodbye, for I dare say you are right, and that we shall never trek south again."

' "Is your master really going to Suliman's Berge, Jim, or are you lying?"

' "No," he answered, "he is going. He told me he was bound to make his fortune somehow, or try to; so he might as well have a fling for the diamonds."

' "Oh!" I said; "wait a bit, Jim; will you take a note to your master, Jim, and promise not to give it to him till you reach Inyati?" which was some hundred miles off.

' "Yes, baas."

'So I took a scrap of paper, and wrote on it, "Let him who comes . . . climb the snow of Sheba's left breast, till he reaches the nipple, on the north side of which is Solomon's great road."

' "Now, Jim," I said, "when you give this to your master, tell him he had better follow the advice on it implicitly. You are not to give it to him now, because I don't want him back asking me questions which I won't answer. Now be off, you idle fellow, the wagon is nearly out of sight."

'Jim took the note and went, and that is all I know about your brother, Sir Henry; but I am much afraid . . . '

'Mr Quatermain,' said Sir Henry, 'I am going to look for my brother; I am going to trace him to Suliman's Mountains, and over them if necessary, till I find him, or until I know that he is dead. Will you come with me?'

I am, as I think I have said, a cautious man, indeed a timid one, and this suggestion frightened me. It seemed to me that to undertake such a journey would be to go to certain death, and putting other considerations aside, as I had a son to support, I could not afford to die just then.

'No, thank you, Sir Henry, I think I had rather not,' I answered. 'I am too old for wild-goose chases of that sort, and we should only end up like my poor friend Silvestre. I have a son dependent on me, so I cannot afford to risk my life foolishly.'

Both Sir Henry and Captain Good looked very disappointed.

'Mr Quatermain,' said the former, 'I am well off and I am bent upon this business. You may put the remuneration for your services at whatever figure you like in reason, and it shall be paid over to you before we start. Moreover, I will arrange in the event of anything untoward happening to us or to you, that your son shall be suitably provided for. You will see from this offer how necessary I think your presence. Also, if by chance we should reach this place and find diamonds they shall belong to you and Good equally. I do not want them. But of course that promise is worth nothing at all, though the same thing would apply to any ivory we may get. You may pretty well make your own terms with me, Mr Quatermain; and of course I shall pay all expenses.'

'Sir Henry,' said I, 'this is about the most liberal proposal I ever had; one not to be sneezed at by a poor hunter and trader. But the job is the biggest I have come across, and I must take time to think it over. I will give you my answer before we get to Durban.'

'Very good,' answered Sir Henry.

Then I said good-night and turned in, and dreamt about poor long-dead Silvestre and the diamonds.

CHAPTER 3

Umbopa Enters Our Service

It takes from four to five days, according to the speed of the vessel and the state of the weather, to run up from the Cape to Durban. Sometimes, if the landing is bad at East London, where they have not yet made that wonderful harbour they talk so much of, and sink such a mint of money in, a ship is delayed for twenty-four hours before the cargo boats can get out to take off the goods. But on this occasion we had not to wait at all, for there were no breakers on the bar to speak of, and the tugs came out at once with the long strings of ugly flat-bottomed boats behind them, into which the packages were bundled with a crash. It did not matter what they might be, over they went slapbang; whether they contained china or woollen goods they met with the same treatment. I saw one case holding four dozen of champagne smashed all to bits, and there was the champagne fizzing and boiling about in the bottom of the dirty cargo boat. It was a wicked waste, and evidently so the Kafirs in the boat thought, for they found a couple of unbroken bottles, and knocking off the necks drank the contents. But they had not allowed for the expansion caused by the fizz in the wine, and, feeling themselves swelling, rolled about in the bottom of the boat, calling out that the good liquor was *tagati* – that is, bewitched. I spoke to them from the vessel, and told them it was the white man's strongest medicine, and that they were as good as dead men. Those Kafirs went to the shore in a very great fright, and I do not think that they will touch champagne again.

Well, all the time that we were steaming up to Natal I was thinking over Sir Henry Curtis's offer. We did not speak any more on the subject for a day or two, though I told them many hunting yarns, all true ones. There is no need to tell lies about hunting, for so many curious things happen within the knowledge of a man whose business it is to hunt; but this is by the way.

At last, one beautiful evening in January, which is our hottest month, we steamed past the coast of Natal expecting to make Durban Point by sunset. It is a lovely coast all along from East London, with its red sandhills and wide sweeps of vivid green, dotted here and there with Kafir kraals, and bordered by a ribbon of white surf, which spouts up in pillars of foam where it hits the rocks. But just before you come to Durban there is a peculiar richness about the landscape. There are the sheer kloofs cut in the hills by the rushing rains of centuries, down which the rivers sparkle; there are the deep green of the bush, growing as God planted it, and the other greens of the mealie gardens and the sugar patches, while now and again a white house, smiling out at the placid sea, puts a finish and gives an air of homeliness to the scene. For to my mind, however beautiful a view may be, it requires the presence of man to make it complete, but perhaps that is because I have lived so much in the wilderness, and therefore know the value of civilisation, though to be sure it drives away the game. The Garden of Eden, no doubt, looked fair before man was, but I always think that it must have been fairer when Eve adorned it.

To return, we had miscalculated a little, and the sun was well down before we dropped anchor off the point, and heard the gun which told the good folks of Durban that the English mail was in. It was too late to think of getting over the bar that night, so we went comfortably to dinner, after seeing the mails carried off in the lifeboat.

When we came up again the moon was out, and shining so brightly over sea and shore that she almost paled the quick, large flashes from the lighthouse. From the shore floated sweet spicy odours that always remind me of hymns and missionaries, and in the windows of the houses on the Berea sparkled a hundred lights. From a large brig lying near also came the music of the sailors as they worked at getting the anchor up in order to be ready for the wind. Altogether it was a perfect night, such a night as you sometimes get in Southern Africa, and it threw a garment of peace over everybody as the moon threw a garment of silver over everything. Even the great bulldog, belonging to a sporting passenger, seemed to yield to its gentle influences, and forgetting his yearning to come to close quarters with a baboon in its cage on the fo'c'sle, snored heavily at the door of the cabin, dreaming no doubt that he had finished it, and happy in his dream.

We three – that is, Sir Henry Curtis, Captain Good and myself – went and sat by the wheel, and were quiet for a while.

'Well, Mr Quatermain,' said Sir Henry presently, 'have you been thinking about my proposals?'

'Aye,' echoed Captain Good, 'what do you think of them, Mr Quatermain? I hope that you are going to give us the pleasure of your company so far as Solomon's Mines, or wherever the gentleman you knew as Neville may have got to.'

I rose and knocked out my pipe before I answered. I had not made up my mind, and wanted an additional moment to decide. Before the burning tobacco had fallen into the sea I had decided; just that little extra second did the trick. It is often the way when you have been bothering a long time over a thing.

'Yes, gentlemen,' I said, sitting down again, 'I will go, and by your leave I will tell you why, and on what conditions. First for the terms which I ask.

'One. You are to pay all expenses, and any ivory or other valuables we may get is to be divided between Captain Good and myself.

'Two. That you give me five hundred pounds for my services on the trip before we start, I undertaking to serve you faithfully till you choose to abandon the enterprise or till we succeed, or disaster overtakes us.

'Three. That before we trek you execute a deed agreeing, in the event of my death or disablement, to pay my boy Harry, who is studying medicine over there in London, at Guy's Hospital, a sum of two hundred pounds a year for five years, by which time he ought to be able to earn a living for himself if he is worth his salt. That is all, I think, and I dare say you will say quite enough too.'

'No,' answered Sir Henry, 'I accept very gladly. I am bent upon this project, and would pay more than that for your help, considering the peculiar and exclusive knowledge which you possess.'

'Pity I did not ask it, then, but I won't go back on my word. And now that I have got my terms I will give you my reasons for making up my mind to go. First of all, gentlemen, I have been observing you both for the last few days, and if you will not think me impertinent I may say that I like you, and believe that we shall come up well to the yoke together. That is something, let me remark, when one has a long journey like this before one.

'And now as to the journey itself, I tell you flatly, Sir Henry and Captain Good, that I do not think it probable we can come out of it alive, that is, if we attempt to cross the Suliman Mountains. What was the fate of the old Dom da Silvestra three hundred years ago? What was the fate of his descendant twenty years ago? What has been your brother's fate? I tell you frankly, gentlemen, that as their fates were so I believe ours will be.'

I paused to watch the effect of my words. Captain Good looked a little uncomfortable, but Sir Henry's face did not change. 'We must take our chance,' he said.

'You may perhaps wonder,' I went on, 'why, if I think this, I, who am, as I told you, a timid man, should undertake such a journey. It is for two reasons. First, I am a fatalist, and believe that my time is appointed to come without reference to my own movements and will, and that if I am to go to Suliman's Mountains to be killed, I shall go there and shall be killed. God Almighty, no doubt, knows His mind about me, so I need not trouble on that point. Secondly, I am a poor man. For nearly forty years I have hunted and traded, but I have never made more than a living. Well, gentlemen, I don't know if you are aware that the average life of an elephant hunter from the time he takes to the trade is between four and five years. So you see I have lived through about seven generations of my class, and I should think that my time cannot be far off, anyway. Now, if anything were to happen to me in the ordinary course of business, by the time my debts are paid there would be nothing left to support my son Harry whilst he was getting in the way of earning his bread, whereas now he will be set up for five years. There is the whole affair in a nutshell.'

'Mr Quatermain,' said Sir Henry, who had been giving me his most serious attention, 'your motives for undertaking an enterprise which you believe can only end in disaster reflect a great deal of credit on you. Whether or not you are right, of course time and the event alone can show. But whether you are right or wrong, I may as well tell you at once that I am going through with it to the end, sweet or bitter. If we are to be knocked on the head, all I have to say is, that I hope we get a little shooting first, eh, Good?'

'Yes, yes,' put in the captain. 'We have all three of us been accustomed to face danger, and to hold our lives in our hands in various ways, so it is no good turning back now. And so I vote we go down to the saloon and take an observation just for luck, you know.' And we did – through the bottom of a tumbler.

Next day we went ashore, and I put up Sir Henry and Captain Good at the little grey shanty I have built on the Berea, which I call my home. There are only three rooms and a kitchen in it, and it is constructed of green brick with a galvanised iron roof, but there is a good garden with the best loquot trees in it that I know, and some nice young mangoes, of which I hope great things. The curator of the botanical gardens gave them to me. It is looked after by an old hunter of mine named Jack, whose thigh was so badly broken by a buffalo cow in Sikukuni's country that he will never hunt again. But he can potter about and garden, being a Griqua by birth. You will never persuade a Zulu to take much interest in gardening. It is a peaceful art, and peaceful arts are not in his line.

Sir Henry and Good slept in a tent pitched in my little grove of orange trees at the end of the garden, for there was no room for them in the house. What with the smell of the bloom, and the sight of the green and golden fruit – in Durban you will see all three on the tree together – I dare say it is a pleasant place enough, for we have few mosquitoes here on the Berea, unless there happens to come an unusually heavy rain.

Well, to get on – for if I do not, Harry, you will be tired of my story before ever we fetch up at Suliman's Mountains – having once made up my mind to go I set about making the necessary preparations. First I secured the deed from Sir Henry, providing for you, my boy, in case of accidents. There was some difficulty about its legal execution, as Sir Henry was a stranger here, and the property to be charged is over the water; but it was ultimately got over with the help of a lawyer, who charged twenty pounds for the job – a price that I thought outrageous. Then I pocketed my cheque for five hundred pounds.

Having paid this tribute to my bump of caution, I purchased a wagon and a span of oxen on Sir Henry's behalf, and beauties they were. It was a twenty-two-foot wagon with iron axles, very strong, very light, and built throughout of stinkwood; not quite a new one, having been to the Diamond Fields and back, but, in my opinion, all the better for that, for I could see that the wood was well seasoned. If anything is going to give in a wagon, or if there is green wood in it, it will show out on the first trip. This particular vehicle was what we call a half-tented wagon, that is to say, only covered in over and after twelve feet, leaving all the front part free for the necessaries we had to carry with us. In this after part were a hide *cartle*, or bed, on which two people could sleep, also racks for rifles, and many other little conveniences. I gave one hundred and twenty-five pounds for it, and think that it was cheap at the price.

Then I bought a beautiful team of twenty Zulu oxen which I had kept my eye on for a year or two. Sixteen oxen is the usual number for a team, but I took four extra to allow for casualties. These Zulu cattle are small and light, not more than half the size of the Africander oxen which are generally used for transport purposes; but they will live where the Africanders would starve, and with a moderate load can make five miles a day better going, being quicker and not so liable to become footsore. What is more, this lot were thoroughly salted, that is, they had worked all over South Africa, and so had become proof, comparatively speaking, against redwater, which so frequently destroys whole teams of oxen when they get on to strange *veld* or grass country. As for lung-sick, which is a dreadful form of pneumonia, very prevalent in this country, they had all been inoculated against it. This is done by cutting a slit in the tail of an ox, and binding in a piece of the diseased lung of an animal which has died of the sickness. The result is that the ox sickens, takes the disease in a mild form, which causes its tail to drop off, as a rule about a foot from the root, and becomes proof against future attacks. It seems cruel to rob the animal of his tail, especially in a country where there are so many flies, but it is better to sacrifice the tail and keep the ox than to lose both tail and ox, for a tail without an ox is not much good, except to dust with. Still it does look odd to trek along behind twenty stumps, where there ought to be tails. It seems as though nature had made a trifling mistake, and stuck the stern ornaments of a lot of prize bulldogs on to the rumps of the oxen.

Next came the question of provisioning and medicines, one which required the most careful consideration, for what we had to do was to avoid lumbering the wagon, and yet to take everything absolutely necessary. Fortunately, it turned out that Good is a bit of a doctor, having at some period in his previous career managed to pass through a course of medical and surgical instruction, which he has more or less kept up. He is not, of course, qualified, but he knows more about it than many a man who can write MD after his name, as we found out afterwards, and he had a splendid travelling medicine chest and a set of instruments. Whilst we were at Durban he cut off a Kafir's big toe in a way which it was a pleasure to see. But he was quite nonplussed when the Kafir, who had sat stolidly watching the operation, asked him to put on another, saying that a white one would do at a pinch.

There remained, when these questions were satisfactorily settled, two further important points for consideration, namely, that of arms and that of servants. As to the arms I cannot do better than put down a list of those which we finally decided on from among the ample store that Sir Henry had brought with him from England, and those which I owned. I copy it from my pocketbook, where I made the entry at the time.

'Three heavy breech-loading double-eight elephant guns, weighing about fifteen pounds each, to carry a charge of eleven drachms of black powder.' Two of these were by a well-known London firm, most excellent makers, but I do not know by whom mine, which is not so highly finished, was made. I have used it on several trips, and shot a good many elephants with it, and it has always proved a most superior weapon, thoroughly to be relied on.

'Three double-500 Expresses, constructed to stand a charge of six drachms' – sweet weapons, and admirable for medium-sized game, such as eland or sable antelope, or for men, especially in open country and with the semi-hollow bullet.

'One double No. 12 central-fire Keeper's shotgun, full choke both barrels.' This gun proved of the greatest service to us afterwards in shooting birds for the pot.

'Three Winchester repeating rifles (not carbines), spare guns.

'Three single-action Colt's revolvers, with the heavier or American pattern of cartridge.'

This was our total armament, and doubtless the reader will observe that the weapons of each class were of the same make and calibre, so that the cartridges were interchangeable, a very important point. I make no apology for detailing it at length, as every experienced hunter will know how vital a proper supply of guns and ammunition is to the success of an expedition.

Now as to the men who were to go with us. After much consultation, we decided that their number should be limited to five, namely, a driver, a leader and three servants.

The driver and leader I found without much difficulty, two Zulus, named respectively Goza and Tom; but to get the servants proved a more difficult matter. It was necessary that they should be thoroughly trustworthy and brave men, as in a business of this sort our lives might depend upon their conduct. At last I secured two, one a Hottentot called Ventvögel, or windbird, and one a little Zulu named Khiva, who had the merit of speaking English perfectly. Ventvögel I had known before, he was one of the most perfect spoorers, that is, game trackers, I ever had to do with, and tough as whipcord. He never seemed to tire. But he had one failing, so common with his race – drink. Put him within reach of a bottle of gin and you could not trust him. However, as we were going beyond the region of grog-shops this little weakness of his did not so much matter.

Having secured these two men I looked in vain for a third to suit my purpose, so we determined to start without one, trusting to luck to find a suitable man on our way up country. But, as it happened, on the evening before the day we had fixed for our departure the Zulu Khiva informed me that a Kafir was waiting to see me. Accordingly, when we had done dinner, for we were at table at the time, I told Khiva to bring him in. Presently a tall, handsome-looking man, somewhere about thirty years of age, and very light-coloured for a Zulu, entered, and, lifting his knob-stick by way of salute, squatted himself down in the corner on his haunches, and sat silent. I did not take any notice of him for a while, for it is a great mistake to do so. If you rush into conversation at once, a Zulu is apt to think you a person of little dignity or consequence. I observed, however, that he was a *keshla* or ringed man; that is, he wore on his head the black ring, made of a species of gum polished with fat and worked up in the hair, which is usually assumed by Zulus on attaining a certain age or dignity. Also it struck me that his face was familiar to me.

'Well,' I said at last, 'what is your name?'

'Umbopa,' answered the man in a slow, deep voice.

'I have seen your face before.'

'Yes; the chief, my father, saw my face at the place of the Little Hand' – that is Isandhlwana – 'on the day before the battle.'

Then I remembered. I was one of Lord Chelmsford's guides in that unlucky Zulu War, and took part in the battle, which I had the good fortune to survive. I will say nothing about it here, indeed the subject is painful to me. On the day before it happened, however, I fell into conversation with this man, who held some small command among the native auxiliaries, and he had expressed to me his doubts as to the safety of the camp. At the time I told him to hold his tongue, and leave such matters to wiser heads; but afterwards I thought of his words.

'I remember,' I said; 'what is it you want?'

'It is this, Macumazahn. That is my Kafir name, and means the man who gets up in the middle of the night, or, in vulgar English, he who keeps his eyes open. 'I hear that you go on a great expedition far into the north with the white chiefs from over the water. Is it a true word?'

'It is.'

'I hear that you go even to the Lukanga River, a moon's journey beyond the Manick country. Is this so also, Macumazahn?'

'Why do you ask whither we go? What is it to you?' I answered suspiciously, for the objects of our journey had been kept a dead secret.

'It is this, O white men, that if indeed you travel so far I would travel with you.'

There was a certain assumption of dignity in the man's mode of speech, and especially in his use of the words 'O white men', instead of 'O *inkosis*', or chiefs, which struck me.

'You forget yourself a little,' I said. 'Your words run out unawares. That is not the way to speak. What is your name, and where is your kraal? Tell us, that we may know with whom we have to deal.'

'My name is Umbopa. I am of the Zulu people, yet not of them. The house of my tribe is in the far north; it was left behind when the Zulus came down here a thousand years ago, long before Chaka reigned in Zululand. I have no kraal. I have wandered for many years. I came from the north as a child to Zululand. I was Cetewayo's man in the Nkomabakosi Regiment, serving there under the great captain, Umslopogaasi of the Axe,* who taught my hands to fight. Afterwards I ran away from Zululand and came to Natal because I wanted to see the white man's ways. Next I fought against Cetewayo in the war. Since then I have been working in Natal. Now I am tired, and would go north again. Here is not my place. I want no money, but I am a brave man and well worth my place and meat. I have spoken.'

I was rather puzzled by this man and his way of speech. It was evident to me from his manner that in the main he was telling the truth, but somehow he seemed different from the ordinary run of Zulus, and I rather mistrusted his offer to come without pay. Being in a difficulty, I translated his words to Sir Henry and Good, and asked them their opinion.

* For the history of Umslopogaasi and his axe, the reader is referred to the books called *Allan Quatermain* and *Nada the Lily*. ED.

Sir Henry told me to ask him to stand up. Umbopa did so, at the same time slipping off the long military greatcoat which he wore, and revealing himself naked except for the *moocha* round his centre and a necklace of lions' claws. Certainly he was a magnificent-looking man; I never saw a finer native. Standing about six foot three high, he was broad in proportion, and very shapely. In that light, too, his skin looked scarcely more than dark, except here and there where deep black scars marked old assegai wounds. Sir Henry walked up to him and looked into his proud, handsome face.

'They make a good pair, don't they?' said Good, 'one as big as the other.'

'I like your looks, Mr Umbopa, and I will take you as my servant,' said Sir Henry in English

Umbopa evidently understood him, for he answered in Zulu, 'It is well;' and then added, with a glance at the white man's great stature and breadth, 'We are men, thou and I.'

CHAPTER 4

An Elephant Hunt

Now I do not propose to narrate at full length all the incidents of our long trek up to Sitanda's Kraal, near the junction of the Lukanga and Kalukwe Rivers. It was a journey of more than a thousand miles from Durban, the last three hundred or so of which we had to make on foot, owing to the frequent presence of the dreadful tsetse fly, whose bite is fatal to all animals except donkeys and men.

We left Durban at the end of January, and it was in the second week of May that we camped near Sitanda's Kraal. Our adventures on the way were many and various, but as they are of the sort which befall every African hunter – with one exception to be presently detailed – I shall not set them down here, lest I should render this history too wearisome.

At Inyati, the outlying trading station in the Matabele country, of which Lobengula (a great and cruel scoundrel) is king, with many regrets we parted from our comfortable wagon. Only twelve oxen remained to us out of the beautiful span of twenty which I had bought at Durban. One we lost from the bite of a cobra, three had perished from 'poverty' and the want of water, one starved and the other three died from eating the poisonous herb called tulip. Five more sickened from this cause, but we managed to cure them with doses of an infusion made by boiling down the tulip leaves. If administered in time this is a very effective antidote.

The wagon and oxen we left in the immediate charge of Goza and Tom, our driver and leader, both trustworthy boys, requesting a worthy Scotch missionary who lived in this distant place to keep an eye to them. Then, accompanied by Umbopa, Khiva, Ventvögel, and half a dozen bearers whom we hired on the spot, we started off on foot upon our wild quest. I remember we were all a little silent on the occasion of this departure, and I think that each of us was wondering if we should ever see our wagon again; for my part I never expected to do so. For a while we tramped on in silence, till Umbopa, who was marching in front, broke into a Zulu chant about how some brave men, tired of life and the tameness of things, started off into a vast wilderness to find new ones or die, and how, lo and behold! when they had travelled far into the wilderness they discovered that it was not a wilderness at all, but a beautiful place full of young wives and fat cattle, of game to hunt, and enemies to kill.

Then we all laughed and took it for a good omen. Umbopa was a cheerful savage, in a dignified sort of way, when he was not suffering from one of his fits of brooding, and he had a wonderful knack of keeping up our spirits. We all grew very fond of him.

And now for the one adventure to which I am going to treat myself, for I do dearly love a hunting yarn.

About a fortnight's march from Inyati we came across a peculiarly beautiful bit of well-watered woodland country. The kloofs in the hills were covered with dense bush, *idoro* bush as the natives call it, and in some places with the *wachteen-beche*, or wait-a-little thorn, and there were great quantities of the lovely machabell tree, laden with refreshing yellow fruit having enormous stones. This tree is the elephant's favourite food, and there were not wanting signs that the great brutes had been about, for not only was their spoor frequent, but in many places the trees were broken down and even uprooted. The elephant is a destructive feeder.

One evening, after a long day's march, we came to a spot of great loveliness. At the foot of a bush-clad hill lay a dry riverbed, in which, however, were to be found pools of crystal water all trodden round with the hoofprints of game. Facing this hill was a park-like plain, where grew clumps of flat-topped mimosa, varied with occasional glossy-leaved machabells, and all round stretched the sea of pathless, silent bush.

As we emerged into this riverbed path suddenly we started a troop of tall giraffes, which galloped, or rather sailed off, with their strange gait, their tails screwed up over their backs, and their hooves rattling like castanets. They were about three hundred yards from us, and therefore practically out of shot, but Good, who was walking ahead, and who had an Express loaded with solid ball in his hand, could not resist temptation. Lifting his gun, he let drive at the last, a young cow. By some extraordinary chance the ball struck it full on the back of the neck, shattering the spinal column, and that giraffe went rolling head over heels just like a rabbit. I never saw a more curious thing.

'Curse it!' said Good – for I am sorry to say he had a habit of using strong language when excited, contracted, no doubt, in the course of his nautical career – 'curse it! I've killed him.'

'Ou, Bougwan,' ejaculated the Kafirs; 'ou! ou!'

They called Good 'Bougwan', or Glass Eye, because of his eyeglass.

'Oh, Bougwan!' re-echoed Sir Henry and I; and from that day Good's reputation as a marvellous shot was established, at any rate among the Kafirs. Really he was a bad one, but whenever he missed we overlooked it for the sake of that giraffe.

Having set some of the boys to cut off the best of the giraffe meat, we went to work to build a *scherm* near one of the pools and about a hundred yards to its right. This is done by cutting a quantity of thorn bushes and piling them in the shape of a circular hedge. Then the space enclosed is smoothed and dry tambouki grass, if obtainable, is made into a bed in the centre, and a fire or fires lighted.

By the time the *scherm* was finished, the moon peeped up, and our dinners of giraffe steaks and roasted marrowbones were ready. How we enjoyed those marrowbones, though it was rather a job to crack them! I know of no greater luxury than giraffe marrow, unless it is elephant's heart, and we had that on the morrow. We ate our simple meal by the light of the moon, pausing at times to thank Good for his wonderful shot; then we began to smoke and yarn, and a curious picture we must have made squatting there round the fire. I, with my short grizzled hair sticking up straight, and Sir Henry, with his yellow locks, which were getting rather long, made rather a contrast, especially as I am thin, and short, and dark, weighing only nine stone and a half, and Sir Henry is tall, and broad, and fair, and weighs fifteen. But perhaps the most curious-looking of the three, taking all the circumstances of the case into consideration, was Captain John Good, RN. There he sat upon a leather bag, looking just as though he had come in from a comfortable day's shooting in a civilised country, absolutely clean, tidy and well dressed. He wore a shooting suit of brown tweed, with a hat to match, and neat gaiters. As usual, he was beautifully shaved, his eyeglass and his false teeth appeared to be in perfect order, and altogether he looked the neatest man I ever had to do with in the wilderness. He even sported a collar, of which he had a supply, made of white gutta-percha.

'You see, they weigh so little,' he said to me innocently, when I expressed my astonishment at the fact; 'and I always like to turn out like a gentleman.' Ah! if he could have foreseen the future and the raiment prepared for him.

Well, there we three sat yarning away in the beautiful moonlight, and watching the Kafirs a few yards off sucking their intoxicating *daccha* from a pipe of which the mouthpiece was made of the horn of an eland, till one by one they rolled themselves up in their blankets and went to sleep by the fire. That is, all except Umbopa, who was a little apart, his chin resting on his hand, and thinking deeply. I noticed that he never mixed much with the other Kafirs.

Presently, from the depths of the bush behind us came a loud 'woof woof!' 'That's a lion,' said I, and we all started up to listen. Hardly had we done so, when from the pool, about a hundred yards off, we heard the strident trumpeting of an elephant. '*Indlovu! Indlovu!*' 'Elephant! Elephant!' whispered the Kafirs, and a few minutes afterwards we saw a succession of vast shadowy forms moving slowly from the direction of the water towards the bush.

Up jumped Good, burning for slaughter, and thinking, perhaps, that it was as easy to kill elephant as he had found it to shoot giraffe, but I caught him by the arm and pulled him down.

'It's no good,' I whispered, 'let them go.'

'It seems that we are in a paradise of game. I vote we stop here a day or two, and have a go at them,' said Sir Henry presently.

I was rather surprised, for hitherto Sir Henry had always been for pushing forward as fast as possible, more especially since we ascertained at Inyati that about two years ago an Englishman of the name of Neville *had* sold his wagon there, and gone on up country. But I suppose his hunter instincts got the better of him for a while.

Good jumped at the idea, for he was longing to have a shot at those elephants. So, to speak the truth, did I, for it went against my conscience to let such a herd as that escape without a pull at them.

'All right, my hearties,' said I. 'I think we want a little recreation. And now let's turn in, for we ought to be off by dawn, and then perhaps we may catch them feeding before they move on.'

The others agreed and we proceeded to make our preparations. Good took off his clothes, shook them, put his eyeglass and his false teeth into his trousers pocket, and folding each article neatly, placed them out of the dew under a corner of his mackintosh sheet. Sir Henry and I contented ourselves with rougher arrangements, and soon were curled up in our blankets, and dropping off into the dreamless sleep that rewards the traveller.

Going, going, go – What was that?

Suddenly from the direction of the water came sounds of violent scuffling, and next instant there broke upon our ears a succession of the most awful roars. There was no mistaking their origin; only a lion could make such a noise as that. We all jumped up and looked towards the water, in the direction of which we saw a confused mass, yellow and black in colour, staggering and struggling towards us. We seized our rifles, and slipping on our *veldschoens*, that is shoes made of untanned hide, ran out of the *scherm*. By this time the mass had fallen, and was rolling over and over on the ground, and when we reached the spot it struggled no longer, but lay quite still.

Now we saw what it was. On the grass there lay a sable antelope bull – the most beautiful of all the African antelope – quite dead, and transfixed by its great curved horns was a magnificent black-maned lion, also dead. Evidently what had happened was this: The sable antelope had come down to drink at the pool where the lion – no doubt the same which we had heard – was lying in wait. While the antelope drank, the lion had sprung upon him, only to be received upon the sharp curved horns and transfixed. Once before I saw a similar thing happen. Then the lion, unable to free himself, had torn and bitten at the back and neck of the bull, which, maddened with fear and pain, had rushed on until it dropped dead.

As soon as we had examined the beasts sufficiently we called the Kafirs, and between us managed to drag their carcasses up to the *scherm*. After that we went in and lay down, to wake no more till dawn.

With the first light we were up and making ready for the fray. We took with us the three eight-bore rifles, a good supply of ammunition, and our large water-bottles, filled with weak cold tea, which I have always found the best stuff to shoot on. After swallowing a little breakfast we started, Umbopa, Khiva and Ventvögel accompanying us. The other Kafirs we left with instructions to skin the lion and the sable antelope, and to cut up the latter.

We had no difficulty in finding the broad elephant trail, which Ventvögel, after examination, pronounced to have been made by between twenty and thirty elephants, most of them full-grown bulls. But the herd had moved on some way during the night, and it was nine o'clock, and already very hot, before, by the broken trees, bruised leaves and bark, and smoking droppings, we knew that we could not be far from them.

Presently we caught sight of the herd, which numbered, as Ventvögel had said, between twenty and thirty, standing in a hollow, having finished their morning meal, and flapping their great ears. It was a splendid sight, for they were only about two hundred yards from us. Taking a handful of dry grass, I threw it into the air to see how the wind was; for if once they winded us I knew they would be off before we could get a shot. Finding that, if anything, it blew from the elephants to us, we crept on stealthily, and thanks to the cover managed to get within forty yards or so of the great brutes. Just in front of us, and broadside on, stood three splendid bulls, one of them with enormous tusks.

I whispered to the others that I would take the middle one; Sir Henry covering the elephant to the left, and Good the bull with the big tusks.

'Now,' I whispered.

Boom! boom! boom! went the three heavy rifles, and down came Sir Henry's elephant dead as a hammer, shot right through the heart. Mine fell on to its knees, and I thought that he was going to die, but in another moment he was up and off, tearing along straight past me. As he went I gave him the second barrel in the ribs, and this brought him down in good earnest. Hastily slipping in two fresh cartridges I ran close up to him, and a ball through the brain put an end to the poor brute's struggles. Then I turned to see how Good had fared with the big bull, which I had heard screaming with rage and pain as I gave mine its quietus. On reaching the captain I found him in a great state of excitement. It appeared that on receiving the bullet the bull had turned and come straight for his assailant, who had barely time to get out of his way, and then charged on blindly past him, in the direction of our encampment. Meanwhile the herd had crashed off in wild alarm in the other direction.

For a while we debated whether to go after the wounded bull or to follow the herd, and finally deciding for the latter alternative, departed, thinking that we had seen the last of those big tusks. I have often wished since that we had. It was easy work to follow the elephants, for they had left a trail like a carriage road behind them, crushing down the thick bush in their furious flight as though it were tambouki grass.

But to come up with them was another matter, and we had struggled on under the broiling sun for over two hours before we found them. With the exception of one bull, they were standing together, and I could see, from their unquiet way and the manner in which they kept lifting their trunks to test the air, that they were on the lookout for mischief. The solitary bull stood fifty yards or so to this side of the herd, over which he was evidently keeping sentry, and about sixty yards from us. Thinking that he would see or wind us, and that it would probably start them off again if we tried to get nearer, especially as the ground was rather open, we all aimed at this bull and at my whispered word we fired. The three shots took effect, and down he went, dead. Again the herd started, but unfortunately for them about a hundred yards farther on was a *nullah*, or dried-out water track with steep banks, a place very much resembling the one where the Prince Imperial was killed in Zululand. Into this the elephants plunged, and when we reached the edge we found them struggling in wild confusion to get up the other bank, filling the air with their screams, and trumpeting as they pushed one another aside in their selfish panic, just like so many human beings. Now was our opportunity, and firing away as quickly as we could load, we killed five of the poor beasts, and no doubt should have bagged the whole herd, had they not suddenly given up their attempts to climb the bank and rushed headlong down the *nullah*. We were too tired to follow them, and perhaps also a little sick of slaughter, eight elephants being a pretty good bag for one day.

So after we were rested a little, and the Kafirs had cut out the hearts of two of the dead elephants for supper, we started homewards, very well pleased with our day's work, having made up our minds to send the bearers on the morrow to chop away the tusks.

Shortly after we re-passed the spot where Good had wounded the patriarchal bull we came across a herd of eland, but did not shoot at them, as we had plenty of meat. They trotted past us, and then stopped behind a little patch of bush about a hundred yards away, wheeling round to look at us. As Good was anxious to get a near view of them, never having seen an eland close, he handed his rifle to Umbopa, and, followed by Khiva, strolled up to the patch of bush. We sat down and waited for him, not sorry of the excuse for a little rest.

The sun was just going down in its reddest glory, and Sir Henry and I were admiring the lovely scene, when suddenly we heard an elephant trumpet, and saw its huge and rushing form with uplifted trunk and tail silhouetted against the great fiery globe of the sun. Next second we saw something else, and that was Good and Khiva tearing back towards us with the wounded bull – for it was he – charging after them. For a moment we did not dare to fire – though at that distance it would have been of little use if we had done so – for fear of hitting one of them. The next a dreadful thing happened – Good fell a victim to his passion for civilised dress. Had he consented to discard his trousers and gaiters like the rest of us, and to hunt in a flannel shirt and a pair of *veldschoens*, it would have been all right. But as it was, his trousers cumbered him in that desperate race, and presently, when he was about sixty yards from us, his boot, polished by the dry grass, slipped, and down he went on his face right in front of the elephant.

We gave a gasp, for we knew that he must die, and ran as hard as we could towards him. In three seconds it had ended, but not as we thought. Khiva, the Zulu boy, saw his master fall, and brave lad as he was, turned and flung his assegai straight into the elephant's face. It stuck in his trunk.

With a scream of pain, the brute seized the poor Zulu, hurled him to earth, and placing one huge foot on to his body about the middle, twined its trunk round his upper part and tore him in two.

We rushed up mad with horror, and fired again and again, till presently the elephant fell upon the fragments of the Zulu.

As for Good, he rose and wrung his hands over the brave man who had given his life to save him, and, though I am an old hand, I felt a lump grow in my throat. Umbopa stood contemplating the huge dead elephant and the mangled remains of poor Khiva.

'Ah, well,' he said presently, 'he is dead, but he died like a man!'

CHAPTER 5

Our March into the Desert

We had killed nine elephants, and it took us two days to cut out the tusks and, having brought them into camp, to bury them carefully in the sand under a large tree, which made a conspicuous mark for miles round. It was a wonderfully fine lot of ivory. I never saw a better, averaging as it did between forty and fifty pounds a tusk. The tusks of the great bull that killed poor Khiva scaled one hundred and seventy pounds the pair, so nearly as we could judge.

As for Khiva himself, we buried what remained of him in an ant-bear hole, together with an assegai to protect himself on his journey to a better world. On the third day we marched again, hoping that we might live to return to dig up our buried ivory, and in due course, after a long and wearisome tramp, and many adventures which I have not space to detail, we reached Sitanda's Kraal, near the Lukanga River, the real starting-point of our expedition. Very well do I recollect our arrival at that place. To the right was a scattered native settlement with a few stone cattle kraals and some cultivated lands down by the water, where these savages grew their scanty supply of grain, and beyond it stretched great tracts of waving veld covered with tall grass, over which herds of smaller game were wandering. To the left lay the vast desert. This spot appears to be the outpost of the fertile country, and it would be difficult to say to what natural causes such an abrupt change in the character of the soil is due. But so it is.

Just below our encampment flowed a little stream, on the farther side of which is a stony slope, the same down which, twenty years before, I had seen poor Silvestre creeping back after his attempt to reach Solomon's Mines. Beyond that slope begins the waterless desert, covered with a species of karoo shrub.

It was evening when we pitched our camp, and the red ball of the sun was sinking into the desert, sending glorious rays of many-coloured light flying over all its vast expanse. Leaving Good to superintend the arrangement of our little camp, I took Sir Henry with me, and walking to the top of the slope opposite, we gazed across the sandy waste. The air was very clear, and far, far away I could distinguish the faint blue outlines of the Suliman Berge, here and there capped with white.

'There,' I said, 'there is the wall round Solomon's Mines, but God knows if we shall ever climb it.'

'My brother should be there, and if he is, I shall reach him somehow,' said Sir Henry, in that tone of quiet confidence which marked the man.

'I hope so,' I answered, and turned to go back to the camp, when I saw that we were not alone. Behind us, also gazing earnestly towards the far-off mountains, stood the great Kafir Umbopa.

The Zulu spoke when he saw that I had observed him, addressing Sir Henry, to whom he had attached himself.

'Is it to that land that thou wouldst journey, Incubu?' (a native word meaning an elephant and the Zulu name given to Sir Henry by the Kafirs), he said, pointing towards the mountains with his broad assegai.

I asked him sharply what he meant by addressing his master in that familiar way. It is very well for natives to have a name for one among themselves, but it is not decent that they should call a white man by their heathenish appellations to his face. The Zulu laughed a quiet little laugh which angered me.

'How dost thou know that I am not the equal of the *inkosi* whom I serve?' he said. 'He is of a royal house, no doubt; one can see it in his size and by his mien; so, mayhap, am I. At least I am as great a man. Be my mouth, O Macumazahn, and say my words to the *inkosi* Incubu, my master, for I would speak to him and to thee.'

I was wroth with the man, for I am not accustomed to be talked to in that way by Kafirs, but somehow he impressed me. Besides, I was curious to know what he had to say. So I translated, expressing my opinion at the same time that he was an impudent fellow, and that his swagger was outrageous.

'Yes, Umbopa,' answered Sir Henry. 'I would journey there.'

'The desert is wide and there is no water in it, the mountains are high and covered with snow, and man cannot say what lies beyond them behind the place where the sun sets; how shalt thou come thither, Incubu, and wherefore dost thou go?'

I translated again.

'Tell him,' answered Sir Henry, 'that I go because I believe that a man of my blood, my brother, has gone there before me, and I journey to seek him.'

'That is so, Incubu; a Hottentot I met on the road told me that a white man went out into the desert two years ago towards those mountains with one servant, a hunter. They never came back.'

'How do you know it was my brother?' asked Sir Henry.

'Nay, I know not. But the Hottentot, when I asked what the white man was like, said that he had thine eyes and a black beard. He said, too, that the name of the hunter with him was Jim; that he was a Bechuana hunter and wore clothes.'

'There is no doubt about it,' said I; 'I knew Jim well.'

Sir Henry nodded. 'I was sure of it,' he said. 'If George set his mind upon a thing he generally did it. It was always so from his boyhood. If he meant to cross the Suliman Berge he has crossed them, unless some accident overtook him, and we must look for him on the other side.'

Umbopa understood English, though he rarely spoke it.

'It is a far journey, Incubu,' he put in, and I translated his remark.

'Yes,' answered Sir Henry, 'it is far. But there is no journey upon this earth that a man may not make if he sets his heart to it. There is nothing, Umbopa, that he cannot do. There are no mountains he may not climb, there are no deserts he cannot cross, save a mountain and a desert of which you are spared the knowledge, if love leads him and he holds his life in his hand counting it as nothing, ready to keep it or lose it as heaven above may order.'

I translated.

'Great words, my father,' answered the Zulu – I always called him a Zulu, though he was not really one – 'great swelling words fit to fill the mouth of a man. Thou art right, my father Incubu. Listen! what is life? It is a feather, it is the seed of the grass, blown hither and thither, sometimes multiplying itself and dying in the act, sometimes carried hence into the heavens. But if that seed be good and heavy it may perchance travel a little way on the road it wills. It is well to try and journey one's road and to fight with the air. Man must die. At the worst he can but die a little sooner. I will go with thee across the desert and over the mountains, unless perchance I fall to the ground on the way, my father.'

He paused awhile, and then went on with one of those strange bursts of rhetorical eloquence that Zulus sometimes indulge in, which to my mind, full though they are of vain repetitions, show that the race is by no means devoid of poetic instinct and of intellectual power.

'What is life? Tell me, O white men, who are wise, who know the secrets of the world, and of the world of stars, and the world that lies above and around the stars; who flash your words from afar without a voice; tell me, white men, the secret of our life – whither it goes and whence it comes!

'You cannot answer me; you know not. Listen, I will answer. Out of the dark we came, into the dark we go. Like a storm-driven bird at night we fly out of the Nowhere; for a moment our wings are seen in the light of the fire, and, lo! we are gone again into the Nowhere. Life is nothing. Life is all. It is the hand with which we hold off death. It is the glow-worm that shines in the night-time and is black in the morning; it is the white breath of the oxen in winter; it is the little shadow that runs across the grass and loses itself at sunset.'

'You are a strange man,' said Sir Henry, when he had ceased.

Umbopa laughed. 'It seems to me that we are much alike, Incubu. Perhaps I seek a brother over the mountains.'

I looked at him suspiciously. 'What dost thou mean?' I asked; 'what dost thou know of those mountains?'

'A little; a very little. There is a strange land yonder, a land of witchcraft and beautiful things; a land of brave people, and of trees, and streams, and snowy peaks, and of a great white road. I have heard of it. But what is the good of talking? It grows dark. Those who live to see will see.'

Again I looked at him doubtfully. The man knew too much.

'You need not fear me, Macumazahn,' he said, interpreting my look. 'I dig no holes for you to fall in. I make no plots. If ever we cross those mountains behind the sun I will tell what I know. But death sits upon them. Be wise and turn back. Go and hunt elephants, my masters. I have spoken.'

And without another word he lifted his spear in salutation, and returned towards the camp, where shortly afterwards we found him cleaning a gun like any other Kafir.

'That is an odd man,' said Sir Henry.

'Yes,' answered I, 'too odd by half. I don't like his little ways. He knows something, and will not speak out. But I suppose it is no use quarrelling with him. We are in for a curious trip, and a mysterious Zulu won't make much difference one way or another.'

Next day we made our arrangements for starting. Of course it was impossible to drag our heavy elephant rifles and other kit with us across the desert, so, dismissing our bearers, we made an arrangement with an old native who had a kraal close by to take care of them till we returned. It went to my heart to leave such things as those sweet tools to the tender mercies of an old thief of a savage whose greedy eyes I could see gloating over them. But I took some precautions.

First of all I loaded all the rifles, placing them at full cock, and informed him that if he touched them they would go off. He tried the experiment instantly with my eight-bore, and it did go off, and blew a hole right through one of his oxen, which were just then being driven up to the kraal, to say nothing of knocking him head over heels with the recoil. He got up considerably startled, and not at all pleased at the loss of the ox, for which he had the impudence to ask me to pay. After that, nothing would induce him to touch the guns again.

'Put the live devils out of the way up there in the thatch,' he said, 'or they will murder us all.'

Then I told him that, when we came back, if one of those things were missing I would kill him and his people by witchcraft; and if we died and he tried to steal the rifles I would come to haunt him and turn his cattle mad and his milk sour till life was a weariness, and would make the devils in the guns jump out and talk to him in a way he did not like, and generally gave him a good idea of judgement to come. After that he promised to look after them as though they were his father's spirit. He was a very superstitious old Kafir and a great villain.

Having thus disposed of our superfluous gear we arranged the kit we five – Sir Henry, Good, myself, Umbopa and the Hottentot Ventvögel – were to take with us on our journey. It was small enough, but do what we would we could not get its weight down under about forty pounds a man. This is what it consisted of:

The three Express rifles and two hundred rounds of ammunition.
The two Winchester repeating rifles (for Umbopa and Ventvögel), with two hundred rounds of cartridge
Three Colt revolvers and sixty rounds of cartridge
Five Cochrane's water-bottles, each holding four pints
Five blankets
Twenty-five pounds' weight of *biltong* – i.e. sun-dried game flesh
Ten pounds' weight of best mixed beads for gifts
A selection of medicine, including an ounce of quinine, and one or two small surgical instruments
Our knives, a few sundries, such as a compass, matches, a pocket filter, tobacco, a trowel, a bottle of brandy, and the clothes we stood in

This was our total equipment, a small one indeed for such a venture, but we dared not attempt to carry more. Indeed, that load was a heavy one per man with which to travel across the burning desert, for in such places every additional ounce tells. But we could not see our way to reducing the amount. There was nothing taken but what was absolutely necessary.

With great difficulty, and by the promise of a present of a good hunting-knife each, I succeeded in persuading three wretched natives from the village to come with us for the first stage, twenty miles, and to carry large gourds holding a gallon of water apiece. My object was to enable us to refill our water-bottles after the first night's march, for we determined to start in the cool of the evening. I gave out to these natives that we were going to shoot ostriches, with which the desert abounded. They jabbered and shrugged their shoulders, saying that we were mad and should perish of thirst, which I must say seemed probable. Still being desirous of obtaining the knives, which were almost unknown treasures up there, they consented to come, having probably reflected that, after all, our subsequent extinction would be no affair of theirs.

All next day we rested and slept, and at sunset ate a hearty meal of fresh beef washed down with tea, the last, as Good remarked sadly, we were likely to drink for many a long day. Then, having made our final preparations, we lay down and waited for the moon to rise. At last, about nine o'clock, up she came in all her glory, flooding the wild country with light, and throwing a silver sheen on the expanse of rolling desert before us, which looked as solemn and quiet and as alien to man as the star-studded firmament above. We rose up, and in a few minutes were ready, and yet we hesitated a little, as human nature is prone to hesitate on the threshold of an irrevocable step. We three white men stood by ourselves. Umbopa, assegai in hand and a rifle slung across his shoulders, looked out fixedly across the desert a few paces ahead of us; while the hired natives, with the gourds of water, and Ventvögel, were gathered in a little knot behind.

'Gentlemen,' said Sir Henry presently, in his deep voice, 'we are going on about as strange a journey as men can make in this world. It is very doubtful if we can succeed in it. But we are three men who will stand together for good or for evil to the last. Now, before we start let us for a moment pray to the power who shapes the destinies of men, and who ages since has marked out our paths, that it may please Him to direct our steps in accordance with His will.'

Taking off his hat, for the space of a minute or so, he covered his face with his hands, and Good and I did likewise.

I do not say that I am a first-rate praying man – few hunters are; and as for Sir Henry, I never heard him speak like that before, and only once since, though deep down in his heart I believe that he is very religious. Good, too, is pious, though apt to swear. Anyhow, I do not remember, excepting on one, no, two occasions, ever putting up a better prayer in my life than I did during that minute, and somehow I felt the happier for it. Our future was so completely unknown, and I think that the unknown and the awful always bring a man nearer to his maker.

'And now,' said Sir Henry, 'trek!'

So we started.

We had nothing to guide ourselves by except the distant mountains and old José da Silvestra's chart, which, considering that it was drawn by a dying and half-distraught man on a fragment of linen three centuries ago, was not a very satisfactory sort of thing to work with. Still, our sole hope of success depended upon it, such as it was. If we failed in finding that pool of bad water which the old dom marked as being situated in the middle of the desert, about sixty miles from our starting-point, and as far from the mountains, in all probability we must perish miserably of thirst. But to my mind the chances of our finding it in that great sea of sand and karoo scrub seemed almost infinitesimal. Even supposing that da Silvestra had marked the pool correctly, what was there to prevent its having been dried up by the sun generations ago, or trampled in by game, or filled with the drifting sand?

On we tramped silently as shades through the night and in the heavy sand. The karoo bushes caught our feet and retarded us, and the sand worked into our veldschoens and Good's shooting-boots, so that every few miles we had to stop and empty them. Still the night kept fairly cool, though the atmosphere was thick and heavy, giving a sort of creamy feel to the air, and we made fair progress. It was very silent and lonely there in the desert, oppressively so indeed. Good felt this, and once began to whistle 'The Girl I Left behind Me', but the notes sounded lugubrious in that vast place, and he gave it up.

Shortly afterwards a little incident occurred which, though it startled us at the time, gave rise to a laugh. Good was leading, as the holder of the compass, which, being a sailor, of course he understood thoroughly, and we were toiling along in single file behind him, when suddenly we heard a half-smothered exclamation, and he vanished. Next second there arose all around us a most extraordinary hubbub: snorts, groans, and wild sounds of rushing feet. In the faint light, too, we could descry dim, galloping forms half-hidden by wreaths of sand. The natives threw down their loads and prepared to bolt, then remembering that there was nowhere to run to, they cast themselves upon the ground and howled something about ghosts. As for Sir Henry and myself, we stood amazed; nor was our amazement lessened when we perceived the form of Good careering off in the direction of the mountains, apparently mounted on the back of a horse and hallooing wildly. In another second he threw up his arms, and we heard him come to the earth with a thud.

Then I saw what had happened; we had stumbled upon a herd of sleeping quagga, on to the back of one of which Good actually had fallen, whereupon the brute naturally got up and made off with him. Calling out to the others that it was all right, I ran towards Good, much afraid lest he should be hurt, but to my great relief I found him sitting in the sand, his eyeglass still fixed firmly in his eye, rather shaken and very much frightened, but not in any way injured.

After this we travelled on without any further misadventure till about one o'clock, when we called a halt, and having drunk a little water, not much, for water was precious, and rested for half an hour, we started again.

On, on we went, till at last the east began to blush like the cheek of a girl. Next appeared faint rays of primrose light, that changed presently to golden bars, through which the dawn glided out across the desert. The stars grew pale and paler still, till at last they vanished; the golden moon waxed wan, and her mountain ridges stood out against her sickly face like the bones on the cheek of a dying man. Then came spear upon spear of light flashing far away across the boundless wilderness, piercing and firing the veils of mist, till the desert was draped in a tremulous golden glow, and it was day.

Still we did not halt, though by this time we should have been glad enough to do so, for we knew that when once the sun was fully up it would be almost impossible for us to travel. At length, about an hour later, we spied a little pile of boulders rising out of the plain, and to this we dragged ourselves. As luck would have it, here we found an overhanging slab of rock carpeted beneath with smooth sand, which afforded a most grateful shelter from the heat. Underneath this we crept, and each of us having drunk some water and eaten a bit of *biltong*, we lay down and soon were sound asleep.

It was three o'clock in the afternoon before we woke, to find our bearers preparing to return. They had seen enough of the desert already, and no number of knives would have tempted them to come a step farther. So we took a hearty drink, and having emptied our water-bottles, filled them up again from the gourds that they had brought with them. Then we watched them depart on their twenty miles' tramp home.

At half-past four we started again. It was lonely and desolate work, for with the exception of a few ostriches there was not a single living creature to be seen on all the vast expanse of sandy plains. Evidently it was too dry for game, and with the exception of a deadly-looking cobra or two we saw no reptiles. One insect, however, we found abundant, and that was the common or house fly. On they came, 'not as single spies but in battalions', as I think the Old Testament* says somewhere. The house fly is a most extraordinary insect. Go where you will you find him, and so it must have been always. I have seen him enclosed in amber which was, I was told, quite half a million years old, looking exactly like his descendant of today, and I have little doubt that when the last man lies dying on the earth he will be buzzing round – if this event should happen to occur in summer – watching for an opportunity to settle on his nose.

---

* Readers must beware of accepting Mr Quatermain's references as accurate, as, it has been found, some are prone to do. Although his reading evidently was limited, the impression produced by it upon his mind was mixed. Thus to him the Old Testament and Shakespeare were interchangeable authorities. ED.

At sunset we halted, waiting for the moon to rise. At last she came up, beautiful and serene as ever, and with one halt about two o'clock in the morning, we trudged on wearily through the night, till at last the welcome sun put a period to our labours. We drank a little and flung ourselves down on the sand, thoroughly tired out, and soon were all asleep. There was no need to set a watch, for we had nothing to fear from anybody or anything in that vast untenanted plain. Our only enemies were heat, thirst and flies, but far rather would I have faced any danger from man or beast than that awful trinity. This time we were not so lucky as to find a sheltering rock to guard us from the glare of the sun, with the result that about seven o'clock we woke up experiencing the exact sensations one would attribute to a beefsteak on a gridiron. We were literally being baked through and through. The burning sun seemed to be sucking our very blood out of us. We sat up and gasped

'Phew,' said I, grabbing at the halo of flies which buzzed cheerfully round my head. The heat did not affect *them*.

'My word!' exclaimed Sir Henry.

'It is devilish hot!' echoed Good.

It was hot, indeed, and there was not a bit of shelter to be found. Look where we would there were no rocks or trees, nothing but an unending glare, rendered dazzling by the heated air that danced over the surface of the desert as it dances over a cooking stove.

'What is to be done?' asked Sir Henry. 'We can't stand this for long.'

We looked at each other blankly.

'I have it,' said Good. 'We must dig a hole, get in it, and cover ourselves with the karoo bushes.'

It did not seem a very promising suggestion, but at least it was better than nothing, so we set to work, and, with the trowel we had brought with us and the help of our hands, in about an hour we succeeded in delving out a patch of ground some ten feet long by twelve wide to the depth of two feet. Then we cut a quantity of low scrub with our hunting-knives, and, creeping into the hole, pulled it over all of us, with the exception of Ventvögel, on whom, being a Hottentot, the heat had no particular effect. This gave us some slight shelter from the burning rays of the sun, but the atmosphere in that amateur grave can be better imagined than described. The Black Hole of Calcutta must have been a fool to it; indeed, to this moment I do not know how we lived through the day. There we lay panting, and every now and again moistening our lips from our scanty supply of water. Had we followed our inclinations we should have finished all we possessed in the first two hours, but we were forced to exercise the most rigid care, for if our water failed us we knew that very soon we must perish miserably.

But everything has an end, if only you live long enough to see it, and somehow that miserable day wore on towards evening. About three o'clock in the afternoon we determined that we could bear it no longer. It would be better to die walking than to be killed slowly by heat and thirst in this dreadful pit. So taking each of us a little drink from our fast diminishing supply of water, now warmed to about the same temperature as a man's blood, we staggered forward.

We had now covered some fifty miles of wilderness. If the reader will refer to the rough copy and translation of old da Silvestra's map, he will see that the desert is marked as measuring forty leagues across, and the 'pan bad water' is set down as being about in the middle of it. Now forty leagues is one hundred and twenty miles, consequently we ought at the most to be within twelve or fifteen miles of the water if any should really exist.

Through the afternoon we crept slowly and painfully along, scarcely doing more than a mile and a half in an hour. At sunset we rested again, waiting for the moon, and after drinking a little managed to get some sleep.

Before we lay down, Umbopa pointed out to us a slight and indistinct hillock on the flat surface of the plain about eight miles away. At that distance it looked like an ant-hill, and as I was dropping off to sleep I fell to wondering what it could be.

With the moon we marched again, feeling dreadfully exhausted, and suffering tortures from thirst and prickly heat. Nobody who has not felt it can know what we went through. We walked no longer, we staggered, now and again falling from exhaustion, and being obliged to call a halt every hour or so. We had scarcely energy left in us to speak. Up to this Good had chatted and joked, for he is a merry fellow; but now he had not a jest in him.

At last, about two o'clock, utterly worn out in body and mind, we came to the foot of the queer hill, or sand *koppie*, which at first sight resembled a gigantic ant-heap about a hundred feet high, covering at its base nearly two acres of ground.

Here we halted, and driven to it by our desperate thirst, sucked down our last drops of water. We had but half a pint a head, and each of us could have drunk a gallon.

Then we lay down. Just as I was dropping off to sleep I heard Umbopa remark to himself in Zulu, 'If we cannot find water we shall all be dead before the moon rises tomorrow.'

I shuddered, hot as it was. The near prospect of such an awful death is not pleasant, but even the thought of it could not keep me from sleeping.

CHAPTER 6

Water! Water!

Two hours later, that is, about four o'clock, I woke up, for so soon as the first heavy demand of bodily fatigue had been satisfied, the torturing thirst from which I was suffering asserted itself. I could sleep no more. I had been dreaming that I was bathing in a running stream, with green banks and trees upon them, and I awoke to find myself in this arid wilderness, and to remember, as Umbopa had said, that if we did not find water this day we must perish miserably. No human creature could live long without water in that heat. I sat up and rubbed my grimy face with my dry and horny hands, as my lips and eyelids were stuck together, and it was only after some friction and with an effort that I was able to open them. It was not far from dawn, but there was none of the bright feel of dawn in the air, which was thick with a hot murkiness that I cannot describe. The others were still sleeping.

Presently it began to grow light enough to read so I drew out a little pocket copy of the *Ingoldsby Legends* which I had brought with me, and read 'The Jackdaw of Rheims'. When I got to where

> A nice little boy held a golden ewer,
> Embossed, and filled with water as pure
> As any that flows between Rheims and Namur,

literally I smacked my cracking lips, or rather tried to smack them. The mere thought of that pure water made me mad. If the cardinal had been there with his bell, book and candle, I would have whipped in and drunk his water up; yes, even if he had filled it already with the suds of soap 'worthy of washing the hands of the Pope', and I knew that the whole concentrated curse of the

Catholic Church should fall upon me for so doing. I almost think that I must have been a little light-headed with thirst, weariness and the want of food; for I fell to thinking how astonished the cardinal and his nice little boy and the jackdaw would have looked to see a burnt up, brown-eyed, grizzly-haired little elephant hunter suddenly bound between them, put his dirty face into the basin, and swallow every drop of the precious water. The idea amused me so much that I laughed, or rather cackled aloud, which woke the others, and they began to rub *their* dirty faces and to drag *their* gummed-up lips and eyelids apart.

As soon as we were all well awake we began to discuss the situation, which was serious enough. Not a drop of water was left. We turned the bottles upside down, and licked their tops, but it was a failure; they were dry as a bone. Good, who had charge of the flask of brandy, got it out and looked at it longingly; but Sir Henry promptly took it away from him, for to drink raw spirit would only have been to precipitate the end.

'If we do not find water we shall die,' he said.

'If we can trust to the old Dom's map there should be some about,' I said; but nobody seemed to derive much satisfaction from this remark. It was so evident that no great faith could be put in the map. Now it was gradually growing light, and as we sat staring blankly at each other, I observed the Hottentot Ventvögel rise and begin to walk about with his eyes on the ground. Presently he stopped short, and uttering a guttural exclamation, pointed to the earth.

'What is it?' Good exclaimed; and rising simultaneously we went to where Ventvögel was standing staring at the sand.

'Well,' I said, 'it is fresh springbok spoor; what of it?'

'Springbok do not go far from water,' the Hottentot answered in Dutch.

'No,' I answered, 'I forgot; and thank God for it.'

This new discovery put new life into us; for it is wonderful, when a man is in a desperate position, how he catches at the slightest hope and feels almost happy. On a dark night a single star is better than nothing.

Meanwhile Ventvögel was lifting his snub nose and sniffing the hot air for all the world like an old Impala ram who scents danger. Presently he spoke again.

'I *smell* water,' he said.

Then we felt quite jubilant, for we knew what a wonderful instinct these wild-bred men possess.

Just at that moment the sun came up gloriously, and revealed so grand a sight to our astonished eyes that for a moment or two we even forgot our thirst.

There, not more than forty or fifty miles from us, glittering like silver in the early rays of the morning sun, soared Sheba's Breasts; and stretching away for hundreds of miles on either side of them ran the great Suliman Berge. Now that, sitting here, I attempt to describe the extraordinary grandeur and beauty of that sight, language seems to fail me. I am impotent even at its memory. Before us rose two enormous mountains, the like of which are not, I believe, to be seen in Africa, if indeed there are any to match them in the world, measuring, each of them, at least fifteen thousand feet in height, standing not more than a dozen miles apart, linked together by a precipitous cliff of rock, and towering in awful white solemnity straight into the sky. These mountains, placed thus, like the pillars of a gigantic gateway, are shaped after the fashion of a woman's breasts, and at times the mists and shadows beneath them take the form of a recumbent woman, veiled mysteriously in sleep. Their bases swell gently from the plain, looking at that distance perfectly round and smooth; and upon the top of each is a vast hillock covered with snow, exactly corresponding to the nipple on the female breast. The stretch of cliff that connects them appears to be some thousands of feet in height, and perfectly precipitous, and on each flank of them, so far as the eye can reach, extend similar lines of cliff, broken only here and there by flat table-topped mountains, something like the world-famed one at Cape Town; a formation, by the way, that is very common in Africa.

To describe the comprehensive grandeur of that view is beyond my powers. There was something so inexpressibly solemn and overpowering about those huge volcanoes – for doubtless they are extinct volcanoes – that it quite awed us. For a while the morning lights played upon the snow and the brown and swelling masses beneath, and then, as though to veil the majestic sight from our curious eyes, strange vapours and clouds gathered and increased around the mountains, till presently we could only trace their pure and gigantic outlines, showing ghost-like through that fleecy envelope. Indeed, as we afterwards discovered, usually they were wrapped in this gauze-like mist, which doubtless accounted for our not having seen them more clearly before.

Sheba's Breasts had scarcely vanished into cloud-clad privacy, before our thirst – literally a burning question – reasserted itself.

It was all very well for Ventvögel to say that he smelt water, but we could see no signs of it, look which way we would. So far as the eye might reach there was nothing but arid sweltering sand and karoo scrub. We walked round the hillock and gazed about anxiously on the other side, but it was the same story, not a drop of water could be found; there was no indication of a pan, a pool or a spring.

'You are a fool,' I said angrily to Ventvögel; 'there is no water.'

But still he lifted his ugly snub nose and sniffed.

'I smell it, baas,' he answered; 'it is somewhere in the air.'

'Yes,' I said, 'no doubt it is in the clouds, and about two months hence it will fall and wash our bones.'

Sir Henry stroked his yellow beard thoughtfully. 'Perhaps it is on the top of the hill,' he suggested.

'Rot,' said Good; 'whoever heard of water being found at the top of a hill!'

'Let us go and look,' I put in, and hopelessly enough we scrambled up the sandy sides of the hillock, Umbopa leading. Presently he stopped as though he was petrified.

'*Nanzia amanzi!*' ('Here is water!') he cried with a loud voice.

We rushed up to him, and there, sure enough, in a deep cut or indentation on the very top of the sand *koppie*, was an undoubted pool of water. How it came to be in such a strange place we did not stop to enquire, nor did we hesitate at its black and unpleasant appearance. It was water, or a good imitation of it, and that was enough for us. We gave a bound and a rush, and in another second we were all down on our stomachs sucking up the uninviting fluid as though it were nectar fit for the gods. Heavens, how we did drink! Then when we had done drinking we tore off our clothes and sat down in the pool, absorbing the moisture through our parched skins. You, Harry my boy, who have only to turn on a couple of taps to summon 'hot' and 'cold' from a vast and unseen cistern, can have little idea of the luxury of that muddy wallow in brackish tepid water.

After a while we rose from it, refreshed indeed, and fell to on our *biltong*, of which we had scarcely been able to touch a mouthful for twenty-four hours, and ate our fill. Then we smoked a pipe, and lay down by the side of that blessed pool, under the overhanging shadow of its bank, and slept till noon.

All that day we rested there by the water, thanking our stars that we had been lucky enough to find it, bad as it was, and not forgetting to render a due share of gratitude to the shade of the long-departed da Silvestra, who had set its position down so accurately on the tail of his shirt. The wonderful thing to us was that the pan should have lasted so long, and the only way in which I can account for this is on the supposition that it is fed by some spring deep down in the sand.

Having filled both ourselves and our water-bottles as full as possible, in far better spirits we started off again with the moon. That night we covered nearly five-and-twenty miles; but, needless to say, found no more water, though we were lucky enough on the following day to get a little shade behind some ant-heaps. When the sun rose, and, for awhile, cleared away the mysterious mists, Suliman's Berge with the two majestic Breasts, now only about twenty miles off, seemed to be towering right above us, and looked grander than ever. At the approach of evening we marched again, and, to cut a long story short, by daylight next morning found ourselves upon the lowest slopes of Sheba's left Breast, for which we had been steadily steering. By this time our water was exhausted once more, and we were suffering severely from thirst, nor indeed could we see any chance of relieving it till we reached the snow-line far, far above us. After resting an hour or two, driven to it by our torturing thirst, we went on, toiling painfully in the burning heat up the lava slopes, for we found that the huge base of the mountain was composed entirely of lava beds belched from the bowels of the earth in some far past age.

By eleven o'clock we were utterly exhausted, and generally speaking, in a very bad state indeed. The lava clinker, over which we must drag ourselves, though smooth compared with some clinker I have heard of, such as that on the Island of Ascension, for instance, was yet rough enough to make our feet very sore, and this, together with our other miseries, had pretty well finished us. A few hundred yards above us were some large lumps of lava, and towards these we steered with the intention of lying down beneath their shade. We reached them, and to our surprise, so far as we had a capacity for surprise left in us, on a little plateau or ridge close by we saw that the clinker was covered with a dense green growth. Evidently soil formed of decomposed lava had rested there, and in due course had become the receptacle of seeds deposited by birds. But we did not take much further interest in the green growth, for one cannot live on grass like Nebuchadnezzar. That requires a special dispensation of providence and peculiar digestive organs.

So we sat down under the rocks and groaned, and for one I wished heartily that we had never started on this fool's errand. As we were sitting there I saw Umbopa get up and hobble towards the patch of green, and a few minutes afterwards, to my great astonishment, I perceived that usually very dignified individual dancing and shouting like a maniac, and waving something green. Off we all scrambled towards him as fast as our wearied limbs would carry us, hoping that he had found water.

'What is it, Umbopa, son of a fool?' I shouted in Zulu.

'It is food and water, Macumazahn,' and again he waved the green thing.

Then I saw what he had found. It was a melon. We had hit upon a patch of wild melons, thousands of them, and dead ripe.

'Melons!' I yelled to Good, who was next me; and in another minute his false teeth were fixed in one of them.

I think that we ate about six each before we had done, and poor fruit as they were, I doubt if I ever thought anything nicer.

But melons are not very nutritious, and when we had satisfied our thirst with their pulpy substance, and put a stock to cool by the simple process of cutting them in two and setting them end on in the hot sun to grow cold by evaporation, we began to feel exceedingly hungry. We had still some *biltong* left, but our stomachs turned from *biltong*, and besides, we were obliged to be very sparing of it, for we could not say when we should find more food. Just at this moment a lucky thing chanced. Looking across the desert I saw a flock of about ten large birds flying straight towards us.

'*Skit, baas, skit!*' (Shoot, master, shoot!) whispered the Hottentot, throwing himself on his face, an example which we all followed.

Then I saw that the birds were a flock of *pauw* or bustards, and that they would pass within fifty yards of my head. Taking one of the repeating Winchesters, I waited till they were nearly over us, and then jumped to my feet. On seeing me the *pauw* bunched up together, as I expected that they would, and I fired two shots straight into the thick of them, and, as luck would have it, brought one down, a fine fellow, that weighed about twenty pounds. In half an hour we had a fire made of dry melon stalks, and he was toasting over it, and we made such a feed as we had not tasted for a week. We ate that *pauw*; nothing was left of him but his leg-bones and his beak, and we felt not a little better afterwards.

That night we went on again with the moon, carrying as many melons as we could with us. As we ascended we found the air grow cooler and cooler, which was a great relief to us, and at dawn, so far as we could judge, we were not more than about a dozen miles from the snow-line. Here we discovered more melons, and so had no longer any anxiety about water, for we knew that we should soon get plenty of snow. But the ascent had now become very precipitous, and we made slow progress, not more than a mile an hour. Also that night we ate our last morsel of *biltong*. As yet, with the exception of the *pauw*, we had seen no living thing on the mountain, nor had we come across a single spring or stream of water, which struck us as very odd, considering the expanse of snow above us, which must, we thought, melt sometimes. But as we afterwards discovered, owing to a cause which it is quite beyond my power to explain, all the streams flowed down upon the north side of the mountains.

Now we began to grow very anxious about food. We had escaped death by thirst, but it seemed probable that it was only to die of hunger. The events of the next three miserable days are best described by copying the entries made at the time in my notebook.

21st May – Started 11 a.m., finding the atmosphere quite cold enough to travel by day, and carrying some watermelons with us. Struggled on all day, but found no more melons, having evidently passed out of their district. Saw no game of any sort. Halted for the night at sundown, having had no food for many hours. Suffered much during the night from cold.

22nd – Started at sunrise again, feeling very faint and weak. Only made about five miles all day; found some patches of snow, of which we ate, but nothing else. Camped at night under the edge of a great plateau. Cold bitter. Drank a little brandy each, and huddled ourselves together, each wrapped up in his blanket, to keep ourselves alive. Are now suffering frightfully from starvation and weariness. Thought that Ventvögel would have died during the night.

23rd – Struggled forward once more as soon as the sun was well up, and had thawed our limbs a little. We are now in a dreadful plight, and I fear that unless we get food this will be our last day's journey. But little brandy left. Good, Sir Henry and Umbopa bear up wonderfully, but Ventvögel is in a very bad way. Like most Hottentots, he cannot stand cold. Pangs of hunger not so bad, but have a sort of numb feeling about the stomach. Others say the same. We are now on a level with the precipitous chain, or wall of lava, linking the two breasts, and the view is glorious. Behind us the glowing desert rolls away to the horizon, and before us lie miles of smooth hard snow almost level, but swelling gently upwards, out of the centre of which the nipple of the mountain, that appears to be some miles in circumference, rises about four thousand feet into the sky. Not a living thing is to be seen. God help us; I fear that our time has come.

And now I will drop the journal, partly because it is not very interesting reading; also what follows requires telling rather more fully.

All that day – the 23rd May – we struggled slowly up the incline of snow, lying down from time to time to rest. A strange gaunt crew we must have looked, while, laden as we were, we dragged our weary feet over the dazzling plain, glaring round us with hungry eyes. Not that there was much use in glaring, for we could see nothing to eat. We did not accomplish more than seven miles that day. Just before sunset we found ourselves exactly under the nipple of Sheba's left Breast, which towered thousands of feet into the air, a vast smooth hillock of frozen snow. Weak as we were, we could not but appreciate the wonderful scene, made even more splendid by the flying rays of light from the setting sun, which here and there stained the snow blood-red, and crowned the great dome above us with a diadem of glory.

'I say,' gasped Good, presently, 'we ought to be somewhere near that cave the old gentleman wrote about.'

'Yes,' said I, 'if there is a cave.'

'Come, Quatermain,' groaned Sir Henry, 'don't talk like that; I have every faith in the dom; remember the water! We shall find the place soon.'

'If we don't find it before dark we are dead men, that is all about it,' was my consolatory reply.

For the next ten minutes we trudged in silence, when suddenly Umbopa, who was marching along beside me, wrapped in his blanket, and with a leather belt strapped so tightly round his stomach, to 'make his hunger small' as he said, that his waist looked like a girl's, caught me by the arm.

'Look!' he said, pointing towards the springing slope of the nipple.

I followed his glance, and some two hundred yards from us perceived what appeared to be a hole in the snow.

'It is the cave,' said Umbopa.

We made the best of our way to the spot, and found sure enough that the hole was the mouth of a cavern, no doubt the same as that of which da Silvestra wrote. We were not too soon, for just as we reached shelter the sun went down with startling rapidity, leaving the world nearly dark, for in these latitudes there is but little twilight. So we crept into the cave, which did not appear to be very big, and huddling ourselves together for warmth, swallowed what remained of our brandy – barely a mouthful each – and tried to forget our miseries in sleep. But the cold was too intense to allow us to do so, for I am convinced that at this great altitude the thermometer cannot have marked less than fourteen or fifteen degrees below freezing point. What such a temperature meant to us, enervated as we were by hardship, want of food, and the great heat of the desert, the reader may imagine better than I can describe. Suffice it to say that it was something as near death from exposure as I have ever felt. There we sat for hour after hour through the still and bitter night, feeling the frost wander round and nip us now in the finger, now in the foot, now in the face. In vain did we huddle up closer and closer; there was no warmth in our miserable starved carcasses. Sometimes one of us would drop into an uneasy slumber for a few minutes, but we could not sleep much, and perhaps this was fortunate, for if we had I doubt if we should ever have woken again. Indeed, I believe that it was only by force of will that we kept ourselves alive at all.

Not very long before dawn I heard the Hottentot Ventvögel, whose teeth had been chattering all night like castanets, give a deep sigh. Then his teeth stopped chattering. I did not think anything of it at the time, concluding that he had gone to sleep. His back was resting against mine, and it seemed to grow colder and colder, till at last it felt like ice.

At length the air began to grow grey with light, then golden arrows sped across the snow, and at last the glorious sun peeped above the lava wall and looked in upon our half-frozen forms. Also it looked upon Ventvögel, sitting there amongst us, stone dead. No wonder his back felt cold, poor fellow. He had died when I heard him sigh, and was now frozen almost stiff. Shocked beyond measure, we dragged ourselves from the corpse – how strange is that horror we mortals have of the companionship of a dead body – and left it sitting there, its arms clasped about its knees.

By this time the sunlight was pouring its cold rays, for here they were cold, straight into the mouth of the cave. Suddenly I heard an exclamation of fear from someone, and turned my head.

This was what I saw. Sitting at the end of the cavern – it was not more than twenty feet long – was another form, of which the head rested on the chest and the long arms hung down. I stared at it, and saw that this too was a dead man, and, what was more, a white man.

The others saw also, and the sight proved too much for our shattered nerves. One and all we scrambled out of that cave as fast as our half-frozen limbs would carry us.

CHAPTER 7

Solomon's Road

Outside the cavern we halted, feeling rather foolish.

'I am going back,' said Sir Henry.

'Why?' asked Good.

'Because it has struck me that – what we saw – may be my brother.'

This was a new idea, and we re-entered the place to put it to the proof. After the bright light outside, our eyes, weak as they were with staring at the snow, could not pierce the gloom of the cave for a while. Presently, however, they grew accustomed to the semi-darkness, and we advanced towards the dead man.

Sir Henry knelt down and peered into his face.

'Thank God,' he said, with a sigh of relief, 'it is *not* my brother.'

Then I drew near and looked. The body was that of a tall man in middle life with aquiline features, grizzled hair and a long black moustache. The skin was perfectly yellow, and stretched tightly over the bones. Its clothing, with the exception of what seemed to be the remains of a woollen pair of hose, had been removed, leaving the skeleton-like frame naked. Round the neck of the corpse, which was frozen perfectly stiff, hung a yellow ivory crucifix.

'Who on earth can it be?' said I.

'Can't you guess?' asked Good.

I shook my head.

'Why, the old dom, José da Silvestra, of course – who else?'

'Impossible,' I gasped; 'he died three hundred years ago.'

'And what is there to prevent him from lasting for three thousand years in this atmosphere, I should like to know?' asked Good. 'If only the temperature is sufficiently low, flesh and blood will keep fresh as New Zealand mutton for ever, and heaven knows it is cold enough here. The sun never gets in here; no animal comes here to tear or destroy. No doubt his slave, of whom he speaks in the writing, took off his clothes and left him. He could not have buried him alone. Look!' he went on, stooping down to pick up a queerly-shaped bone scraped at the end into a sharp point, 'here is the cleft bone that Silvestra used to draw the map with.'

We gazed for a moment astonished, forgetting our own miseries in this extraordinary and, as it seemed to us, semi-miraculous sight.

'Aye,' said Sir Henry, 'and this is where he got his ink from,' and he pointed to a small wound on the Dom's left arm. 'Did ever a man see such a thing before?'

There was no longer any doubt about the matter, which for my own part, I confess, perfectly appalled me. There he sat, the dead man, whose directions, written some ten generations ago, had led us to this spot. Here in my own hand was the rude pen with which he had written them, and about his neck hung the crucifix that his dying lips had kissed. Gazing at him, my imagination could reconstruct the last scene of the drama – the traveller dying of cold and starvation, yet striving to convey to the world the great secret which he had discovered – and the awful loneliness of his death, of which the evidence sat before us. It even seemed to me that I could trace in his strongly-marked features a likeness to those of my poor friend Silvestre his descendant, who had died twenty years before in my arms, but perhaps that was fancy. At any rate, there he sat, a sad memento of the fate that so often overtakes those who would penetrate into the unknown; and there doubtless he will still sit, crowned with the dread majesty of death, for centuries to come, to startle the eyes of wanderers like ourselves, if ever any such should come again to invade his loneliness. The thing overpowered us, already almost perished as we were with cold and hunger.

'Let us go,' said Sir Henry in a low voice; 'stay, we will give him a companion,' and lifting up the dead body of the Hottentot Ventvögel, he placed it near to that of the old dom. Then he stooped, and with a jerk broke the rotten string of the crucifix which hung round da Silvestra's neck, for his fingers were too cold to attempt to unfasten it. I believe that he has it still. I took the bone pen, and it is before me as I write – sometimes I use it to sign my name.

Then leaving these two, the proud white man of a past age, and the poor Hottentot, to keep their eternal vigil in the midst of the eternal snows, we crept out of the cave into the welcome sunshine and resumed our path, wondering in our hearts how many hours it would be before we were even as they are.

When we had walked about half a mile we came to the edge of the plateau, for the nipple of the mountain does not rise out of its exact centre, though from the desert side it had seemed to do so. What lay before us we could not see, for the landscape was wreathed in billows of morning fog. Presently, however, the higher layers of mist cleared a little, and revealed, at the end of the long slope of snow, a patch of green grass, some five hundred yards beneath us, through which a stream was running. Nor was this all. By the stream basking in the bright sun stood and lay a group of from ten to fifteen large antelopes – at that distance we could not see of what species.

The sight filled us with an unreasoning joy. If only we could get it, there was food in plenty. But the question was how to get it. The beasts were fully six hundred yards off, a very long shot, and one not to be depended on when our lives hung upon the results.

Rapidly we discussed the advisability of trying to stalk the game, but in the end dismissed it reluctantly. To begin with, the wind was not favourable, and further, we must certainly be perceived, however careful we were, against the blinding background of the snow, which we should be obliged to traverse.

'Well, we must have a try from where we are,' said Sir Henry. 'Which shall it be, Quatermain, the repeating rifles or the Expresses?'

Here again was a question. The Winchester repeaters – of which we had two, Umbopa carrying poor Ventvögel's as well as his own – were sighted up to a thousand yards, whereas the Expresses were only sighted to three hundred and fifty, beyond which distance shooting with them was more or less guesswork. On the other hand, if they did hit, the Express bullets, being expanding, were much more likely to bring the game down. It was a knotty point, but I made up my mind that we must risk it and use the Expresses.

'Let each of us take the buck opposite to him. Aim well at the point of the shoulder and high up,' said I; 'and Umbopa, do you give the word, so that we may all fire together.'

Then came a pause, each of us aiming his level best, as indeed a man is likely to do when he knows that life itself depends upon the shot.

'Fire,' said Umbopa in Zulu, and at almost the same instant the three rifles rang out loudly; three clouds of smoke hung for a moment before us, and a hundred echoes went flying over the silent snow. Presently the smoke cleared, and revealed – oh, joy!– a great buck lying on its back and kicking furiously in its death agony. We gave a yell of triumph – we were saved, we should not starve. Weak as we were, we rushed down the intervening slope of snow, and in ten minutes from the time of shooting, that animal's heart and liver were lying before us. But now a new difficulty arose, we had no fuel, and therefore could make no fire to cook them. We gazed at each other in dismay.

'Starving men should not be fanciful,' said Good; 'we must eat raw meat.'

There was no other way out of the dilemma, and our gnawing hunger made the proposition less distasteful than it would otherwise have been. So we took the heart and liver and buried them for a few minutes in a patch of snow to cool them. Then we washed them in the ice-cold water of the stream, and lastly ate them greedily. It sounds horrible enough, but honestly, I never tasted anything so good as that raw meat. In a quarter of an hour we were changed men. Our life and vigour came back to us, our feeble pulses grew strong again, and the blood went coursing through our veins. But mindful of the results of over-feeding on starved stomachs, we were careful not to eat too much, stopping whilst we were still hungry.

'Thank heaven!' said Sir Henry; 'that brute has saved our lives. What is it, Quatermain?'

I rose and went to look at the antelope, for I was not certain. It was about the size of a donkey, with large curved horns. I had never seen one like it before; the species was new to me. It was brown in colour, with faint red stripes, and grew a thick coat. I afterwards discovered that the natives of that wonderful country call these bucks *inco*. They are very rare, and only found at a great altitude where no other game will live. This animal was fairly hit up in the shoulder, though whose bullet knocked it over we could not, of course, discover. I believe that Good, mindful of his marvellous shot at the giraffe, secretly set it down to his own prowess, and we did not contradict him.

We had been so busy satisfying our hunger that hitherto we had not found time to look about us. But now, having set Umbopa to cut off as much of the best meat as we were likely to be able to carry, we began to inspect our surroundings. The mist had cleared away, for it was eight o'clock, and the sun had sucked it up, so we were able to take in all the country before us at a glance. I know not how to describe the glorious panorama which unfolded itself to our gaze. I have never seen anything like it before, nor shall, I suppose, again.

Behind and over us towered Sheba's snowy Breasts, and below, some five thousand feet beneath where we stood, lay league on league of the most lovely champaign. Here were dense patches of lofty forest, there a great river wound its silvery way. To the left stretched a vast expanse of rich, undulating veld or grassland, whereon we could just make out countless herds of game or cattle, at that distance we could not tell which. This expanse appeared to be ringed in by a wall of distant mountains. To the right the country was more or less mountainous; that is, solitary hills stood up from its level, with stretches of cultivated land between, amongst which we could see groups of dome-shaped huts. The landscape lay before us as a map, wherein rivers flashed like silver snakes and alp-like peaks, crowned with wildly twisted snow wreaths, rose in grandeur, whilst over all was the glad sunlight and the breath of nature's happy life.

Two curious things struck us as we gazed. First, that the country before us must lie at least three thousand feet higher than the desert we had crossed, and secondly, that all the rivers flowed from south to north. As we had painful reason to know, there was no water upon the southern side of the vast range on which we stood, but on the northern face were many streams, most of which appeared to unite with the great river we could see winding away farther than our eyes could follow.

We sat down for a while and gazed in silence at this wonderful view.

Presently Sir Henry spoke. 'Isn't there something on the map about Solomon's Great Road?' he said.

I nodded, for I was still gazing out over the far country.

'Well, look; there it is!' and he pointed a little to our right.

Good and I looked accordingly, and there, winding away towards the plain, was what appeared to be a wide turnpike road. We had not seen it at first because, on reaching the plain, it turned behind some broken country. We did not say anything, at least, not much; we were beginning to lose the sense of wonder. Somehow it did not seem particularly unnatural that we should find a sort of Roman road in this strange land. We accepted the fact, that was all.

'Well,' said Good, 'it must be quite near us if we cut off to the right. Hadn't we better be making a start?'

This was sound advice, and as soon as we had washed our faces and hands in the stream we acted on it. For a mile or more we made our way over boulders and across patches of snow, till suddenly, on reaching the top of the little rise, we found the road at our feet. It was a splendid road cut out of the solid rock, at least fifty feet wide, and apparently well kept; though the odd thing was that it seemed to begin there. We walked down and stood on it, but one single hundred paces behind us, in the direction of Sheba's Breasts, it vanished, the entire surface of the mountain being strewn with boulders interspersed with patches of snow.

'What do you make of this, Quatermain?' asked Sir Henry.

I shook my head, I could make nothing of the thing.

'I have it!' said Good; 'the road no doubt ran right over the range and across the desert on the other side, but the sand there has covered it up, and above us it has been obliterated by some volcanic eruption of molten lava.'

This seemed a good suggestion; at any rate, we accepted it, and proceeded down the mountain. It proved a very different business travelling along downhill on that magnificent pathway with full stomachs from what it was travelling uphill over the snow quite starved and almost frozen. Indeed, had it not been for melancholy recollections of poor Ventvögel's sad fate, and of that grim cave where he kept company with the old dom, we should have felt positively cheerful, notwithstanding the sense of unknown dangers before us. Every mile we walked the atmosphere grew softer and balmier, and the country before us shone with a yet more luminous beauty. As for the road itself, I never saw such an engineering work, though Sir Henry said that the great road over the St Gothard in Switzerland is very similar. No difficulty had been too great for the old-world engineer who laid it out. At one place we came to a ravine three hundred feet broad and at least a hundred deep. This vast gulf was actually filled in with huge blocks of dressed stone, having arches pierced through them at the bottom for a waterway, over which the road went on sublimely. At another place it was cut in zigzags out of the side of a precipice five hundred feet deep, and in a third it tunnelled through the base of an intervening ridge, a space of thirty yards or more.

Here we noticed that the sides of the tunnel were covered with quaint sculptured reliefs, mostly of mailed figures driving in chariots. One, which was exceedingly beautiful, represented a whole battle scene, with a convoy of captives being marched off in the distance.

'Well,' said Sir Henry, after inspecting this ancient work of art, 'it is very well to call this Solomon's Road, but my humble opinion is that the Egyptians had been here before Solomon's people ever set foot on it. If this isn't Egyptian or Phoenician handiwork, I must say that it is very like it.'

By midday we had advanced sufficiently down the mountain to reach the region where wood was to be met with. First we came to scattered bushes, which grew more and more frequent till at last we found the road winding through a vast grove of silver trees similar to those which are to be seen on the slopes of Table Mountain at Cape Town. I had never before met with them in all my wanderings, except at the Cape, and their appearance here astonished me greatly.

'Ah!' said Good, surveying these shining-leaved trees with evident enthusiasm, 'here is lots of wood, let us stop and cook some dinner; I have about digested that raw heart.'

Nobody objected to this, so leaving the road we made our way to a stream which was babbling away not far off, and soon had a goodly fire of dry boughs blazing. Cutting off some substantial hunks from the flesh of the *inco* which we had brought with us, we proceeded to toast them on the end of sharp sticks, as one sees the Kafirs do, and ate them with relish. After filling ourselves, we lit our pipes and gave ourselves up to enjoyment that, compared with the hardships we had recently undergone, seemed almost heavenly.

The brook, of which the banks were clothed with dense masses of a gigantic species of maidenhair fern interspersed with feathery tufts of wild asparagus, sang merrily at our side, the soft air murmured through the foliage of the silver trees, doves cooed around and bright-winged birds flashed like living gems from bough to bough. It was a paradise.

The magic of the place, combined with an overwhelming sense of dangers left behind, and of the promised land reached at last, seemed to charm us into silence. Sir Henry and Umbopa sat conversing in a mixture of broken English and kitchen Zulu in low voices, but earnestly enough, and I lay, with my eyes half shut, upon that fragrant bed of fern and watched them.

Presently I missed Good and looked to see what had become of him. Soon I observed him sitting by the bank of the stream, in which he had been bathing. He had nothing on but his flannel shirt, and his natural habits of extreme neatness having reasserted themselves, he was actively employed in making a most elaborate toilet. He had washed his gutta-percha collar, had thoroughly shaken out his trousers, coat and waistcoat, and was now folding them up neatly till he was ready to put them on, shaking his head sadly as he scanned the numerous rents and tears in them, which naturally had resulted from our frightful journey. Then he took his boots, scrubbed them with a handful of fern, and finally rubbed them over with a piece of fat which he had carefully saved from the *inco* meat, till they looked, comparatively speaking, respectable. Having inspected them judicially through his eyeglass, he put the boots on and began a fresh operation. From a little bag that he carried he produced a pocket-comb in which was fixed a tiny looking-glass, and in this he surveyed himself. Apparently he was not satisfied, for he proceeded to do his hair with great care. Then came a pause whilst he again contemplated the effect; still it was not satisfactory. He felt his chin, on which the accumulated scrub of a ten days' beard was flourishing.

'Surely,' thought I, 'he is not going to try to shave.' But so it was. Taking the piece of fat with which he had greased his boots, Good washed it thoroughly in the stream. Then diving again into the bag he brought out a little pocket razor with a guard to it, such as are bought by people who are afraid of cutting themselves, or by those about to undertake a sea voyage. Then he rubbed his face and chin vigorously with the fat and began. Evidently it proved a painful process, for he groaned very much over it, and I was convulsed with inward laughter as I watched him struggling with that stubbly beard. It seemed so very odd that a man should take the trouble to shave himself with a piece of fat in such a place and in our circumstances. At last he succeeded in getting the hair off the right side of his face and chin, when suddenly I, who was watching, became conscious of a flash of light that passed just by his head.

Good sprang up with a profane exclamation (if it had not been a safety razor he would certainly have cut his throat), and so did I, without the exclamation, and this was what I saw. Standing not more than twenty paces from where I was, and ten from Good, were a group of men. They were very tall and copper-coloured, and some of them wore great plumes of black feathers and short cloaks of leopard-skin; this was all I noticed at the moment. In front of them stood a youth of about seventeen, his hand still raised and his body bent forward in the attitude of a Grecian statue of a spear thrower. Evidently the flash of light had been caused by a weapon which he had hurled.

As I looked, an old soldier-like man stepped forward out of the group, and catching the youth by the arm, said something to him. Then they advanced upon us.

Sir Henry, Good and Umbopa by this time had seized their rifles and lifted them threateningly. The party of natives still came on. It struck me that they could not know what rifles were, or they would not have treated them with such contempt.

'Put down your guns!' I hallooed to the others, seeing that our only chance of safety lay in conciliation. They obeyed, and walking to the front I addressed the elderly man who had checked the youth.

'Greetings,' I said in Zulu, not knowing what language to use. To my surprise I was understood.

'Greetings,' answered the man, not, indeed, in the same tongue, but in a dialect so closely allied to it that neither Umbopa nor myself had any difficulty in understanding him. Indeed, as we afterwards found out, the language spoken by this people is an old-fashioned form of the Zulu tongue, bearing about the same relationship to it that the English of Chaucer does to the English of the nineteenth century.

'Whence come you?' he went on, 'who are you? And why are the faces of three of you white, and the face of the fourth as the face of our mother's sons?' and he pointed to Umbopa. I looked at Umbopa as he said it, and it flashed across me that he was right. The face of Umbopa was like the faces of the men before me, and so was his great form like their forms. But I had not time to reflect on this coincidence.

'We are strangers, and come in peace,' I answered, speaking very slowly, so that he might understand me, 'and this man is our servant.'

'Ye lie,' he answered; 'no strangers can cross the mountains where all things perish. But what do your lies matter? If ye are strangers then ye must die, for no strangers may live in the land of the Kukuanas. It is the king's law. Prepare then to die, O strangers!'

I was slightly staggered at this, more especially as I saw the hands of some of the men steal down to their sides, where hung on each what looked to me like a large and heavy knife.

'What does that beggar say?' asked Good.

'He says we are going to be killed,' I answered grimly.

'Oh, Lord!' groaned Good; and, as was his way when perplexed, he put his hand to his false teeth, dragging the top set down and allowing them to fly back to his jaw with a snap. It was a most fortunate move, for next second the dignified crowd of Kukuanas uttered a simultaneous yell of horror, and bolted back some yards.

'What's up?' said I.

'It's his teeth,' whispered Sir Henry excitedly. 'He moved them. Take them out, Good, take them out!'

He obeyed, slipping the set into the sleeve of his flannel shirt.

In another second curiosity had overcome fear, and the men advanced slowly. Apparently they had now forgotten their amiable intention of killing us.

'How is it, O strangers,' asked the old man solemnly, 'that this fat man' (pointing to Good, who was clad in nothing but boots and a flannel shirt, and had only half finished his shaving), 'whose body is clothed, and whose legs are bare, who grows hair on one side of his sickly face and not on the other, and who wears one shining and transparent eye – how is it, I ask, that he has teeth which move of themselves, coming away from the jaws and returning of their own will?'

'Open your mouth,' I said to Good, who promptly curled up his lips and grinned at the old gentleman like an angry dog, revealing to his astonished gaze two thin red lines of gum as utterly innocent of ivories as is a newborn elephant. The audience gasped.

'Where are his teeth?' they shouted; 'with our eyes we saw them.'

Turning his head slowly and with a gesture of ineffable contempt, Good swept his hand across his mouth. Then he grinned again, and lo, there were two rows of lovely teeth.

Now the young man who had flung the knife threw himself down on the grass and gave vent to a prolonged howl of terror; and as for the old gentleman, his knees knocked together with fear.

'I see that ye are spirits,' he said falteringly; 'did ever man born of woman have hair on one side of his face and not on the other, or a round and transparent eye, or teeth which moved and melted away and grew again? Pardon us, O my lords.'

Here was luck indeed, and, needless to say, I jumped at the chance.

'It is granted,' I said with an imperial smile. 'Nay, ye shall know the truth. We come from another world, though we are men such as ye. We come,' I went on, 'from the biggest star that shines at night.'

'Oh! oh!' groaned the chorus of astonished aborigines.

'Yes,' I went on, 'we do, indeed,' and again I smiled benignly, as I uttered that amazing lie. 'We come to stay with you a little while, and to bless you by our sojourn. Ye will see, O friends, that I have prepared myself for this visit by the learning of your language.'

'It is so, it is so,' said the chorus.

'Only, my lord,' put in the old gentleman, 'thou hast learnt it very badly.'

I cast an indignant glance at him, and he quailed. 'Now, friends,' I continued, 'ye might think that after so long a journey we should find it in our hearts to avenge such a reception, mayhap to strike cold in death the impious hand that – that, in short – threw a knife at the head of him whose teeth come and go.'

'Spare him, my lords,' said the old man in supplication; 'he is the king's son, and I am his uncle. If anything befalls him his blood will be required at my hands.'

'Yes, that is certainly so,' put in the young man with great emphasis.

'Ye may perhaps doubt our power to avenge,' I went on, heedless of this by-play. 'Stay, I will show you. Here, thou dog and slave' (addressing Umbopa in a savage tone), 'give me the magic tube that speaks,' and I tipped a wink towards my Express rifle.

Umbopa rose to the occasion. With something as nearly resembling a grin as I have ever seen on his dignified face he handed me the gun.

'It is here, O lord of lords,' he said with a deep obeisance.

Now just before I asked for the rifle I had perceived a little *klipspringer* standing on a mass of rock about seventy yards away, and determined to risk the shot.

'Ye see that buck,' I said, pointing the animal out to the party before me. 'Tell me, is it possible for man born of woman to kill it from here with a noise?'

'It is not possible, my lord,' answered the old man.

'Yet shall I kill it,' I said quietly.

The old man smiled. 'That my lord cannot do,' he answered.

I raised the rifle and covered the buck. It was a small animal, and one which a man might well be excused for missing, but I knew that it would not do to miss.

I drew a deep breath, and slowly pressed on the trigger. The buck stood still as a stone.

'Bang! thud!' The antelope sprang in the air and fell on the rock dead as a doornail.

A simultaneous groan of terror burst from the group before us.

'If you want meat,' I remarked coolly, 'go fetch that buck.'

The old man made a sign; one of his followers departed, and presently returned bearing the *klipspringer*. I noticed with satisfaction that I had hit it fairly behind the shoulder. They gathered round the poor creature's body, gazing at the bullet-hole in consternation.

'Ye see,' I said, 'I do not speak empty words.'

There was no answer.

'If ye yet doubt our power,' I went on, 'let one of you go stand upon that rock that I may make him as this buck.'

None of them seemed at all inclined to take the hint, till at last the king's son spoke. 'It is well said. Do thou, my uncle, go stand upon the rock. It is but a buck that the magic has killed. Surely it cannot kill a man.'

The old gentleman did not take the suggestion in good part. Indeed, he seemed hurt.

'No! no!' he ejaculated hastily, 'my old eyes have seen enough. These are wizards, indeed. Let us bring them to the king. Yet if any should wish a further proof, let him stand upon the rock, that the magic tube may speak with him.'

There was a most general and hasty expression of dissent.

'Let not good magic be wasted on our poor bodies,' said one; 'we are satisfied. All the witchcraft of our people cannot show the like of this.'

'It is so,' remarked the old gentleman, in a tone of intense relief; 'without any doubt it is so. Listen, children of the stars, children of the shining eye and the movable teeth, who roar out in thunder and slay from afar. I am Infadoos, son of Kafa, once king of the Kukuana people. This youth is Scragga.'

'He nearly scragged me,' murmured Good.

'Scragga, son of Twala, the great king – Twala, husband of a thousand wives, chief and lord paramount of the Kukuanas, keeper of the great road, terror of his enemies, student of the black arts, leader of a hundred thousand warriors, Twala the One-Eyed, the Black, the Terrible.'

'So,' said I superciliously, 'lead us then to Twala. We do not talk with low people and underlings.'

'It is well, my lords, we will lead you; but the way is long. We are hunting three days' journey from the place of the king. But let my lords have patience, and we will lead them.'

'So be it,' I said carelessly; 'all time is before us, for we do not die. We are ready; lead on. But Infadoos, and thou Scragga, beware! Play us no monkey tricks, set for us no foxes' snares, for before your brains of mud have thought of them we shall know and avenge. The light from the transparent eye of him with the bare legs and the half-haired face shall destroy you, and go through your land; his vanishing teeth shall fix themselves fast in you and eat you up, you and your wives and children; the magic tubes shall argue with you loudly, and make you as sieves. Beware!'

This magnificent address did not fail of its effect; indeed, it might almost have been spared, so deeply were our friends already impressed with our powers.

The old man made a deep obeisance, and murmured the words, '*Koom! Koom!*' which I afterwards discovered was their royal salute, corresponding to the *Bayéte* of the Zulus, and turning, addressed his followers. These at once proceeded to lay hold of all our goods and chattels, in order to bear them for us, excepting only the guns, which they would on no account touch. They even seized Good's clothes, that, as the reader may remember, were neatly folded up beside him.

He saw and made a dive for them, and a loud altercation ensued.

'Let not my lord of the transparent eye and the melting teeth touch them,' said the old man. 'Surely his slave shall carry the things.'

'But I want to put 'em on!' roared Good, in nervous English.

Umbopa translated.

'Nay, my lord,' answered Infadoos; 'would my lord cover up his beautiful white legs' (although he is so dark, Good has a singularly white skin) 'from the eyes of his servants? Have we offended my lord that he should do such a thing?'

Here I nearly exploded with laughing; and meanwhile one of the men started on with the garments.

'Damn it!' roared Good, 'that black villain has got my trousers.'

'Look here, Good,' said Sir Henry; 'you have appeared in this country in a certain character, and you must live up to it. It will never do for you to put on trousers again. Henceforth you must exist in a flannel shirt, a pair of boots, and an eyeglass.'

'Yes,' I said, 'and with whiskers on one side of your face and not on the other. If you change any of these things the people will think that we are impostors. I am very sorry for you, but, seriously, you must. If once they begin to suspect us, our lives will not be worth a brass farthing.'

'Do you really think so?' asked Good gloomily.

'I do, indeed. Your beautiful white legs and your eyeglass are now *the* features of our party, and as Sir Henry says, you must live up to them. Be thankful that you have got your boots on, and that the air is warm.'

Good sighed, and said no more, but it took him a fortnight to become accustomed to his new and scant attire.

CHAPTER 8

We Enter Kukuanaland

All that afternoon we travelled along the magnificent roadway, which trended steadily in a northwesterly direction. Infadoos and Scragga walked with us, but their followers marched about one hundred paces ahead.

'Infadoos,' I said at length, 'who made this road?'

'It was made, my lord, of old time, none know how or when, not even the wise woman Gagool, who has lived for generations. We are not old enough to remember its making. None can fashion such roads now, but the king suffers no grass to grow upon it.'

'And whose are the writings on the walls of the caves through which we have passed on the road?' I asked referring to the Egyptian-like reliefs that we had seen.

'My lord, the hands that made the road wrote the wonderful writings. We know not who wrote them.'

'When did the Kukuana people come into this country?'

'My lord, the race came down hither like the breath of a storm ten thousand thousand moons ago, from the great lands which lie there beyond,' and he pointed to the north. 'They could travel no farther because of the high mountains which ring in the land, so say the old voices of our fathers that have descended to us the children, and so says Gagool, the wise woman, the smeller out of witches,' and again he pointed to the snow-clad peaks. 'The country, too, was good, so they settled here and grew strong and powerful, and now our numbers are like the sea sand, and when Twala the king calls up his regiments their plumes cover the plain so far as the eye of man can reach.'

'And if the land is walled in with mountains, who is there for the regiments to fight with?'

'Nay, my lord, the country is open there towards the north, and now and again warriors sweep down upon us in clouds from a land we know not, and we slay them. It is the third part of the life of a man since there was a war. Many thousands died in it, but we destroyed those who came to eat us up. So since then there has been no war.'

'Your warriors must grow weary of resting on their spears, Infadoos.'

'My lord, there was one war, just after we destroyed the people that came down upon us, but it was a civil war; dog ate dog.'

'How was that?'

'My lord, the king, my half-brother, had a brother born at the same birth, and of the same woman. It is not our custom, my lord, to suffer twins to live; the weaker must always die. But the mother of the king hid away the feebler child, which was born the last, for her heart yearned over it, and that child is Twala the king. I am his brother, born of another wife.'

'Well?'

'My lord, Kafa, our father, died when we came to manhood, and my brother Imotu was made king in his place, and for a space reigned and had a son by his favourite wife. When the babe was three years old, just after the great war, during which no man could sow or reap, a famine came upon the land, and the people murmured because of the famine, and looked round like a starved lion for something to rend. Then it was that Gagool, the wise and terrible woman, who does not die, made a proclamation to the people, saying, "The king Imotu is no king." And at the time Imotu was sick with a wound, and lay in his kraal not able to move.

'Then Gagool went into the hut and led out Twala, my half-brother, and twin brother to the king, whom she had hidden among the caves and rocks since he was born, and stripping the *moocha* off his loins, showed the people of the Kukuanas the mark of the sacred snake coiled round his middle, wherewith the eldest son of the king is marked at birth, and cried out loud, "Behold your king whom I have saved for you even to this day!"

'Now the people being mad with hunger, and altogether bereft of reason and the knowledge of truth, cried out – "*The king! The king!*" but I knew that it was not so, for Imotu my brother was the elder of the twins, and our lawful king. Then just as the tumult was at its height Imotu the king, though he was very sick, crawled from his hut holding his wife by the hand, and followed by his little son Ignosi – that is, by interpretation, Son of the Lightning.

' "What is this noise?" he asked. "Why cry ye, *The king! The king!*"

'Then Twala, his own brother, born of the same woman, and in the same hour, ran to him, and taking him by the hair, stabbed him through the heart with his knife. And the people being fickle, and ever ready to worship the rising sun, clapped their hands and cried, "*Twala is king!* Now we know that Twala is king!" '

'And what became of Imotu's wife and her son Ignosi? Did Twala kill them too?'

'Nay, my lord. When she saw that her lord was dead the queen seized the child with a cry and ran away. Two days afterwards she came to a kraal very hungry, and none would give her milk or food, now that her lord the king was dead, for all men hate the unfortunate. But at nightfall a little child, a girl, crept out and brought her corn to eat, and she blessed the child, and went on towards the mountains with her boy before the sun rose again. There she must have perished, for none have seen her since, nor the child Ignosi.'

'Then if this child Ignosi had lived he would be the true king of the Kukuana people?'

'That is so, my lord; the sacred snake is round his middle. If he lives he is king; but, alas! he is long dead.'

'See, my lord,' and Infadoos pointed to a vast collection of huts surrounded by a fence, which was in its turn encircled by a great ditch, that lay on the plain beneath us. 'That is the kraal where the wife of Imotu was last seen with the child Ignosi. It is there that we shall sleep tonight, if, indeed,' he added doubtfully, 'my lords sleep at all upon this earth.'

'When we are among the Kukuanas, my good friend Infadoos, we do as the Kukuanas do,' I said majestically, and turned round quickly to address Good, who was tramping along sullenly behind, his mind fully occupied with unsatisfactory attempts to prevent his flannel shirt from flapping in the evening breeze. To my astonishment I butted into Umbopa, who was walking along immediately behind me, and very evidently had been listening with the greatest interest to my conversation with Infadoos. The expression on his face was most curious, and gave me the idea of a man who was struggling with partial success to bring something long ago forgotten back into his mind.

All this while we had been pressing on at a good rate towards the undulating plain beneath us. The mountains we had crossed now loomed high above our heads, and Sheba's Breasts were veiled modestly in diaphanous wreaths of mist. As we went the country grew more and more lovely. The vegetation was luxuriant, without being tropical; the sun was bright and warm, but not burning; and a gracious breeze blew softly along the odorous slopes of the mountains. Indeed, this new land was little less than an earthly paradise; in beauty, in natural wealth, and in climate I have never seen its like. The Transvaal is a fine country in parts, but it is nothing to Kukuanaland.

So soon as we started, Infadoos had despatched a runner to warn the people of the kraal, which, by the way, was in his military command, of our arrival. This man had departed at an extraordinary speed, which Infadoos informed me he would keep up all the way, as running was an exercise much practised among his people.

The result of this message now became apparent. When we arrived within two miles of the kraal we could see that company after company of men were issuing from its gates and marching towards us.

Sir Henry laid his hand upon my arm, and remarked that it looked as though we were going to meet with a warm reception. Something in his tone attracted Infadoos' attention.

'Let not my lords be afraid,' he said hastily, 'for in my breast there dwells no guile. This regiment is one under my command, and comes out by my orders to greet you.'

I nodded easily, though I was not quite easy in my mind.

About half a mile from the gates of this kraal is a long stretch of rising ground sloping gently upwards from the road, and here the companies formed. It was a splendid sight to see them, each company about three hundred strong, charging swiftly up the rise, with flashing spears and waving plumes, to take their appointed place. By the time we reached the slope twelve such companies, or in all three thousand six hundred men, had passed out and taken up their positions along the road.

Presently we came to the first company, and were able to gaze in astonishment on the most magnificent set of warriors that I have ever seen. They were all men of mature age, mostly veterans of about forty, and not one of them was under six feet in height, whilst many stood six feet three or four. They wore upon their heads heavy black plumes of sakaboola feathers, like those which adorned our guides. About their waists and beneath the right knees were bound circlets of white ox tails, while in their left hands they carried round shields measuring about twenty inches across. These shields are very curious. The framework is made of an iron plate, beaten out thin, over which is stretched milk-white oxhide.

The weapons that each man bore were simple, but most effective, consisting of a short and very heavy two-edged spear with a wooden shaft, the blade being about six inches across at the widest part. These spears are not used for throwing, but like the Zulu *bangwan*, or stabbing assegai, are for close quarters only, when the wound inflicted by them is terrible. In addition to his *bangwan* every man carried three large and heavy knives, each knife weighing about two pounds. One knife was fixed in the oxtail girdle, and the other two at the back of the round shield. These knives, which are called *tollas* by the Kukuanas, take the place of the throwing assegai of the Zulus. The Kukuana warriors can cast them with great accuracy to a distance of fifty yards, and it is their custom on charging to hurl a volley of them at the enemy as they come to close quarters.

Each company remained still as a collection of bronze statues till we were opposite to it. Then at a signal given by its commanding officer, who, distinguished by a leopard-skin cloak, stood some paces in front, every spear was raised into the air, and from three hundred throats sprang forth with a sudden roar the royal salute of *Koom*. So soon as we had passed, the company formed up behind us and followed us towards the kraal, till at last the whole regiment of the Greys – thus called from their white shields – the crack corps of the Kukuana people, was marching in our rear with a tread that shook the ground.

At length, branching off from Solomon's Great Road, we came to the wide fosse surrounding the kraal, which is at least a mile round, and fenced with a strong palisade of piles formed of the trunks of trees. At the gateway this fosse is spanned by a primitive drawbridge, which was let down by the guard to allow us to pass in. The kraal is exceedingly well laid out. Through the centre runs a wide pathway intersected at right angles by other pathways so arranged as to cut the huts into square blocks, each block being the quarters of a company. The huts are dome-shaped and built, like those of the Zulus, of a framework of wattle, beautifully thatched with grass; but, unlike the Zulu huts, they have doorways through which men can walk. Also they are much larger, and surrounded by a verandah about six feet wide, beautifully paved with powdered lime trodden hard.

All along each side of this wide pathway that pierces the kraal were ranged hundreds of women, brought out by curiosity to look at us. These women, for a native race, are exceedingly handsome. They are tall and graceful, and their figures are wonderfully fine. The hair, though short, is rather curly than woolly, the features are frequently aquiline, and the lips are not unpleasantly thick, as is the case among most African races. But what struck us most was their exceedingly quiet and dignified air. They were as wellbred in their way as the *habituées* of a fashionable drawing-room, and in this respect they differ from Zulu women and their cousins the Masai who inhabit the district behind Zanzibar. Their curiosity had brought them out to see us, but they allowed no rude expressions of astonishment or savage criticism to pass their lips as we trudged wearily in front of them. Not even when old Infadoos with a surreptitious motion of his hand pointed out the crowning wonder of poor Good's 'beautiful white legs', did they suffer the feelings of intense admiration which evidently mastered their minds to find expression. They fixed their dark eyes upon this new and snowy loveliness, for, as I think I have said, Good's skin is exceedingly white, and that was all. But it was quite enough for Good, who is modest by nature.

When we reached the centre of the kraal, Infadoos halted at the door of a large hut, which was surrounded at a distance by a circle of smaller ones.

'Enter, sons of the stars,' he said in a magniloquent voice, 'and deign to rest awhile in our humble habitations. A little food shall be brought to you, so that ye may have no need to draw your belts tight from hunger; some honey and some milk, and an ox or two, and a few sheep; not much, my lords, but still a little food.'

'It is good,' said I. 'Infadoos, we are weary with travelling through realms of air; now let us rest.'

Accordingly we entered into the hut, which we found amply prepared for our comfort. Couches of tanned skins were spread for us to lie on, and water was placed for us to wash in.

Presently we heard a shouting outside, and stepping to the door, saw a line of damsels bearing milk and roasted mealies, and honey in a pot. Behind these were some youths driving a fat young ox. We received the gifts, and then one of the young men drew a knife from his girdle and dexterously cut the ox's throat. In ten minutes it was dead, skinned, and jointed. The best of the meat was then cut off for us, and the rest, in the name of our party, I presented to the warriors round us, who took it and distributed the 'white lords' gift'.

Umbopa set to work, with the assistance of an extremely prepossessing young woman, to boil our portion in a large earthenware pot over a fire which was built outside the hut, and when it was nearly ready we sent a message to Infadoos, and asked him and Scragga, the king's son, to join us.

Presently they came, and sitting down upon little stools, of which there were several about the hut, for the Kukuanas do not in general squat upon their haunches like the Zulus, they helped us to get through our dinner. The old gentleman was most affable and polite, but it struck me that the young one regarded us with doubt. Together with the rest of the party, he had been overawed by our white appearance and by our magic properties; but it seemed to me that, on discovering that we ate, drank and slept like other mortals, his awe was beginning to wear off, and to be replaced by a sullen suspicion – which made me feel rather uncomfortable.

In the course of our meal Sir Henry suggested to me that it might be well to try to discover if our hosts knew anything of his brother's fate, or if they had ever seen or heard of him; but, on the whole, I thought that it would be wiser to say nothing of the matter at this time. It was difficult to explain a relative lost from 'the stars'.

After supper we produced our pipes and lit them; a proceeding which filled Infadoos and Scragga with astonishment. The Kukuanas were evidently unacquainted with the divine delights of tobacco-smoke. The herb is grown among them extensively; but, like the Zulus, they use it for snuff only, and quite failed to identify it in its new form.

Presently I asked Infadoos when we were to proceed on our journey, and was delighted to learn that preparations had been made for us to leave on the following morning, messengers having already departed to inform Twala the king of our coming.

It appeared that Twala was at his principal place, known as Loo, making ready for the great annual feast which was to be held in the first week of June. At this gathering all the regiments, with the exception of certain detachments left behind for garrison purposes, are brought up and paraded before the king; and the great annual witch-hunt, of which more by and by, is held.

We were to start at dawn; and Infadoos, who was to accompany us, expected that we should reach Loo on the night of the second day, unless we were detained by accident or by swollen rivers.

When they had given us this information, our visitors bade us good-night; and, having arranged to watch turn and turn about, three of us flung ourselves down and slept the sweet sleep of the weary, whilst the fourth sat up on the lookout for possible treachery.

CHAPTER 9

Twala the King

It will not be necessary for me to detail at length the incidents of our journey to Loo. It took two full days' travelling along Solomon's Great Road, which pursued its even course right into the heart of Kukuanaland. Suffice it to say that as we went the country seemed to grow richer and richer, and the kraals, with their wide surrounding belts of cultivation, more and more numerous. They were all built upon the same principles as the first camp which we had reached, and were guarded by ample garrisons of troops. Indeed, in Kukuanaland, as among the Germans, the Zulu and the Masai, every able-bodied man is a soldier, so that the whole force of the nation is available for its wars, offensive or defensive. As we travelled we were overtaken by thousands of warriors hurrying up to Loo to be present at the great annual review and festival, and more splendid troops I never saw.

At sunset on the second day, we stopped to rest awhile upon the summit of some heights over which the road ran, and there on a beautiful and fertile plain before us lay Loo itself. For a native town it is an enormous place, quite five miles round, I should say, with outlying kraals, projecting from it, that serve on grand occasions as cantonments for the regiments, and a curious horseshoe-shaped hill, with which we were destined to become better acquainted, about two miles to the north. It is beautifully situated, and through the centre of the kraal, dividing it into two portions, runs a river – the same indeed that we had seen from the slopes of Sheba's Breasts – which appeared to be bridged in several places. Sixty or seventy miles away three great snow-capped mountains, placed at the points of a triangle, started out of the level plain. The conformation of these mountains is unlike that of Sheba's Breasts, being sheer and precipitous, instead of smooth and rounded.

Infadoos saw us looking at them, and volunteered a remark.

'The road ends there,' he said, pointing to these mountains which are known among the Kukuanas as the Three Witches.

'Why does it end?' I asked.

'Who knows?' he answered with a shrug. 'The mountains are full of caves, and there is a great pit between them. It is there that the wise men of old time used to go to get whatever it was they came for to this country, and now it is there that our kings are buried in the Place of Death.'

'What was it they came for?' I asked eagerly.

'Nay, I know not. My lords who have dropped from the stars should know,' he answered with a quick look. Evidently he knew more than he chose to say.

'Yes,' I went on, 'you are right; in the stars we learn many things. I have heard, for instance, that the wise men of old came to these mountains to find bright stones, pretty playthings, and yellow iron.'

'My lord is wise,' he answered coldly; 'I am but a child and cannot talk with my lord on such matters. My lord must speak with Gagool the old, at the king's place, who is wise as my lord,' and he went away.

So soon as he was gone I turned to the others, and pointed out the mountains. 'There are Solomon's diamond mines,' I said.

Umbopa was standing with them, apparently plunged in one of the fits of abstraction which were common to him, and caught my words.

'Yes, Macumazahn,' he put in, in Zulu, 'the diamonds are surely there, and you shall have them, since you white men are so fond of toys and money.'

'How dost thou know that, Umbopa?' I asked sharply, for I did not like his mysterious ways.

He laughed. 'I dreamed it in the night, white men,' he said. Then he turned on his heel and went.

'Now what,' said Sir Henry, 'is our black friend driving at? He knows more than he chooses to say, that is clear. By the way, Quatermain, has he heard anything of – of my brother?'

'Nothing; he has asked everyone he has become friendly with, but they declare that no white man has ever been seen in the country before.'

'Do you suppose that he got here at all?' suggested Good; 'we have only fetched up by a miracle; is it likely he could have reached it without the map?'

'I don't know,' said Sir Henry gloomily, 'but somehow I think that I shall find him.'

Slowly the sun sank, then sudden darkness rushed down on the land like a tangible thing. There was no breathing-space between the day and night, no soft transformation scene, for in these latitudes twilight does not exist. The change from day to night is as quick and as absolute as the change from life to death. The sun sank and the world was wreathed in shadows. But not for long, for see in the west there is a glow, then come rays of silver light, and at last the full and glorious moon lights up the plain and shoots its gleaming arrows far and wide, filling the earth with a faint refulgence.

We stood and watched the lovely sight, whilst the stars grew pale before this chastened majesty, and felt our hearts lifted up in the presence of a beauty that I cannot describe. Mine has been a rough life, but there are a few things for which I am thankful to have lived, and one of them is to have seen that moon shine over Kukuanaland.

Presently our meditations were broken in upon by our polite friend Infadoos.

'If my lords are rested we will journey on to Loo, where a hut is made ready for my lords tonight. The moon is now bright, so that we shall not fall by the way.'

We assented, and in an hour's time were at the outskirts of the town, of which the extent, mapped out as it was by thousands of camp fires, appeared absolutely endless. Indeed, Good, who is always fond of a bad joke, christened it 'Unlimited Loo'. Soon we came to a moat with a drawbridge, where we were met by the rattling of arms and the hoarse challenge of a sentry. Infadoos gave some password that I could not catch, which was met with a salute, and we marched on through the central street of the great grass city. After nearly half an hour's tramp, past endless lines of huts, Infadoos halted at last by the gate of a little group of huts which surrounded a small courtyard of powdered limestone, and informed us that these were to be our poor quarters.

We entered, and found that a hut had been assigned to each of us. These huts were superior to any that we had yet seen, and in each was a most comfortable bed made of tanned skins, spread upon mattresses of aromatic grass. Food too was ready for us, and so soon as we had washed ourselves with water, which stood ready in earthenware jars, some young women of handsome appearance brought us roasted meats and mealie cobs, daintily served on wooden platters, and presented them to us with deep obeisances.

We ate and drank, and then, the beds having been all moved into one hut by our request, a precaution at which the amiable young ladies smiled, we flung ourselves down to sleep, thoroughly wearied with our long journey.

When we woke it was to find the sun high in the heavens, and our female attendants, who did not seem to be troubled by any false shame, already standing inside the hut, having been ordered to attend and help us to make ready.

'Make ready, indeed,' growled Good; 'when one has only a flannel shirt and a pair of boots, that does not take long. I wish you would ask them for my trousers, Quatermain.'

I asked accordingly, but was informed that these sacred relics had already been taken to the king who would see us in the forenoon.

Having requested the young ladies to step outside, somewhat to their astonishment and disappointment, we proceeded to make the best toilet of which the circumstances admitted. Good even went the length of again shaving the right side of his face; the left, on which now appeared a very fair crop of whiskers, we impressed upon him he must on no account touch. Curtis and I were contented with a good wash and combing our hair. Sir Henry's yellow locks were now almost upon his shoulders, and he looked more like an ancient Dane than ever, while my grizzled scrub was fully an inch long, instead of half an inch, which in a general way I considered my maximum length.

By the time that we had eaten our breakfasts, and smoked a pipe, a message was brought to us by Infadoos himself to the effect that Twala the king was ready to see us, if we would be pleased to come.

We remarked in reply that we should prefer to wait till the sun was a little higher, we were yet weary with our journey, etc., etc. It is always well, when dealing with uncivilised people, not to be in too great a hurry. They are apt to mistake politeness for awe or servility. So although we were quite as anxious to see Twala as Twala could be to see us, we sat down and waited for an hour, employing the interval in preparing such presents as our slender stock of goods permitted – namely, the Winchester rifle which had been used by poor Ventvögel, and some beads. The rifle and ammunition we determined to present to his royal highness, and the beads were for his wives and courtiers. We had already given a few to Infadoos and Scragga, and found that they were delighted with them, never having seen such things before. At length we declared that we were ready, and guided by Infadoos, we started off to the audience, Umbopa carrying the rifle and beads.

After walking a few hundred yards we came to an enclosure, something like that surrounding the huts which had been allotted to us, only fifty times as big, for it could not have covered less than six or seven acres of ground. All round the outside fence stood a row of huts, which were the habitations of the king's wives. Exactly opposite the gateway, on the farther side of the open space, was a very large hut, built by itself, in which his majesty resided. All the rest was open ground; that is to say, it would have been open had it not been filled by company after company of warriors, who were mustered there to the number of seven or eight thousand. These men stood still as statues as we advanced through them, and it would be impossible to give an adequate idea of the grandeur of the spectacle which they presented, with their waving plumes, their glancing spears and iron-backed oxhide shields.

The space in front of the large hut was empty, but before it were placed several stools. On three of these, at a sign from Infadoos, we seated ourselves, Umbopa standing behind us. As for Infadoos, he took up a position by the door of the hut. So we waited for ten minutes or more in the midst of a dead silence, but conscious that we were the object of the concentrated gaze of some eight thousand pairs of eyes. It was a somewhat trying ordeal, but we went through it as best we could. At length the door of the hut opened, and a gigantic figure, having a splendid tiger-skin *karross* flung over its shoulders, stepped out, followed by the boy Scragga, and what appeared to us to be a withered-up monkey, wrapped in a fur cloak. The figure seated itself upon a stool, Scragga took his stand behind it, and the withered-up monkey crept on all fours into the shade of the hut and squatted down.

Still there was silence.

Then the gigantic figure slipped off the *karross* and stood up before us, a truly alarming spectacle. It was that of an enormous man with the most entirely repulsive countenance we had ever beheld. This man's lips were thick as a negro's, the nose was flat, he had but one gleaming black eye, for the other was represented by a hollow in the face, and his whole expression was cruel and sensual to a degree. From the large head rose a magnificent plume of white ostrich feathers, his body was clad in a shirt of shining chain armour, whilst round the waist and right knee were the usual circlets of white oxtails. In his right hand he held a huge spear, about his neck was a thick torque of gold, and bound on his forehead shone a single and enormous uncut diamond.

Still there was silence; but not for long. Presently this man, whom we rightly guessed to be the king, raised the great javelin in his hand. Instantly eight thousand spears were lifted in answer, and from eight thousand throats rang out the royal salute of '*Koom*'. Three times this was repeated, and each time the earth shook with a noise that can only be compared to the deepest notes of thunder.

'Be humble, O people!' piped out a thin voice which seemed to come from the monkey in the shade, 'it is the king!'

'*It is the king!*' boomed the answer from eight thousand throats. '*Be humble, O people, it is the king!*'

Then there was silence again – dead silence. Presently, however, it was broken. A soldier on our left dropped his shield, which fell with a clatter to the limestone flooring.

Twala turned his one fierce eye in the direction of the noise. 'Come hither, thou,' he said, in a cold voice.

A fine young man stepped out of the ranks, and stood before him.

'It was thy shield that fell, thou awkward dog. Wilt thou make me a reproach in the eyes of these strangers from the stars? What hast thou to say for thyself?'

We saw the poor fellow turn pale under his dusky skin.

'It was by chance, O Calf of the Black Cow,' he murmured.

'Then it is a chance for which thou must pay. Thou hast made me foolish; prepare for death.'

'I am the king's ox,' was the low answer.

'Scragga,' roared the king, 'let me see how thou canst use thy spear. Kill me this blundering fool.'

Scragga stepped forward with an ill-favoured grin, and lifted his spear. The poor victim covered his eyes with his hand and stood still. As for us, we were petrified with horror.

Once, twice, he waved the spear and then struck, ah! right home – the spear stood out a foot behind the soldier's back. He flung up his hands and dropped dead. From the multitude about us rose something like a murmur, it rolled round and round, and died away. The tragedy was finished; there lay the corpse, and we had not yet realised that it had been enacted. Sir Henry sprang up and swore a great oath, then, overpowered by the sense of silence, sat down again.

'The thrust was a good one,' said the king; 'take him away.'

Four men stepped out of the ranks, and lifting the body of the murdered man, carried it thence.

'Cover up the bloodstains, yes, cover them up,' piped the thin voice that proceeded from the monkey-like figure; 'the king's word is spoken, the king's doom is done!'

Thereupon a girl came forward from behind the hut, bearing a jar filled with powdered lime, which she scattered over the red mark, blotting it from sight.

Sir Henry meanwhile was boiling with rage at what had happened; indeed, it was with difficulty that we could keep him still.

'Sit down, for heaven's sake,' I whispered; 'our lives depend on it.'

He yielded and remained quiet.

Twala sat silent until the traces of the tragedy had been removed, then he addressed us. 'White people,' he said, 'who come hither, whence I know not, and why I know not, greetings.'

'Greetings, Twala, King of the Kukuanas,' I answered.

'White people, whence come ye, and what seek ye?'

'We come from the stars, ask us not how. We come to see this land.'

'Ye journey from far to see a little thing. And that man with you,' pointing to Umbopa, 'does he also come from the stars?'

'Even so; there are people of thy colour in the heavens above; but ask not of matters too high for thee, Twala the king.'

'Ye speak with a loud voice, people of the stars,' Twala answered in a tone which I scarcely liked. 'Remember that the stars are far off, and ye are here. How if I make you as him whom they bore away?'

I laughed out loud, though there was little laughter in my heart.

'O king,' I said, 'be careful, walk warily over hot stones, lest thou shouldst burn thy feet; hold the spear by the handle lest thou shouldst cut thy hands. Touch but one hair of our heads, and destruction shall come upon thee. What, have not these' – pointing to Infadoos and Scragga, who, young villain that he was, was employed in cleaning the blood of the soldier off his spear – 'told thee what manner of men we are? Hast thou seen the like of us?' and I pointed to Good, feeling quite sure that he had never seen anybody before in the least resembling the captain as he then appeared.

'It is true, I have not,' said the king, surveying Good with intense interest.

'Have they not told thee how we strike with death from afar?' I went on.

'They have told me, but I believe them not. Let me see you kill.

Kill me a man among those who stand yonder' – and he pointed to the opposite side of the kraal – 'and I will believe.'

'Nay,' I answered; 'we shed no blood of men except in just punishment. Yet if thou wilt see, bid thy servants drive an ox through the kraal gates, and before he has run twenty paces I will strike him dead.'

'Nay,' laughed the king, 'kill me a man and I will believe.'

'Good, O king, so be it,' I answered coolly; 'do thou walk across the open space and before thy feet reach the gate thou shalt be dead; or if thou wilt not, send thy son Scragga' (whom at that moment it would have given me much pleasure to shoot).

On hearing this suggestion Scragga uttered a sort of howl, and bolted into the hut.

Twala frowned majestically; the suggestion did not please him.

'Let a young ox be driven in,' he said.

Two men at once departed, running swiftly.

'Now, Sir Henry,' said I, 'do you shoot. I want to show this ruffian that I am not the only magician of the party, and we can't trust Good.'

Sir Henry accordingly took his Express, and made ready.

'I hope I shall make a good shot,' he groaned.

'You must,' I answered. 'If you miss with the first barrel, let him have the second. Sight for one hundred and fifty yards, and wait till the beast turns broadside on.'

Then came a pause, until presently we caught sight of an ox running straight for the kraal gate. It came on through the gate, then, catching sight of the vast concourse of people, stopped stupidly, turned round, and bellowed.

'Now's your time,' I whispered.

Up went the rifle.

Bang! *thud!* and the ox was kicking on his back, shot in the ribs. The semi-hollow bullet had done its work well, and a sigh of astonishment went up from the assembled thousands.

I turned round coolly. 'Have I lied, O king?'

'Nay, white man, it is the truth,' was the somewhat awed answer.

'Listen, Twala,' I went on. 'Thou hast seen. Now know we

come in peace, not in war. See,' and I held up the Winchester repeater; 'here is a hollow staff that shall enable thee to kill even as we kill, only I lay this charm upon it, thou shalt kill no man with it. If thou liftest it against a man, it shall kill thee. Stay, I will show thee. Bid a soldier step forty paces and place the shaft of a spear in the ground so that the flat blade looks towards us.'

In a few seconds it was done.

'Now, see, I will break yonder spear.'

Taking a careful sight I fired. The bullet struck the flat of the spear, and shattered the blade into fragments.

Again the sigh of astonishment went up.

'Now, Twala, we give this magic tube to thee. By and by I will show thee how to use it; but beware how thou turnest the magic of the stars against a man of earth,' and I handed him the rifle.

The king took it very gingerly and laid it down at his feet. As he did so I observed the wizened, monkey-like figure creeping from the shadow of the hut. It crept on all fours, but when it reached the place where the king sat it rose upon its feet, and throwing the furry covering from its face, revealed a most extraordinary and weird countenance. Apparently it was that of a woman of great age so shrunken that in size it seemed little larger than the face of a year-old child, but made up of countless deep and yellow wrinkles. Set among these wrinkles was a sunken slit that represented the mouth, beneath which the chin curved outwards to a point. There was no nose to speak of; indeed, the visage might have been taken for that of a sun-dried corpse, had it not been for a pair of large black eyes, still full of fire and intelligence, which gleamed and played under the snow-white eyebrows and the projecting parchment-coloured skull like jewels in a charnel-house. The head itself was perfectly bare, and yellow in hue, while the naked wrinkled scalp moved and contracted like the head of a cobra.

The figure to which this fearful countenance belonged – a countenance so fearful indeed that it caused a shiver of fear to pass through us as we gazed on it – stood still for a moment. Then suddenly it projected a skinny claw armed with nails nearly an inch long, and laying it on the shoulder of Twala the king, began to speak in a thin and piercing voice: 'Listen, O king! Listen, O warriors! Listen, O mountains and plains and rivers, home of the Kukuana race! Listen, O stars and sun, O rain and storm and mist! Listen, O men and matrons, O youths and maidens and O ye babes unborn! Listen, all things that live and must die! Listen, all dead things that shall live again – again to die! Listen, the spirit of life is in me, and I prophesy. I prophesy! I prophesy!'

The words died away in a faint wail, and dread seemed to seize upon the hearts of all who heard them, including our own. This old woman was very terrible.

'*Blood! blood! blood!* rivers of blood; blood everywhere. I see it, I smell it, I taste it – it is salt! it runs red upon the ground, it rains down from the skies.

'*Footsteps! footsteps! footsteps!* the tread of the white man coming from afar. It shakes the earth; the earth trembles before her master.

'Blood is good, the red blood is bright; there is no smell like the smell of new-shed blood. The lions shall lap it and roar, the vultures shall wash their wings in it and shriek with joy.

'I am old! I am old! I have seen much blood; *ha, ha!* but I shall see more ere I die, and be merry. How old am I, think ye? Your grandfathers knew me, and *their* fathers knew me, and *their* fathers' fathers' fathers. I have seen the white man and his desires. I am old, but the mountains are older than I. Who made the great road, tell me? Who wrote the pictures on the rocks, tell me? Who reared up the three Silent Ones yonder, that gaze across the pit, tell me?' and she pointed towards the three precipitous mountains which we had noticed on the previous night.

'Ye know not, but I know. It was a white people who were before ye are, who shall be when ye are not, who shall eat you up and destroy you. *Yea, yea, yea!*'

'And what came they for, the White Ones, the Terrible Ones, the skilled in magic and all learning, the strong, the unswerving? What is that bright stone upon thy forehead, O king? Whose hands made the iron garments upon thy breast, O king? Ye know not, but I know. I the Old One, I the Wise One, I the *isanusi*, the witch-doctress!'

Then she turned her bald vulture-head towards us.

'What seek ye, white men of the stars – ah, yes, of the stars? Do ye seek a lost one? Ye shall not find him here. He is not here. Never for ages upon ages has a white foot pressed this land; never save once, and I remember that he left it but to die. Ye come for bright stones; I know it – I know it; ye shall find them when the blood is dry; but shall ye return whence ye came, or shall ye stop with me? *Ha! ha! ha!*

'And thou, thou with the dark skin and the proud bearing,' and she pointed her skinny fingers at Umbopa, 'who art *thou*, and what seekest *thou*? Not stones that shine, not yellow metal that gleams, these thou leavest to "white men from the stars". Methinks I know thee; methinks I can smell the smell of the blood in thy heart. Strip off the girdle – '

Here the features of this extraordinary creature became convulsed, and she fell to the ground foaming in an epileptic fit and was carried into the hut.

The king rose up trembling and waved his hand. Instantly the regiments began to file off, and in ten minutes, save for ourselves, the king and a few attendants, the great space was left empty.

'White people,' he said, 'it passes in my mind to kill you. Gagool has spoken strange words. What say ye?'

I laughed. 'Be careful, O king, we are not easy to slay. Thou hast seen the fate of the ox; wouldst thou be as the ox is?'

The king frowned. 'It is not well to threaten a king.'

'We threaten not; we speak what is true. Try to kill us, O king, and learn.'

The great savage put his hand to his forehead and thought.

'Go in peace,' he said at length. 'Tonight is the great dance. Ye shall see it. Fear not that I shall set a snare for you. Tomorrow I will think.'

'It is well, O king,' I answered unconcernedly, and then, accompanied by Infadoos, we rose and went back to our kraal.

CHAPTER 10

The Witch-Hunt

On reaching our hut I motioned to Infadoos to enter with us.

'Now, Infadoos,' I said, 'we would speak with thee.'

'Let my lords say on.'

'It seems to us, Infadoos, that Twala the king is a cruel man.'

'It is so, my lords. Alas! the land cries out because of his cruelties. Tonight ye shall see. It is the great witch-hunt, and many will be smelt out as wizards and slain. No man's life is safe. If the king covets a man's cattle, or a man's wife, or if he fears a man that he should excite a rebellion against him, then Gagool, whom ye saw, or some of the witch-finding women that she has taught, will smell that man out as a wizard, and he will be killed. Many must die before the moon grows pale tonight. It is ever so. Perhaps I too shall be killed. As yet I have been spared because I am skilled in war, and beloved by the soldiers; but I know not how long I have to live. The land groans at the wickedness of Twala the king; it is wearied of him and his red ways.'

'Then why is it, Infadoos, that the people do not cast him down?'

'Nay, my lords, he is the king, and if he were killed Scragga would reign in his place, and the heart of Scragga is blacker than the heart of Twala his father. If Scragga were king his yoke upon our neck would be heavier than the yoke of Twala. If Imotu had never been slain, or if Ignosi his son had lived, it might have been otherwise; but they are both dead.'

'How knowest thou that Ignosi is dead?' said a voice behind us. We looked round astonished to see who spoke. It was Umbopa.

'What meanest thou, boy?' asked Infadoos; 'who told thee to speak?'

'Listen, Infadoos,' was the answer, 'and I will tell thee a story.

Years ago the king Imotu was killed in this country and his wife fled with the boy Ignosi. Is it not so?'

'It is so.'

'It was said that the woman and her son died upon the mountains. Is it not so?'

'It is even so.'

'Well, it came to pass that the mother and the boy Ignosi did not die. They crossed the mountains, and were led by a tribe of wandering desert men across the sands beyond, till at last they came to water and grass and trees again.'

'How knowest thou this?'

'Listen. They travelled on and on, many months' journey, till they reached a land where a people called the Amazulu, who also are of the Kukuana stock, live by war, and with them they tarried many years, till at length the mother died. Then the son Ignosi became a wanderer again, and journeyed into a land of wonders, where white people live, and for many more years he learned the wisdom of the white people.'

'It is a pretty story,' said Infadoos, incredulously.

'For years he lived there working as a servant and a soldier, but holding in his heart all that his mother had told him of his own place, and casting about in his mind to find how he might journey thither to see his people and his father's house before he died. For long years he lived and waited, and at last the time came, as it comes ever to him who can wait, and he met certain white men who would seek the unknown land, and joined himself to them. The white men started and travelled on and on seeking for one who is lost. They crossed the burning desert, they crossed the snow-clad mountains, and at last reached the land of the Kukuanas, and there they found *thee*, O Infadoos.'

'Surely thou art mad to talk thus,' exclaimed the astonished old soldier.

'Thou thinkest so; see, I will show thee, O my uncle. I am Ignosi, rightful king of the Kukuanas!' Then with a single movement Umbopa slipped off his *moocha*, or girdle, and stood naked before us. 'Look,' he said, 'what is this?' and he pointed to the picture of a great snake tattooed in blue round his middle, its tail disappearing into its open mouth just above where the thighs are set into the body.

Infadoos looked, his eyes starting nearly out of his head. Then he fell upon his knees.

'*Koom! Koom!*' he ejaculated; 'it is my brother's son; it is the king.'

'Did I not tell thee so, my uncle? Rise; I am not yet the king, but with thy help, and with the help of these brave white men who are my friends, I shall be. Yet the old witch Gagool was right, the land will run with blood first, and hers shall run with it, if she has any and can die, for she killed my father with her words, and drove my mother forth. And now, Infadoos, choose thou. Wilt thou lay thy hands between my hands and be my man? Wilt thou share the dangers that lie before me, and help me to overthrow this tyrant and murderer, or wilt thou not? Choose thou.'

The old man put his hand to his head and thought. Then he rose, and advancing to where Umbopa, or rather Ignosi, stood, he knelt before him and took his hand.

'Ignosi, rightful king of the Kukuanas, I lay my hand between thy hands, and am thy man till death. When thou wast a babe I dandled thee upon my knees, now shall my old arm strike for thee and freedom.'

'It is well, Infadoos; if I conquer, thou shalt be the greatest man in my kingdom after the king. If I fail, thou canst only die, and death is not far off from thee. Rise, my uncle.

'And ye, white men, will ye help me? What have I to offer you? The white stones! If I conquer and can find them, ye shall have as many as ye can carry hence. Will that suffice you?'

I translated this remark.

'Tell him,' answered Sir Henry, 'that he mistakes an Englishman. Wealth is good, and if it comes in our way we will take it; but a gentleman does not sell himself for wealth. Still, speaking for myself, I say this. I have always liked Umbopa, and so far as lies in me I will stand by him in this business. It will be very pleasant to me to try to square matters with that cruel devil Twala. What do you say, Good, and you, Quatermain?'

'Well,' said Good, 'to adopt the language of hyperbole, in

which all these people seem to indulge, you can tell him that a row is surely good, and warms the cockles of the heart, and, in short, so far as I am concerned I'm his boy. My only stipulation is that he allows me to wear trousers.'

I translated the substance of these answers.

'It is well, my friends,' said Ignosi, late Umbopa. 'But what sayest thou, Macumazahn, art thou also with me, old Watcher-by-Night, cleverer than a wounded buffalo?'

I thought awhile and scratched my head.

'Umbopa, or Ignosi,' I said, 'I don't like revolutions. I am a man of peace, and a bit of a coward' – here Umbopa smiled – 'but, on the other hand, I stick to my friends, Ignosi. You have stuck to us and played the part of a man, and I will stick to you. But mind you, I am a trader, and have to make my living, so I accept your offer about those diamonds in case we should ever be in a position to avail ourselves of it. Another thing: we came, as you know, to look for Incubu's – Sir Henry's – lost brother. You must help us to find him.'

'That I will do,' answered Ignosi. 'Stay, Infadoos; by the sign of the snake about my middle, tell me the truth. Has any white man to thy knowledge set his foot within the land?'

'None, O Ignosi.'

'If any white man had been seen or heard of, wouldst thou have known?'

'I should certainly have known.'

'Thou hearest, Incubu,' said Ignosi to Sir Henry; 'he has not been here.'

'Well, well,' said Sir Henry, with a sigh; 'there it is; I suppose that he never got so far. Poor fellow, poor fellow! So it has all been for nothing. God's will be done.'

'Now for business,' I put in, anxious to escape from a painful subject. 'It is very well to be a king by right divine, Ignosi, but how dost thou propose to become a king indeed?'

'Nay, I know not. Infadoos, hast thou a plan?'

'Ignosi, Son of the Lightning,' answered his uncle, 'tonight is the great dance and witch-hunt. Many must be smelt out and perish, and in the hearts of many others there will be grief and anguish and fury against the king Twala. When the dance is over, then I will speak to some of the great chiefs, who in turn, if I can win them over, will speak to their regiments. I shall speak to the chiefs softly at first, and bring them to see that thou art indeed the king, and I think that by tomorrow's light thou wilt have twenty thousand spears at thy command. And now I must go and think, and hear, and make ready. After the dance is done, if I am yet alive, and we are all alive, I will meet thee here and we can talk. At the best there must be war.'

At this moment our conference was interrupted by the cry that messengers had come from the king. Advancing to the door of the hut we ordered that they should be admitted, and presently three men entered, each bearing a shining shirt of chain armour, and a magnificent battle-axe.

'The gifts of my lord the king to the white men from the stars!' said a herald who came with them.

'We thank the king,' I answered; 'withdraw.'

The men went, and we examined the armour with great interest. It was the most wonderful chain work that any of us had ever seen. A whole coat fell together so closely that it formed a mass of links scarcely too big to be covered with both hands.

'Do you make these things in this country, Infadoos?' I asked; 'they are very beautiful.'

'Nay, my lord, they came down to us from our forefathers. We know not who made them, and there are but few left.* None but those of royal blood may be clad in them. They are magic coats through which no spear can pass, and those who wear them are well-nigh safe in the battle. The king is well pleased or much afraid, or he would not have sent you these garments of steel. Clothe yourselves in them tonight, my lords.'

The remainder of that day we spent quietly, resting and talking over the situation, which was sufficiently exciting. At last the sun went down, the thousand watch-fires glowed out, and through the darkness we heard the tramp of many feet and the clashing of

---

* In the Sudan swords and coats of mail are still worn by Arabs, whose ancestors must have stripped them from the bodies of Crusaders. ED.

hundreds of spears, as the regiments passed to their appointed places to be ready for the great dance. Then the full moon shone out in splendour, and as we stood watching her rays, Infadoos arrived, clad in his war dress, and accompanied by a guard of twenty men to escort us to the dance. As he had recommended, we had already donned the shirts of chain armour which the king had sent us, putting them on under our ordinary clothing, and finding to our surprise that they were neither very heavy nor uncomfortable. These steel shirts, which evidently had been made for men of a very large stature, hung somewhat loosely upon Good and myself, but Sir Henry's fitted his magnificent frame like a glove. Then strapping our revolvers round our waists, and taking in our hands the battle-axes which the king had sent with the armour, we started.

On arriving at the great kraal, where we had that morning been received by the king, we found that it was closely packed with some twenty thousand men arranged round it in regiments. These regiments were in turn divided into companies, and between each company ran a little path to allow space for the witch-finders to pass up and down. Anything more imposing than the sight that was presented by this vast and orderly concourse of armed men it is impossible to conceive. There they stood perfectly silent, and the moon poured her light upon the forest of their raised spears, upon their majestic forms, waving plumes and the harmonious shading of their various-coloured shields. Wherever we looked were lines upon lines of dim faces surmounted by range upon range of shimmering spears.

'Surely,' I said to Infadoos, 'the whole army is here?'

'Nay, Macumazahn,' he answered, 'but a third of it. One third part is present at this dance each year, another third is mustered outside in case there should be trouble when the killing begins, ten thousand more garrison the outposts round Loo, and the rest watch at the kraals in the country. Thou seest it is a great people.'

'They are very silent,' remarked Good; and indeed the intense stillness among such a vast concourse of living men was almost overpowering.

'What says Bougwan?' asked Infadoos.

I translated. 'Those over whom the shadow of death is hovering are silent,' he answered grimly.

'Will many be killed?'

'Very many.'

'It seems,' I said to the others, 'that we are going to assist at a gladiatorial show arranged regardless of expense.'

Sir Henry shivered, and Good said he wished that we could get out of it.

'Tell me,' I asked Infadoos, 'are we in danger?'

'I know not, my lords, I trust not; but do not seem afraid. If ye live through the night all may go well with you. The soldiers murmur against the king.'

All this while we had been advancing steadily towards the centre of the open space, in the midst of which were placed some stools. As we proceeded we perceived another small party coming from the direction of the royal hut.

'It is the king Twala, Scragga his son and Gagool the old; and see, with them are those who slay,' said Infadoos, pointing to a little group of about a dozen gigantic and savage-looking men, armed with spears in one hand and heavy kerries in the other.

The king seated himself upon the centre stool, Gagool crouched at his feet and the others stood behind him.

'Greetings, white lords,' Twala cried, as we came up; 'be seated, waste not precious time – the night is all too short for the deeds that must be done. Ye come in a good hour, and shall see a glorious spectacle. Look round, white lords; look round,' and he rolled his one wicked eye from regiment to regiment. 'Can the stars show you such a sight as this? See how they shake in their wickedness, all those who have evil in their hearts and fear the judgement of "heaven above".'

'*Begin! begin!*' piped Gagool, in her thin piercing voice; 'the hyaenas are hungry, they howl for food. *Begin! begin!*'

Then for a moment there was intense stillness, made horrible by a presage of what was to come.

The king lifted his spear, and suddenly twenty thousand feet were raised, as though they belonged to one man, and brought down with a stamp upon the earth. This was repeated three times, causing the solid ground to shake and tremble. Then from a far point of the circle a solitary voice began a wailing song, of which the refrain ran something as follows – '*What is the lot of man born of woman?*'

Back came the answer rolling out from every throat in that vast company – '*Death!*'

Gradually, however, the song was taken up by company after company, till the whole armed multitude were singing it, and I could no longer follow the words, except in so far as they appeared to represent various phases of human passions, fears and joys. Now it seemed to be a love song, now a majestic swelling war chant, and last of all a death dirge ending suddenly in one heartbreaking wail that went echoing and rolling away in a volume of blood-curdling sound.

Again silence fell upon the place, and again it was broken by the king lifting his hand. Instantly we heard a pattering of feet, and from out of the masses of warriors strange and awful figures appeared running towards us. As they drew near we saw that these were women, most of them aged, for their white hair, ornamented with small bladders taken from fish, streamed out behind them. Their faces were painted in stripes of white and yellow; down their backs hung snake-skins, and round their waists rattled circlets of human bones, while each held a small forked wand in her shrivelled hand. In all there were ten of them. When they arrived in front of us they halted, and one of them, pointing with her wand towards the crouching figure of Gagool, cried out, 'Mother, Old Mother, we are here.'

'*Good! good! good!*' answered that aged Iniquity. 'Are your eyes keen, *isanusi* (witch-doctoresses), 'ye seers in dark places?'

'Mother, they are keen.'

'*Good! good! good!* Are your ears open, *isanusi*, ye who hear words that come not from the tongue?'

'Mother they are open.'

'*Good! good! good!* Are your senses awake, *isanusi* – can ye smell blood, can ye purge the land of the wicked ones who compass evil against the king and against their neighbours? Are ye ready to do the justice of "heaven above", ye whom I have taught, ye who have eaten of the bread of my wisdom and drunk of the water of my magic?'

'Mother, we can.'

'Then go! Tarry not, ye vultures; see, the slayers' (pointing to the ominous group of executioners behind), 'make sharp their spears; the white men from afar are hungry to see. Go!'

With a wild yell Gagool's horrid ministers broke away in every direction, like fragments from a shell, the dry bones round their waists rattling as they ran, and headed for various points of the dense human circle. We could not watch them all, so we fixed our eyes upon the *isanusi* nearest to us. When she came to within a few paces of the warriors she halted and began to dance wildly, turning round and round with an almost incredible rapidity, and shrieking out sentences such as, 'I smell him, the evildoer!' 'He is near, he who poisoned his mother!' 'I hear the thoughts of him who thought evil of the king!'

Quicker and quicker she danced, till she lashed herself into such a frenzy of excitement that the foam flew in flecks from her gnashing jaws, till her eyes seemed to start from her head and her flesh to quiver visibly. Suddenly she stopped dead and stiffened all over, like a pointer dog when he scents game, and then with outstretched wand she began to creep stealthily towards the soldiers before her. It seemed to us that as she came their stoicism gave way, and that they shrank from her. As for ourselves, we followed her movements with a horrible fascination. Presently, still creeping and crouching like a dog, the *isanusi* was before them. Then she halted and pointed, and again crept on a pace or two.

Suddenly the end came. With a shriek she sprang in and touched a tall warrior with her forked wand. Instantly two of his comrades, those standing immediately next to him, seized the doomed man, each by one arm, and advanced with him towards the king.

He did not resist, but we saw that he dragged his limbs as though they were paralysed, and that his fingers, from which the spear had fallen, were limp like those of a man newly dead.

As he came, two of the villainous executioners stepped forward to meet him. Presently they met, and the executioners turned round, looking towards the king as though for orders.

'*Kill!*' said the king.

'*Kill!*' squeaked Gagool.

'*Kill!*' re-echoed Scragga, with a hollow chuckle.

Almost before the words were uttered the horrible deed was done. One man had driven his spear into the victim's heart, and to make assurance doubly sure, the other had dashed out his brains with a great club.

'*One*,' counted Twala the king, just like a black Madame Defarge, as Good said, and the body was dragged a few paces away and stretched out.

Hardly was the thing done before another poor wretch was brought up, like an ox to the slaughter. This time we could see, from the leopard-skin cloak which he wore, that the man was a person of rank. Again the awful syllables were spoken, and the victim fell dead.

'*Two*,' counted the king.

And so the deadly game went on, till about a hundred bodies were stretched in rows behind us. I have heard of the gladiatorial shows of the Caesars, and of the Spanish bullfights, but I take the liberty of doubting if either of them could be half so horrible as this Kukuana witch-hunt. Gladiatorial shows and Spanish bullfights at any rate contributed to the public amusement, which certainly was not the case here. The most confirmed sensation-monger would fight shy of sensation if he knew that it was well on the cards that he would, in his own proper person, be the subject of the next event.

Once we rose and tried to remonstrate, but were sternly repressed by Twala.

'Let the law take its course, white men. These dogs are magicians and evildoers; it is well that they should die,' was the only answer vouchsafed to us.

About half-past ten there was a pause. The witch-finders gathered themselves together, apparently exhausted with their bloody work, and we thought that the performance was done with. But it was not so, for presently, to our surprise, the ancient woman, Gagool, rose from her crouching position and, supporting herself with a stick, staggered off into the open space. It was an extra-ordinary sight to see this frightful, vulture-headed old creature, bent nearly double with extreme age, gather strength by degrees, until at last she rushed about almost as actively as her ill-omened pupils. To and fro she ran, chanting to herself, till suddenly she made a dash at a tall man standing in front of one of the regiments, and touched him. As she did this a sort of groan went up from the regiment which evidently he commanded. But two of its officers seized him all the same, and brought him up for execution. We learned afterwards that he was a man of great wealth and importance, being indeed a cousin of the king.

He was slain and Twala counted one hundred and three. Then Gagool again sprang to and fro, gradually drawing nearer and nearer to ourselves.

'Hang me if I don't believe she is going to try her games on us,' ejaculated Good in horror.

'Nonsense!' said Sir Henry.

As for myself, when I saw that old fiend dancing nearer and nearer, my heart positively sank into my boots. I glanced behind us at the long rows of corpses, and shivered.

Nearer and nearer waltzed Gagool looking for all the world like an animated crooked stick or comma, her horrid eyes gleaming and glowing with a most unholy lustre.

Nearer she came, and yet nearer, every creature in that vast assemblage watching her movements with intense anxiety. At last she stood still and pointed.

'Which is it to be?' asked Sir Henry to himself.

In a moment all doubts were set at rest, for the old hag had rushed in and touched Umbopa, alias Ignosi, on the shoulder.

'I smell him out,' she shrieked. 'Kill him, kill him, he is full of evil; kill him, the stranger, before blood flows for him. Slay him, O king.'

There was a pause, of which I instantly took advantage.

'O king,' I called out, rising from my seat, 'this man is the servant of thy guests, he is their dog; whosoever sheds the blood of our dog sheds our blood. By the sacred law of hospitality I claim protection for him.'

'Gagool, old mother of the witch-finders, has smelt him out; he must die, white man,' was the sullen answer.

'Nay, he shall not die,' I replied; 'he who tries to touch him shall die indeed.'

'Seize him!' roared Twala to the executioners, who stood round red to the eyes with the blood of their victims.

They advanced towards us, and then hesitated. As for Ignosi, he clutched his spear, and raised it as though determined to sell his life dearly.

'Stand back, ye dogs!' I shouted, 'if ye would see tomorrow's light. Touch one hair of his head and your king dies,' and I covered Twala with my revolver. Sir Henry and Good also drew their pistols, Sir Henry pointing his at the leading executioner, who was advancing to carry out the sentence, and Good taking a deliberate aim at Gagool.

Twala winced perceptibly as my barrel came in a line with his broad chest.

'Well,' I said, 'what is it to be, Twala?'

Then he spoke.

'Put away your magic tubes,' he said; 'ye have adjured me in the name of hospitality, and for that reason, but not from fear of what you can do, I spare him. Go in peace.'

'It is well,' I answered unconcernedly; 'we are weary of slaughter and would sleep. Is the dance ended?'

'It is ended,' Twala answered sulkily. 'Let these dead dogs,' pointing to the long row of corpses, 'be flung out to the hyaenas and the vultures,' and he lifted his spear.

Instantly the regiments began to defile through the kraal gateway in perfect silence, a fatigue party only remaining behind to drag away the corpses of those who had been sacrificed.

Then we rose also, and making our salaam to his majesty, which he hardly deigned to acknowledge, we departed to our huts.

'Well,' said Sir Henry, as we sat down, having first lit a lamp of the sort used by the Kukuanas, of which the wick is made from the fibre of a species of palm-leaf, and the oil from clarified hippopotamus fat. 'Well, I feel uncommonly inclined to be sick.'

'If I had any doubts about helping Umbopa to rebel against that infernal blackguard,' put in Good, 'they are gone now. It was as much as I could do to sit still while that slaughter was going on. I tried to keep my eyes shut, but they would open just at the wrong time. I wonder where Infadoos is. Umbopa, my friend, you ought to be grateful to us; your skin came near to having an air-hole made in it.'

'I am grateful, Bougwan,' was Umbopa's answer, when I had translated, 'and I shall not forget. As for Infadoos, he will be here by and by. We must wait.'

So we lit our pipes and waited.

CHAPTER 11

We Give a Sign

For a long while – two hours, I should think – we sat there in silence, being too much overwhelmed by the recollection of the horrors we had seen to talk. At last, just as we were thinking of turning in – for the night drew nigh to dawn – we heard a sound of steps. Then came the challenge of a sentry posted at the kraal gate, which apparently was answered, though not in an audible tone, for the steps still advanced. In another second Infadoos had entered the hut, followed by some half-dozen stately-looking chiefs.

'My lords,' he said, 'I have come according to my word. My lords and Ignosi, rightful king of the Kukuanas, I have brought with me these men,' pointing to the row of chiefs, 'who are great men among us, having each one of them the command of three thousand soldiers that live but to do their bidding, under the king's. I have told them of what I have seen, and what my ears have heard. Now let them also behold the sacred snake around thee, and hear thy story, Ignosi, that they may say whether or no they will make cause with thee against Twala the king.'

By way of answer Ignosi again stripped off his girdle, and exhibited the snake tattooed about him. Each chief in turn drew near and examined the sign by the dim light of the lamp, and without saying a word passed on to the other side.

Then Ignosi resumed his *moocha*, and addressing them, repeated the history he had detailed in the morning.

'Now ye have heard, chiefs,' said Infadoos, when he had done, 'what say ye; will ye stand by this man and help him to his father's throne, or will ye not? The land cries out against Twala, and the blood of the people flows like the waters in spring. Ye have seen tonight. Two other chiefs there were with whom I had it in my mind to speak, and where are they now? The hyaenas howl over their corpses. Soon shall ye be as they are if ye strike not. Choose then, my brothers.'

The eldest of the six men, a short, thickset warrior, with white hair, stepped forward a pace and answered: 'Thy words are true, Infadoos; the land cries out. My own brother is among those who died tonight; but this is a great matter and the thing is hard to believe. How know we that if we lift our spears it may not be for a cheat and a liar? It is a great matter, I say, of which none can see the end. For of this be sure, blood will flow in rivers before the deed is done; many will still cleave to the king, for men worship the sun that still shines bright in the heavens, rather than that which has not risen. These white men from the stars, their magic is great, and Ignosi is under the cover of their wing. If he be indeed the rightful king, let them give us a sign, and let the people have a sign, that all may see. So shall men cleave to us, knowing of a truth that the white man's magic is with them.'

'Ye have the sign of the snake,' I answered.

'My lord, it is not enough. The snake may have been placed there since the man's childhood. Show us a sign, and it will suffice. But we will not move without a sign.'

The others gave a decided assent, and I turned in perplexity to Sir Henry and Good, and explained the situation.

'I think that I have it,' said Good, exultingly; 'ask them to give us a moment to think.'

I did so, and the chiefs withdrew. As soon as they had gone Good went to the little box where he kept his medicines, unlocked it and took out a notebook in the fly-leaves of which was an almanack. 'Now look here, you fellows, isn't tomorrow the 4th of June?' he said.

We had kept a careful note of the days, so were able to answer that it was.

'Very good; then here we have it – "4 June, total eclipse of the moon commences at 8.15 Greenwich time, visible in Tenerife, South Africa, etc." There's a sign for you. Tell them we will darken the moon tomorrow night.'

The idea was a splendid one; indeed, the only weak spot about it was a fear lest Good's almanack might be incorrect. If we made a false prophecy on such a subject, our prestige would be gone for ever, and so would Ignosi's chance of the throne of the Kukuanas.

'Suppose that the almanack is wrong,' suggested Sir Henry to Good, who was busily employed in working out something on a blank page of the book.

'I see no reason to suppose anything of the sort,' was his answer. 'Eclipses always come up to time; at least that is my experience of them, and it especially states that this one will be visible in South Africa. I have worked out the reckonings as well as I can, without knowing our exact position; and I make out that the eclipse should begin here about ten o'clock tomorrow night, and last until half-past twelve. For an hour and a half or so there should be almost total darkness.'

'Well,' said Sir Henry, 'I suppose we had better risk it.'

I acquiesced, though doubtfully, for eclipses are queer cattle to deal with – it might be a cloudy night, for instance, or our dates might be wrong – and sent Umbopa to summon the chiefs back. Presently they came, and I addressed them thus: 'Great men of the Kukuanas, and thou, Infadoos, listen. We love not to show our powers, for to do so is to interfere with the course of nature, and to plunge the world into fear and confusion. But since this matter is a great one, and as we are angered against the king because of the slaughter we have seen, and because of the act of the *isanusi* Gagool, who would have put our friend Ignosi to death, we have determined to break a rule, and to give such a sign as all men may see. Come hither'; and I led them to the door of the hut and pointed to the red ball of the moon. 'What see ye there?'

'We see the sinking moon,' answered the spokesman of the party.

'It is so. Now tell me, can any mortal man put out that moon before the hour of setting, and bring the curtain of black night down on to the land?'

The chief laughed a little at the question.

'No, my lord, that no man can do. The moon is stronger than man who looks on her, nor can she vary in her courses.'

'Ye say so. Yet I tell you that tomorrow night, about two hours before midnight, we will cause the moon to be eaten up for a space of an hour and the half of an hour. Yes, deep darkness shall cover the earth, and it shall be for a sign that Ignosi is indeed king of the Kukuanas. If we do this thing, will ye be satisfied?'

'Yea, my lords,' answered the old chief with a smile, which was reflected on the faces of his companions; 'if ye do this thing, we will be satisfied indeed.'

'It shall be done; we three, Incubu, Bougwan and Macumazahn, have said it, and it shall be done. Dost thou hear, Infadoos?'

'I hear, my lord, but it is a wonderful thing that ye promise, to put out the moon, the mother of the world, when she is at her full.'

'Yet shall we do it, Infadoos.'

'It is well, my lords. Today, two hours after sunset, Twala will send for my lords to witness the Girls' Dance, and one hour after the dance begins the girl whom Twala thinks the fairest shall be killed by Scragga, the king's son, as a sacrifice to the silent Stone Ones, who sit and keep watch by the mountains yonder,' and he pointed towards the three strange-looking peaks where Solomon's Road was supposed to end. 'Then let my lords darken the moon, and save the maiden's life, and the people will believe indeed.'

'Aye,' said the old chief, still smiling a little, 'the people will believe indeed.'

'Two miles from Loo,' went on Infadoos, 'there is a hill curved like a new moon, a stronghold, where are stationed my regiment, and three other regiments which these chiefs command. This morning we will make a plan whereby two or three other regiments may be moved there also. Then, if in truth my lords can darken the moon, in the darkness I will take my lords by the hand and lead them out of Loo to this place, where they shall be safe, and thence we can make war upon Twala the king.'

'It is good,' said I. 'Now let us sleep awhile before we make ready our magic.'

Infadoos rose, and, having saluted us, departed with the chiefs.

'My friends,' said Ignosi, so soon as they were gone, 'can ye do this wonderful thing, or were we speaking empty words to the captains?'

'We believe that we can do it, Umbopa – Ignosi, I mean.'

'It is strange,' he answered, 'and had ye not been Englishmen I would not have believed it; but I have learned that English gentlemen tell no lies. If we live through the matter, be sure that I will repay you.'

'Ignosi,' said Sir Henry, 'promise me one thing.'

'I will promise, Incubu, my friend, even before I hear it,' answered the big man with a smile. 'What is it?'

'This: that if ever you come to be king of this people you will do away with the smelling out of wizards such as we saw last night; and that the killing of men without trial shall no longer take place in the land.'

Ignosi thought for a moment after I had translated this request, and then answered: 'The ways of black people are not as the ways of white men, Incubu, nor do we value life so highly. Yet I will promise. If it be in my power to hold them back, the witch-finders shall hunt no more, nor shall any man die without trial and judgment.'

'That's a bargain, then,' said Sir Henry; 'and now let us get a little rest.'

Thoroughly wearied out, we were soon sound asleep, and slept till Ignosi woke us about eleven o'clock. Then we rose, washed, and ate a hearty breakfast. After that we went outside the hut and walked about, amusing ourselves with examining the structure of the Kukuana huts and observing the customs of the women.

'I hope that eclipse will come off,' said Sir Henry presently.

'If it does not it will soon be all up with us,' I answered mournfully; 'for so sure as we are living men some of those chiefs will tell the whole story to the king. Then there will be another sort of eclipse, and one that we shall certainly not like.'

Returning to the hut we ate some dinner, and passed the rest of the day in receiving visits of ceremony and curiosity. At length the sun set, and we enjoyed a couple of hours of such quiet as our melancholy forebodings would allow to us. Finally, about half-past eight, a messenger came from Twala to bid us to the great annual Dance of Girls which was about to be celebrated.

Hastily we put on the chain shirts that the king had sent us, and taking our rifles and ammunition with us, so as to have them handy in case we must fly, as suggested by Infadoos, we started boldly enough, though with inward fear and trembling. The great space in front of the king's kraal bore a very different appearance from that which it had presented on the previous evening. In place of the grim ranks of serried warriors were company after company of Kukuana girls, not overdressed, so far as clothing went, but each crowned with a wreath of flowers, and holding a palm leaf in one hand and a white arum lily in the other. In the centre of the open moonlit space sat Twala the king, with old Gagool at his feet, attended by Infadoos, the boy Scragga, and twelve guards. There were also present about a score of chiefs, amongst whom I recognised most of our friends of the night before.

Twala greeted us with much apparent cordiality, though I saw him fix his one eye viciously on Umbopa.

'Welcome, white men from the stars,' he said; 'this is another sight from that which your eyes gazed on by the light of last night's moon, but it is not so good a sight. Girls are pleasant, and were it not for such as these,' and he pointed round him, 'we should none of us be here this day; but men are better. Kisses and the tender words of women are sweet, but the sound of the clashing of the spears of warriors, and the smell of men's blood, are sweeter far! Would ye have wives from among our people, white men? If so, choose the fairest here, and ye shall have them, as many as ye will,' and he paused for an answer.

The prospect did not seem to be without attractions for Good, who, like most sailors, is of a susceptible nature. But being elderly and wise, I foresaw the endless complications that anything of the sort would involve, for women bring trouble so surely as the night follows the day, and put in a hasty answer, 'Thanks to thee, O king, but we white men wed only with white women like ourselves. Your maidens are fair, but they are not for us!'

The king laughed. 'It is well. In our land there is a proverb which runs, "Women's eyes are always bright, whatever the colour;" and another that says, "Love her who is present, for be sure she who is absent is false to thee." But perhaps these things are not so in the stars. In a land where men are white all things are possible. So be it, white men; the girls will not go begging! Welcome again; and welcome, too, thou black one; if Gagool here had won her way, thou wouldst have been stiff and cold by now. It is lucky for thee that thou too camest from the stars; ha! ha!'

'I can kill thee before thou killest me, O king,' was Ignosi's calm answer, 'and thou shalt be stiff before my limbs cease to bend.'

Twala started. 'Thou speakest boldly, boy,' he replied angrily; 'presume not too far.'

'He may well be bold in whose lips are truth. The truth is a sharp spear which flies home and misses not. It is a message from the stars, O king.'

Twala scowled, and his one eye gleamed fiercely, but he said nothing more. 'Let the dance begin,' he cried.

Then the flower-crowned girls sprang forward in companies, singing a sweet song and waving the delicate palms and white lilies. On they danced, looking faint and spiritual in the soft, sad light of the risen moon; now whirling round and round, now meeting in mimic warfare; swaying, eddying here and there, coming forward, falling back in an ordered confusion delightful to witness. At last they paused, and a beautiful young woman sprang out of the ranks and began to pirouette in front of us with a grace and vigour which would have put most ballet girls to shame. At length she retired exhausted, and another took her place, then another and another, but none of them, either in grace, skill or personal attractions, came up to the first.

When the chosen girls had all danced, the king lifted his hand.

'Which deem ye the fairest, white men?' he asked.

'The first,' said I unthinkingly. Next second I regretted it, for I remembered that Infadoos had told us that the fairest woman must be offered up as a sacrifice.

'Then is my mind as your minds, and my eyes are as your eyes. She is the fairest! and a sorry thing it is for her, since she must die!'

'*Aye, must die!*' piped out Gagool, casting a quick glance in the direction of the poor girl, who, as yet ignorant of the awful fate in store for her, was standing some ten yards off in front of a company of maidens, engaged in nervously picking a flower from her wreath to pieces, petal by petal.

'Why, O king?' said I, restraining my indignation with difficulty. 'The girl has danced well and pleased us; she is fair too; it would be hard to reward her with death.'

Twala laughed as he answered: 'It is our custom, and the Shapes who sit in stone yonder,' and he pointed towards the three distant peaks, 'must have their due. Did I fail to put the fairest girl to death today, misfortune would fall upon me and my house. Thus runs the prophecy of my people: "If the king offer not a sacrifice of a fair girl on the day of the Dance of Maidens to the Old Ones who sit and watch on the mountains, then shall he fall and his House." Look ye, white men, my brother who reigned before me offered not the sacrifice, because of the tears of the woman, and he fell, and his house, and I reign in his stead. It is finished; she must die!' Then turning to the guards – 'Bring her hither. Scragga, make sharp thy spear.'

Two of the men stepped forward, and as they advanced, the girl, for the first time realising her impending fate, screamed aloud and turned to fly. But strong hands caught her fast, and brought her, struggling and weeping, before us.

'What is thy name, girl?' piped Gagool. 'What! wilt thou not answer! Shall the king's son do his work at once?'

At this hint, Scragga, looking more evil than ever, advanced a step and lifted his great spear, and at that moment I saw Good's hand creep to his revolver. The poor girl caught the faint glint of steel through her tears, and it sobered her anguish. She ceased struggling and, clasping her hands convulsively, stood shuddering from head to foot.

'See,' cried Scragga in high glee, 'she shrinks from the sight of my little plaything even before she has tasted it,' and he tapped the broad blade of his spear.

'If ever I get the chance you shall pay for that, you young hound!' I heard Good mutter beneath his breath.

'Now that thou art quiet, give us thy name, my dear. Come, speak out, and fear not,' said Gagool in mockery.

'Oh, mother,' answered the girl, in trembling accents, 'my name is Foulata, of the house of Suko. Oh, mother, why must I die? I have done no wrong!'

'Be comforted,' went on the old woman in her hateful tone of mockery. 'Thou must die, indeed, as a sacrifice to the Old Ones who sit yonder,' and she pointed to the peaks. 'It is better to sleep in the night than to toil in the daytime; it is better to die than to live, and thou shalt die by the royal hand of the king's own son.'

The girl Foulata wrung her hands in anguish, and cried out aloud, 'Oh, cruel! and I so young! What have I done that I should never again see the sun rise out of the night, or the stars come following on his track in the evening, that I may no more gather flowers when the dew is heavy or listen to the laughing of the waters? Woe is me, that I shall never see my father's hut again, nor feel my mother's kiss, nor tend the lamb that is sick! Woe is me, that no lover shall put his arm around me and look into my eyes, nor shall men children be born of me! Oh, cruel, cruel!'

And again she wrung her hands and turned her tear-stained, flower-crowned face to heaven, looking so lovely in her despair – for she was indeed a beautiful woman – that assuredly the sight of her would have melted the hearts of any less cruel than were the three fiends before us. Prince Arthur's appeal to the ruffians who came to blind him was not more touching than that of this savage girl.

Still it did not move Gagool or Gagool's master, though I saw signs of pity among the guards behind, and on the faces of the chiefs. As for Good, he gave a fierce snort of indignation, and made a motion as though to go to her assistance. With all a woman's quickness, the doomed girl interpreted what was passing in his mind. By a sudden movement she flung herself before him, and clasped his 'beautiful white legs' with her hands.

'Oh, white father from the stars!' she cried, 'throw over me the mantle of protection; let me creep into the shadow of thy strength, that I may be saved. Oh, keep me from these cruel men and from the mercies of Gagool!'

'All right, my hearty, I'll look after you,' sang out Good, in nervous Saxon. 'Come, get up, there's a good girl,' and he stooped and caught her hand.

Twala turned and motioned to his son, who advanced with his spear lifted.

'Now's your time,' whispered Sir Henry to me; 'what are you waiting for?'

'I am waiting for that eclipse,' I answered; 'I have had my eye on the moon for the last half-hour, and I never saw it look healthier.'

'Well, you must risk it now, or the girl will be killed. Twala is losing patience.'

Recognising the force of the argument, and having cast one more despairing look at the bright face of the moon, for never did the most ardent astronomer with a theory to prove await a celestial event with such anxiety, I stepped with all the dignity that I could command between the prostrate girl and the advancing spear of Scragga.

'King,' I said, 'it shall not be; we will not endure this thing; let the girl go in safety.'

Twala rose from his seat in wrath and astonishment, and from the chiefs and serried ranks of maidens who had closed in slowly upon us in anticipation of the tragedy came a murmur of amazement.

'*Shall not be!* thou white dog, that yappest at the lion in his cave; *shall not be!* art thou mad? Be careful, lest this chicken's fate should overtake thee, and those with thee. How canst thou save her or thyself? Who art thou that thou settest thyself between me and my will? Back, I say. Scragga, kill her! Ho, guards! seize these men.'

At his words armed men ran swiftly from behind the hut, where they had evidently been placed beforehand.

Sir Henry, Good and Umbopa ranged themselves alongside of me, and lifted their rifles.

'Stop!' I shouted boldly, though at the moment my heart was in my boots. 'Stop! we, the white men from the stars, say that it shall not be. Come but one pace nearer, and we will put out the moon like a windblown lamp, as we who dwell in her house can do, and plunge the land in darkness. Dare to disobey, and ye shall taste of our magic.'

My threat produced an effect; the men halted, and Scragga stood still before us, his spear lifted.

'Hear him! hear him!' piped Gagool; 'hear the liar who says he will put out the moon like a lamp. Let him do it and the girl shall be spared. Yes, let him do it, or die by the girl, he and those with him.'

I glanced up at the moon despairingly, and now to my intense joy and relief saw that we – or rather the almanack – had made no mistake. On the edge of the great orb lay a faint rim of shadow, while a smoky shade grew and gathered upon its bright surface. Never shall I forget that supreme, that superb moment of relief.

Then I lifted my hand solemnly towards the sky, an example which Sir Henry and Good followed, and quoted a line or two from the *Ingoldsby Legends* at it in the most impressive tones that I could command. Sir Henry followed suit with a verse out of the Old Testament, and something about Balbus building a wall, in Latin, whilst Good addressed the Queen of Night in a volume of the most classical bad language which he could think of.

Slowly the penumbra, the shadow of a shadow, crept on over the bright surface, and as it crept I heard deep gasps of fear rising from the multitude around.

'Look, O king!' I cried; 'look, Gagool! Look, chiefs and people and women, and see if the white men from the stars keep their word, or if they be but empty liars!

'The moon grows black before your eyes; soon there will be darkness – aye, darkness in the hour of the full moon. Ye have asked for a sign; it is given to you. Grow dark, O moon! withdraw thy light, thou pure and holy one; bring the proud heart of usurping murderers to the dust, and eat up the world with shadows.'

A groan of terror burst from the onlookers. Some stood petrified with dread, others threw themselves upon their knees and cried aloud. As for the king, he sat still and turned pale beneath his dusky skin. Only Gagool kept her courage.

'It will pass,' she cried; 'I have often seen the like before; no man can put out the moon; lose not heart; sit still – the shadow will pass.'

'Wait, and ye shall see,' I replied, hopping with excitement. 'O moon! moon! moon! wherefore art thou so cold and fickle?' This appropriate quotation I took from the pages of a popular romance that I chanced to have read recently. Yet now I come to think of it, it was ungrateful to abuse the Lady of the heavens –

> That orbéd maiden with white fire laden
> Whom mortals call the moon –

who was showing herself to be the truest of friends to us, however she may have behaved to the impassioned lover in the novel. Then I added: 'Keep it up, Good, I can't remember any more poetry. Curse away, there's a good fellow.'

Good responded nobly to this tax upon his inventive faculties. Never before had I the faintest conception of the breadth and depth and height of a naval officer's objurgatory powers. For ten minutes he went on in several languages without stopping, and he scarcely ever repeated himself.

Meanwhile the dark ring crept on, while all that great assembly fixed their eyes upon the sky and stared and stared in fascinated silence. Strange and unholy shadows encroached upon the moonlight; an ominous quiet filled the place. Everything grew still as death. Slowly and in the midst of this most solemn silence the minutes sped away, and while they sped the full moon passed deeper and deeper into the shadow of the earth, as the inky segment of its circle slid in awful majesty across the lunar craters. The great pale orb seemed to draw near and to grow in size. She turned a coppery hue, then that portion of her surface which was unobscured as yet, grew grey and ashen, and at length, as totality approached, her mountains and her plains were to be seen glowing luridly through a crimson gloom.

On, yet on, crept the ring of darkness; it was now more than half across the blood-red orb. The air grew thick, and still more deeply tinged with dusky crimson. On, yet on, till we could scarcely see the fierce faces of the group before us. No sound rose now from the spectators, and at last Good stopped swearing.

'The moon is dying – the white wizards have killed the moon,' yelled the prince Scragga at last. 'We shall perish in the dark.' Then animated by fear or fury, or by both, he lifted his spear and drove it with all his force at Sir Henry's breast. But he forgot the mail shirts that the king had given us, which we wore beneath our clothing. The steel rebounded harmless, and before he could repeat the blow Curtis had snatched the spear from his hand and sent it straight through him.

Scragga dropped dead.

At the sight, and driven mad with fear of the gathering darkness, and of the unholy shadow which, as they believed, was swallowing the moon, the companies of girls broke up in wild confusion and ran screeching for the gateways. Nor did the panic stop there. The king himself, followed by his guards, some of the chiefs and Gagool, who hobbled away after them with marvellous alacrity, fled for the huts. Thus in another minute we ourselves, the intended victim Foulata, Infadoos and most of the chiefs who had interviewed us on the previous night, were left alone upon the scene, together with the dead body of Scragga, Twala's son.

'Chiefs,' I said, 'we have given you the sign. If ye are satisfied, let us fly swiftly to the place of which ye spoke. The charm cannot now be stopped. It will work for an hour and the half of an hour. Let us cover ourselves with the darkness.'

'Come,' said Infadoos, turning to go, an example which was followed by the awed captains, ourselves and the girl Foulata, whom Good took by the arm.

Before we reached the gate of the kraal the moon went out utterly, and from every quarter of the firmament stars rushed forth into the inky sky.

Holding each other by the hand we stumbled on through the darkness.

CHAPTER 12

Before the Battle

Luckily for us, Infadoos and the chiefs knew all the paths of the great town perfectly, so that we passed by side-ways unmolested, and notwithstanding the gloom we made fair progress.

For an hour or more we journeyed on, till at length the eclipse began to pass, and that edge of the moon which had disappeared the first became again visible. Suddenly, as we watched, there burst from it a silver streak of light, accompanied by a wondrous ruddy glow, which hung upon the blackness of the sky like a celestial lamp. A wild and lovely sight it was. In another five minutes the stars began to fade, and there was sufficient light to see our whereabouts. We then discovered that we were clear of the town of Loo and approaching a large flat-topped hill, measuring some two miles in circumference. This hill, which was of a formation common in South Africa, was not very high; indeed, its greatest elevation was scarcely more than two hundred feet, but it was shaped like a horseshoe, and its sides were rather precipitous and strewn with boulders. On the grass tableland at its summit was ample camping-ground, which had been utilised as a military cantonment of no mean strength. Its ordinary garrison was one regiment of three thousand men but, as we toiled up the steep side of the mountain, in the returning moonlight we perceived that there were several such regiments encamped there.

Reaching the tableland at last, we found crowds of men roused from their sleep, shivering with fear and huddled up together in the utmost consternation at the natural phenomenon which they were witnessing. Passing through these without a word, we gained a hut in the centre of the ground. Here we were astonished to find two men waiting, laden with our few goods and chattels, which of course we had been obliged to leave behind in our hasty flight.

'I sent for them,' explained Infadoos; 'also for these,' and he lifted up Good's long-lost trousers.

With an exclamation of rapturous delight Good sprang at them, and instantly proceeded to put them on.

'Surely my lord will not hide his beautiful white legs!' exclaimed Infadoos regretfully.

But Good persisted, and once only did the Kukuana people get the chance of seeing his beautiful legs again. Good is a very modest man. Henceforward they had to satisfy their aesthetic longings with his one-sided whiskers, his transparent eye and his movable teeth.

Still gazing with fond remembrance at Good's trousers, Infadoos next informed us that he had commanded the regiments to muster so soon as the day broke, in order to explain to them fully the origin and circumstances of the rebellion which was decided on by the chiefs, and to introduce to them the rightful heir to the throne, Ignosi.

Accordingly, when the sun was up, the troops – in all some twenty thousand men, and the flower of the Kukuana army – mustered on a large open space to which we went. The men were drawn up in the three sides of a dense square, and presented a magnificent spectacle. We took our station on the open side of the square, and were speedily surrounded by all the principal chiefs and officers.

These, after silence had been proclaimed, Infadoos proceeded to address. He narrated to them in vigorous and graceful language – for, like most Kukuanas of high rank, he was a born orator – the history of Ignosi's father, and of how he had been basely murdered by Twala the king, and his wife and child driven out to starve. Then he pointed out that the people suffered and groaned under Twala's cruel rule, instancing the proceedings of the previous night, when, under pretence of their being evildoers, many of the noblest in the land had been dragged forth and wickedly done to death. Next he went on to say that the white lords from the stars, looking down upon their country, had perceived its trouble, and determined, at great personal inconvenience, to alleviate its lot; that they had accordingly taken the real king of the Kukuanas, Ignosi, who was languishing in exile, by the hand, and led him over the mountains; that they had seen the wickedness of Twala's doings, and for a sign to the wavering, and to save the life of the girl Foulata, actually, by the exercise of their high magic, had put out the moon and slain the young fiend Scragga; and that they were prepared to stand by them, to assist them to overthrow Twala, and to set up the rightful king, Ignosi, in his place.

He finished his discourse amidst a murmur of approbation. Then Ignosi stepped forward and began to speak. Having reiterated all that Infadoos his uncle had said, he concluded with a powerful speech in these words: 'O chiefs, captains, soldiers and people, ye have heard my words. Now must ye make choice between me and him who sits upon my throne, the uncle who killed his brother, and hunted his brother's child forth to die in the cold and the night. That I am indeed the king these' – pointing to the chiefs – 'can tell you, for they have seen the snake about my middle. If I were not the king, would these white men be on my side with all their magic? Tremble, chiefs, captains, soldiers and people! Is not the darkness they have brought upon the land to confound Twala and cover our flight, darkness even in the hour of the full moon, yet before your eyes?'

'It is,' answered the soldiers.

'I am the king; I say to you, I am the king,' went on Ignosi, drawing up his great stature to its full, and lifting the broad-bladed battle-axe above his head. 'If there be any man among you who says that it is not so, let him stand forth and I will fight him now, and his blood shall be a red token that I tell you true. Let him stand forth, I say!' and he shook the great axe till it flashed in the sunlight.

As nobody seemed inclined to respond to this heroic version of 'Dilly, Dilly, come and be killed', our late henchman proceeded with his address.

'I am indeed the king, and should ye stand by my side in the battle, if I win the day ye shall go with me to victory and honour.

I will give you oxen and wives, and ye shall take precedence among all the regiments; and if ye fall, I will fall with you.

'Behold, I give you this promise also, that when I sit upon the seat of my fathers, bloodshed shall cease in the land. No longer shall ye cry for justice to find slaughter, no longer shall the witch-finder hunt you out so that ye may be slain without a cause. No man shall die save he who offends against the laws. The "eating up" of your kraals shall cease; each one of you shall sleep secure in his own hut and fear nought, and justice shall walk blindfold throughout the land. Have ye chosen, chiefs, captains, soldiers and people?'

'We have chosen, O king,' came back the answer.

'It is well. Turn your heads and see how Twala's messengers go forth from the great town, east and west and north and south, to gather a mighty army to slay me and you, and these my friends and protectors. Tomorrow, or perchance the next day, he will come against us with all who are faithful to him. Then I shall see the man who is indeed my man, the man who fears not to die for his cause; and I tell you that he shall not be forgotten in the time of spoil. I have spoken, O chiefs, captains, soldiers and people. Now go to your huts and make you ready for war.'

There was a pause, till presently one of the chiefs lifted his hand and out rolled the royal salute, '*Koom*'. It was a sign that the soldiers accepted Ignosi as their king. Then they marched off in battalions.

Half an hour afterwards we held a council of war, at which all the commanders of regiments were present. It was evident to us that before very long we should be attacked in overwhelming force. Indeed, from our point of vantage on the hill we could see troops mustering, and runners going forth from Loo in every direction, doubtless to summon soldiers to the king's assistance. We had on our side about twenty thousand men, composed of seven of the best regiments in the country. Twala, so Infadoos and the chiefs calculated, had at least thirty to thirty-five thousand on whom he could rely at present assembled in Loo, and they thought that by midday on the morrow he would be able to gather another five thousand or more to his aid. It was, of course, possible that some of the troops would desert and come over to us, but it was not a contingency which could be reckoned on. Meanwhile, it was clear that active preparations were being made by Twala to subdue us. Already strong bodies of armed men were patrolling round and round the foot of the hill; also there were other signs of coming assault.

Infadoos and the chiefs, however, were of the opinion that no attack would take place that day, which would be devoted to preparation and to the removal by every available means of the moral effect produced upon the minds of the soldiery by the supposed magical darkening of the moon. The onslaught would be on the morrow, they said, and they proved to be right.

Meanwhile we set to work to strengthen the position in all ways possible. Almost every man was turned out, and in the course of the day, which seemed far too short, much was done. The paths up the hill – that was rather a sanatorium than a fortress, being used generally as the camping place of regiments suffering from recent service in unhealthy portions of the country – were carefully blocked with masses of stones, and every other approach was made as impregnable as time would allow. Piles of boulders were collected at various spots to be rolled down upon an advancing enemy, stations were appointed to the different regiments, and all preparation was made which our joint ingenuity could suggest.

Just before sundown, as we rested after our toil, we perceived a small company of men advancing towards us from the direction of Loo, one of whom bore a palm leaf in his hand for a sign that he came as a herald.

As he drew near, Ignosi, Infadoos, one or two chiefs and ourselves went down to the foot of the mountain to meet him. He was a gallant-looking fellow, wearing the regulation leopard-skin cloak.

'Greetings!' he cried, as he came; 'the king's greeting to those who make unholy war against the king; the lion's greeting to the jackals that snarl around his heels.'

'Speak,' I said.

'These are the king's words. Surrender to the king's mercy ere a worse thing befall you. Already the shoulder has been torn from the black bull, and the king drives him bleeding about the camp.'*

'What are Twala's terms?' I asked from curiosity.

'His terms are merciful, worthy of a great king. These are the words of Twala, the one-eyed, the mighty, the husband of a thousand wives, lord of the Kukuanas, keeper of the Great Road (Solomon's Road), beloved of the Strange Ones who sit in silence at the mountains yonder (the Three Witches), Calf of the Black Cow, Elephant whose tread shakes the earth, Terror of the evildoer, Ostrich whose feet devour the desert, huge One, black One, wise One, King from generation to generation! these are the words of Twala: "I will have mercy and be satisfied with a little blood. One in every ten shall die, the rest shall go free; but the white man Incubu, who slew Scragga my son, and the black man his servant, who pretends to my throne, and Infadoos my brother, who brews rebellion against me, these shall die by torture as an offering to the Silent Ones." Such are the merciful words of Twala.'

After consulting with the others a little, I answered him in a loud voice, so that the soldiers might hear, thus: 'Go back, thou dog, to Twala, who sent thee, and say that we, Ignosi, veritable king of the Kukuanas, Incubu, Bougwan and Macumazahn, the wise ones from the stars, who make dark the moon, Infadoos, of the royal house, and the chiefs, captains and people here gathered, make answer and say that we will not surrender; that before the sun has gone down twice, Twala's corpse shall stiffen at Twala's gate, and Ignosi, whose father Twala slew, shall reign in his stead. Now go, ere we whip thee away, and beware how thou dost lift a hand against such as we are.'

The herald laughed loudly. 'Ye frighten not men with such swelling words,' he cried out. 'Show yourselves as bold tomorrow, O ye who darken the moon. Be bold, fight and be merry, before the crows pick your bones till they are whiter than your faces.

* This cruel custom is not confined to the Kukuanas, but is common amongst African tribes on the occasion of the outbreak of war or any other important public event. A.Q.

Farewell; perhaps we may meet in the fight; fly not to the stars, but wait for me, I pray, white men.' With this shaft of sarcasm he retired, and almost immediately the sun sank.

That night was a busy one, for weary as we were, so far as was possible by the moonlight all preparations for the morrow's fight were continued, and messengers were constantly coming and going from the place where we sat in council. At last, about an hour after midnight, everything that could be done was done, and the camp, save for the occasional challenge of a sentry, sank into silence. Sir Henry and I, accompanied by Ignosi and one of the chiefs, descended the hill and made a round of the pickets. As we went, suddenly, from all sorts of unexpected places, spears gleamed out in the moonlight, only to vanish again when we uttered the password. It was clear to us that none were sleeping at their posts. Then we returned, picking our way warily through thousands of sleeping warriors, many of whom were taking their last earthly rest.

The moonlight, flickering along their spears, played upon their features and made them ghastly; the chilly night wind tossed their tall and funereal plumes. There they lay in wild confusion, with arms outstretched and limbs twisted; their stern, stalwart forms looking weird and unhuman in the moonlight.

'How many of these do you suppose will be alive at this time tomorrow?' asked Sir Henry.

I shook my head and looked again at the sleeping men, and to my tired yet excited imagination it seemed as though death had already touched them. My mind's eye singled out those who were sealed to slaughter, and there rushed in upon my heart a great sense of the mystery of human life, and an overwhelming sorrow at its futility and sadness. Tonight these thousands slept their healthy sleep, tomorrow they, and many others with them, ourselves perhaps among them, would be stiffening in the cold; their wives would be widows, their children fatherless, and their place know them no more for ever. Only the old moon would shine on serenely, the night wind would stir the grasses, and the wide earth would take its rest, even as it did aeons before we were, and will do aeons after we have been forgotten.

Yet man dies not whilst the world, at once his mother and his monument, remains. His name is lost, indeed, but the breath he breathed still stirs the pine-tops on the mountains; the sound of the words he spoke yet echoes on through space; the thoughts his brain gave birth to we have inherited today; his passions are our cause of life; the joys and sorrows that he knew are our familiar friends – the end from which he fled aghast will surely overtake us also!

Truly the universe is full of ghosts, not sheeted, churchyard spectres, but the inextinguishable elements of individual life, which having once been, can never *die*, though they blend and change, and change again for ever.

All sorts of reflections of this nature passed through my mind – for as I grow older I regret to say that a detestable habit of thinking seems to be getting a hold of me – while I stood and stared at those grim yet fantastic lines of warriors, sleeping, as their saying goes, 'upon their spears'.

'Curtis,' I said, ' I am in a condition of pitiable fear.'

Sir Henry stroked his yellow beard and laughed, as he answered: 'I have heard you make that sort of remark before, Quatermain.'

'Well, I mean it now. Do you know, I very much doubt if one of us will be alive tomorrow night. We shall be attacked in over-whelming force, and it is quite a chance if we can hold this place.'

'We'll give a good account of some of them, at any rate. Look here, Quatermain, this business is nasty, and one with which, properly speaking, we ought not to be mixed up, but we are in for it, so we must make the best of our job. Speaking personally, I had rather be killed fighting than any other way, and now that there seems little chance of our finding my poor brother, it makes the idea easier to me. But fortune favours the brave, and we may succeed. Anyway, the battle will be awful, and having a reputation to keep up, we shall need to be in the thick of the thing.'

He made this last remark in a mournful voice, but there was a gleam in his eye which belied its melancholy. I have an idea that Sir Henry Curtis actually likes fighting.

After this we went to sleep for a couple of hours or so.

Just about dawn we were awakened by Infadoos, who came to say that great activity was to be observed in Loo, and that parties of the king's skirmishers were driving in our outposts.

We rose and dressed ourselves for the fray, each putting on his chain armour shirt, for which garments at the present juncture we felt exceedingly thankful. Sir Henry went the whole length about the matter, and dressed himself like a native warrior. 'When you are in Kukuanaland, do as the Kukuanas do,' he remarked, as he drew the shining steel over his broad breast, which it fitted like a glove. Nor did he stop there. At his request Infadoos had provided him with a complete set of native war uniform. Round his throat he fastened the leopard-skin cloak of a commanding officer, on his brows he bound the plume of black ostrich feathers worn only by generals of high rank, and about his middle a magnificent *moocha* of white ox tails. A pair of sandals, a leglet of goat's hair, a heavy battle-axe with a rhinoceros-horn handle, a round iron shield covered with white oxhide, and the regulation number of *tollas*, or throwing-knives, made up his equipment, to which, however, he added his revolver. The dress was, no doubt, a savage one, but I am bound to say that I seldom saw a finer sight than Sir Henry Curtis presented in this guise. It showed off his magnificent physique to the greatest advantage, and when Ignosi arrived presently, arrayed in a similar costume, I thought to myself that I had never before seen two such splendid men.

As for Good and myself, the armour did not suit us nearly so well. To begin with, Good insisted upon wearing his new-found trousers, and a stout, short gentleman with an eyeglass and one half of his face shaved, arrayed in a mail shirt, carefully tucked into a very seedy pair of corduroys, looks more remarkable than imposing. In my case, the chain shirt being too big for me, I put it on over all my clothes, which caused it to bulge in a somewhat ungainly fashion. I discarded my trousers, however, retaining only my *veldschoens*, having determined to go into battle with bare legs, in order to be the lighter for running, in case it became necessary to retire quickly. The mail coat, a spear, a shield that I did not know how to use, a couple of *tollas*, a revolver and a huge plume, which I pinned into the top of my shooting hat, in order to give a bloodthirsty finish to my appearance, completed my modest equipment. In addition to all these articles, of course, we had our rifles, but as ammunition was scarce, and as they would be useless in case of a charge, we arranged that they should be carried behind us by bearers.

When at length we had equipped ourselves, we swallowed some food hastily, and then started out to see how things were going on. At one point in the tableland of the mountain, there was a little *koppie* of brown stone, which served the double purpose of headquarters and of a conning tower. Here we found Infadoos surrounded by his own regiment, the Greys, which was undoubtedly the finest in the Kukuana army, and the same that we had first seen at the outlying kraal. This regiment, now three thousand five hundred strong, was being held in reserve, and the men were lying down on the grass in companies and watching the king's forces creep out of Loo in long ant-like columns. There seemed to be no end to the length of these columns – three in all, and each of them numbering, as we judged, at least eleven or twelve thousand men.

As soon as they were clear of the town the regiments formed up. Then one body marched off to the right, one to the left and the third came on slowly towards us.

'Ah,' said Infadoos, 'they are going to attack us on three sides at once.'

This seemed rather serious news, for our position on the top of the mountain, which measured a mile and a half in circumference, being an extended one, it was important to us to concentrate our comparatively small defending force as much as possible. But since it was impossible for us to dictate in what way we should be assailed, we had to make the best of it, and accordingly sent orders to the various regiments to prepare to receive the separate onslaughts.

CHAPTER 13

The Attack

Slowly, and without the slightest appearance of haste or excitement, the three columns crept on. When within about five hundred yards of us, the main or centre column halted at the root of a tongue of open plain which ran up into the hill, to give time to the other divisions to circumvent our position, which was shaped more or less in the form of a horseshoe, with its two points facing towards the town of Loo. The object of this manoeuvre was that the threefold assault should be delivered simultaneously.

'Oh, for a Gatling!' groaned Good, as he contemplated the serried phalanxes beneath us. 'I would clear that plain in twenty minutes.'

'We have not got one, so it is no use yearning for it; but suppose you try a shot, Quatermain,' said Sir Henry. 'See how near you can go to that tall fellow who appears to be in command. Two to one you miss him, and an even sovereign, to be honestly paid if ever we get out of this, that you don't drop the bullet within five yards.'

This piqued me, so, loading the Express with solid ball, I waited till my friend walked some ten yards out from his force, in order to get a better view of our position, accompanied only by an orderly; then, lying down and resting the Express upon a rock, I covered him. The rifle, like all Expresses, was only sighted to three hundred and fifty yards, so to allow for the drop in trajectory I took him halfway down the neck, which ought, I calculated, to find him in the chest. He stood quite still and gave me every opportunity, but whether it was the excitement or the wind, or the fact of the man being a long shot, I don't know, but this was what happened. Getting dead on, as I thought, and taking a fine sight, I pressed. When the puff of smoke had cleared away, to my disgust, I saw my man standing unharmed, whilst his orderly, who was at least three paces to the left, was stretched upon the ground apparently dead. Turning swiftly, the officer I had aimed at began to run towards his men in evident alarm.

'Bravo, Quatermain!' sang out Good; 'you've frightened him.'

This made me very angry, for, if possible to avoid it, I hate to miss in public. When a man is master of only one art he likes to keep up his reputation in that art. Moved quite out of myself at my failure, I did a rash thing. Rapidly covering the general as he ran, I let drive with the second barrel. Instantly the poor man threw up his arms, and fell forward on to his face. This time I had made no mistake; and – I say it as a proof of how little we think of others when our own safety, pride and reputation are in question – I was brute enough to feel delighted at the sight.

The regiments who had seen the feat cheered wildly at this exhibition of the white man's magic, which they took as an omen of success, while the force the general had belonged to – which, indeed, as we ascertained afterwards, he had commanded – fell back in confusion. Sir Henry and Good now took up their rifles and began to fire, the latter industriously 'browning' the dense mass before him with a Winchester repeater, and I also had another shot or two, with the result, so far as we could judge, that we put some six or eight men *hors de combat* before they were out of range.

Just as we stopped firing there came an ominous roar from our far right, then a similar roar rose on our left. The two other divisions were engaging us.

At the sound, the mass of men before us opened out a little, and advanced towards the hill and up the spit of bare grassland at a slow trot, singing a deep-throated song as they ran. We kept up a steady fire from our rifles as they came, Ignosi joining in occasionally, and accounted for several men, but of course we produced no more effect upon that mighty rush of armed humanity than he who throws pebbles does on the breaking wave.

On they came, with a shout and the clashing of spears; now they were driving in the pickets we had placed among the rocks at the foot of the hill. After that the advance was a little slower, for though as yet we had offered no serious opposition, the attacking forces must climb uphill, and they came slowly to save their breath. Our first line of defence was about halfway down the side of the slope, our second fifty yards farther back, while our third occupied the edge of the plateau.

On they stormed, shouting their war-cry, '*Twala! Twala! Chiele! Chiele!*' (Twala! Twala! Smite! Smite!) '*Ignosi! Ignosi! Chiele! Chiele!*' answered our people. They were quite close now, and the *tollas*, or throwing-knives, began to flash backwards and forwards. With an awful yell, battle was joined.

To and fro swayed the mass of struggling warriors, men falling fast as leaves in an autumn wind; but before long the superior weight of the attacking force began to tell, and our first line of defence was slowly pressed back, till it merged into the second. Here the struggle was very fierce, but again our people were driven back and up, till at length, within twenty minutes of the commencement of the fight, our third line came into action.

But by this time the assailants were much exhausted, and besides had lost many men killed and wounded, and to break through that third impenetrable hedge of spears proved beyond their powers. For a while the seething lines of savages swung backwards and forwards, in the fierce ebb and flow of battle, and the issue was doubtful. Sir Henry watched the desperate struggle with a kindling eye, and then without a word he rushed off, followed by Good, and flung himself into the hottest of the fray. As for myself, I stopped where I was.

The soldiers caught sight of his tall form as he plunged into battle, and there rose a cry of: '*Nanzia Incubu! Nanzia Incubu!*' (Here is the Elephant!) '*Chiele! Chiele!*'

From that moment the end was no longer in doubt. Inch by inch, fighting with splendid gallantry, the attacking force was pressed back down the hillside, till at last it retreated upon its reserves in something like confusion. At that instant, too, a messenger arrived to say that the left attack had been repulsed; and I was just beginning to congratulate myself, believing that the affair was over for the present, when, to our horror, we perceived our men who had been engaged in the right defence being driven towards us across the plain, followed by swarms of the enemy, who had evidently succeeded at this point.

Ignosi, who was standing by me, took in the situation at a glance and issued a rapid order. Instantly the reserve regiment around us, the Greys, extended itself.

Again Ignosi gave a word of command, which was taken up and repeated by the captains, and in another second, to my intense disgust, I found myself involved in a furious onslaught upon the advancing foe. Getting as much as I could behind Ignosi's huge frame, I made the best of a bad job, and toddled along to be killed as though I liked it. In a minute or two – the time seemed all too short to me – we were plunging through the flying groups of our men, who at once began to reform behind us, and then I am sure I do not know what happened. All I can remember is a dreadful rolling noise of the meeting of shields, and the sudden apparition of a huge ruffian, whose eyes seemed literally to be starting out of his head, making straight at me with a bloody spear. But – I say it with pride – I rose – or rather sank – to the occasion. It was one before which most people would have collapsed once and for all. Seeing that if I stood where I was I must be killed, as the horrid apparition came I flung myself down in front of him so cleverly that, being unable to stop himself, he took a header right over my prostrate form. Before he could rise again, I was up and had settled the matter from behind with my revolver.

Shortly after this somebody knocked me for six, and I remember no more of that charge.

When I came to I found myself back at the *koppie*, with Good bending over me holding some water in a gourd.

'How do you feel, old fellow?' he asked anxiously.

I got up and shook myself before replying.

'Pretty well, thank you,' I answered.

'Thank heaven! When I saw them carry you in, I felt quite sick; I thought that you were done for.'

'Not this time, my boy. I fancy I only got a rap on the head, which knocked me stupid. How has it ended?'

'They are repulsed at every point for a while. The loss is

dreadfully heavy; we have quite two thousand killed and wounded, and they must have lost three. Look, there's a sight!' and he pointed to long lines of men advancing by fours.

In the centre of every group of four, and being borne by it, was a kind of hide tray, of which a Kukuana force always carries a quantity, with a loop for a handle at each corner. On these trays – and their number seemed endless – lay wounded men, who as they arrived were hastily examined by the medicine men, of whom ten were attached to a regiment. If the wound was not of a fatal character the sufferer was taken away and attended to as carefully as circumstances would allow. But if, on the other hand, the injured man's condition proved hopeless, what followed was very dreadful, though doubtless it may have been the truest mercy. One of the doctors, under pretence of carrying out an examination, swiftly opened an artery with a sharp knife, and in a minute or two the sufferer expired painlessly. There were many cases that day in which this was done. In fact, it was done in the majority of cases when the wound was in the body, for the gash made by the entry of the enormously broad spears used by the Kukuanas generally rendered recovery impossible. In most instances the poor sufferers were already unconscious, and in others the fatal 'nick' of the artery was inflicted so swiftly and painlessly that they did not seem to notice it. Still it was a ghastly sight, and one from which we were glad to escape. Indeed, I never remember anything of the kind that affected me more than seeing those gallant soldiers thus put out of pain by the red-handed medicine men, except, perhaps, on one occasion when, after an attack, I saw a force of Swazis burying their hopelessly wounded *alive*.

Hurrying from this dreadful scene to the farther side of the *koppie*, we found Sir Henry, who still held a battle-axe in his hand, Ignosi, Infadoos and one or two of the chiefs in deep consultation.

'Thank heaven, here you are, Quatermain! I can't quite make out what Ignosi wants to do. It seems that though we have beaten off the attack, Twala is now receiving large reinforcements, and is showing a disposition to invest us, with a view of starving us out.'

'That's awkward.'

'Yes, especially as Infadoos says that the water supply has given out.'

'My lord, that is so,' said Infadoos; 'the spring cannot supply the wants of so great a multitude, and it is failing rapidly. Before night we shall all be thirsty. Listen, Macumazahn. Thou art wise, and hast doubtless seen many wars in the lands from whence thou camest – that is if indeed they make wars in the stars. Now tell us, what shall we do? Twala has brought up many fresh men to take the place of those who have fallen. Yet Twala has learnt his lesson; the hawk did not think to find the heron ready; but our beak has pierced his breast; he fears to strike at us again. We too are wounded, and he will wait for us to die; he will wind himself round us like a snake round a buck, and fight the fight of "sit down".'

'I hear thee,' I said.

'So, Macumazahn, thou seest we have no water here, and but a little food, and we must choose between these three things – to languish like a starving lion in his den, or to strive to break away towards the north, or,' and here he rose and pointed towards the dense mass of our foes, 'to launch ourselves straight at Twala's throat. Incubu, the great warrior – for today he fought like a buffalo in a net, and Twala's soldiers went down before his axe like young corn before the hail; with these eyes I saw it – Incubu says "Charge"; but the Elephant is ever prone to charge. Now what says Macumazahn, the wily old fox, who has seen much, and loves to bite his enemy from behind? The last word is in Ignosi the king, for it is a king's right to speak of war; but let us hear thy voice, O Macumazahn, who watchest by night, and the voice too of him of the transparent eye.'

'What sayest thou, Ignosi?' I asked.

'Nay, my father,' answered our quondam servant, who now, clad as he was in the full panoply of savage war, looked every inch a warrior king, 'do thou speak, and let me, who am but a child in wisdom beside thee, hearken to thy words.'

Thus adjured, after taking hasty counsel with Good and Sir Henry, I delivered my opinion briefly to the effect that, being trapped, our best chance, especially in view of the failure of our water supply, was to initiate an attack upon Twala's forces. Then I recommended that the attack should be delivered at once, 'before our wounds grew stiff'; also before the sight of Twala's overpowering force caused the hearts of our soldiers 'to wax small like fat before a fire'. Otherwise, I pointed out, some of the captains might change their minds, and, making peace with Twala, desert to him, or even betray us into his hands.

This expression of opinion seemed, on the whole, to be favourably received; indeed, among the Kukuanas my utterances met with a respect which has never been accorded to them before or since. But the real decision as to our plans lay with Ignosi, who, since he had been recognised as rightful king, could exercise the almost unbounded rights of sovereignty, including, of course, the final decision on matters of generalship, and it was to him that all eyes were now turned.

At length, after a pause, during which he appeared to be thinking deeply, he spoke.

'Incubu, Macumazahn and Bougwan, brave white men, and my friends; Infadoos, my uncle, and chiefs; my heart is fixed. I will strike at Twala this day, and set my fortunes on the blow, aye, and my life – my life and your lives also. Listen; thus will I strike. Ye see how the hill curves round like the half-moon, and how the plain runs like a green tongue towards us within the curve?'

'We see,' I answered.

'Good; it is now midday, and the men eat and rest after the toil of battle. When the sun has turned and travelled a little way towards the darkness, let thy regiment, my uncle, advance with one other down to the green tongue; and it shall be that when Twala sees it he will hurl his force at it to crush it. But the spot is narrow, and the regiments can come against thee one at a time only; so may they be destroyed one by one, and the eyes of all Twala's army shall be fixed upon a struggle the like of which has not been seen by living man. And with thee, my uncle, shall go Incubu my friend, that when Twala sees his battle-axe flashing in the first rank of the Greys his heart may grow faint. And I will come with the second regiment, that which follows thee, so that if ye are destroyed, as it might happen, there may yet be a king left to fight for; and with me shall come Macumazahn the wise.'

'It is well, O king,' said Infadoos, apparently contemplating the certainty of the complete annihilation of his regiment with perfect calmness. Truly, these Kukuanas are a wonderful people. Death has no terrors for them when it is incurred in the course of duty.

'And whilst the eyes of the multitude of Twala's soldiers are thus fixed upon the fight,' went on Ignosi, 'behold, one-third of the men who are left alive to us' (i.e. about six thousand) 'shall creep along the right horn of the hill and fall upon the left flank of Twala's force and one-third shall creep along the left horn and fall upon Twala's right flank. And when I see that the horns are ready to toss Twala, then will I, with the men who remain to me, charge home in Twala's face, and if fortune goes with us the day will be ours, and before night drives her black oxen from the mountains to the mountains we shall sit in peace at Loo. Now let us eat and make ready; and, Infadoos, do thou prepare, that the plan be carried out without fail; and stay, let my white father Bougwan go with the right horn, that his shining eye may give courage to the captains.'

The arrangements for attack thus briefly indicated were set in motion with a rapidity that spoke well for the perfection of the Kukuana military system. Within little more than an hour rations had been served out and devoured, the divisions were formed, the scheme of onslaught was explained to the leaders, and the whole force, numbering about eighteen thousand men, was ready to move, with the exception of a guard left in charge of the wounded.

Presently Good came up to Sir Henry and myself.

'Goodbye, you fellows,' he said; 'I am off with the right wing according to orders. So I have come to shake hands, in case we should not meet again, you know,' he added significantly.

We shook hands in silence, and not without the exhibition of as much emotion as Anglo-Saxons are wont to show.

'It is a queer business,' said Sir Henry, his deep voice shaking a little, 'and I confess I never expect to see tomorrow's sun. So far as I can make out, the Greys, with whom I am to go, are to fight until they are wiped out in order to enable the wings to slip round unawares and outflank Twala. Well, so be it; at any rate, it will be a man's death. Goodbye, old fellow. God bless you! I hope you will pull through and live to collar the diamonds; but if you do, take my advice and don't have anything more to do with pretenders to thrones!'

In another second Good had wrung us both by the hand and gone. Then Infadoos came up and led off Sir Henry to his place in the forefront of the Greys, whilst, with many misgivings, I departed with Ignosi to my station in the second attacking regiment.

CHAPTER 14

The Last Stand of the Greys

In a few more minutes the regiments destined to carry out the flanking movements had tramped off in silence, keeping carefully under the lee of the rising ground in order to conceal their advance from the keen eyes of Twala's scouts.

Half an hour or more was allowed to elapse after the setting out of the horns or wings of the army before any stir was made by the Greys and their supporting regiments, known as the Buffaloes, which formed its chest, and were destined to bear the brunt of the battle.

Both of these regiments were almost perfectly fresh, and of full strength, the Greys having been in reserve in the morning, and having lost but a small number of men in sweeping back that part of the attack which had proved successful in breaking the line of defence, on the occasion when I charged with them and was stunned for my pains. As for the Buffaloes, they had formed the third line of defence on the left, and since the attacking force at that point had not succeeded in breaking through the second, they had scarcely come into action at all.

Infadoos, who was a wary old general, and knew the absolute importance of keeping up the spirits of his men on the eve of such a desperate encounter, employed the pause in addressing his own regiment, the Greys, in poetical language. He explained to them the honour that they were receiving in being set thus in the forefront of the battle, and in having the great white warrior from the stars to fight with them in their ranks. Also he promised large rewards of cattle and promotion to all who survived, in the event of Ignosi's arms being successful.

I looked down the long lines of waving black plumes and of

stern faces beneath them, and sighed to think that within one short hour most, if not all, of those magnificent veteran warriors, not a man of whom was under forty years of age, would be laid dead or dying in the dust. It could not be otherwise; with that sagacious recklessness of human life which marks the great general, and often saves his forces and attains his ends, they were being condemned to inevitable slaughter, in order to give their cause and the remainder of the army a chance of success. They were foredoomed to die, and they knew the truth. It was to be their task to engage regiment after regiment of Twala's army on the narrow strip of green beneath us, till they were exterminated, or until the wings found a favourable opportunity for their onslaught. And yet they never hesitated, nor could I detect a sign of fear upon the face of a single warrior. There they stood – going to certain death, about to walk the dreadful bridge of spears, about to quit the blessed light of day, and yet able to contemplate their doom without a tremor. Even at that moment I could not help contrasting their state of mind with my own, which was far from comfortable, and breathing a sigh of envy and admiration. Never before had I seen such an absolute devotion to the idea of duty, and such a complete indifference to its bitter fruits.

'Behold your king!' ended old Infadoos, pointing to Ignosi; 'fight and fall for him, as is the duty of brave men, and cursed and shameful for ever be the name of him who shrinks from death for his king, or who turns his back to the foe. Chiefs, captains and soldiers, behold your king! Now do your homage to the sacred snake, and follow on, that Incubu and I may show you a road to the heart of Twala's host.'

There was a moment's pause, then suddenly a murmur arose from the serried phalanxes before us, a sound like the distant whisper of the sea, caused by the gentle tapping of the handles of six thousand spears against their holders' shields. Slowly it swelled, till its growing volume deepened and widened into a roar of rolling noise, that echoed like thunder against the mountains, and filled the air with heavy waves of sound. Then it decreased, until by faint degrees it died away into nothing, and suddenly out crashed the royal salute.

Ignosi, I thought to myself, might well be a proud man that day, for no Roman emperor ever had such a salutation from gladiators about to die.

Ignosi acknowledged this magnificent act of homage by lifting his battle-axe, and then the Greys filed off in a triple-line formation, each line containing about one thousand fighting men, exclusive of officers. When the last companies had advanced some five hundred yards, Ignosi put himself at the head of the Buffaloes, which regiment was drawn up in a similar threefold formation, and gave the word to march. Off we went, I, needless to say, uttering the most heartfelt prayers that I might emerge from that entertainment with a whole skin. Many a queer position have I found myself in, but seldom before in one quite so unpleasant, or one in which my chance of coming off safe was smaller.

By the time that we reached the edge of the plateau, the Greys were already halfway down the slope ending in the tongue of grassland that ran up into the bend of the mountain, something as the frog of a horse's foot runs up into the shoe. The excitement in Twala's camp on the plain beyond seemed very great. Regiment after regiment was starting forward at a long swinging trot in order to reach the root of the tongue of land before the attacking force could emerge into the plain of Loo.

This tongue, which was some four hundred yards in depth, even at its root or widest part was not more than six hundred and fifty paces across, while at its tip it scarcely measured ninety. The Greys, who, in passing down the side of the hill and on to the tip of the tongue, had formed into a column, on reaching the spot where it broadened out again, reassumed their triple-line formation, and halted dead.

Then we – that is, the Buffaloes – moved down the tip of the tongue and took our stand in reserve, about one hundred yards behind the last line of the Greys, and on slightly higher ground. Meanwhile we had leisure to observe Twala's entire force, which evidently had been reinforced since the morning attack, and could not now, notwithstanding their losses, number fewer than forty thousand, moving swiftly up towards us. But as they drew near the root of the tongue they hesitated, having discovered that only one regiment could advance into the gorge at a time, and that there, some seventy yards from the mouth of it, unassailable except in front, on account of the high walls of boulder-strewn ground on each side, stood the famous regiment of Greys, the pride and glory of the Kukuana army, ready to hold the way against their power as the three Romans once held the bridge against the ranks of Tusculum.

They hesitated, and finally stopped their advance; there was no eagerness to cross spears with these three grim ranks of warriors who stood so firm and ready. Presently, however, a tall general, wearing the customary headdress of nodding ostrich plumes, appeared, attended by a group of chiefs and orderlies, being, I thought, none other than Twala himself. He gave an order, and the first regiment, raising a shout, charged up towards the Greys, who remained perfectly still and silent till the attacking troops were within forty yards, and a volley of *tollas*, or throwing-knives, came rattling among the ranks.

Then suddenly with a bound and a roar, the Greys sprang forward with uplifted spears, and the regiments met in deadly strife. Next second the roll of the meeting shields came to our ears like the sound of thunder, and the plain seemed to be alive with flashes of light reflected from the shimmering spears. To and fro swung the surging mass of struggling, stabbing humanity, but not for long. Suddenly the attacking lines began to grow thinner, and then with a slow, long heave the Greys passed over them, just as a great wave heaves up its bulk and passes over a sunken ridge. It was done; that regiment was completely destroyed, but now the Greys had but two lines left; a third of their number were dead.

Closing up shoulder to shoulder, once more they halted in silence and awaited attack; and I was rejoiced to catch sight of Sir Henry's yellow beard as he moved to and fro arranging the ranks. So he was yet alive!

Meanwhile we moved on to the ground of the encounter, which was cumbered by about four thousand prostrate human beings, dead, dying and wounded, and literally stained red with blood. Ignosi issued an order, which was rapidly passed down the ranks, to the effect that none of the enemy's wounded were to be killed, and so far as we could see this command was scrupulously carried out. It would have been a shocking sight, if we had found time to think of such things.

But now a second regiment, distinguished by white plumes, kilts and shields, was moving to the attack of the two thousand remaining Greys, who stood waiting in the same ominous silence as before till the foe was within thirty yards or so, when they hurled themselves with irresistible force upon them. Again there came the awful roll of the meeting shields, and as we watched the tragedy repeated itself.

But this time the issue was left longer in doubt; indeed, it seemed for a while almost impossible that the Greys should again prevail. The attacking regiment, which was formed of young men, fought with the utmost fury, and at first seemed by sheer weight to be driving the veterans back. The slaughter was truly awful, hundreds falling every minute; and from among the shouts of the warriors and the groans of the dying, set to the music of clashing spears, came a continuous hissing undertone of 'S'gee, s'gee', the note of triumph of each victor as he passed his assegai through and through the body of his fallen foe.

But perfect discipline and steady and unchanging valour can do wonders, and one veteran soldier is worth two young ones, as soon became apparent in the present case. For just when we thought that it was all over with the Greys, and were preparing to take their place so soon as they made room by being destroyed, I heard Sir Henry's deep voice ringing through the din, and caught a glimpse of his circling battle-axe as he waved it high above his plumes. Then came a change; the Greys ceased to give; they stood still as a rock, against which the furious waves of spearmen broke again and again, only to recoil. Presently they began to move once more – forward this time; as they had no firearms there was no smoke, so we could see it all. Another minute and the onslaught grew fainter.

'Ah, these are *men*, indeed; they will conquer again,' called out Ignosi, who was grinding his teeth with excitement at my side. 'See, it is done!'

Suddenly, like puffs of smoke from the mouth of a cannon, the attacking regiment broke away in flying groups, their white headdresses streaming behind them in the wind, and left their opponents victors, indeed, but, alas! no more a regiment. Of the gallant triple line, which forty minutes before had gone into action three thousand strong, there remained at most some six hundred blood-bespattered men; the rest were underfoot. And yet they cheered and waved their spears in triumph, and then, instead of falling back upon us as we expected, they ran forward, for a hundred yards or so, after the flying groups of foemen, took possession of a rising knoll of ground, and, resuming their triple formation, formed a threefold ring around its base. And there, thanks be to heaven, standing on the top of the mound for a minute, I saw Sir Henry, apparently unharmed, and with him our old friend Infadoos. Then Twala's regiments rolled down upon the doomed band, and once more the battle closed in.

As those who read this history will probably long ago have gathered, I am, to be honest, a bit of a coward, and certainly in no way given to fighting, though somehow it has often been my lot to get into unpleasant positions, and to be obliged to shed man's blood. But I have always hated it, and kept my own blood as undiminished in quantity as possible, sometimes by a judicious use of my heels. At this moment, however, perhaps for the first time in my life, I felt my bosom burn with martial ardour. Warlike fragments from the *Ingoldsby Legends*, together with numbers of sanguinary verses in the Old Testament, sprang up in my brain like mushrooms in the dark; my blood, which hitherto had been half-frozen with horror, went beating through my veins, and there came upon me a savage desire to kill and spare not. I glanced round at the serried ranks of warriors behind us, and somehow, all in an instant, I began to wonder if my face looked like theirs. There they stood, their heads craned forward over their shields, the hands twitching, the lips apart, the fierce features instinct with the hungry lust of battle, and in the eyes a look like the glare of a bloodhound when after long pursuit he sights his quarry.

Only Ignosi's heart, to judge from his comparative self-possession, seemed, to all appearance, to beat as calmly as ever beneath his leopard-skin cloak, though even *he* still ground his teeth. I could bear it no longer.

'Are we to stand here till we put out roots, Umbopa – Ignosi, I mean – while Twala swallows our brothers yonder?' I asked.

'Nay, Macumazahn,' was the answer; 'see, now is the ripe moment: let us pluck it.'

As he spoke a fresh regiment rushed past the ring upon the little mound, and wheeling round, attacked it from the hither side.

Then, lifting his battle-axe, Ignosi gave the signal to advance, and, screaming the wild Kukuana war-cry, the Buffaloes charged home with a rush like the rush of the sea.

What followed immediately on this it is out of my power to tell. All I can remember is an irregular yet ordered advance, that seemed to shake the ground; a sudden change of front and forming up on the part of the regiment against which the charge was directed; then an awful shock, a dull roar of voices, and a continuous flashing of spears, seen through a red mist of blood.

When my mind cleared I found myself standing inside the remnant of the Greys near the top of the mound, and just behind no less a person than Sir Henry himself. How I got there I had at the moment no idea, but Sir Henry afterwards told me that I was borne up by the first furious charge of the Buffaloes almost to his feet, and there left, as they in turn were pressed back. Thereon he dashed out of the circle and dragged me into shelter.

As for the fight that followed, who can describe it? Again and again the multitudes surged against our momentarily lessening circle, and again and again we beat them back.

> The stubborn spearmen still made good
> The dark impenetrable wood,
> Each stepping where his comrade stood
> The instant that he fell,

as someone or other beautifully says.

It was a splendid sight to see those brave battalions come on time after time over the barriers of their dead, sometimes lifting corpses before them to receive our spear thrusts, only to leave their own corpses to swell the rising piles. It was a gallant thing to hear that sturdy old warrior, Infadoos, as cool as though he were on parade, shouting out orders, taunts and even jests, to keep up the spirit of his few remaining men, and then, as each charge rolled on, to watch him spring to wherever the fighting was thickest, to bear his share in its repulse. And yet more gallant was the vision of Sir Henry, whose ostrich plumes had been shorn off by a spear thrust, so that his long yellow hair streamed out in the breeze behind him. There he stood, the great Norseman, for he was nothing else, his hands, his axe and his armour all red with blood, and none could live before his stroke. Time after time I saw it sweeping down, as some great warrior ventured to give him battle, and as he struck he shouted 'O-hoy! O-hoy!' like his Berserker forefathers, and the blow went crashing through shield and spear, through headdress, hair and skull, till at last none would of their own will come near the tall white *umtagati*, the wizard, who killed and failed not.

But suddenly there arose a cry of, '*Twala, y' Twala*,' and out of the press sprang forward none other than the gigantic one-eyed king himself, also armed with battle-axe and shield, and clad in chain armour.

'Where art thou, Incubu, thou white man, who slewest Scragga my son – see if thou canst slay me!' he shouted, and at the same time hurled a *tolla* straight at Sir Henry, who fortunately saw it coming, and caught it on his shield, which it transfixed, remaining wedged in the iron plate behind the hide.

Then, uttering a cry, Twala sprang straight at Curtis, and with his battle-axe struck him such a blow upon the shield that the mere force and shock of it brought him, strong man as he is, down upon his knees.

But at this time the matter went no further, for that instant there rose from the regiments pressing round us something like a shout of dismay, and on looking up I saw the cause.

To the right and to the left the plain was alive with the plumes of charging warriors. The outflanking squadrons had come to our relief. The time could not have been better chosen. All Twala's army, as Ignosi predicted would be the case, had fixed their attention on the bloody struggle which was raging round the

remnant of the Greys and that of the Buffaloes, who were now
carrying on a battle of their own at a little distance, which two
regiments had formed the chest of our army. It was not until our
horns were about to close upon them that they had dreamed of
their approach, for they believed these forces to be hidden in
reserve upon the crest of the moon-shaped hill. And now, before
they could even assume a proper formation for defence, the
outflanking *impis* had leapt, like greyhounds, on their flanks.

In five minutes the fate of the battle was decided.

Taken on both flanks, and dismayed at the awful slaughter
inflicted upon them by the Greys and Buffaloes, Twala's
regiments broke into flight, and soon the whole plain between us
and Loo was scattered with groups of running soldiers making
good their retreat. As for the hosts that had so recently
surrounded us and the Buffaloes, they melted away as though by
magic, and presently we were left standing there like a rock from
which the sea has retreated. But what a sight it was! Around us
the dead and dying lay in heaped-up masses, and of the gallant
Greys there remained but ninety-five men upon their feet. More
than three thousand four hundred had fallen in this one
regiment, most of them never to rise again.

'Men,' said Infadoos calmly, as between the intervals of binding
a wound in his arm he surveyed what remained to him of his
corps, 'ye have kept up the reputation of your regiment, and this
day's fighting will be well spoken of by your children's children.'
Then he turned round and shook Sir Henry Curtis by the hand.
'Thou art a great captain, Incubu,' he said simply; 'I have lived a
long life among warriors, and I have known many a brave one, yet
have I never seen a man like unto thee.'

At this moment the Buffaloes began to march past our position
on the road to Loo, and as they went a message was brought to us
from Ignosi requesting Infadoos, Sir Henry and myself to join
him. Accordingly, orders having been issued to the remaining
men of the Greys to employ themselves in collecting the
wounded, we joined Ignosi, who informed us that he was
pressing on to Loo to complete the victory by capturing Twala, if
that should be possible. Before we had gone far, suddenly we

discovered the figure of Good sitting on an ant-heap about one hundred paces from us. Close beside him was the body of a Kukuana.

'He must be wounded,' said Sir Henry, anxiously. As he made the remark, an untoward thing happened. The dead body of the Kukuana soldier, or rather what had appeared to be his dead body, suddenly sprang up, knocked Good head over heels off the ant-heap, and began to spear him. We rushed forward in terror, and as we drew near we saw the brawny warrior making dig after dig at the prostrate Good, who at each prod jerked all his limbs into the air. Seeing us coming, the Kukuana gave one final and most vicious dig, and with a shout of, 'Take that, wizard!' bolted away. Good did not move, and we concluded that our poor comrade was done for. Sadly we came towards him, and were astonished to find him pale and faint indeed, but with a serene smile upon his face, and his eyeglass still fixed in his eye.

'Capital armour this,' he murmured, on catching sight of our faces bending over him. 'How irked that beggar must have been,' and then he fainted. On examination we discovered that he had been seriously wounded in the leg by a *tolla* in the course of the pursuit, but that the chain armour had prevented his last assailant's spear from doing anything more than bruise him badly. It was a merciful escape. As nothing could be done for him at the moment, he was placed on one of the wicker shields used for the wounded, and carried along with us.

On arriving before the nearest gate of Loo we found one of our regiments watching it in obedience to orders received from Ignosi. The other regiments were in the same way guarding the different exits from the town. The officer in command of this regiment saluted Ignosi as king, and informed him that Twala's army had taken refuge in the town, whither Twala himself had also escaped, but he thought that they were thoroughly demoralised and would surrender. Thereupon Ignosi, after taking counsel with us, sent forward heralds to each gate ordering the defenders to open, and promising on his royal word life and forgiveness to every soldier who laid down his arms, but saying that if they did not do so, before nightfall he would certainly burn Loo and all within its gates. This message was not without its effect. Half an hour later, amid the shouts and cheers of the Buffaloes, the bridge was dropped across the fosse, and the gates upon the farther side were flung open.

Taking due precautions against treachery, we marched on into the town. All along the roadways stood thousands of dejected warriors, their heads drooping, and their shields and spears at their feet, who, headed by their officers, saluted Ignosi as king as he passed. On we marched, straight to Twala's kraal. When we reached the great space, where a day or two previously we had seen the review and the witch-hunt, we found it deserted. No, not quite deserted, for there, on the farther side, in front of his hut, sat Twala himself with but one attendant – Gagool.

It was a melancholy sight to see him seated thus, his battle-axe and shield by his side, his chin upon his mailed breast, with but one old crone for companion, and notwithstanding his cruelties and misdeeds, a pang of compassion shot through me as I looked upon Twala so fallen from his high estate. Not a soldier of all his armies, not a courtier out of the hundreds who had cringed round him, not even a solitary wife, remained to share his fate or halve the bitterness of his fall. Poor savage! he was learning the lesson which Fate teaches to most of us who live long enough, that the eyes of mankind are blind to the discredited, and that he who is defenceless and undone finds few friends and little mercy. Nor, indeed, in this case did he deserve any.

Filing through the kraal gate, we marched across the open space to where the ex-king sat. When within about fifty yards of him, the regiment was halted, and accompanied only by a small guard we advanced towards him, Gagool reviling us bitterly as we came. As we drew near, Twala, for the first time, lifted his plumed head, and fixed his one eye, which seemed to flash with suppressed fury almost as brightly as the great diamond bound round his forehead, upon his successful rival – Ignosi.

'Hail, O king!' he said, with bitter mockery; 'thou who hast eaten of my bread, and now by the aid of the white man's magic hast seduced my regiments and defeated mine army, hail! What fate hast thou for me, O king?'

'The fate thou gavest to my father, whose throne you hast sat on these many years!' was the stern answer.

'It is good. I will show thee how to die, that thou mayest remember it against thine own time. See, the sun sinks in blood,' and he pointed with his battle-axe towards the setting orb; 'it is well that my sun should go down in its company. And now, O king! I am ready to die, but I crave the boon of the Kukuana royal house to die fighting.* Thou canst not refuse it, or even those cowards who fled today will hold thee shamed.'

'It is granted. Choose – with whom wilt thou fight? Myself I cannot fight with thee, for the king fights not except in war.'

Twala's sombre eye ran up and down our ranks, and I felt, as for a moment it rested on myself, that the position had developed a new horror. What if he chose to begin by fighting me? What chance should I have against a desperate savage six feet five high, and broad in proportion? I might as well commit suicide at once. Hastily I made up my mind to decline the combat, even if I were hooted out of Kukuanaland as a consequence. It is, I think, better to be hooted than be quartered with a battle-axe.

Presently Twala spoke.

'Incubu, what sayest thou, shall we end what we began today, or shall I call thee coward, white – even to the liver?'

'Nay,' interposed Ignosi hastily; 'thou shalt not fight with Incubu.'

'Not if he is afraid,' said Twala.

Unfortunately Sir Henry understood this remark, and the blood flamed up into his cheeks.

'I will fight him,' he said; 'he shall see if I am afraid.'

'For heaven's sake,' I entreated, 'don't risk your life against that of a desperate man. Anybody who saw you today will know that you are brave enough.'

'I will fight him,' was the sullen answer. 'No living man shall call

---

* It is a law amongst the Kukuanas that no man of the direct royal blood can be put to death, unless by his own consent, which is, however, never refused. He is allowed to choose a succession of antagonists, to be approved by the king, with whom he fights, till one of them kills him.   A.Q.

me a coward. I am ready now!' and he stepped forward and lifted his axe.

I wrung my hands over this absurd piece of Quixotism; but if he was determined on this duel, of course I could not stop him.

'Fight not, my white brother,' said Ignosi, laying his hand affectionately on Sir Henry's arm; 'thou hast fought enough, and if aught befell thee at his hands it would cut my heart in twain.'

'I will fight, Ignosi,' was Sir Henry's answer.

'It is well, Incubu; thou art a brave man. It will be a good fray. Behold, Twala, the Elephant is ready for thee.'

The ex-king laughed savagely, and stepping forward faced Curtis. For a moment they stood thus, and the light of the sinking sun caught their stalwart frames and clothed them both in fire. They were a well-matched pair.

Then they began to circle round each other, their battle-axes raised.

Suddenly Sir Henry sprang forward and struck a fearful blow at Twala, who stepped to one side. So heavy was the stroke that the striker half overbalanced himself, a circumstance of which his antagonist took a prompt advantage. Circling his massive battle-axe round his head, he brought it down with tremendous force. My heart jumped into my mouth; I thought that the affair was already finished. But no; with a quick upward movement of the left arm Sir Henry interposed his shield between himself and the axe, with the result that its outer edge was shorn away, the axe falling on his left shoulder, but not heavily enough to do any serious damage. In another moment Sir Henry got in a second blow, which was also received by Twala upon his shield.

Then followed blow upon blow, each, in turn, either received upon the shield or avoided. The excitement grew intense; the regiment which was watching the encounter forgot its discipline, and, drawing near, shouted and groaned at every stroke. Just at this time, too, Good, who had been laid upon the ground by me, recovered from his faint, and, sitting up, perceived what was going on. In an instant he was up, and catching hold of my arm, hopped about from place to place on one leg, dragging me after him, and yelling encouragement to Sir Henry: 'Go it, old fellow!' he hallooed. 'That was a good one! Give it him amidships,' and so on.

Presently Sir Henry, having caught a fresh stroke upon his shield, hit out with all his force. The blow cut through Twala's shield and through the tough chain armour behind it, gashing him in the shoulder. With a yell of pain and fury Twala returned the blow with interest, and, such was his strength, shore right through the rhinoceros-horn handle of his antagonist's battle-axe, strengthened as it was with bands of steel, wounding Curtis in the face.

A cry of dismay rose from the Buffaloes as our hero's broad axe-head fell to the ground; and Twala, again raising his weapon, flew at him with a shout. I shut my eyes. When I opened them again it was to see Sir Henry's shield lying on the ground and Sir Henry himself with his great arms twined round Twala's middle. To and fro they swung, hugging each other like bears, straining with all their mighty muscles for dear life, and dearer honour. With a supreme effort Twala swung the Englishman clean off his feet. Down they came together, rolling over and over on the lime paving, Twala striking out at Curtis's head with the battle-axe and Sir Henry trying to drive the *tolla* he had drawn from his belt through Twala's armour.

It was a mighty struggle, and an awful thing to see.

'Get his axe!' yelled Good; and perhaps our champion heard him.

At any rate, dropping the *tolla*, he snatched at the axe, which was fastened to Twala's wrist by a strip of buffalo hide, and still rolling over and over, they fought for it like wild cats, drawing their breath in heavy gasps. Suddenly the hide string burst, and then, with a great effort, Sir Henry freed himself, the weapon remaining in his hand. Another second and he was upon his feet, the red blood streaming from the wound in his face, and so was Twala. Drawing the heavy *tolla* from his belt, he reeled straight at Curtis and struck him upon the breast. The stab came home true and strong, but whoever it was who made that chain armour understood his art, for it turned the steel. Again Twala struck out with a savage yell; again the sharp knife rebounded, and Sir Henry went staggering back. Once more Twala came on, and as he came our great Englishman gathered himself together, and swinging the big axe round his head with both hands, hit at him with all his force.

There was a shriek of excitement from a thousand throats, and, behold! Twala's head seemed to spring from his shoulders. It fell and came rolling and bounding along the ground toward Ignosi, stopping just at his feet. For a second the corpse stood upright; then with a dull crash it came to the earth, and the gold torque from its neck rolled away across the pavement. As it did so Sir Henry, overpowered by faintness and loss of blood, fell heavily across the body of the dead king.

In a second he was lifted up, and eager hands were pouring water on his face. Another minute and the grey eyes opened wide.

He was not dead.

Now I, just as the sun sank, stepping to where Twala's head lay in the dust, unloosed the diamond from the dead brow and handed it to Ignosi. 'Take it,' I said, 'lawful king of the Kukuanas – king by birth and victory.'

Ignosi bound the diadem upon his brow. Then advancing, he placed his foot upon the broad chest of his headless foe and broke out into a chant, or rather a paean of triumph, so beautiful, and yet so utterly savage, that I despair of being able to give an adequate version of his words. Once I heard a scholar with a fine voice read aloud from the Greek poet Homer, and I remember that the sound of the rolling lines seemed to make my blood stand still. Ignosi's chant, uttered as it was in a language as beautiful and sonorous as the old Greek, produced exactly the same effect on me, although I was exhausted with toil and many emotions.

'Now, *now our rebellion is swallowed up in victory, and our evildoing is justified by strength.*

'*In the morning the oppressors arose and stretched themselves; they bound on their harness and made themselves ready for war.*

'*They rose up and tossed their spears: the soldiers called to the captains, "Come, lead us" – and the captains cried to the king, "Direct thou the battle."*

'They laughed in their pride, twenty thousand men, and again twenty thousand.

'Their plumes covered the valleys as the plumes of a bird cover her nest; they shook their shields and shouted, yea; they shook their shields in the sunlight; they lusted for the battle and were glad.

'They came up against me; their strong ones ran swiftly to slay me; they cried, "Ha! ha! he is as one already dead."

'Then breathed I on them, and my breath was as the breath of a wind, and lo! they were not.

'My lightning pierced them; I licked up their strength with the lightning of my spears; I shook them to the ground with the thunder of my shoutings.

'They broke – they scattered – they were gone as the mists of the morning.

'They are food for the kites and the foxes, and the place of battle is fat with their blood.

'Where are the mighty ones who rose up in the morning?

'Where are the proud ones who tossed their spears and cried, "He is as a man already dead "?

'They bow their heads, but not in sleep; they are stretched out, but not in sleep.

'They are forgotten; they have gone into the blackness; they dwell on the dead moons; yea, others shall lead away their wives, and their children shall remember them no more.

'And I! – the king – like an eagle I have found my eyrie.

'Behold! far have I flown in the night season, yet have I returned to my young at the daybreak.

'Shelter ye under the shadow of my wings, O people, and I will comfort ye, and ye shall not be dismayed.

'Now is the good time, the time of spoil.

'Mine are the cattle on the mountains, mine are the virgins in the kraals.

'The winter is overpast with storms, the summer is come with flowers.

'Now Evil shall cover up her face, now Mercy and Gladness shall dwell in the land.

'Rejoice, rejoice, my people!

'Let all the world rejoice in that this tyranny is trodden down, in that I am the king.'

Ignosi ceased his song, and out of the gathering gloom came back the deep reply: 'Thou art the king!'

Thus was my prophecy to the herald fulfilled, and within the forty-eight hours Twala's headless corpse was stiffening at Twala's gate.

CHAPTER 15

Good Falls Sick

After the fight was ended Sir Henry and Good were carried into Twala's hut, where I joined them. They were both utterly exhausted by exertion and loss of blood, and, indeed, my own condition was little better. I am very wiry, and can stand more fatigue than most men, probably on account of my light weight and long training; but this night I was quite done up, and, as is always the case with me when exhausted, that old wound which the lion gave me began to pain. Also my head was aching violently from the blow I had received in the morning, when I was knocked senseless. Altogether, a more miserable trio than we were that evening it would have been difficult to discover. Our only comfort lay in the reflection that we were exceedingly fortunate to be there to feel miserable, instead of being stretched dead upon the plain, as so many thousands of brave men were that night, who had risen well and strong in the morning.

Somehow, with the assistance of the beautiful Foulata, who, since we had been the means of saving her life, had constituted herself our handmaiden, and especially Good's, we managed to get off the chain shirts, which had certainly saved the lives of two of us that day. As I expected, we found that the flesh underneath was terribly contused, for though the steel links had kept the weapons from entering, they had not prevented them from bruising. Both Sir Henry and Good were a mass of contusions, and I was by no means free. As a remedy Foulata brought us some pounded green leaves, with an aromatic odour, which, when applied as a plaster, gave us considerable relief.

But though the bruises were painful, they did not give us such anxiety as Sir Henry's and Good's wounds. Good had a hole right through the fleshy part of his 'beautiful white leg', from which he had lost a great deal of blood; and Sir Henry, with other hurts, had a deep cut over the jaw, inflicted by Twala's battle-axe. Luckily, Good is a very decent surgeon, and so soon as his small box of medicines was forthcoming, having thoroughly cleansed the wounds, he managed to stitch up first Sir Henry's and then his own pretty satisfactorily, considering the imperfect light given by the primitive Kukuana lamp in the hut. Afterwards he smeared the injured places plentifully with some antiseptic ointment, of which there was a pot in the little box, and we covered them with the remains of a pocket-handkerchief which we possessed.

Meanwhile Foulata had prepared us some strong broth, for we were too weary to eat. This we swallowed, and then threw ourselves down on the piles of magnificent *karrosses*, or fur rugs, which were scattered about the dead king's great hut. By a very strange instance of the irony of fate, it was on Twala's own couch, and wrapped in Twala's own particular *karross*, that Sir Henry, the man who had slain him, slept that night.

I say slept; but after that day's work sleep was indeed difficult. To begin with, in very truth the air was full

> Of farewells to the dying
> And mournings for the dead.

From every direction came the sound of the wailing of women whose husbands, sons and brothers had perished in the battle. No wonder that they wailed, for over twelve thousand men, or nearly a fifth of the Kukuana army, had been destroyed in that awful struggle. It was heart-rending to lie and listen to their cries for those who never would return, and it made me understand the full horror of the work done that day to further man's ambition. Towards midnight, however, the crying of the women gradually abated, till at length the silence was only broken at intervals of a few minutes by a long piercing howl that came from a hut in our immediate rear. This, as I afterwards discovered, proceeded from Gagool 'keening' over the dead king Twala.

After that I got a little fitful sleep, only to wake from time to time with a start, thinking that I was once more an actor in the terrible events of the past twenty-four hours. Now I seemed to see that warrior whom my hand had sent to his account charging at me on the mountain-top; now I was once more in that glorious ring of Greys, which made its immortal stand against all Twala's regiments upon the little mound; and now again I saw Twala's plumed and gory head roll past my feet with gnashing teeth and glaring eye.

At last, somehow or other, the night passed away; but when dawn broke I found that my companions had slept no better than myself. Good, indeed, was in a high fever, and very soon afterwards began to grow light-headed, and also, to my alarm, to spit blood, the result, no doubt, of some internal injury, inflicted during the desperate efforts made by the Kukuana warrior on the previous day to force his big spear through the chain armour. Sir Henry, however, though he was so sore and stiff that he could scarcely stir, seemed pretty fresh, notwithstanding his wound on the face, which made eating difficult and laughter an impossibility.

About eight o'clock we had a visit from Infadoos, who appeared but little the worse – tough old warrior that he was – for his exertions in the battle, although he informed us that he had been up all night. He shook our hands cordially, and was delighted to see us, but much grieved at Good's condition. I noticed, however, that he addressed Sir Henry with a kind of reverence, as though he were something more than human; and, indeed, as we found out afterwards, the great Englishman was looked on throughout Kukuanaland as a supernatural being. No man, the soldiers said, could have fought as he fought or, at the end of a day of such toil and bloodshed, could have slain Twala, who, in addition to being the king, was supposed to be the strongest warrior in the country, in single combat, shearing through his bull-neck at a stroke. Indeed, that stroke became proverbial in Kukuanaland, and any extraordinary blow or feat of strength was henceforth known as 'Incubu's blow'.

Infadoos told us also that all Twala's regiments had submitted to Ignosi, and that like submissions were beginning to arrive from chiefs in the outlying country. Twala's death at the hands of Sir Henry had put an end to all further chance of disturbance; for

Scragga had been his only legitimate son, so there was no rival claimant to the throne left alive.

I remarked that Ignosi had swum to power through blood. The old chief shrugged his shoulders. 'Yes,' he answered; 'but the Kukuana people can only be kept cool by letting their blood flow sometimes. Many are killed, indeed, but the women are left, and others must soon grow up to take the places of the fallen. After this the land will be quiet for a while.'

Afterwards, in the course of the morning, we had a short visit from Ignosi, on whose brows the royal diadem was now bound. As I contemplated him advancing with kingly dignity, an obsequious guard following his steps, I could not help recalling to my mind the tall Zulu who had presented himself to us at Durban some few months before, asking to be taken into our service, and reflected on the strange revolutions of the wheel of fortune.

'Hail, O king!' I said, rising.

'Yes, Macumazahn. King at last, by the might of your three right hands,' was the ready answer.

All was, he said, going on well; and he hoped to arrange a great feast in two weeks' time in order to show himself to the people.

I asked him what he had settled to do with Gagool.

'She is the evil genius of the land,' he answered, 'and I shall kill her and all the witch doctors with her! She has lived so long that none can remember when she was not very old, and she it is who has always trained the witch-hunters, and made the land wicked in the sight of the heavens above.'

'Yet she knows much,' I replied; 'it is easier to destroy knowledge, Ignosi, than to gather it.'

'That is so,' he said thoughtfully. 'She, and she only, knows the secret of the Three Witches, yonder, whither the Great Road runs, where the kings are buried, and the Silent Ones sit.'

'Yes, and the diamonds are. Forget not thy promise, Ignosi; thou must lead us to the mines, even if thou hast to spare Gagool alive to show the way.'

'I will not forget, Macumazahn, and I will think on what thou sayest.'

After Ignosi's visit I went to see Good, and found him quite delirious. The fever set up by his wound seemed to have taken a firm hold of his system, and to be complicated with an internal injury. For four or five days his condition was most critical; indeed, I believe firmly that had it not been for Foulata's indefatigable nursing he must have died.

Women are women all the world over, whatever their colour. Yet somehow it seemed curious to watch this dusky beauty bending night and day over the fevered man's couch, and performing all the merciful errands of a sickroom swiftly, gently and with as fine an instinct as that of a trained hospital nurse. For the first night or two I tried to help her, and so did Sir Henry as soon as his stiffness allowed him to move. But Foulata bore our interference with impatience, and finally insisted upon our leaving him to her, saying that our movements made him restless, which I think was true. Day and night she watched and tended him, giving him his only medicine, a native cooling drink made of milk, in which was infused juice from the bulb of a species of tulip, and keeping the flies from settling on him. I can see the whole picture now as it appeared night after night by the light of our primitive lamp: Good tossing to and fro, his features emaciated, his eyes shining large and luminous, and jabbering nonsense by the yard; and seated on the ground by his side, her back resting against the wall of the hut, the soft-eyed, shapely Kukuana beauty, her face, weary as it was with her long vigil, animated by a look of infinite compassion – or was it something more than compassion?

For two days we thought that he must die, and crept about with heavy hearts. Only Foulata would not believe it.

'He will live,' she said.

For three hundred yards or more around Twala's chief hut, where the sufferer lay, there was silence; for by the king's order all who lived in the habitations behind it, except Sir Henry and myself, had been removed, lest any noise should come to the sick man's ears. One night – it was the fifth of Good's illness – as was my habit, I went across to see how he was doing before turning in for a few hours.

I entered the hut carefully. The lamp placed upon the floor

showed the figure of Good tossing no more, but lying quite still. So it had come at last! In the bitterness of my heart I gave something like a sob.

'Hush—h—h!' came from the patch of dark shadow behind Good's head.

Then, creeping closer, I saw that he was not dead, but sleeping soundly, with Foulata's taper fingers clasped tightly in his poor white hand. The crisis had passed, and he would live. He slept like that for eighteen hours; and I scarcely like to say it, for fear I should not be believed, but during the entire period did this devoted girl sit by him, fearing that if she moved and drew away her hand it would wake him. What she must have suffered from cramp and weariness, to say nothing of want of food, nobody will ever know; but it is a fact that, when at last he woke, she had to be carried away — her limbs were so stiff that she could not move them.

After the turn had once been taken, Good's recovery was rapid and complete. It was not till he was nearly well that Sir Henry told him of all he owed to Foulata; and when he came to the story of how she sat by his side for eighteen hours, fearing lest by moving she should wake him, the honest sailor's eyes filled with tears. He turned and went straight to the hut where Foulata was preparing the midday meal, for we were back in our old quarters now, taking me with him to interpret in case he could not make his meaning clear to her, though I am bound to say that she understood him marvellously as a rule, considering how extremely limited was his foreign vocabulary.

'Tell her,' said Good, 'that I owe her my life, and that I will never forget her kindness to my dying day.'

I interpreted, and under her dark skin she actually seemed to blush.

Turning to him with one of those swift and graceful motions that in her always reminded me of the flight of a wild bird, Foulata answered softly, glancing at him with her large brown eyes: 'Nay, my lord; my lord forgets! Did he not save my life; am I not my lord's handmaiden?'

It will be noted that the young lady appeared to be oblivious of

the share which Sir Henry and myself had taken in her preserva-
tion from Twala's clutches. But that is the way of women! I
remember others who were just the same. Well, I retired from
that little interview sad at heart. I did not like Miss Foulata's soft
glances, for I knew the fatal amorous propensities of sailors in
general, and of Good in particular.

There are two things in the world, as I have found out, which
cannot be prevented: you cannot keep a Zulu from fighting, or a
sailor from falling in love upon the slightest provocation! And
here the provocation was not slight.

A few days after this last touching occurrence Ignosi held his
great *indaba*, or council, and was formally recognised as king by
the *induna*, or head men, of Kukuanaland. The spectacle was a
most imposing one, including as it did a grand review of troops.
On this day the remaining fragments of the Greys were formally
paraded, and in the face of the army thanked for their splendid
conduct in the great battle. To each man the king made a large
present of cattle, promoting them one and all to the rank of
officers in the new corps of Greys then in process of formation.

An order was also promulgated throughout the length and
breadth of Kukuanaland that, whilst we honoured the country by
our presence, we three were to be greeted with the royal salute,
and to be treated with the same ceremony and respect that was by
custom accorded to the king. Also the power of life and death was
publicly conferred upon us. Ignosi, too, in the presence of his
people, reaffirmed the promises which he had made, to the effect
that no man's blood should be shed without trial, and that witch-
hunting should cease in the land.

When the ceremony was over we waited upon Ignosi, and
informed him that we were now anxious to investigate the
mystery of the mines to which Solomon's Road ran, asking him if
he had discovered anything about them.

'My friends,' he answered, 'I have discovered this. It is yonder
that the three great figures sit, who here are called the Silent
Ones, and to whom Twala would have offered the girl Foulata as
a sacrifice. It is there, too, in a great cave deep in the mountain,
that the kings of the land are buried; there ye shall find Twala's

body, sitting with those who went before him. There, also, is a deep pit, which, at sometime, long-dead men dug out, mayhap for the stones ye speak of, such as I have heard men in Natal tell of at Kimberley. There, too, in the Place of Death, is a hidden chamber, secret to all save the king and Gagool. But Twala, who knew it, is dead, and I know it not, nor know I what is in it. Yet there is a legend in the land that once, many generations gone, a white man crossed the mountains, and was led by a woman to the dark chamber and shown the wealth concealed in it. But before he could take it she betrayed him, and he was driven by the king of that day back to the mountains, and since then no man has entered the ancient place.'

'The story is surely true, Ignosi, for on the mountains we found the white man,' I said.

'Yes, we found him. And now I have promised you that if ye can come to that chamber, and the stones are there – '

'The gem upon thy forehead proves that they are there,' I put in, pointing to the great diamond I had taken from Twala's dead brow.

'Mayhap; and if they are there,' he said, 'ye shall have as many as ye can take hence – if indeed ye would leave me, my brothers.'

'First we must find the chamber,' said I

'There is but one who can show it to thee – Gagool.'

'And if she will not?'

'Then she must die,' said Ignosi sternly. 'I have saved her alive but for this. Stay, she shall choose,' and calling to a messenger he ordered Gagool to be brought before him.

In a few minutes she came, hurried along by two guards, whom she was cursing as she walked.

'Leave her,' said the king to the guards.

So soon as their support was withdrawn, the withered old bundle – for she resembled a bundle more than anything else, out of which her two bright and wicked eyes gleamed like those of a snake – sank in a heap on the floor.

'What will ye with me, Ignosi?' she piped. 'Ye dare not touch me. If ye touch me I will slay you all as ye sit. Beware of my magic.'

'Thy magic could not save Twala, old she-wolf, and it cannot hurt us,' was the answer. 'Listen; I will this of thee, that thou reveal to us the chamber where are the shining stones.'

'Ha! ha!' she piped, 'none know its key but I, and I will never tell it thee. The white devils shall go hence empty-handed.'

'Thou shalt tell me. I will make thee tell me.'

'How, O king? Thou art great, but can thy power wring the truth from a woman?'

'It is difficult, yet will I do so.'

'How, O king?'

'Nay, thus; if thou dost refuse thou shalt slowly die.'

'Die!' she shrieked in terror and fury; 'ye dare not touch me – man, ye know not who I am! How old am I, think ye? I knew your fathers, and their fathers' fathers' fathers. When the country was young I was here; when the country grows old I shall still be here. I cannot die unless I be killed by chance, for none dare slay me.'

'Yet will I slay thee. See, Gagool, mother of evil, thou art so old that thou canst no longer love thy life. What can life be worth to such a hag as thou, who hast no shape, nor form, nor hair, nor teeth – hast naught, save wickedness and evil eyes? It will be mercy to make an end of thee, Gagool.'

'Thou fool,' shrieked the old fiend, 'thou accursed fool, deemest thou that life is sweet only to the young? It is not so, and naught thou knowest of the heart of man to think it. To the young, indeed, death is sometimes welcome, for the young can feel. They love and suffer, and it wrings them to see their beloved pass to the land of shadows. But the very old feel not, they love not, and, *ha! ha!* they laugh to see another go out into the dark; *ha! ha!* they laugh to see the evil that is done under the stars. All they love is life, the warm, warm sun, and the sweet, sweet air. They are afraid of the cold, afraid of the cold and the dark, *ha! ha! ha!*' and the old hag writhed in ghastly merriment on the ground.

'Cease thine evil talk and answer me,' said Ignosi angrily. 'Wilt thou show the place where the stones are, or wilt thou not? If thou wilt not thou diest, even now,' and he seized a spear and held it over her.

'I will not show it; thou darest not kill me, darest not! He who slays me will be accursed for ever. In life and death woe shall be his bedfellow.'

Slowly Ignosi brought down the spear till it pricked the prostrate heap of rags.

With a thin scream Gagool sprang to her feet, then fell again and rolled upon the floor.

'Nay, I will show thee. Only let me live on, let me sit in the sun for one more short hundred years and have my meat to suck, and I will show thee.'

'It is well. I thought that I should find a way to reason with thee. Tomorrow shalt thou go with Infadoos and my white brothers to the place, and beware how thou failest, for if thou showest it not, then thou shalt slowly die of hunger. I have spoken.'

'I will not fail, Ignosi. I always keep my word – *ha! ha! ha!* Once before a woman showed the chamber to a white man, and, behold! evil befell him,' here her wicked eyes glinted. 'Her name was Gagool also. Perchance I was that woman.'

'Thou liest,' I said, 'that was ten generations gone.'

'Mayhap, mayhap; when one lives long one forgets. Perhaps it was my mother's mother who told me; surely her name was Gagool also. But mark, ye will find, in the place where the bright playthings are, a bag of hide full of stones. The man filled that bag, but he never took it away. Evil befell him, I say, evil befell him! Perhaps it was my mother's mother who told me. It will be a merry journey – we can see the bodies of those who died in the battle as we go. Their eyes will be sunk by now, and their ribs will be hollow. *Ha! ha! ha!*'

CHAPTER 16

The Place of Death

It was already dark on the third day after the scene described in the previous chapter when we camped in some huts at the foot of the Three Witches, as the triangle of mountains is called to which Solomon's Great Road runs. Our party consisted of our three selves and Foulata, who waited on us – especially on Good – Infadoos, Gagool, who was borne along in a litter, inside which she could be heard muttering and cursing all day long, and a party of guards and attendants. The mountains, or rather the three peaks of the mountain, for their mass was evidently the result of a solitary upheaval, were, as I have said, in the form of a triangle, of which the base was towards us, one peak being on our right, one on our left, and one straight in front of us. Never shall I forget the sight afforded by those three towering peaks in the early sunlight of the following morning.

High, high above us, up into the blue air, soared their twisted snow-wreaths. Beneath the snow-line the peaks were purple with heather, and so were the wild moors that ran up the slopes towards them. Straight before us the white ribbon of Solomon's Great Road stretched away uphill to the foot of the centre peak, about five miles away, and there stopped. It was its terminus.

I had better leave the feelings of intense excitement with which we set out on our march that morning to the imagination of those who read this history. At last we were drawing near to the wonderful mines that had been the cause of the miserable death of the old Portuguese dom three centuries ago; of my poor friend, his ill-starred descendant; and also, we feared, of George Curtis, Sir Henry's brother. Were we destined, after all that we had gone through, to fare any better? Evil befell them, as that old fiend

Gagool said; would it also befall us? Somehow, as we were marching up that last stretch of beautiful road, I could not help feeling a little superstitious about the matter, and so I think did Good and Sir Henry.

For an hour and a half or more we tramped on up the heather-fringed way, going so fast in our excitement that the bearers of Gagool's hammock could scarcely keep pace with us, and its occupant piped out to us to stop.

'Walk more slowly, white men,' she said, projecting her hideous, shrivelled countenance between the grass curtains, and fixing her gleaming eyes upon us. 'Why will ye run to meet the evil that shall befall you, ye seekers after treasure?' and she laughed that horrible laugh which always sent a cold shiver down my back, and for a while quite took the enthusiasm out of us.

However, on we went, till we saw before us, and between ourselves and the peak, a vast circular hole with sloping sides, three hundred feet or more in depth, and over half a mile round.

'Can't you guess what that is?' I said to Sir Henry and Good, who were staring in astonishment at the awful pit before us.

They shook their heads.

'Then it is clear that you have never seen the diamond diggings at Kimberley. You may depend on it that this is Solomon's diamond Mine. Look there,' I said, pointing to the strata of stiff blue clay which were yet to be seen among the grass and bushes that clothed the sides of the pit, 'the formation is the same. I'll be bound that if we went down there we should find "pipes" of soapy, brecciated rock. Look, too,' and I pointed to a series of worn, flat slabs of stone that were placed on a gentle slope below the level of a watercourse which in some past age had been cut out of the solid rock; 'if those are not tables once used to wash the "stuff", I'm a Dutchman.'

At the edge of this vast hole, which was none other than the pit marked on the old Dom's map, the Great Road branched into two and circumvented it. In many places, by the way, this surrounding road was built entirely of blocks of stone, apparently with the object of supporting the edges of the pit and preventing falls of reef. Along this path we pressed, driven by curiosity to see what the three towering objects might be which we discerned from the hither side of the great gulf. As we drew nearer we perceived that they were colossi of some strange sort, and rightly conjectured that before us sat the three 'Silent Ones' that are held in such awe by the Kukuana people. But it was not until we were quite close to them that we recognised the full majesty of these 'Silent Ones'.

There, upon huge pedestals of dark rock, sculpted with rude emblems of phallus worship, separated from each other by a distance of forty paces and looking down the road which crossed some sixty miles of plain to Loo, were three colossal seated forms – two male and one female – each measuring about fifty feet from the crown of its head to the pedestal.

The female form, which was nude, was of great though severe beauty, but unfortunately the features had been injured by centuries of exposure to the weather. Rising from either side of her head were the points of a crescent. The two male colossi, on the contrary, were draped, and presented a terrifying cast of features, especially the one to our right, which had the face of a devil. That to our left was serene in countenance, but the calm upon it seemed dreadful. It was the calm of that inhuman cruelty, Sir Henry remarked, which the ancients attributed to beings potent for good, who could yet watch the sufferings of humanity, if not with rejoicing, at least without sorrow. These three statues formed a most awe-inspiring trinity, as they sat there in their solitude, gazing eternally out across the plain.

Contemplating these 'Silent Ones', as the Kukuanas call them, an intense curiosity again seized us to know whose were the hands which had shaped them, who it was that had dug the pit and made the road. Whilst I was gazing and wondering, suddenly it occurred to me, being familiar with the Old Testament, that Solomon went astray after strange gods, the names of three of whom I remembered – Ashtoreth, the goddess of the Zidonians, Chemosh, the god of the Moabites, and Milcom, the god of the children of Ammon – and I suggested to my companions that the figures before us might represent these false and discredited divinities.

'Hum,' said Sir Henry, who is a scholar, having taken a high degree in classics at college, 'there may be something in that; Ashtoreth of the Hebrews was the Astarte of the Phoenicians, who were the great traders of Solomon's time. Astarte, who afterwards became the Aphrodite of the Greeks, was represented with horns like the half-moon, and there on the brow of the female figure are distinct horns. Perhaps these colossi were designed by some Phoenician official who managed the mines. Who can say?'*

Before we had finished examining these extraordinary relics of remote antiquity, Infadoos came up, and having saluted the Silent Ones by lifting his spear, asked us if we intended entering the Place of Death at once, or if we would wait till after we had taken food at midday. If we were ready to go at once, Gagool had announced her willingness to guide us. As it was not later than eleven o'clock – driven to it by a burning curiosity – we announced our intention of proceeding instantly, and I suggested that, in case we should be detained in the cave, we should take some food with us.

Accordingly Gagool's litter was brought up, and that witch herself assisted to descend. Meanwhile Foulata, at my request, stored some *biltong*, or dried game-flesh, together with a couple of gourds of water, in a reed-basket with a hinged cover. Straight in front of us, at a distance of some fifty paces from the backs of the colossi, rose a sheer wall of rock, eighty feet or more in height, that gradually sloped upwards till it formed the base of the lofty snow-wreathed peak, which soared into the air three thousand feet above.

As soon as she was lifted from her hammock Gagool cast one evil glare upon us; then, leaning on a stick, she hobbled off towards the face of this wall. We followed her till we came to a narrow portal solidly arched that looked like the opening of a gallery of a mine.

Here Gagool was waiting for us, with a devilish grin upon her horrid face.

---

* Compare Milton, *Paradise Lost*, Book i –

> With these in troop
> Came Ashtoreth whom the Phoenicians called
> Astarté, Queen of Heaven, with crescent horns;
> To whose bright image nightly by the moon
> Sidonian virgins paid their vows and songs.   A.Q.

'Now, white men from the stars,' she piped; 'great warriors, Incubu, Bougwan and Macumazahn the wise, are ye ready? Behold, I am here to do the bidding of my lord the king, and to show you the store of bright stones. *Ha! ha! ha!*'

'We are ready,' I said.

'Good, good! Make strong your hearts to bear what ye shall see. Comest thou too, Infadoos, thou who didst betray thy master?'

Infadoos frowned as he answered: 'Nay, I come not; it is not for me to enter there. But thou, Gagool, curb thy tongue, and beware how thou dealest with my lords. At thy hands will I require them and if a hair of them be hurt, Gagool, be thou fifty times a witch, thou shalt die. Hearest thou?'

'I hear, Infadoos; I know thee, thou didst ever love big words; when thou wast a babe I remember thou didst threaten thine own mother. That was but the other day. But, fear not, fear not, I live only to do the bidding of the king. I have done the bidding of many kings, Infadoos, till in the end they did mine. *Ha! ha!* I go to look upon their faces once more, and Twala's also! Come on, come on, here is the lamp,' and she drew a large gourd full of oil, and fitted with a rush wick, from under her fur cloak.

'Art thou coming, Foulata?' asked Good in his villainous kitchen Kukuana, in which he had been improving himself under that young lady's tuition.

'I fear, my lord,' the girl answered timidly.

'Then give me the basket.'

'Nay, my lord, whither thou goest there I go also.'

'The deuce you do!' thought I to myself; 'that may be rather awkward if ever we get out of this.'

Without further ado Gagool plunged into the passage, which was wide enough to admit of two walking abreast, and quite dark. We followed the sound of her voice, as she piped to us to be swift, in some fear and trembling, which was not allayed by the flutter of a sudden rush of wings.

'Hallo! what's that?' hallooed Good, 'somebody hit me in the face.'

'Bats,' said I; 'on you go.'

When, so far as we could judge, we had gone some fifty paces, we perceived that the passage was growing faintly light. Another minute, and we were in perhaps the most wonderful place that the eyes of any living man have beheld.

Let the reader picture to himself the hall of the vastest cathedral he ever stood in, windowless indeed, but dimly lighted from above, presumably by shafts connected with the outer air and driven in the roof, which arched away a hundred feet above our heads, and he will get some idea of the size of the enormous cave in which we found ourselves, with the difference that this cathedral designed by nature was loftier and wider than any built by man.

But its stupendous size was the least of the wonders of the place, for running in rows down its length were gigantic pillars of what looked like ice, but were, in reality, huge stalactites. It is impossible for me to convey any idea of the overpowering beauty and grandeur of these pillars of white spar, some of which were not less than twenty feet in diameter at the base, and sprang up in lofty and yet delicate beauty, sheer to the distant roof. Others again were in process of formation. On the rock floor there was in these instances what looked, Sir Henry said, exactly like a broken column in an old Grecian temple, whilst high above, depending from the roof, the point of a huge lime icicle could be dimly seen.

Even as we gazed we heard the process going on, for now and again with a tiny splash a drop of water would fall from the far-off icicle on to the column below. On some columns the drops only fell once in two or three minutes, and in these cases it would be an interesting calculation to discover how long, at that rate of dripping, it would take to form a pillar, say eighty feet high by ten in diameter. That the process, in at least one instance, was incalculably slow, the following example will suffice to show. Cut on one of these pillars we discovered the rude likeness of a mummy, by which sat what appeared to be the beast-headed figure of an Egyptian god, doubtless the handiwork of some old-world labourer in the mine. This work of art was executed at the natural height at which an idle fellow, be he Phoenician workman or British cad, is in the habit of trying to immortalise himself at the expense of nature's masterpieces, namely, about five feet from the ground. Yet at the time that we saw it, which must have been nearly three thousand years after the date of the execution of the carving, the column was only eight feet high, and was still in process of formation, which gives a rate of growth of a foot to a thousand years, or an inch and a fraction to a century. This we knew because, as we were standing by it, we heard a drop of water fall.

Sometimes the stalagmites below took strange forms, presumably where the dropping of the water had not always been on the same spot. Thus, one huge mass, which must have weighed a hundred tons or so, was in the shape of a pulpit, beautifully fretted over outside with a design that looked like lace. Others resembled strange beasts, and on the sides of the cave were fanlike ivory tracings, such as frost leaves upon a pane.

Out of the vast main aisle there opened here and there smaller caves, exactly, Sir Henry said, as chapels open out of great cathedrals. Some were large, but one or two – and this is a wonderful instance of how nature carries out her handiwork by the same unvarying laws, utterly irrespective of size – were tiny. One little nook, for instance, was no larger than an unusually big doll's house, and yet it might have been a model of the whole place, for the water dropped, tiny icicles of lime hung, and spar columns were forming in just the same way.

We had not, however, enough time to examine this beautiful cavern so thoroughly as we should have liked to do, since, unfortunately, Gagool seemed to be indifferent to stalactites, and only anxious to get her business over. This annoyed me the more, as I was particularly anxious to discover, if possible, by what system the light was admitted into the cave, and whether it was by the hand of man or by that of nature that this was done; also if the place had been used in any way in ancient times, as seemed probable. However, we consoled ourselves with the idea that we would investigate it thoroughly on our way back, and followed quickly at the heels of our uncanny guide.

On she led us, straight to the top of the mighty, silent cave, where we found another doorway, not arched as the first was, but square at the top, something like the doorways of Egyptian temples.

'Are ye prepared to enter the Place of Death, white men?' asked Gagool, evidently with a view to making us feel uncomfortable.

'Lead on, Macduff,' said Good solemnly, trying to look as

though he was not at all alarmed, as indeed we all did except Foulata, who caught Good by the arm for protection.

'This is getting rather ghastly,' said Sir Henry, peeping into the dark doorway. 'Come on, Quatermain – *seniores priores!* We mustn't keep the old lady waiting!' and he politely made way for me to lead the van, for which inwardly I did not bless him.

Tap, tap, went old Gagool's stick down the passage, as she trotted along, chuckling hideously; and still overcome by some unaccountable presentiment of evil, I hung back.

'Come, get on, old fellow,' said Good, 'or we shall lose our fair guide.'

Thus adjured, I started down the passage, and after about twenty paces found myself in a gloomy apartment some fifty feet long, by thirty broad and twenty high, which in some past age evidently had been hollowed, by hand-labour, out of the mountain. This apartment was not nearly so well lighted as the vast stalactite ante-cave, and at first glance all I could discern was a massive stone table running down its length, with a colossal white figure at its head, and life-sized white figures all round it. Next I discovered a brown thing, seated on the table in the centre. In another moment my eyes grew accustomed to the light, and I saw what all these things were, and was tailing out of the place as hard as my legs would carry me.

I am not a nervous man in a general way, nor greatly troubled with superstitions, of which I have lived to see the folly. Yet I am free to own that this sight quite upset me, and had it not been that Sir Henry caught me by the collar and held me, I do honestly believe that in another five minutes I should have been outside the stalactite cave, and that a promise of all the diamonds in Kimberley would not have induced me to enter it again. But he held me tight, so I stopped because I could not help myself. Very soon, however, *his* eyes became focused on the sight, and he let go of me, and began to mop the perspiration off his forehead. As for Good, he swore feebly, while Foulata threw her arms round his neck and shrieked.

Only Gagool chuckled loud and long.

It *was* a ghastly sight. There at the end of the long stone table, holding in his skeleton fingers a great white spear, sat Death himself, shaped in the form of a colossal human skeleton, fifteen feet or more in height. High above his head he held the spear, as though in the act to strike. One bony hand rested on the stone table before him, in the position a man assumes on rising from a seat, whilst his frame was bent forward so that the vertebrae of the neck and the grinning, gleaming skull projected towards us, and fixed its hollow eye-places upon us, the jaws a little open, as though it were about to speak.

'Great heavens!' I exclaimed faintly, at last, 'what can it be?'

'And what are *those things*?' asked Good, pointing to the white company round the table.

'And what on earth is *that thing*?' said Sir Henry, pointing to the brown creature seated on the table.

'*Hee! hee! hee!*' laughed Gagool. 'To those who enter the Hall of the Dead, evil draws near. *Hee! hee! hee! ha! ha!*'

'Come, Incubu, brave in battle, come and see him thou slewest;' and the old creature caught Curtis's coat in her skinny fingers, and led him away towards the table. We followed.

Presently she stopped and pointed at the brown object seated on the table. Sir Henry looked, and started back with an exclamation. No wonder, for there, quite naked, the head which Curtis's battle-axe had shorn from the body resting on its knees, was the gaunt corpse of Twala, the last king of the Kukuanas! Yes, there, the head perched upon the knees, it sat in all its ugliness, the vertebrae projecting a full inch above the level of the shrunken flesh of the neck, for all the world like a black double of Hamilton Tighe.* Over the surface of the black corpse was gathered a thin glassy film, that made its appearance yet more appalling. For this we were, at the moment, quite unable to account, till presently we observed that from the roof of the chamber the water fell steadily, *drip! drop! drip!* on to the neck of the dead man, whence it trickled over the entire surface, and finally escaped into the rock through a tiny hole in the table. Then I guessed what the film was – Twala's body was being transformed into a stalactite!

---

* Now haste ye, my hand-maidens, haste and see
  How he sits there and glowers with his head on his knee.

A look at the white forms seated on the stone bench which ran round that ghastly board confirmed this view. They were human bodies indeed, or rather they had been human; now they were stalactites. This was the way in which the Kukuana people had from time immemorial preserved their royal dead. They petrified them. What the exact system might be, if there was any, beyond the placing of them for a long period of years under the drip, I never discovered, but there they sat, iced over and preserved for ever by the silicious fluid.

Anything more awe-inspiring than the spectacle of this long line of departed royalties (there were twenty-seven of them, the last being Ignosi's father), wrapped, each one, in a shroud of ice-like spar, through which the features could be dimly discovered, and seated round that inhospitable board, with Death himself for a host, it is impossible to imagine. That the practice of thus preserving their kings must have been ancient is very evident from the number, which, allowing for an average reign of fifteen years, and supposing that every king who reigned was placed here – an improbable thing, as some are sure to have perished in battle far from home – would fix the date of its commencement at four and a quarter centuries ago.

But the colossal White Death, who sat at the head of the board, was far older than that, and, unless I am much mistaken, owed his origin to the same artist who designed the three colossi. He was hewn out of a single stalactite, and, looked at as a work of art, was most admirably conceived and executed. Good, who understands such things, declared that, so far as he could see, the anatomical design of the skeleton was perfect down to the smallest bones.

My own idea is that this terrific object was a freak of fancy on the part of some old-world sculptor, and that its presence had suggested to the Kukuanas the idea of placing their royal dead under its awful presidency. Or perhaps it was set there to frighten away any marauders who might have designs upon the treasure chamber beyond. I cannot say. All I can do is to describe it as it was, and the reader must form his own conclusion.

Such, at any rate, was the White Death and such were the White Dead!

CHAPTER 17

Solomon's Treasure Chamber

While we were engaged in recovering from our fright, and in examining the grisly wonders of the Place of Death, Gagool had been differently occupied. Somehow or other – for she was marvellously active when she chose – she had scrambled on to the great table, and made her way to where our departed friend Twala was placed, under the drip, to see, suggested Good, how he was 'pickling', or for some dark purpose of her own. Then, after bending down to kiss his icy lips as though in affectionate greeting, she hobbled back, stopping now and again to address a remark, the tenor of which I could not catch, to one or other of the shrouded forms, just as you or I might welcome an old acquaintance. Having gone through this mysterious and horrible ceremony, she squatted herself down on the table immediately under the White Death, and began, so far as I could make out, to offer up prayers. The spectacle of this wicked creature pouring out supplications, evil ones, no doubt, to the arch-enemy of mankind, was so uncanny that it caused us to hasten our inspection.

'Now, Gagool,' said I, in a low voice – somehow one did not dare to speak above a whisper in that place – 'lead us to the chamber.'

The old witch promptly scrambled down from the table.

'My lords are not afraid?' she said, leering up into my face.

'Lead on.'

'Good, my lords;' and she hobbled round to the back of the White Death. 'Here is the chamber; let my lords light the lamp, and enter,' and she placed the gourd full of oil upon the floor, and leaned herself against the side of the cave. I took out a match, of which we had still a few in a box, and lit the rush wick. Then looked for the doorway, but there was nothing before us except the solid rock.

Gagool grinned, and said: 'The way is there, my lords. *Ha! ha! ha!*'

'Do not jest with us,' I answered sternly.

'I jest not, my lords. See!' and she pointed to the rock.

As she did so, on holding up the lamp we perceived that a mass of stone was rising slowly from the floor and vanishing into the roof above, where doubtless there was a cavity prepared to receive it. The mass was of the width of a good-sized door, about ten feet high and not less than five feet thick. It must have weighed at least twenty or thirty tons, and was clearly moved upon some simple balance principle of counterweights, probably the same as that by which the opening and shutting of an ordinary modern window is arranged. How that principle was set in motion, of course, none of us saw; Gagool was careful to avoid this; but I have little doubt that there was some primitive lever, which was moved ever so little by pressure at a secret spot, thereby throwing additional weight on to the hidden counter-balances, and causing the monolith to be lifted from its bed.

Very slowly and gently the great stone raised itself, till at last it had vanished altogether, and a dark hole presented itself to us in the place which the door had filled.

Our excitement was so intense, as we saw the way to Solomon's treasure chamber thrown open at last, that I for one began to tremble and shake. Would it prove a hoax after all, I wondered, or was old da Silvestra right? Were there vast hoards of wealth hidden in that dark place, hoards which would make us the richest men in the whole world? We should know in a minute or two.

'Enter, white men from the stars,' said Gagool, advancing into the doorway; 'but first hear your servant, Gagool the Old. The bright stones that ye will see were dug out of the pit over which the Silent Ones are set, and stored here, I know not by whom, for that was done longer ago than even I remember. Only once has this place been entered since the time that those who hid the stones departed in haste, leaving them behind. The report of the treasure went down indeed among the peoples who lived in the country from age to age, but none knew where the chamber was, nor the secret of the door. But it happened that a white man reached this country from over the mountains – perchance he too came from "the stars" – and was well received by the king of that day. He it is who sits yonder,' and she pointed to the fifth king at the table of the dead. 'And it came to pass that he and a woman of the country who was with him journeyed to this place, and that by chance, or magic, the woman learnt the secret of the door – a thousand years might ye search, but ye would never find that secret. Then the white man entered with the woman, and found the treasure, and filled with stones the skin of a small goat, which the woman had with her to hold food. Also as he was going from the chamber he took up one more stone, a large one, and held it in his hand.'

Here she paused.

'Well,' I asked, breathless with interest as we all were, 'what happened to da Silvestra?'

The old hag started at the mention of the name.

'How knowest thou the dead man's name?' she asked sharply; and then, without waiting for an answer, went on: 'None can tell what happened; but it came about that the white man was frightened, for he flung down the goatskin, with the stones, and fled out with only the one stone in his hand, and that the king seized, and it is the stone which thou, Macumazahn, didst take from Twala's brow.'

'Have none entered here since?' I asked, peering again down the dark passage.

'None, my lords. Only the secret of the door has been kept, and every king has opened it in his day, though he has not entered. There is a saying, that those who enter there will die within a moon, even as the white man died in the cave upon the mountain, where ye found him, Macumazahn, and therefore the kings do not enter. *Ha! ha!* mine are true words.'

Our eyes met as she said it, and I turned sick and cold. How did the old hag know all these things?

'Enter, my lords. If I speak truth, the goatskin with the stones will lie upon the floor; and if there is truth as to whether it is death to enter here, that ye will learn afterwards. *Ha! ha! ha!*' and she hobbled through the doorway, bearing the light with her; but I confess that once more I hesitated about following.

'Oh, confound it all!' said Good; 'here goes. I am not going to be frightened by that old devil;' and followed by Foulata, who, however, evidently did not at all like the business, for she was shivering with fear, he plunged into the passage after Gagool – an example which we quickly followed.

A few yards down the passage, in the narrow way hewn out of the living rock, Gagool had paused, and was waiting for us.

'See, my lords,' she said, holding the light before her, 'those who stored the treasure here fled in haste, and bethought them to guard against any who should find the secret of the door, but had not the time,' and she pointed to large square blocks of stone, which, to the height of two courses (about two foot three), had been placed across the passage with the object of walling it up. Along the side of the passage were similar blocks ready for use, and, most curious of all, a heap of mortar and a couple of trowels, which tools, so far as we had time to examine them, appeared to be of a similar shape and make to those used by workmen to this day.

Here Foulata, who had been in a state of great fear and agitation throughout, said that she felt faint, and could go no further, but would wait there. Accordingly we set her down on the unfinished wall, placing the basket of provisions by her side, and left her to recover.

Following the passage for about fifteen paces further, we came suddenly to an elaborately painted wooden door. It was standing wide open. Whoever was last there either had not found the time to shut it, or had forgotten to do so.

Across the threshold of this door lay a skin bag, fashioned from a goatskin, that appeared to be full of pebbles.

'*Hee! Hee!* white men,' sniggered Gagool, as the light from the lamp fell upon it. 'What did I tell you – that the white man who came here fled in haste, and dropped the woman's bag; behold it! Look within also and ye will find a water-gourd amongst the stones.'

Good stooped down and lifted it. It was heavy, and jingled.

'By Jove! I believe it's full of diamonds,' he said in an awed whisper; and, indeed, the idea of a small goatskin full of diamonds is enough to awe anybody.

'Go on,' said Sir Henry impatiently. 'Here, old lady, give me the lamp,' and taking it from Gagool's hand, he stepped through the doorway and held it high above his head.

We pressed in after him, forgetful for the moment of the bag of diamonds, and found ourselves in King Solomon's treasure chamber.

At first, all that the somewhat faint light of the lamp revealed was a lofty room hewn out of the living rock, and apparently not more than fifteen feet square. Next there came into sight, stored one on the other to the arch of the roof a splendid collection of elephant-tusks. How many of them there were we did not know, for of course we could not see to what depth they went back, but there could not have been less than the ends of four or five hundred tusks of the first quality visible to our eyes. There, alone, was enough ivory before us to make a man wealthy for life. Perhaps, I thought, it was from this very store that Solomon drew the raw material for his 'great throne of ivory', of which 'there was not the like made in any kingdom'.

On the opposite side of the chamber were about a score of wooden boxes, something like Martini–Henry ammunition boxes, only rather larger and painted red. 'There are the diamonds,' cried I; 'bring the light.'

Sir Henry did so, holding it close to the top box, of which the lid, rendered rotten by time even in that dry place, appeared to have been smashed in, probably by da Silvestra himself. Pushing my hand through the hole in the lid I drew it out full, not of diamonds, but of gold pieces, of a shape that none of us had seen before, and with what looked like Hebrew characters stamped upon them.

'Ah!' I said, replacing the coin, 'we shan't go back empty-handed, anyhow. There must be a couple of thousand pieces in each box, and there are eighteen boxes. I suppose this was the money to pay the workmen and merchants.'

'Well,' put in Good, 'I think that is the lot; I don't see any diamonds – it seems the old Portuguese put them all into his bag.'

'Let my lords look yonder where it is darkest, if they would find the stones,' said Gagool, interpreting our looks. 'There my lords will find a nook, and three stone chests in the nook, two sealed and one open.'

Before translating this to Sir Henry, who carried the light, I could not resist asking how she knew these things, if no one had entered the place since the white man, generations ago.

'Ah, Macumazahn, the Watcher-by-Night,' was the mocking answer, 'ye who dwell in the stars, do ye not know that some live long, and that some have eyes which can see through rock? *Ha! ha! ha!*'

'Look in that corner, Curtis,' I said, indicating the spot Gagool had pointed out.

'Great heavens! you fellows,' he cried presently, 'see here.'

We hurried up to where he was standing in a nook shaped something like a small bow window. Against the wall of this recess were placed three stone chests, each about two feet square. Two were fitted with stone lids; the lid of the third rested against the side of the chest, which was open.

'*See!*' he repeated hoarsely, holding the lamp over the open chest. We looked, and for a moment could make out nothing, on account of a silvery sheen which dazzled us. When our eyes grew used to it we saw that the chest was three-parts full of uncut diamonds, most of them of considerable size. Stooping, I picked up a handful. Yes, there was no doubt of it, they had that unmistakable soapy feel.

I gasped as I dropped them.

'We are the richest men in the whole world,' I exclaimed. 'Monte Cristo was a fool to us.'

'We shall flood the market with diamonds,' said Good.

'Got to get them there first,' suggested Sir Henry.

We stood still with pale faces and stared at each other, the lantern in the middle and the glimmering gems below, as though we were conspirators about to commit a crime, instead of being, as we thought, the most fortunate men on earth.

'*Hee! hee! hee!*' cackled old Gagool as she flitted about like a vampire bat behind us. 'There are the bright stones ye love, white men, as many as ye will; take them, run them through your fingers, *eat* of them, *hee! hee! drink* of them, *ha! ha!*'

At that moment there was something so ridiculous to my mind in the idea of eating and drinking diamonds, that I began to laugh outrageously, an example which the others followed, without knowing why. There we stood and shrieked with laughter over the gems that were *ours*, which had been found for us thousands of years ago by the patient delvers in the great hole yonder, and stored for us by Solomon's long-dead overseer, whose name, perchance, was written in the characters stamped on the faded wax that yet adhered to the lids of the chests. Solomon never got them, nor David, nor da Silvestra, nor anybody else. We had got them; there before us were millions of pounds' worth of diamonds, and tens of thousands of pounds' worth of gold and ivory only waiting to be taken away.

Suddenly the fit passed off, and we stopped laughing.

'Open the other chests, white men,' croaked Gagool, 'there are surely more therein. Take your fill, white lords! *Ha! ha!* take your fill.'

Thus adjured, we set to work to pull up the stone lids on the other two, first – not without a feeling of sacrilege – breaking the seals that fastened them.

Hurrah! they were full too, full to the brim; at least the second one was; no wretched, burglarious da Silvestra had been filling goatskins out of that. As for the third chest, it was only about a fourth full, but the stones were all picked ones; none less than twenty carats, and some of them as large as pigeon-eggs. A good many of these bigger ones, however, we could see by holding them up to the light, were a little yellow, 'off-coloured', as they call it at Kimberley. Some, too, were black.

What we did *not* note, however, was the look of fearful malevolence that old Gagool favoured us with as she crept, crept like a snake, out of the treasure chamber and down the passage towards the door of solid rock.

*　　　*　　　*

Hark! Cry upon cry comes ringing up the vaulted path. It is Foulata's voice!

'Oh, Bougwan! help! help! the stone falls!'

'Leave go, girl!'

Then – 'Help! help! she has stabbed me!'

By now we are running down the passage, and this is what the light from the lamp shows us. The door of rock is closing down slowly; it is not three feet from the floor. Near it struggle Foulata and Gagool. The red blood of Foulata runs to her knee, but still the brave girl holds the old witch, who fights like a wild cat. Look! she is free! Foulata falls, and Gagool throws herself on the ground, to twist like a snake beneath the lip of the closing stone. She is under – ah! God! too late! too late! The stone nips her, and she yells in agony. Down, down, it comes, all the thirty tons of it, slowly pressing her old body against the rock below. Shriek upon shriek, such as we had never heard, then a long sickening *crunch*, and the door is shut just as, rushing down the passage, we hurl ourselves against its mass.

It was all done in four seconds.

Then we turned to Foulata. The poor girl was stabbed in the body, and I saw that she could not live for long.

'Ah! Bougwan, I die!' gasped the beautiful creature. 'She crept out – Gagool; I did not see her, I was faint – and the door began to fall. Then she came back, and was looking up the path – I saw her come in through the slowly falling door, and caught her and held her, and she stabbed me, and I *die*, Bougwan!'

'Poor girl! poor girl!' Good cried in his distress. Then, as he could do nothing else, he fell to kissing her.

'Bougwan,' she said, after a pause, 'is Macumazahn there? It grows so dark – I cannot see.'

'Here I am, Foulata.'

'Macumazahn, be my tongue for a moment, I pray thee, for Bougwan cannot understand me, and before I go into the night I would speak a word to him.'

'Say on, Foulata, I will render it.'

'Say to my lord, Bougwan, that – I love him, and that I am glad to die because I know that he cannot cumber his life with such as I am, for the sun may not mate with the moon, nor the white with the black.

'Say that, since I saw him, at times I have felt as though there were a bird in my bosom, which would one day fly hence and sing elsewhere. Even now, though I cannot lift my hand, and my brain grows cold, I do not feel as though my heart were dying; it is so full of love that it could live ten thousand years, and yet be young. Say that if I live again, mayhap I shall see him in the stars, and that – I will search them all, though perchance there I must still be black and he will – still be white. Say – nay, Macumazahn, say no more, save that I love – Oh, hold me closer, Bougwan, I cannot feel thine arms – *oh! oh!*'

'She is dead – she is dead!' muttered Good presently as he rose, the tears of grief running down his honest face.

'You need not let that trouble you, old fellow,' said Sir Henry.

'Eh!' exclaimed Good; 'what do you mean?'

'I mean that you will soon be in a position to join her. Man, don't you see that we are buried alive?'

Until Sir Henry uttered these words I do not think that the full horror of what had happened came home to us, preoccupied as we were with the sight of poor Foulata's end. But now we understood. The ponderous mass of rock had closed, probably for ever, for the only brain which knew its secret was crushed to powder beneath its weight. This was a door that none could hope to force with anything short of dynamite in large quantities. And we were on its wrong side!

For a few minutes we stood horrified – there, over the corpse of Foulata. All the manhood seemed to have gone out of us. The first shock of the knowledge of the slow and miserable end that awaited us was overpowering. We saw it all now; that fiend Gagool had planned this snare for us from the first.

It must have been exactly the jest that her evil mind would have rejoiced in, this idea of the three white men whom, for some reason of her own, she had always hated, slowly perishing of thirst and hunger in the company of the treasure they had coveted. Now I saw the point of that sneer of hers about our eating and drinking the diamonds. Probably somebody had tried to serve the poor old dom in the same way, when he abandoned the skin full of jewels. And who was that somebody?

'This will never do,' said Sir Henry hoarsely; 'the lamp will soon go out. Let us see if we can't find the lever that works the rock.'

We sprang forward with desperate energy, and, standing in a bloody ooze, began to feel up and down the door and the sides of the passage. But no knob or spring could we discover.

'Depend on it,' I said, 'it does not work from the inside; if it did, Gagool would not have risked trying to crawl underneath the stone. It was this knowledge that made her try to escape at all hazards, curse her.'

'At any rate,' answered Sir Henry with a hard little laugh, 'retribution was swift; hers was almost as awful an end as ours is likely to be. We can do nothing with the door; let us go back to the treasure room.'

We turned and went, and as we passed it I perceived by the unfinished wall across the passage the basket of food which poor Foulata had carried. I took it up, and brought it with me to the accursed treasure chamber that was to be our grave. Then we returned and reverently bore in Foulata's corpse, laying it on the floor by the boxes of coin.

Next we seated ourselves, leaning our backs against the three stone chests which contained the priceless treasure.

'Let us divide the food,' said Sir Henry, 'so as to make it last as long as possible.'

Accordingly we did so. It would, we reckoned, make four infinitesimally small meals for each of us, enough, say, to support life for a couple of days. Besides the *biltong*, or dried game-flesh, there were two gourds of water, each of which held not more than a quart.

'Now,' said Sir Henry grimly, 'let us eat and drink, for tomorrow we die.'

We each ate a small portion of the *biltong*, and drank a sip of water. Needless to say, we had but little appetite, though we were sadly in need of food, and felt better after swallowing it. Then we got up and made a systematic examination of the walls of our prison-house, in the faint hope of finding some means of exit, sounding them and the floor carefully.

There was none. It was not probable that there would be any to a treasure chamber.

Our lamp began to burn dim. The fat was nearly exhausted.

'Quatermain,' said Sir Henry, 'what is the time – your watch goes?'

I drew it out, and looked at it. It was six o'clock; we had entered the cave at eleven.

'Infadoos will miss us,' I suggested. 'If we do not return tonight he will search for us in the morning, Curtis.'

'He may search in vain. He does not know the secret of the door, nor even where it is. No living person knew it yesterday, except Gagool. Today no one knows it. Even if he found the door he could not break it down. All the Kukuana army could not break through five feet of living rock. My friends, I see nothing for it but to bow ourselves to the will of the Almighty. The search for treasure has brought many to a bad end; we shall go to swell their number.'

The lamp grew dimmer yet.

Presently it flared up and showed the whole scene in strong relief, the great mass of white tusks, the boxes of gold, the corpse of poor Foulata stretched before them, the goatskin full of treasure, the dim glimmer of the diamonds, and the wild, wan faces of us three white men, seated there awaiting death by starvation.

Then the flame sank and expired.

CHAPTER 18

We Abandon Hope

I can give no adequate description of the horrors of the night which followed. Mercifully these were to some extent mitigated by sleep, for even in such a position as ours wearied nature will sometimes assert itself. But I, at any rate, found it impossible to sleep much. Putting aside the terrifying thought of our impending doom – for the bravest man on earth might well quail from such a fate as awaited us, and I never made any pretensions to be brave – the *silence* itself was too great to allow of it.

Reader, you may have lain awake at night and thought the quiet oppressive, but I say with confidence that you can have no idea what a vivid, tangible thing is perfect stillness. On the surface of the earth there is always some sound or motion, and though it may in itself be imperceptible, yet it deadens the sharp edge of absolute silence. But here there was none. We were buried in the bowels of a huge snow-clad peak. Thousands of feet above us the fresh air rushed over the white snow, but no sound of it reached us. We were separated by a long tunnel and five feet of rock even from the awful chamber of the dead; and the dead make no noise. Did we not know it who lay by poor Foulata's side? The crashing of all the artillery of earth and heaven could not have come to our ears in that living tomb. We were cut off from every echo of the world – we were as men already in the grave.

Then the irony of the situation forced itself upon me. There around us lay treasures enough to pay off a moderate national debt, or to build a fleet of ironclads, and yet we would have bartered them all gladly for the faintest chance of escape. Soon, doubtless, we should be rejoiced to exchange them for a bit of food or a cup of water, and, after that, even for the privilege of a speedy close to our sufferings. Truly wealth, which men spend their lives in acquiring, is a valueless thing at the last.

And so the night wore on.

'Good,' said Sir Henry's voice at last, and it sounded awful in the intense stillness, 'how many matches have you in the box?'

'Eight, Curtis.'

'Strike one and let us see the time.'

He did so, and in contrast to the dense darkness the flame nearly blinded us. It was five o'clock by my watch. The beautiful dawn was now blushing on the snow-wreaths far over our heads, and the breeze would be stirring the night mists in the hollows.

'We had better eat something and keep up our strength,' I suggested.

'What is the good of eating?' answered Good; 'the sooner we die and get it over the better.'

'While there is life there is hope,' said Sir Henry.

Accordingly we ate and sipped some water, and another period of time passed. Then Sir Henry suggested that it might be well to get as near the door as possible and halloo, on the faint chance of somebody catching a sound outside. Accordingly Good, who, from long practice at sea, has a fine piercing note, groped his way down the passage and set to work. I must say that he made a most diabolical noise. I never heard such yells; but it might have been a mosquito buzzing for all the effect they produced.

After a while he gave it up and came back very thirsty, and had to drink. Then we stopped yelling, as it encroached on the supply of water.

So we sat down once more against the chests of useless diamonds in that dreadful inaction which was one of the hardest circumstances of our fate; and I am bound to say that, for my part, I gave way to despair. Laying my head against Sir Henry's broad shoulder I burst into tears; and I think that I heard Good gulping away on the other side, and swearing hoarsely at himself for doing so.

Ah, how good and brave that great man was! Had we been two frightened children, and he our nurse, he could not have treated us more tenderly. Forgetting his own share of miseries, he did all he could to soothe our broken nerves, telling stories of men who had been in somewhat similar circumstances, and miraculously escaped; and when these failed to cheer us, pointing out how, after all, it was only anticipating an end which must come to us all; that it would soon be over, and that death from exhaustion was a merciful one (which is not true). Then, in a different sort of way, as once before I had heard him do, he suggested that we should throw ourselves on the mercy of a higher power, which for my part I did with great vigour.

His is a beautiful character, very quiet, but very strong.

And so somehow the day went as the night had gone, if, indeed, one can use these terms where all was densest night, and when I lit a match to see the time it was seven o'clock.

Once more we ate and drank, and as we did so an idea occurred to me.

'How is it,' said I, 'that the air in this place keeps fresh? It is thick and heavy, but it is perfectly fresh.'

'Great heavens!' said Good, starting up, 'I never thought of that. It can't come through the stone door, for it's airtight, if ever a door was. It must come from somewhere. If there were no current of air in the place we should have been stifled or poisoned when we first came in. Let us have a look.'

It was wonderful what a change this mere spark of hope wrought in us. In a moment we were all three groping about on our hands and knees, feeling for the slightest indication of a draught. Presently my ardour received a check. I put my hand on something cold. It was dead Foulata's face!

For an hour or more we went on feeling about, till at last Sir Henry and I gave it up in despair, having been considerably hurt by constantly knocking our heads against tusks, chests and the sides of the chamber. But Good still persevered, saying, with an approach to cheerfulness, that it was better than doing nothing.

'I say, you fellows,' he said presently, in a constrained sort of voice, 'come here.'

Needless to say we scrambled towards him quickly enough.

'Quatermain, put your hand here, where mine is. Now do you feel anything?'

'I *think* I feel air coming up.'

'Now listen.' He rose and stamped upon the place, and a flame of hope shot up in our hearts. It rang *hollow*.

With trembling hands I lit a match. I had only three left, and we saw that we were in the angle of the far corner of the chamber, a fact that accounted for our not having noticed the hollow sound of the place during our former exhaustive examination. As the match burnt we scrutinised the spot. There was a join in the solid rock floor, and, great heavens! there, let in level with the rock, was a stone ring. We said no word, we were too excited, and our hearts beat too wildly with hope to allow us to speak. Good had a knife, at the back of which was one of those hooks that are made to extract stones from horses' hoofs. He opened it, and with it scratched round the ring. Finally he worked it under, and levered away gently for fear of breaking the hook. The ring began to move. Being of stone it had not rusted fast in all the centuries it had lain there, as would have been the case had it been of iron. Presently the ring was upright. Then he thrust his hands into it and tugged with all his force, but nothing budged.

'Let me try,' I said impatiently, for the situation of the stone, right in the angle of the corner, was such that it was impossible for two to pull at once. I took hold and strained away, but no results.

Next Sir Henry tried and failed.

Taking the hook again, Good scratched all round the crack where we felt the air coming up.

'Now, Curtis,' he said, 'tackle on, and put your back into it; you are as strong as two. Stop,' and he took off a stout, black silk handkerchief, which, true to his habits of neatness, he still wore, and ran it through the ring. 'Quatermain, get Curtis round the middle and pull for dear life when I give the word. Now!'

Sir Henry put out all his enormous strength, and Good and I did the same, with such power as nature had given us.

'Heave! heave! it's giving,' gasped Sir Henry; and I heard the muscles of his great back cracking. Suddenly there was a grating sound, then a rush of air, and we were all on our backs on the floor with a heavy flagstone lying upon the top of us. Sir Henry's strength had done it, and never did muscular power stand a man in better stead.

'Light a match, Quatermain,' he said, so soon as we had picked ourselves up and got our breath; 'carefully, now.'

I did so, and there before us, heaven be praised! was the first step of a stone stair.

'Now what is to be done?' asked Good.

'Follow the stair, of course, and trust to providence.'

'Stop!' said Sir Henry; 'Quatermain, get the bit of *biltong* and the water that are left; we may want them.'

I went, creeping back to our place by the chests for that purpose, and as I was coming away an idea struck me. We had not thought much of the diamonds for the last twenty-four hours or so; indeed, the very idea of diamonds was nauseous, seeing what they had entailed upon us; but, reflected I, I may as well pocket some in case we ever should get out of this ghastly hole. So I just put my fist into the first chest and filled all the available pockets of my old shooting-coat and trousers, topping up – this was a happy notion – with a few handfuls of big ones out of the third chest. Also, by an afterthought, I stuffed Foulata's basket, which, except for one water-gourd and a little *biltong*, was empty now, with great quantities of the stones.

'I say, you fellows,' I sang out, 'won't you take some diamonds with you? I've filled my pockets and the basket.'

'Oh, come on, Quatermain! and hang the diamonds!' said Sir Henry. 'I hope that I may never see another.'

As for Good, he made no answer. He was, I think, taking his last farewell of all that was left of the poor girl who had loved him so well.

Curious as it may seem to you, my reader, sitting at home at ease and reflecting on the vast, indeed the immeasurable wealth which we were thus abandoning, I can assure you that if you had passed some twenty-eight hours with next to nothing to eat and drink in that place, you would not have cared to cumber yourself with diamonds whilst plunging down into the unknown bowels of the earth, in the wild hope of escape from an agonising death. If, from the habits of a lifetime, it had not become a sort of second nature with me never to leave anything worth having behind if there was the slightest chance of my being able to carry it away, I am sure that I should not have bothered to fill my pockets and that basket.

'Come on, Quatermain,' repeated Sir Henry, who was already standing on the first step of the stone stair. 'Steady, I will go first.'

'Mind where you put your feet, there may be some awful hole underneath,' I answered.

'Much more likely to be another room,' said Sir Henry, while he descended slowly, counting the steps as he went.

When he got to fifteen he stopped. 'Here's the bottom,' he said. 'Thank goodness! I think it's a passage. Follow me down.'

Good went next, and I came last, carrying the basket, and on reaching the bottom lit one of the two remaining matches. By its light we could just see that we were standing in a narrow tunnel, which ran right and left at right angles to the staircase we had descended. Before we could make out any more, the match burnt my fingers and went out. Then arose the delicate question of which way to go. Of course, it was impossible to know what the tunnel was, or where it led to, and yet to turn one way might lead us to safety, and to turn the other, to destruction. We were utterly perplexed, till suddenly it struck Good that when I had lit the match the draught of the passage had blown the flame to the left.

'Let us go against the draught,' he said; 'air draws inwards, not outwards.'

We took this suggestion, and feeling along the wall with our hands, whilst trying the ground before us at every step, we departed from that accursed treasure chamber on our terrible quest for life. If ever it should be entered again by living man, which I do not think probable, he will find tokens of our visit in the open chests of jewels, the empty lamp, and the white bones of poor Foulata.

When we had groped our way for about a quarter of an hour along the passage, suddenly it took a sharp twist, or else was bisected by another, which we followed, only in the course of time to be led into a third. And so it went on for some hours. We seemed to be in a stone labyrinth which led nowhere. What all these passages are, of course I cannot say, but we thought that they must be the ancient workings of a mine, of which the various shafts and adits travelled hither and thither as the ore chutes led them. This is the only way in which we could account for such a multitude of galleries.

At length we halted, thoroughly worn out with fatigue and with that hope deferred which makes the heart sick, and ate up our poor remaining piece of *biltong* and drank our last sup of water, for our throats were like lime-kilns. It seemed to us that we had escaped Death in the darkness of the treasure chamber only to meet him in the darkness of the tunnels.

As we stood, once more utterly depressed, I thought that I caught a sound, to which I called the attention of the others. It was very faint and very far off, but it was a sound, a faint murmuring sound, for the others heard it too, and no words can describe the blessedness of it after all those hours of utter, awful stillness.

'By heaven! it's running water,' said Good. 'Come on.'

Off we started again in the direction from which the faint murmur seemed to come, groping our way as before along the rocky walls. I remember that I laid down the basket full of diamonds, wishing to be rid of its weight, but on second thoughts took it up again. One might as well die rich as poor, I reflected. As we went the sound became more and more audible, till at last it seemed quite loud in the quiet. On, yet on; now we could distinctly descry the unmistakable swirl of rushing water. And yet how could there be running water in the bowels of the earth? Now we were quite near it, and Good, who was leading, swore that he could smell it.

'Go gently, Good,' said Sir Henry, 'we must be close.' *Splash!* and a cry from Good.

He had fallen in.

'Good! Good! where are you?' we shouted, in terrified distress. To our intense relief an answer came back in a choky voice.

'All right; I've got hold of a rock. Strike a light to show me where you are.'

Hastily I lit the last remaining match. Its faint gleam discovered to us a dark mass of water running at our feet. How wide it was we could not see, but there, some way out, was the dark form of our companion hanging on to a projecting rock.

'Stand clear to catch me,' sang out Good. 'I must swim for it.'

Then we heard a splash, and a great struggle. Another minute and he had grabbed at and caught Sir Henry's outstretched hand, and we had pulled him up high and dry into the tunnel.

'My word!' he said, between his gasps, 'that was touch and go. If I hadn't managed to catch that rock, and known how to swim, I should have been done. It runs like a mill-race, and I could feel no bottom.'

We dared not follow the banks of the subterranean river for fear lest we should fall into it again in the darkness. So after Good had rested a while, and we had drunk our fill of the water, which was sweet and fresh, and washed our faces, that needed it sadly, as well as we could, we started from the banks of this African Styx, and began to retrace our steps along the tunnel, Good dripping unpleasantly in front of us. At length we came to another gallery leading to our right.

'We may as well take it,' said Sir Henry wearily; 'all roads are alike here; we can only go on till we drop.'

Slowly, for a long, long while, we stumbled, utterly exhausted, along this new tunnel, Sir Henry now leading the way. Again I thought of abandoning that basket, but did not.

Suddenly he stopped, and we bumped up against him. 'Look!' he whispered, 'is my brain going, or is that light?'

We stared with all our eyes, and there, yes there, far ahead of us, was a faint, glimmering spot, no larger than a cottage window pane. It was so faint that I doubt if any eyes, except those which, like ours, had for days seen nothing but blackness, could have perceived it at all.

With a gasp of hope we pushed on. In five minutes there was no longer any doubt; it was a patch of faint light. A minute more and a breath of real live air was fanning us. On we struggled. All at once the tunnel narrowed. Sir Henry went on his knees. Smaller yet it grew, till it was only the size of a large fox's earth – it was *earth* now, mind you; the rock had ceased.

A squeeze, a struggle, and Sir Henry was out, and so was Good, and so was I, dragging Foulata's basket after me; and there above us were the blessed stars, and in our nostrils was the sweet air.

Then suddenly something gave, and we were all rolling over and over through grass and bushes and soft, wet soil.

The basket caught in something and I stopped. Sitting up I hallooed lustily. An answering shout came from just below, where Sir Henry's wild career had been checked by some level ground. I scrambled to him, and found him unhurt, though breathless. Then we looked for Good. A little way off we discovered him also, jammed in a forked root. He was a good deal knocked about, but soon came to himself.

We sat down together, there on the grass, and the intensity of feeling was so great that really I think we cried with joy. We had escaped from that awful dungeon, which was so near to becoming our grave. Surely some merciful power guided our footsteps to the jackal hole, for that is what it must have been, at the termination of the tunnel. And see, yonder on the mountains the dawn we had never thought to look upon again was blushing rosy red.

Presently the grey light stole down the slopes, and we saw that we were at the bottom, or rather, nearly at the bottom, of the vast pit in front of the entrance to the cave. Now we could make out the dim forms of the three colossi who sat upon its verge. Doubtless those awful passages, along which we had wandered the livelong night, had been originally in some way connected with the great diamond mine. As for the subterranean river in the bowels of the mountain, heaven only knows what it is, or whence it flows, or whither it goes. I, for one, have no anxiety to trace its course.

Lighter it grew, and lighter yet. We could see each other now, and such a sight as we presented I have never set eyes on before or since. Gaunt-cheeked, hollow-eyed wretches, smeared all over with dust and mud, bruised, bleeding, the long fear of imminent death yet written on our countenances, we were, indeed, a spectacle to frighten the daylight. And yet it is a solemn fact that Good's eyeglass was still fixed in Good's eye. I doubt whether he had ever taken it out at all. Neither the darkness, nor the plunge in the subterranean river, nor the roll down the slope, had been able to separate Good and his eyeglass.

Presently we rose, fearing that our limbs would stiffen if we stopped there longer, and commenced with slow and painful steps to struggle up the sloping sides of the great pit. For an hour or more we toiled steadfastly over the blue clay, dragging ourselves on by the help of the roots and grasses with which it was clothed. But now I had no more thought of leaving the basket; indeed, nothing but death would have parted us.

At last it was done, and we stood by the great road, on that side of the pit which was opposite to the colossi.

At the side of the road, a hundred yards off, a fire was burning in front of some huts, and round the fire were figures. We staggered towards them, supporting one another, and halting every few paces. Presently one of the figures rose, saw us and fell on to the ground, crying out for fear.

'Infadoos, Infadoos! it is we, thy friends.'

He rose; he ran to us, staring wildly, and still shaking with fear.

'Oh, my lords, my lords, it is indeed you come back from the dead! – come back from the dead!'

And the old warrior flung himself down before us, and clasping Sir Henry's knees, he wept aloud for joy.

CHAPTER 19

Ignosi's Farewell

Ten days from that eventful morning found us once more in our old quarters at Loo; and, strange to say, but little the worse for our terrible experience, except that my stubbly hair came out of the treasure cave about three shades greyer than it went in, and that Good never was quite the same after Foulata's death, which seemed to move him very greatly. I am bound to say, looking at the thing from the point of view of an oldish man of the world, that I consider her removal was a fortunate occurrence, since, otherwise, complications would have been sure to ensue. The poor creature was no ordinary native girl, but a person of great, I had almost said stately, beauty, and of considerable refinement of mind. But no amount of beauty or refinement could have made an entanglement between Good and herself a desirable occurrence – for, as she herself put it, 'Can the sun mate with the moon, or the white with the black?'

I need hardly state that we never again penetrated into Solomon's treasure chamber. After we had recovered from our fatigue, a process which took us forty-eight hours, we descended into the great pit in the hope of finding the hole by which we had crept out of the mountain, but with no success. To begin with, rain had fallen, and obliterated our spoor; and what is more, the sides of the vast pit were full of ant-bear and other holes. It was impossible to say to which of these we owed our salvation.

Also, on the day before we started back to Loo, we made a further examination of the wonders of the stalactite cave, and, drawn by a kind of restless feeling, even penetrated once more into the chamber of the dead. Passing beneath the spear of the White Death we gazed, with sensations which it would be quite impossible for me to describe, at the mass of rock that had shut us off from escape, thinking the while of the priceless treasures beyond, of the mysterious old hag whose flattened fragments lay crushed beneath it, and of the fair girl of whose tomb it was the portal. I say gazed at the 'rock', for, examine as we would, we could find no traces of the join of the sliding door; nor, indeed, could we hit upon the secret, now utterly lost, that worked it, though we tried for an hour or more. It is certainly a marvellous bit of mechanism, characteristic, in its massive and yet inscrutable simplicity, of the age which produced it; and I doubt if the world has such another to show.

At last we gave it up in disgust; though, if the mass had suddenly risen before our eyes, I doubt if we should have screwed up courage to step over Gagool's mangled remains, and once more enter the treasure chamber, even in the sure and certain hope of unlimited diamonds. And yet I could have cried at the idea of leaving all that treasure, the biggest treasure probably that in the world's history has ever been accumulated in one spot. But there was no help for it. Only dynamite could force its way through five feet of solid rock.

So we left it. Perhaps, in some remote unborn century, a more fortunate explorer may hit upon the 'open sesame', and flood the world with gems. But, myself, I doubt it. Somehow, I seem to feel that the tens of millions of pounds' worth of jewels which lie in the three stone coffers will never shine round the neck of an earthly beauty. They and Foulata's bones will keep cold company to the end of all things. And yet who can tell?

With a sigh of disappointment we made our way back, and next day started for Loo. Still it was really very ungrateful of us to be disappointed; for, as the reader will remember, by a lucky thought I had taken the precaution to fill the wide pockets of my old shooting coat and trousers with gems before we left our prison-house, also Foulata's basket, which held twice as many more, notwithstanding that the water-bottle had occupied some of its space. A good many of these fell out in the course of our roll down the side of the pit, including several of the big ones, which I had crammed in on the top in my coat pockets. But, comparatively speaking, an enormous quantity still remained, including ninety-three large stones ranging from over two hundred to seventy carats in weight. My old shooting coat and the basket still held sufficient treasure to make us all, if not millionaires as the term is understood in America, at least exceedingly wealthy men, and yet to keep enough stones each to form the three finest sets of gems in Europe. So we had not done so badly.

On arriving at Loo we were most cordially received by Ignosi, whom we found well, and busily engaged in consolidating his power and reorganising the regiments which had suffered most in the great struggle with Twala.

He listened with intense interest to our wonderful story; but when we told him of old Gagool's frightful end he grew thoughtful.

'Come hither,' he called to a very old *induna*, or councillor, who was sitting with others in a circle round the king, but out of earshot. The ancient man rose, approached, saluted, and seated himself.

'Thou art aged,' said Ignosi.

'Aye, my lord the king! Thy father's father and I were born on the same day.'

'Tell me, when thou wast little, didst thou know Gagaool the witch-doctress?'

'Aye, my lord the king!'

'How was she then – young, like thee?'

'Not so, my lord the king! She was even as she is now and as she was in the days of my great grandfather before me; old and dried, very ugly, and full of wickedness.'

'She is no more; she is dead.'

'So, O king! then is an ancient curse taken from the land.'

'Go!'

'*Koom!* I go, Black Puppy, who tore out the old dog's throat. *Koom!*'

'Ye see, my brothers,' said Ignosi, 'this was a strange woman, and I rejoice that she is dead. She would have let you die in the dark place, and mayhap afterwards she had found a way to slay me, as she found a way to slay my father and to set up Twala, whom her black heart loved, in his place. Now go on with the tale; surely there never was its like!'

After I had narrated all the story of our escape, as we had agreed between ourselves that I should, I took the opportunity to address Ignosi on the matter of our departure from Kukuanaland.

'And now, Ignosi,' I said, 'the time has come for us to bid thee farewell, and start to see our own land once more. Behold, Ignosi, thou camest with us as a servant, and now we leave thee a mighty king. If thou art grateful to us, remember to do even as thou didst promise: to rule justly, to respect the law, and to put none to death without a cause. So shalt thou prosper. Tomorrow, at break of day, Ignosi, thou wilt give us an escort who shall lead us across the mountains. Is it not so, O king?'

Ignosi covered his face with his hands for a while before answering.

'My heart is sore,' he said at last; 'your words split my heart in twain. What have I done to you, Incubu, Macumazahn and Bougwan, that ye should leave me desolate? Ye who stood by me in rebellion and in battle, will ye leave me in the day of peace and victory? What will ye – wives? Choose from among the maidens! A place to live in? Behold, the land is yours as far as ye can see. The white man's houses? Ye shall teach my people how to build them. Cattle for beef and milk? Every married man shall bring you an ox or a cow. Wild game to hunt? Does not the elephant walk through my forests, and the river-horse sleep in the reeds? Would ye make war? My *impis* wait your word. If there is anything more which I can give, that will I give you.'

'Nay, Ignosi, we want none of these things,' I answered; 'we would seek our own place.'

'Now do I learn,' said Ignosi bitterly, and with flashing eyes, 'that ye love the bright stones more than me, your friend. Ye have the stones; now ye would go to Natal and across the moving black water and sell them, and be rich, as it is the desire of a white man's heart to be. Cursed for your sake be the white stones and cursed he who seeks them. Death shall it be to him who sets foot in the Place of death to find them. For they are yours, and yours alone. I have spoken. White men, ye can go.'

I laid my hand upon his arm. 'Ignosi,' I said, 'tell us, when thou didst wander in Zululand, and among the white people of Natal, did not thine heart turn to the land thy mother told thee of, thy native land, where thou didst see the light, and play when thou wast little, the land where thy place was?'

'It was even so, Macumazahn.'

'In like manner, Ignosi, do our hearts turn to our land and to our own place.'

Then came a silence. When Ignosi broke it, it was in a different voice. 'I perceive that now, as ever, thy words are wise and full of reason, Macumazahn; that which flies in the air loves not to run along the ground; the white man loves not to live on the level of the black or to house among his kraals. Well, ye must go, and leave my heart sore, because ye will be as dead to me, since from where ye are no tidings can come to me.

'But listen, and let all your brothers know my words. No other white man shall cross the mountains, even if any man live to come so far. I will see no traders with their guns and gin. My people shall fight with the spear, and drink water, like their forefathers before them. I will have no praying-men to put a fear of death into men's hearts, to stir them up against the law of the king, and make a path for the white folk who follow to run on. If a white man comes to my gates I will send him back; if a hundred come I will push them back; if armies come I will make war on them with all my strength, and they shall not prevail against me. None shall ever seek for the shining stones; no, not an army, for if they come I will send a regiment and fill up the pit, and break down the white columns in the caves and choke them with rocks, so that none can reach even to that door of which ye speak, whereof the way to move it is lost. But for you three, Incubu, Macumazahn and Bougwan, the path is always open; for, behold, ye are dearer to me than aught that breathes.

'So ye would go. Infadoos, my uncle and my *induna*, shall take you by the hand and guide you with a regiment. There is, as I have learned, another way across the mountains that he shall show you. Farewell, my brothers, brave white men. See me no more, for I have no heart to bear it. Behold! I make a decree, and it shall be published from the mountains to the mountains; your names, Incubu, Macumazahn and Bougwan, shall be *hlonipa* even as the names of dead kings, and he who speaks them shall die.* So shall your memory be preserved in the land for ever.

'Go now, ere my eyes rain tears like a woman's. At times as ye look back down the path of life, or when ye are old and gather yourselves together to crouch before the fire, because for you the sun has no more heat, ye will think of how we stood shoulder to shoulder in that great battle which thy wise words planned, Macumazahn; of how thou wast the point of the horn that galled Twala's flank, Bougwan; whilst thou stoodst in the ring of the Greys, Incubu, and men went down before thine axe like corn before a sickle; aye, and of how thou didst break that wild bull Twala's strength, and bring his pride to dust. Fare ye well, perchance for ever, Incubu, Macumazahn and Bougwan, my lords and my friends.'

Ignosi rose and looked earnestly at us for a few seconds. Then he threw the corner of his *karross* over his head, so as to cover his face from us.

We went in silence.

Next day at dawn we left Loo, escorted by our old friend Infadoos, who was heartbroken at our departure, and by the regiment of Buffaloes. Early as was the hour, we found the main street of the town lined with multitudes of people, who gave us the royal salute as we passed at the head of the regiment, while the women blessed us for having rid the land of Twala, throwing flowers before us as we went. It was really very affecting, and not the sort of thing one is accustomed to meet with from natives.

One ludicrous incident occurred, however, which I rather welcomed, as it gave us something to laugh at.

Just before we reached the confines of the town, a pretty young

---

* This extraordinary and negative way of showing intense respect is by no means unknown among African people, and the result is that if, as is usual, the name in question has a significance, the meaning must be expressed by an idiom or another word. In this way a memory is preserved for generations, or until the new word utterly supplants the old one.   A.Q.

girl, with some lovely lilies in her hand, ran forward and presented them to Good – somehow they all seemed to like Good; I think his eyeglass and unilateral whiskers gave him a fictitious value – and then said that she had a boon to ask.

'Speak on,' he answered.

'Let my lord show his servant his beautiful white legs, that his servant may look on them and remember them all her days, and tell of them to her children; his servant has travelled four days' journey to see them, for the fame of them has gone throughout the land.'

'I'll be hanged if I do!' exclaimed Good excitedly.

'Come, come, my dear fellow,' said Sir Henry, 'you can't refuse to oblige a lady.'

'I won't,' replied Good obstinately; 'it is positively indecent.'

However, in the end he consented to draw up his trousers to the knee, amidst notes of rapturous admiration from all the women present, especially the gratified young lady, and in this guise he had to walk till we got clear of the town.

Good's legs, I fear, will never be so greatly admired again. Of his melting teeth, and even of his 'transparent eye', the Kukuanas wearied more or less, but of his legs, never.

As we travelled, Infadoos told us that there was another pass over the mountains to the north of the one followed by Solomon's Great Road, or rather that there was a place where it is possible to climb down the wall of cliff which separates Kukuanaland from the desert and is broken by the towering shapes of Sheba's Breasts. It appeared, also, that rather more than two years previously a party of Kukuana hunters had descended this path into the desert in search of ostriches, whose plumes are much prized among them for war headdresses, and that in the course of their hunt they had been led far from the mountains and were much troubled by thirst. Seeing trees on the horizon, however, they walked towards them and discovered a large and fertile oasis some miles in extent, and plentifully watered. It was by way of this oasis that Infadoos suggested we should return, and the idea seemed to us a good one, for it appeared that we should thus escape the rigours of the mountain pass. Also some of the hunters were in attendance to guide us to the oasis, from which, they stated, they could perceive other fertile spots far away in the desert.*

Travelling easily, on the night of the fourth day's journey we found ourselves once more on the crest of the mountains that separate Kukuanaland from the desert which rolled away in sandy billows at our feet, and about twenty-five miles to the north of Sheba's Breasts.

At dawn on the following day, we were led to the edge of a very precipitous chasm, by which we were to descend, and gain the plain two thousand or more feet below.

Here we bade farewell to that true friend and sturdy old warrior, Infadoos, who solemnly wished all good upon us, and nearly wept with grief. 'Never, my lords,' he said, 'shall mine old eyes see the like of you again. Ah! the way that Incubu cut his men down in the battle! Ah! for the sight of that stroke with which he swept off my brother Twala's head! It was beautiful – beautiful! I may never hope to see such another, except perchance in happy dreams.'

We were very sorry to part from him; indeed, Good was so moved that he gave him as a souvenir – what do you think? – an *eyeglass*; afterwards we discovered that it was a spare one. Infadoos was delighted, foreseeing that the possession of such an article would increase his prestige enormously, and after several vain attempts he actually succeeded in screwing it into his own eye. Anything more incongruous than the old warrior looked with an

---

* It often puzzled all of us to understand how it was possible that Ignosi's mother, bearing the child with her, should have survived the dangers of her journey across the mountains and the desert, dangers which so nearly proved fatal to ourselves. It has since occurred to me, and I give the idea to the reader for what it is worth, that she must have taken this second route, and wandered out like Hagar into the wilderness. If she did so, there is no longer anything inexplicable about the story, since, as Ignosi himself related, she may well have been picked up by some ostrich hunters before she or the child was exhausted, and led by them to the oasis. Thence she may have travelled by stages to the fertile country, and so on by slow degrees southwards to Zululand.

A.Q.

eyeglass I never saw. Eyeglasses do not go well with leopard-skin cloaks and black ostrich plumes.

Then, after seeing that our guides were well laden with water and provisions, and having received a thundering farewell salute from the Buffaloes, we wrung Infadoos by the hand, and began our downward climb. A very arduous business it proved to be, but somehow that evening we found ourselves at the bottom without accident.

'Do you know,' said Sir Henry that night, as we sat by our fire and gazed up at the beetling cliffs above us, 'I think that there are worse places than Kukuanaland in the world, and that I have known unhappier times than the last month or two, though I have never spent such queer ones. Eh! you fellows?'

'I almost wish I were back,' said Good with a sigh.

As for myself, I reflected that all's well that ends well; but that in the course of a long life of peril, I never had such shaves as those which I had recently experienced. The thought of that battle still makes me feel cold all over, and as for our experience in the treasure chamber – !

Next morning we started on a toilsome trudge across the desert, having with us a good supply of water carried by our five guides, and camped that night in the open, marching again at dawn on the morrow.

By noon of the third day's journey we could see the trees of the oasis of which the guides spoke, and within an hour of sundown we were walking once more upon grass and listening to the sound of running water.

CHAPTER 20

Found

And now I come to perhaps the strangest adventure that happened to us in all this strange business; one, too, which shows how wonderfully things are brought about.

I was walking along quietly, some way in front of the other two, down the banks of the stream which runs from the oasis till it is swallowed up in the hungry desert sands, when suddenly I stopped and rubbed my eyes, as well I might. There, not twenty yards in front of me, placed in a charming situation, under the shade of a species of fig tree, and facing to the stream, was a cosy hut, built more or less on the Kafir principle with grass and withies, but having a full-length door instead of a bee-hole.

'What the dickens,' said I to myself, 'can a hut be doing here?' Even as I said it the door of the hut opened, and there limped out of it a white man clothed in skins and an enormous black beard. I thought that I must have got a touch of the sun. It was impossible. No hunter ever came to such a place as this. Certainly no hunter would ever settle in it. I stared and stared, and so did the other man, and just at that juncture Sir Henry and Good walked up.

'Look here, you fellows,' I said, 'is that a white man, or am I mad?'

Sir Henry looked, and Good looked, and then all of a sudden the lame white man with the black beard uttered a great cry, and began hobbling towards us. When he was close he fell down in a sort of faint.

With a spring Sir Henry was by his side.

'Great Powers!' he cried. '*It is my brother George!*'

At the sound of the disturbance, another figure, also clad in skins, emerged from the hut, a gun in his hand, and ran towards us. On seeing me he too gave a cry.

'Macumazahn,' he hallooed, 'don't you know me, baas? I'm Jim the hunter. I lost the note you gave me to give to the baas, and we have been here nearly two years.' And the fellow fell at my feet, and rolled over and over, weeping for joy.

'You careless scroundrel!' I said. 'You ought to be well *sjambocked*' – that is hided.

Meanwhile the man with the black beard had recovered and risen, and he and Sir Henry were pump-handling away at each other apparently without a word to say. But whatever they had quarrelled about in the past – I suspect it was a lady, though I never asked – it was evidently forgotten now.

'My dear old fellow,' burst out Sir Henry at last, 'I thought that you were dead. I have been over Solomon's Mountains to find you. I had given up all hope of ever seeing you again, and now I come across you perched in the desert, like an old *aasvögel*.'

'I tried to cross Solomon's Mountains nearly two years ago,' was the answer, spoken in the hesitating voice of a man who has had little recent opportunity of using his tongue, 'but when I reached here a boulder fell on my leg and crushed it, and I have been able to go neither forward nor back.'

Then I came up. 'How do you do, Mr Neville?' I said; 'do you remember me?'

'Why,' he said, 'isn't it Hunter Quatermain, eh, and Good, too? Hold on a minute, you fellows, I am getting dizzy again. It is all so very strange, and, when a man has ceased to hope, such happiness is too much!'

That evening, over the camp fire, George Curtis told us his story, which, in its way, was almost as eventful as our own, and, put shortly, amounted to this. A little less than two years before, he had started from Sitanda's Kraal, to try to reach Suliman's Berge. As for the note I had sent him by Jim, that worthy lost it, and he had never heard of it till today. But, acting upon information he received from the natives, he headed not for Sheba's Breasts, but for the ladder-like descent of the mountains down which we had just come, clearly a much better route than that marked out in old Dom da Silvestra's plan. In the desert he and Jim suffered great hardship but finally they reached this oasis, where a terrible accident befell George Curtis. On the day of their arrival he was sitting by the stream, and Jim was extracting the honey from the nest of a stingless bee which is to be found in the desert, on the top of a bank immediately above him. In so doing he loosened a great boulder of rock, which fell upon George Curtis's right leg, crushing it frightfully. From that day he had been so lame that he found it impossible to go either forward or back, and had preferred to take the chance of dying in the oasis to the certainty of perishing in the desert.

As for food, however, they got on pretty well, for they had a good supply of ammunition, and the oasis was frequented, especially at night, by large quantities of game, which came thither for water. These they shot, or trapped in pitfalls, using the flesh to eat, and, after their clothes wore out, the hides for clothing.

'And so,' George Curtis ended, 'we have lived for nearly two years, like a second Robinson Crusoe and his man Friday, hoping against hope that some natives might come here to help us away, but none have come. Only last night we settled that Jim should leave me, and try to reach Sitanda's Kraal to get assistance. He was to go tomorrow, but I had little hope of ever seeing him back again. And now you, of all people in the world, you, who, as I fancied, had long ago forgotten all about me, and were living comfortably in old England, turn up in a promiscuous way and find me where you least expected. It is the most wonderful thing that I have ever heard of, and the most merciful too.'

Then Sir Henry set to work and told him the main facts of our adventures, sitting till late into the night to do so.

'By Jove!' said George Curtis, when I showed him some of the diamonds. 'Well, at least you have got something for your pains, besides my worthless self.'

Sir Henry laughed. 'They belong to Quatermain and Good. It was a part of the bargain that they should divide any spoils there might be.'

This remark set me thinking, and having spoken to Good, I told Sir Henry that it was our joint wish that he should take a third portion of the diamonds, or, if he would not, that his share should be handed to his brother, who had suffered even more than ourselves on the chance of getting them. Finally, we prevailed upon him to consent to this arrangement, but George Curtis did not know of it until some time afterwards.

*   *   *

Here, at this point, I think that I shall end my history. Our journey across the desert back to Sitanda's Kraal was most arduous, especially as we had to support George Curtis, whose right leg was very weak indeed, and continually threw out splinters of bone. But we did accomplish it somehow, and to give its details would only be to reproduce much of what happened to us on the former occasion.

Six months from the date of our re-arrival at Sitanda's, where we found our guns and other goods quite safe, though the old rascal in charge was much disgusted at our surviving to claim them, saw us all once more safe and sound at my little place in the Berea, near Durban, where I am now writing. Thence I bid farewell to all who have accompanied me throughout the strangest trip I ever made in the course of a long and varied experience.

PS – Just as I had written the last word, a Kafir came up my avenue of orange trees, carrying a letter in a cleft stick, which he had brought from the post. It turned out to be from Sir Henry, and as it speaks for itself I give it in full.

October 1, 1880
Brayley Hall, Yorkshire

MY DEAR QUATERMAIN – I sent you a line a few mails back to say that the three of us, George, Good and myself, fetched up all right in England. We got off the boat at Southampton, and went up to town. You should have seen what a swell Good turned out the very next day, beautifully shaved, frock-coat fitting like a glove, brand-new eyeglass, etc., etc. I went for a walk in the park with him, where I met some people I know, and at once told them the story of his 'beautiful white legs'.

He is furious, especially as an ill-natured person has printed it in a society paper.

To come to business, Good and I took the diamonds to Streeter's to be valued, as we arranged, and really I am afraid to tell you what they put them at, it seems so enormous. They say that of course it is more or less guesswork as such stones have never to their knowledge been put on the market in anything like such quantities. It appears that (with the exception of one or two of the largest) they are of the finest water, and equal in every way to the best Brazilian stones. I asked them if they would buy them, but they said that it was beyond their power to do so, and recommended us to sell by degrees, over a period of years indeed, for fear lest we should flood the market. They offer, however, a hundred and eighty thousand pounds for a very small portion of them.

You must come home, Quatermain, and see about these things, especially if you insist upon making the magnificent present of the third share, which does not belong to me, to my brother George. As for Good, he is *no good*. His time is too much occupied in shaving, and other matters connected with the vain adorning of the body. But I think he is still down on his luck about Foulata. He told me that since he had been home he hadn't seen a woman to touch her, either as regards her figure or the sweetness of her expression.

I want you to come home, my dear old comrade, and to buy a house near here. You have done your day's work, and have lots of money now, and there is a place for sale quite close which would suit you admirably. Do come; the sooner the better; you can finish writing the story of our adventures on board ship. We have refused to tell the tale till it is written by you, for fear lest we shall not be believed. If you start on receipt of this you will reach here by Christmas, and I book you to stay with me for that. Good is coming, and George; and so, by the way, is your boy Harry (there's a bribe for you). I have had him down for a week's shooting, and like him. He is a cool young hand; he shot me in the leg, cut out the pellets, and then remarked upon the advantages of having a medical student with every shooting party!

Goodbye, old boy; I can't say any more, but I know that you will come, if it is only to oblige

Your sincere friend,

HENRY CURTIS

PS – The tusks of the great bull that killed poor Khiva have now been put up in the hall here, over the pair of buffalo horns you gave me, and look magnificent; and the axe with which I chopped off Twala's head is fixed above my writing-table. I wish that we could have managed to bring away the coats of chain armour. Don't lose poor Foulata's basket in which you carried off the diamonds.   H. C.

Today is Tuesday. There is a steamer going on Friday, and I really think that I must take Curtis at his word, and sail by her for England, if it is only to see you, Harry, my boy, and to look after the printing of this history, which is a task that I do not like to trust to anybody else.

ALLAN QUATERMAIN

Allan Quatermain

being an account of his further adventures in
company with Sir Henry Curtis, BART,
Commander John Good, RN,
and one Umslopogaas

EX AFRICA SEMPER ALIQUID NOVI

[*Always something new out of Africa*]

I inscribe this book of adventure to my son

ARTHUR JOHN RIDER HAGGARD

*in the hope that in days to come he, and many other boys
whom I shall never know may, in the acts and thoughts of
Allan Quatermain and his companions, as herein recorded,
find something to help him and them to reach to what,
with Sir Henry Curtis, I hold to be the highest rank whereto
we can attain – the state and dignity of English gentlemen.*

INTRODUCTION

I have just buried my boy, my poor handsome boy of whom I was so proud, and my heart is broken. It is very hard having only one son to lose him thus, but God's will be done. Who am I that I should complain? The great wheel of Fate rolls on like a Juggernaut, and crushes us all in turn, some soon, some late – it does not matter when, in the end, it crushes us all. We do not prostrate ourselves before it like the poor Indians; we fly hither and thither – we cry for mercy; but it is of no use, the black Fate thunders on and in its season reduces us to powder.

Poor Harry to go so soon! just when his life was opening to him. He was doing so well at the hospital, he had passed his last examination with honours, and I was proud of them, much prouder than he was, I think. And then he must needs go to that smallpox hospital. He wrote to me that he was not afraid of smallpox and wanted to gain the experience; and now the disease has killed him, and I, old and grey and withered, am left to mourn over him, without a chick or child to comfort me. I might have saved him, too – I have money enough for both of us, and much more than enough – King Solomon's Mines provided me with that; but I said, 'No, let the boy earn his living, let him labour that he may enjoy rest.' But the rest has come to him before the labour. Oh, my boy, my boy!

I am like the man in the Bible who laid up much goods and builded barns – goods for my boy and barns for him to store them in; and now his soul has been required of him, and I am left desolate. I would that it had been my soul and not my boy's!

We buried him this afternoon under the shadow of the grey and ancient tower of the church of this village where my house is. It was a dreary December afternoon, and the sky was heavy with snow, but not much was falling. The coffin was put down by the grave, and a few big flakes lit upon it. They looked very white upon the black cloth! There was a little hitch about getting the coffin down into the grave – the necessary ropes had been forgotten: so we drew back from it, and waited in silence watching the big flakes fall gently one by one like heavenly benedictions, and melt in tears on Harry's pall. But that was not all. A robin redbreast came as bold as could be and lit upon the coffin and began to sing. And then I am afraid that I broke down, and so did Sir Henry Curtis, strong man though he is; and as for Captain Good, I saw him turn away too; even in my own distress I could not help noticing it.

The above, signed 'Allan Quatermain', is an extract from my diary written two years and more ago. I copy it down here because it seems to me that it is the fittest beginning to the history that I am about to write, if it please God to spare me to finish it. If not, well it does not matter. That extract was penned seven thousand miles or so from the spot where I now lie painfully and slowly writing this, with a pretty girl standing by my side fanning the flies from my august countenance. Harry is there and I am here, and yet somehow I cannot help feeling that I am not far off Harry.

When I was in England I used to live in a very fine house – at least I call it a fine house, speaking comparatively, and judging from the standard of the houses I have been accustomed to all my life in Africa – not five hundred yards from the old church where Harry is asleep, and thither I went after the funeral and ate some food; for it is no good starving even if one has just buried all one's earthly hopes. But I could not eat much, and soon I took to walking, or rather limping – being permanently lame from the bite of a lion – up and down, up and down the oak-panelled vestibule; for there is a vestibule in my house in England. On all the four walls of this vestibule were placed pairs of horns – about a hundred pairs altogether, all of which I had shot myself. They are beautiful specimens, as I never keep any horns which are not in every way perfect, unless it may be now and again on account of the associations connected with them. In the centre of the room, however, over the wide fireplace, there was a clear space left on which I had fixed up all my rifles. Some of them I have had for forty years, old muzzle-loaders that nobody would look at nowadays. One was an elephant gun with strips of rimpi, or green hide, lashed round the stock and locks, such as used to be owned by the Dutchmen – a 'roer' they call it. That gun, the Boer I bought it from many years ago told me, had been used by his father at the battle of the Blood River, just after Dingaan swept into Natal and slaughtered six hundred men, women, and children, so that the Boers named the place where they died 'Weenen', or the 'Place of Weeping'; and so it is called to this day, and always will be called. And many an elephant have I shot with that old gun. She always took a handful of black powder and a three-ounce ball, and kicked like the very deuce.

Well, up and down I walked, staring at the guns and the horns which the guns had brought low; and as I did so there rose up in me a great craving: I would go away from this place where I lived idly and at ease, back again to the wild land where I had spent my life, where I met my dear wife and poor Harry was born, and so many things, good, bad, and indifferent, had happened to me. The thirst for the wilderness was on me; I could tolerate this place no more; I would go and die as I had lived, among the wild game and the savages. Yes, as I walked, I began to long to see the moonlight gleaming silvery white over the wide veldt and mysterious sea of bush, and watch the lines of game travelling down the ridges to the water. The ruling passion is strong in death, they say, and my heart was dead that night. But, independently of my trouble, no man who has for forty years lived the life I have, can with impunity go coop himself in this prim English country, with its trim hedgerows and cultivated fields, its stiff formal manners, and its well-dressed crowds. He begins to long – ah, how he longs! – for the keen breath of the desert air; he dreams of the sight of Zulu impis breaking on their foes like surf upon the rocks, and his heart rises up in rebellion against the strict limits of the civilised life.

Ah! this civilisation, what does it all come to? For forty years and more I lived among savages, and studied them and their ways;

and now for several years I have lived here in England, and have in my own stupid manner done my best to learn the ways of the children of light; and what have I found? A great gulf fixed? No, only a very little one, that a plain man's thought may spring across. I say that as the savage is, so is the white man, only the latter is more inventive, and possesses the faculty of combination; save and except also that the savage, as I have known him, is to a large extent free from the greed of money, which eats like a cancer into the heart of the white man. It is a depressing conclusion, but in all essentials the savage and the child of civilisation are identical. I dare say that the highly civilised lady reading this will smile at an old fool of a hunter's simplicity when she thinks of her black bead-bedecked sister; and so will the superfine cultured idler scientifically eating a dinner at his club, the cost of which would keep a starving family for a week. And yet, my dear young lady, what are those pretty things round your own neck? – they have a strong family resemblance, especially when you wear that *very* low dress, to the savage woman's beads. Your habit of turning round and round to the sound of horns and tom-toms, your fondness for pigments and powders, the way in which you love to subjugate yourself to the rich warrior who has captured you in marriage, and the quickness with which your taste in feathered head-dresses varies – all these things suggest touches of kinship; and you remember that in the fundamental principles of your nature you are quite identical. As for you, sir, who also laugh, let some man come and strike you in the face whilst you are enjoying that marvellous-looking dish, and we shall soon see how much of the savage there is in *you*.

There, I might go on for ever, but what is the good? Civilisation is only savagery silver-gilt. A vainglory is it, and like a northern light, comes but to fade and leave the sky more dark. Out of the soil of barbarism it has grown like a tree, and, as I believe, into the soil like a tree it will once more, sooner or later, fall again, as the Egyptian civilisation fell, as the Hellenic civilisation fell, and as the Roman civilisation and many others of which the world has now lost count, fell also. Do not let me, however, be understood as decrying our modern institutions, representing as they do the gathered experience of humanity applied for the good of all. Of course they have great advantages – hospitals for instance; but then, remember, we breed the sickly people who fill them. In a savage land they do not exist. Besides, the question will arise: How many of these blessings are due to Christianity as distinct from civilisation? And so the balance sways and the story runs – here a gain, there a loss, and Nature's great average struck across the two, whereof the sum total forms one of the factors in that mighty equation in which the result will equal the unknown quantity of her purpose.

I make no apology for this digression, especially as this is an introduction which all young people and those who never like to think (and it is a bad habit) will naturally skip. It seems to me very desirable that we should sometimes try to understand the limitations of our nature, so that we may not be carried away by the pride of knowledge. Man's cleverness is almost indefinite, and stretches like an elastic band, but human nature is like an iron ring. You can go round and round it, you can polish it highly, you can even flatten it a little on one side, whereby you will make it bulge out the other, but you will *never*, while the world endures and man is man, increase its total circumference. It is the one fixed unchangeable thing – fixed as the stars, more enduring than the mountains, as unalterable as the way of the Eternal. Human nature is God's kaleidoscope, and the little bits of coloured glass which represent our passions, hopes, fears, joys, aspirations towards good and evil and what not, are turned in His mighty hand as surely and as certainly as it turns the stars, and continually fall into new patterns and combinations. But the composing elements remain the same, nor will there be one more bit of coloured glass nor one less for ever and ever.

This being so, supposing for the sake of argument we divide ourselves into twenty parts, nineteen savage and one civilised, we must look to the nineteen savage portions of our nature, if we would really understand ourselves, and not to the twentieth, which, though so insignificant in reality, is spread all over the other nineteen, making them appear quite different from what they really are, as the blacking does a boot, or the veneer a table.

It is on the nineteen rough serviceable savage portions that we fall back on emergencies, not on the polished but unsubstantial twentieth. Civilisation should wipe away our tears, and yet we weep and cannot be comforted. Warfare is abhorrent to her, and yet we strike out for hearth and home, for honour and fair fame, and can glory in the blow. And so on, through everything.

So, when the heart is stricken, and the head is humbled in the dust, civilisation fails us utterly. Back, back, we creep, and lay us like little children on the great breast of Nature, she that perchance may soothe us and make us forget, or at least rid remembrance of its sting. Who has not in his great grief felt a longing to look upon the outward features of the universal Mother; to lie on the mountains and watch the clouds drive across the sky and hear the rollers break in thunder on the shore, to let his poor struggling life mingle for a while in her life; to feel the slow beat of her eternal heart, and to forget his woes, and let his identity be swallowed in the vast imperceptibly moving energy of her of whom we are, from whom we came, and with whom we shall again be mingled, who gave us birth, and will in a day to come give us our burial also.

And so in my trouble, as I walked up and down the oak-panelled vestibule of my house there in Yorkshire, I longed once more to throw myself into the arms of Nature. Not the Nature which you know, the Nature that waves in well-kept woods and smiles out in cornfields, but Nature as she was in the age when creation was complete, undefiled as yet by any human sinks of sweltering humanity. I would go again where the wild game was, back to the land whereof none know the history, back to the savages, whom I love, although some of them are almost as merciless as Political Economy. There, perhaps, I should be able to learn to think of poor Harry lying in the churchyard, without feeling as though my heart would break in two.

And now there is an end of this egotistical talk, and there shall be no more of it. But if you whose eyes may perchance one day fall upon my written thoughts have got so far as this, I ask you to persevere, since what I have to tell you is not without its interest, and it has never been told before, nor will again.

CHAPTER I

The Consul's Yarn

A week had passed since the funeral of my poor boy Harry, and one evening I was in my room walking up and down and thinking, when there was a ring at the outer door. Going down the steps I opened it myself, and in came my old friends Sir Henry Curtis and Captain John Good, RN. They entered the vestibule and sat themselves down before the wide hearth, where, I remember, a particularly good fire of logs was burning.

'It is very kind of you to come round,' I said by way of making a remark; 'it must have been heavy walking in the snow.'

They said nothing, but Sir Henry slowly filled his pipe and lit it with a burning ember. As he leant forward to do so the fire got hold of a gassy bit of pine and flared up brightly, throwing the whole scene into strong relief, and I thought, What a splendid-looking man he is! Calm, powerful face, clear-cut features, large grey eyes, yellow beard and hair – altogether a magnificent specimen of the higher type of humanity. Nor did his form belie his face. I have never seen wider shoulders or a deeper chest. Indeed, Sir Henry's girth is so great that, though he is six feet two high, he does not strike one as a tall man. As I looked at him I could not help thinking what a curious contrast my little dried-up self presented to his grand face and form. Imagine to yourself a small, withered, yellow-faced man of sixty-three, with thin hands, large brown eyes, a head of grizzled hair cut short and standing up like a half-worn scrubbing-brush – total weight in my clothes, nine stone six – and you will get a very fair idea of Allan Quatermain, commonly called Hunter Quatermain, or by the natives 'Macumazahn' – Anglicè, he who keeps a bright look-out at night, or, in vulgar English, a sharp fellow who is not to be taken in.

Then there was Good, who is not like either of us, being short, dark, stout – *very* stout – with twinkling black eyes, in one of which an eyeglass is everlastingly fixed. I say stout, but it is a mild term; I regret to state that of late years Good has been running to fat in a most disgraceful way. Sir Henry tells him that it comes from idleness and over-feeding, and Good does not like it at all, though he cannot deny it.

We sat for a while, and then I got a match and lit the lamp that stood ready on the table, for the half-light began to grow dreary, as it is apt to do when one has a short week ago buried the hope of one's life. Next, I opened a cupboard in the wainscoting and got a bottle of whisky and some tumblers and water. I always like to do these things for myself: it is irritating to me to have somebody continually at my elbow, as though I were an eighteen-month-old baby. All this while Curtis and Good had been silent, feeling, I suppose, that they had nothing to say that could do me any good, and content to give me the comfort of their presence and unspoken sympathy; for it was only their second visit since the funeral. And it is, by the way, from the *presence* of others that we really derive support in our dark hours of grief, and not from their talk, which often only serves to irritate us. Before a bad storm the game always herd together, but they cease their calling.

They sat and smoked and drank whisky and water, and I stood by the fire also smoking and looking at them.

At last I spoke. 'Old friends,' I said, 'how long is it since we got back from Kukuanaland?'

'Three years,' said Good. 'Why do you ask?'

'I ask because I think that I have had a long enough spell of civilisation. I am going back to the veldt.'

Sir Henry laid his head back in his armchair and laughed one of his deep laughs. 'How very odd,' he said, 'eh, Good?'

Good beamed at me mysteriously through his eyeglass and murmured, 'Yes, odd – very odd.'

'I don't quite understand,' said I, looking from one to the other, for I dislike mysteries.

'Don't you, old fellow?' said Sir Henry; 'then I will explain. As Good and I were walking up here we had a talk.'

'If Good was there you probably did,' I put in sarcastically, for Good is a great hand at talking. 'And what may it have been about?'

'What do you think?' asked Sir Henry.

I shook my head. It was not likely that I should know what Good might be talking about. He talks about so many things.

'Well, it was about a little plan that I have formed – namely, that if you were willing we should pack up our traps and go off to Africa on another expedition.'

I fairly jumped at his words. 'You don't say so!' I said.

'Yes I do, though, and so does Good; don't you, Good?'

'Rather,' said that gentleman.

'Listen, old fellow,' went on Sir Henry, with considerable animation of manner. 'I'm tired of it too, dead-tired of doing nothing more except play the squire in a country that is sick of squires. For a year or more I have been getting as restless as an old elephant who scents danger. I am always dreaming of Kukuanaland and Gagool and King Solomon's Mines. I can assure you I have become the victim of an almost unaccountable craving. I am sick of shooting pheasants and partridges, and want to have a go at some large game again. There, you know the feeling – when one has once tasted brandy and water, milk becomes insipid to the palate. That year we spent together up in Kukuanaland seems to me worth all the other years of my life put together. I dare say that I am a fool for my pains, but I can't help it; I long to go, and, what is more, I mean to go.' He paused, and then went on again. 'And, after all, why should I not go? I have no wife or parent, no chick or child to keep me. If anything happens to me the baronetcy will go to my brother George and his boy, as it would ultimately do in any case. I am of no importance to anyone.'

'Ah!' I said, 'I thought you would come to that sooner or later. And now, Good, what is your reason for wanting to trek; have you got one?'

'I have,' said Good, solemnly. 'I never do anything without a reason; and it isn't a lady – at least, if it is, it's several.'

I looked at him again. Good is so overpoweringly frivolous. 'What is it?' I said.

'Well, if you really want to know, though I'd rather not speak of a delicate and strictly personal matter, I'll tell you: I'm getting too fat.'

'Shut up, Good!' said Sir Henry. 'And now, Quatermain, tell us, where do you propose going to?'

I lit my pipe, which had gone out, before answering.

'Have you people ever heard of Mt Kenia?' I asked.

'Don't know the place,' said Good.

'Did you ever hear of the Island of Lamu?' I asked again.

'No. Stop, though – isn't it a place about three hundred miles north of Zanzibar?'

'Yes. Now listen. What I have to propose is this. That we go to Lamu and thence make our way about two hundred and fifty miles inland to Mt Kenia; from Mt Kenia on inland to Mt Lekakisera, another two hundred miles, or thereabouts, beyond which no white man has to the best of my belief ever been; and then, if we get so far, right on into the unknown interior. What do you say to that, my hearties?'

'It's a big order,' said Sir Henry, reflectively.

'You are right,' I answered, 'it is; but I take it that we are all three of us in search of a big order. We want a change of scene, and we are likely to get one – a thorough change. All my life I have longed to visit those parts, and I mean to do it before I die. My poor boy's death has broken the last link between me and civilisation, and I'm off to my native wilds. And now I'll tell you another thing, and that is, that for years and years I have heard rumours of a great white race which is supposed to have its home somewhere up in this direction, and I have a mind to see if there is any truth in them. If you fellows like to come, well and good; if not, I'll go alone.'

'I'm your man, though I don't believe in your white race,' said Sir Henry Curtis, rising and placing his arm upon my shoulder.

'Ditto,' remarked Good. 'I'll go into training at once. By all means let's go to Mt Kenia and the other place with an unpronounceable name, and look for a white race that does not exist. It's all one to me.'

'When do you propose to start?' asked Sir Henry.

'This day month,' I answered, 'by the British India steamboat;

and don't you be so certain that things have no existence because you do not happen to have heard of them. Remember King Solomon's Mines!'

Some fourteen weeks or so had passed since the date of this conversation, and this history goes on its way in very different surroundings.

After much deliberation and enquiry we came to the conclusion that our best starting-point for Mt Kenia would be from the neighbourhood of the mouth of the Tana River, and not from Mombasa, a place over a hundred miles nearer Zanzibar. This conclusion we arrived at from information given to us by a German trader whom we met upon the steamer at Aden. I think that he was the dirtiest German I ever knew; but he was a good fellow, and gave us a great deal of valuable information. 'Lamu,' said he, 'you goes to Lamu – oh ze beautiful place!' and he turned up his fat face and beamed with mild rapture. 'One year and a half I live there and never change my shirt – never at all.'

And so it came to pass that on arriving at the island we disembarked with all our goods and chattels, and, not knowing where to go, marched boldly up to the house of Her Majesty's Consul, where we were most hospitably received.

Lamu is a very curious place, but the things which stand out most clearly in my memory in connection with it are its exceeding dirtiness and its smells. These last are simply awful. Just below the Consulate is the beach, or rather a mud bank that is called a beach. It is left quite bare at low tide, and serves as a repository for all the filth, offal, and refuse of the town. Here it is, too, that the women come to bury coconuts in the mud, leaving them there till the outer husk is quite rotten, when they dig them up again and use the fibres to make mats with, and for various other purposes. As this process has been going on for generations, the condition of the shore can be better imagined than described. I have smelt many evil odours in the course of my life, but the concentrated essence of stench which arose from that beach at Lamu as we sat in the moonlit night – not under, but *on* our friend the Consul's hospitable roof – and sniffed it, makes the remembrance of them very poor and faint. No wonder people get fever at Lamu. And yet the place was not without a certain quaintness and charm of its own, though possibly – indeed probably – it was one which would quickly pall.

'Well, where are you gentlemen steering for?' asked our friend the hospitable Consul, as we smoked our pipes after dinner.

'We propose to go to Mt Kenia and then on to Mt Lekakisera,' answered Sir Henry. 'Quatermain has got hold of some yarn about there being a white race up in the unknown territories beyond.'

The Consul looked interested, and answered that he had heard something of that, too.

'What have you heard?' I asked.

'Oh, not much. All I know about it is that a year or so ago I got a letter from Mackenzie, the Scotch missionary, whose station, the "Highlands", is placed at the highest navigable point of the Tana River, in which he said something about it.'

'Have you the letter?' I asked.

'No, I destroyed it; but I remember that he said that a man had arrived at his station who declared that two months' journey beyond Mt Lekakisera, which no white man has yet visited – at least, so far as I know – he found a lake called Laga, and that then he went off to the north-east, a month's journey, over desert and thorn veldt and great mountains, till he came to a country where the people are white and live in stone houses. Here he was hospitably entertained for a while, till at last the priests of the country set it about that he was a devil, and the people drove him away, and he journeyed for eight months and reached Mackenzie's place, as I heard, dying. That's all I know; and if you ask me, I believe that it is a lie; but if you want to find out more about it, you had better go up the Tana to Mackenzie's place and ask him for information.'

Sir Henry and I looked at each other. Here was something tangible.

'I think that we will go to Mr Mackenzie's,' I said.

'Well,' answered the Consul, 'that is your best way, but I warn you that you are likely to have a rough journey, for I hear that the Masai are about, and, as you know, they are not pleasant customers. Your best plan will be to choose a few picked men for personal servants and hunters, and to hire bearers from village to village. It will give you an infinity of trouble, but perhaps on the whole it will prove a cheaper and more advantageous course than engaging a caravan, and you will be less liable to desertion.'

Fortunately there were at Lamu at this time a party of Wakwafi Askari (soldiers). The Wakwafi, who are a cross between the Masai and the Wataveta, are a fine manly race, possessing many of the good qualities of the Zulu, and a great capacity for civilisation. They are also great hunters. As it happened, these particular men had recently been on a long trip with an Englishman named Jutson, who had started from Mombasa, a port about a hundred and fifty miles below Lamu, and journeyed right round Kiliman-jaro, one of the highest known mountains in Africa. Poor fellow, he had died of fever when on his return journey, and within a day's march of Mombasa. It does seem hard that he should have gone off thus when within a few hours of safety, and after having survived so many perils, but so it was. His hunters buried him, and then came on to Lamu in a dhow. Our friend the Consul suggested to us that we had better try and hire these men, and accordingly on the following morning we started to interview the party, accompanied by an interpreter.

In due course we found them in a mud hut on the outskirts of the town. Three of the men were sitting outside the hut, and fine frank-looking fellows they were, having a more or less civilised appearance. To them we cautiously opened the object of our visit, at first with very scant success. They declared that they could not entertain any such idea, that they were worn and weary with long travelling, and that their hearts were sore at the loss of their master. They meant to go back to their homes and rest awhile. This did not sound very promising, so by way of effecting a diversion I asked where the remainder of them were. I was told there were six, and I saw but three. One of the men said they slept in the hut, and were yet resting after their labours – 'sleep weighed down their eyelids, and sorrow made their hearts as lead: it was best to sleep, for with sleep came forgetfulness. But the men should be awakened.'

Presently they came out of the hut, yawning – the first two men being evidently of the same race and style as those already before us; but the appearance of the third and last nearly made me jump out of my skin. He was a very tall, broad man, quite six foot three, I should say, but gaunt, with lean, wiry-looking limbs. My first glance at him told me that he was no Wakwafi: he was a pure bred Zulu. He came out with his thin aristocratic-looking hand placed before his face to hide a yawn, so I could only see that he was a 'Keshla' or ringed man,* and that he had a great three-cornered hole in his forehead. In another second he removed his hand, revealing a powerful-looking Zulu face, with a humorous mouth, a short woolly beard, tinged with grey, and a pair of brown eyes keen as a hawk's. I knew my man at once, although I had not seen him for twelve years. 'How do you do, Umslopogaas?' I said quietly in Zulu.

The tall man (who among his own people was commonly known as the 'Woodpecker', and also as the 'Slaughterer') started, and almost let the long-handled battleaxe he held in his hand fall in his astonishment. Next second he had recognised me, and was saluting me in an outburst of sonorous language which made his companions the Wakwafi stare.

'Koos' (chief), he began, 'Koos-y-Pagete! Koos-y-umcool! (Chief from of old – mighty chief) Koos! Baba! (father) Macuma-zahn, old hunter, slayer of elephants, eater up of lions, clever one! watchful one! brave one! quick one! whose shot never misses, who strikes straight home, who grasps a hand and holds it to the death (i.e. is a true friend) Koos! Baba! Wise is the voice of our people that says, "Mountain never meets with mountain, but at daybreak or at even man shall meet again with man." Behold! a messenger came up from Natal, "Macumazahn is dead!" cried he. "The land knows Macumazahn no more." That is years ago. And now, behold, now in this strange place of stinks I find Macumazahn, my

* Among the Zulus a man assumes the ring, which is made of a species of black gum twisted in with the hair, and polished a brilliant black, when he has reached a certain dignity and age, or is the husband of a sufficient number of wives. Till he is in a position to wear a ring he is looked on as a boy, though he may be thirty-five years of age, or even more. A.Q.

friend. There is no room for doubt. The brush of the old jackal has gone a little grey; but is not his eye as keen, and are not his teeth as sharp? Ha! ha! Macumazahn, mindest thou how thou didst plant the ball in the eye of the charging buffalo – mindest thou – '

I had let him run on thus because I saw that his enthusiasm was producing a marked effect upon the minds of the five Wakwafi, who appeared to understand something of his talk; but now I thought it time to put a stop to it, for there is nothing that I hate so much as this Zulu system of extravagant praising – 'bongering' as they call it. 'Silence!' I said. 'Has all thy noisy talk been stopped up since last I saw thee that it breaks out thus, and sweeps us away? What doest thou here with these men – thou whom I left a chief in Zululand? How is it that thou art far from thine own place, and gathered together with strangers?'

Umslopogaas leant himself upon the head of his long battleaxe (which was nothing else but a pole-axe, with a beautiful handle of rhinoceros horn), and his grim face grew sad.

'My father,' he answered, 'I have a word to tell thee, but I cannot speak it before these low people (umfagozana),' and he glanced at the Wakwafi Askari; 'it is for thine own ear. My Father, this will I say,' and here his face grew stern again, 'a woman betrayed me to the death, and covered my name with shame – ay, my own wife, a round-faced girl, betrayed me; but I escaped from death; ay, I broke from the very hands of those who came to slay me. I struck but three blows with this mine axe Inkosikaas – surely my father will remember it – one to the right, one to the left, and one in front, and yet I left three men dead. And then I fled, and, as my father knows, even now that I am old my feet are as the feet of the Sassaby,* and there breathes not the man who, by running, can touch me again when once I have bounded from his side. On I sped, and after me came the messengers of death, and their voice was as the voice of dogs that hunt. From my own kraal I flew, and, as I passed, she who had betrayed me was drawing water from the spring. I fleeted by her like the shadow of Death, and as I went I

* One of the fleetest of the African antelopes. A.Q.

smote with mine axe, and lo! her head fell: it fell into the water pan. Then I fled north. Day after day I journeyed on; for three moons I journeyed, resting not, stopping not, but running on towards forgetfulness, till I met the party of the white hunter who is now dead, and am come hither with his servants. And nought have I brought with me. I who was high-born, ay, of the blood of Chaka, the great king – a chief, and a captain of the regiment of the Nkomabakosi – am a wanderer in strange places, a man without a kraal. Nought have I brought save this mine axe; of all my belongings this remains alone. They have divided my cattle; they have taken my wives; and my children know my face no more. Yet with this axe' – and he swung the formidable weapon round his head, making the air hiss as he clove it – 'will I cut another path to fortune. I have spoken.'

I shook my head at him. 'Umslopogaas,' I said, 'I know thee from of old. Ever ambitious, ever plotting to be great, I fear me that thou hast overreached thyself at last. Years ago, when thou wouldst have plotted against Cetywayo, son of Panda, I warned thee, and thou didst listen. But now, when I was not by thee to stay thy hand, thou hast dug a pit for thine own feet to fall in. Is it not so? But what is done is done. Who can make the dead tree green, or gaze again upon last year's light? Who can recall the spoken word, or bring back the spirit of the fallen? That which Time swallows comes not up again. Let it be forgotten!

'And now, behold, Umslopogaas, I know thee for a great warrior and a brave man, faithful to the death. Even in Zululand, where all the men are brave, they called thee the "Slaughterer", and at night told stories round the fire of thy strength and deeds. Hear me now. Thou seest this great man, my friend' – and I pointed to Sir Henry; 'he also is a warrior as great as thou, and, strong as thou art, he could throw thee over his shoulder. Incubu is his name. And thou seest this one also; him with the round stomach, the shining eye, and the pleasant face. Bougwan (glass eye) is his name, and a good man is he and a true, being of a curious tribe who pass their life upon the water, and live in floating kraals.

'Now, we three whom thou seest would travel inland, past Dongo Egere, the great white mountain (Mt Kenia), and far into the unknown beyond. We know not what we shall find there; we go to hunt and seek adventures, and new places, being tired of sitting still, with the same old things around us. Wilt thou come with us? To thee shall be given command of all our servants; but what shall befall thee, that I know not. Once before we three journeyed thus, in search of adventure, and we took with us a man such as thou – one Umbopa; and, behold, we left him the king of a great country, with twenty Impis (regiments), each of three thousand plumed warriors, waiting on his word. How it shall go with thee, I know not; mayhap death awaits thee and us. Wilt thou throw thyself to Fortune and come, or fearest thou, Umslopogaas?'

The great man smiled. 'Thou art not altogether right, Macumazahn,' he said; 'I have plotted in my time, but it was not ambition that led me to my fall; but, shame on me that I should have to say it, a fair woman's face. Let it pass. So we are going to see something like the old times again, Macumazahn, when we fought and hunted in Zululand? Ay, I will come. Come life, come death, what care I, so that the blows fall fast and the blood runs red? I grow old, I grow old, and I have not fought enough! And yet am I a warrior among warriors; see my scars' – and he pointed to countless cicatrices, stabs and cuts, that marked the skin of his chest and legs and arms. 'See the hole in my head; the brains gushed out therefrom, yet did I slay him who smote, and live. Knowest thou how many men I have slain, in fair hand-to-hand combat, Macumazahn? See, here is the tale of them' – and he pointed to long rows of notches cut in the rhinoceros-horn handle of his axe. 'Number them, Macumazahn – one hundred and three – and I have never counted but those whom I have ripped open,* nor have I reckoned those whom another man had struck.'

'Be silent,' I said, for I saw that he was getting the blood-fever on him; 'be silent; well art thou called the "Slaughterer". We

---

* Alluding to the Zulu custom of opening the stomach of a dead foe. They have a superstition that, if this is not done, as the body of their enemy swells up so will the bodies of those who killed him swell up. A.Q.

would not hear of thy deeds of blood. Remember, if thou comest with us, we fight not save in self-defence. Listen, we need servants. These men,' and I pointed to the Wakwafi, who had retired a little way during our 'indaba' (talk), 'say they will not come.'

'Will not come!' shouted Umslopogaas; 'where is the dog who says he will not come when my father orders? Here, thou' – and with a single bound he sprang upon the Wakwafi with whom I had first spoken, and, seizing him by the arm, dragged him towards us. 'Thou dog!' he said, giving the terrified man a shake, 'didst thou say that thou wouldst not go with my father? Say it once more and I will choke thee' – and his long fingers closed round his throat as he said it – 'thee, and those with thee. Hast thou forgotten how I served thy brother?'

'Nay, we will come with the white man,' gasped the man.

'White man!' went on Umslopogaas, in simulated fury, which a very little provocation would have made real enough; 'of whom speakest thou, insolent dog?'

'Nay, we will go with the great chief.'

'So!' said Umslopogaas, in a quiet voice, as he suddenly released his hold, so that the man fell backward. 'I thought you would.'

'That man Umslopogaas seems to have a curious *moral* ascendency over his companions,' Good afterwards remarked thoughtfully.

CHAPTER 2

The Black Hand

In due course we left Lamu, and ten days afterwards we found ourselves at a spot called Charra, on the Tana River, having gone through many adventures which need not be recorded here. Amongst other things we visited a ruined city, of which there are many on this coast, and which must once, to judge from their extent and the numerous remains of mosques and stone houses, have been very populous places. These ruined cities are immeasurably ancient, having, I believe, been places of wealth and importance as far back as the Old Testament times, when they were centres of trade with India and elsewhere. But their glory has departed now – the slave trade has finished them – and where wealthy merchants from all parts of the then civilised world stood and bargained in the crowded market-places, the lion holds his court at night, and instead of the chattering of slaves and the eager voices of the bidders, his awful note goes echoing down the ruined corridors. At this particular place we discovered on a mound, covered up with rank growth and rubbish, two of the most beautiful stone doorways that it is possible to conceive. The carving on them was simply exquisite, and I only regret that we had no means of getting them away. No doubt they had once been the entrances to a palace, of which, however, no traces were now to be seen, though probably its ruins lay under the rising mound.

Gone! quite gone! the way that everything must go. Like the nobles and the ladies who lived within their gates, these cities have had their day, and now they are as Babylon and Nineveh, and as London and Paris will one day be. Nothing may endure. That is the inexorable law. Men and women, empires and cities, thrones, principalities, and powers, mountains, rivers, and unfathomed seas, worlds, spaces, and universes, all have their day, and all must go. In this ruined and forgotten place the moralist may behold a symbol of the universal destiny. For this system of ours allows no room for standing still – nothing can loiter on the road and check the progress of things upwards towards Life, or the rush of things downwards towards Death. The stern police-man Fate moves us and them on, on, uphill and downhill and across the level; there is no resting-place for the weary feet, till at last the abyss swallows us, and from the shores of the Transitory we are hurled into the sea of the Eternal.

At Charra we had a violent quarrel with the headman of the bearers we had hired to go as far as this, and who now wished to extort large extra payment from us. In the result he threatened to set the Masai – about whom more anon – on to us. That night he, with all our hired bearers, ran away, stealing most of the goods which had been entrusted to them to carry. Luckily, however, they had not happened to steal our rifles, ammunition, and personal effects; not because of any delicacy of feeling on their part, but owing to the fact that they chanced to be in the charge of the five Wakwafis. After that, it was clear to us that we had had enough of caravans and of bearers. Indeed, we had not much left for a caravan to carry. And yet, how were we to get on?

It was Good who solved the question. 'Here is water,' he said, pointing to the Tana River; 'and yesterday I saw a party of natives hunting hippopotami in canoes. I understand that Mr Macken-zie's mission station is on the Tana River. Why not get into canoes and paddle up to it?'

This brilliant suggestion was, needless to say, received with acclamation; and I instantly set to work to buy suitable canoes from the surrounding natives. I succeeded after a delay of three days in obtaining two large ones, each hollowed out of a single log of some light wood, and capable of holding six people and baggage. For these two canoes we had to pay nearly all our remaining cloth, and also many other articles.

On the day following our purchase of the two canoes we effected a start. In the first canoe were Good, Sir Henry, and three of our Wakwafi followers; in the second myself, Umslopogaas, and the other two Wakwafis. As our course lay upstream, we had to keep four paddles at work in each canoe, which meant that the whole lot of us, except Good, had to row away like galley-slaves; and very exhausting work it was. I say, except Good, for, of course, the moment that Good got into a boat his foot was on his native heath, and he took command of the party. And certainly he worked us. On shore Good is a gentle, mild-mannered man, and given to jocosity; but, as we found to our cost, Good in a boat was a perfect demon. To begin with, he knew all about it, and we didn't. On all nautical subjects, from the torpedo fittings of a man-of-war down to the best way of handling the paddle of an African canoe, he was a perfect mine of information, which, to say the least of it, we were not. Also his ideas of discipline were of the sternest, and, in short, he came the royal naval officer over us pretty considerably, and paid us out amply for all the chaff we were wont to treat him to on land; but, on the other hand, I am bound to say that he managed the boats admirably.

After the first day Good succeeded, with the help of some cloth and a couple of poles, in rigging up a sail in each canoe, which lightened our labours not a little. But the current ran very strong against us, and at the best we were not able to make more than twenty miles a day. Our plan was to start at dawn, and paddle along till about half-past ten, by which time the sun got too hot to allow of further exertion. Then we moored our canoes to the bank, and ate our frugal meal; after which we ate or otherwise amused ourselves till about three o'clock, when we again started, and rowed till within an hour of sundown, when we called a halt for the night. On landing in the evening, Good would at once set to work, with the help of the Askari, to build a little 'scherm', or small enclosure, fenced with thorn bushes, and to light a fire. I, with Sir Henry and Umslopogaas, would go out to shoot something for the pot. Generally this was an easy task, for all sorts of game abounded on the banks of the Tana. One night Sir Henry shot a young cow-giraffe, of which the marrow-bones were excellent; on another I got a couple of waterbuck right and left; and once, to his own intense satisfaction, Umslopogaas (who, like most Zulus, was a vile shot with a rifle) managed to kill a fine fat eland with a Martini I had lent him. Sometimes we varied our food by shooting some guinea-fowl, or bush-bustard (paau) – both of which were numerous – with a shotgun, or by catching a supply of beautiful yellow fish, with which the waters of the Tana swarmed, and which form, I believe, one of the chief food-supplies of the crocodiles.

Three days after our start an ominous incident occurred. We were just drawing in to the bank to make our camp as usual for the night, when we caught sight of a figure standing on a little knoll not forty yards away, and intensely watching our approach. One glance was sufficient – although I was personally unacquainted with the tribe – to tell me that he was a Masai Elmoran, or young warrior. Indeed, had I had any doubts, they would have quickly been dispelled by the terrified ejaculation of '*Masai*!' that burst simultaneously from the lips of our Wakwafi followers, who are, as I think I have said, themselves bastard Masai.

And what a figure he presented as he stood there in his savage war-gear! Accustomed as I have been to savages all my life, I do not think that I have ever before seen anything quite so ferocious or awe-inspiring. To begin with, the man was enormously tall, quite as tall as Umslopogaas, I should say, and beautifully, though somewhat slightly, shaped; but with the face of a devil. In his right hand he held a spear about five and a half feet long, the blade being two and a half feet in length, by nearly three inches in width, and having an iron spike at the end of the handle that measured more than a foot. On his left arm was a large and well-made elliptical shield of buffalo hide, on which were painted strange heraldic-looking devices. On his shoulders was a huge cape of hawk's feathers, and round his neck was a 'naibere', or strip of cotton, about seventeen feet long, by one and a half broad, with a stripe of colour running down the middle of it. The tanned goatskin robe, which formed his ordinary attire in times of peace, was tied lightly round his waist, so as to serve the purposes of a belt, and through it were stuck, on the right and left sides respectively, his short pear-shaped sime, or sword, which is made of a single piece of steel, and carried in a wooden sheath, and an enormous knobkerrie. But perhaps the most remarkable feature of his attire consisted of a headdress of ostrich-feathers, which was fixed on the chin, and passed in front of the ears to the forehead, and, being shaped like an ellipse, completely framed the face, so that the diabolical countenance appeared to project from a sort of feather fire-screen. Round the ankles he wore black fringes of hair, and, projecting from the upper portion of the calves, to which they were attached, were long spurs like spikes, from which flowed down tufts of the beautiful black and waving hair of the Colobus monkey. Such was the elaborate array of the Masai Elmoran who stood watching the approach of our two canoes, but it is one which, to be appreciated, must be seen; only those who see it do not often live to describe it. Of course I could not make out all these details of his full dress on the occasion of this my first introduction, being, indeed, amply taken up with the consideration of the general effect, but I had plenty of subsequent opportunities of becoming acquainted with the items that went to make it up.

Whilst we were hesitating what to do, the Masai warrior drew himself up in a dignified fashion, shook his huge spear at us, and, turning, vanished on the further side of the slope.

'Hulloa!' holloaed Sir Henry from the other boat; 'our friend the caravan leader has been as good as his word, and set the Masai after us. Do you think it will be safe to go ashore?'

I did not think it would be at all safe; but, on the other hand, we had no means of cooking in the canoes, and nothing that we could eat raw, so it was difficult to know what to do. At last Umslopogaas simplified matters by volunteering to go and reconnoitre, which he did, creeping off into the bush like a snake, while we hung off in the stream waiting for him. In half an hour he returned, and told us that there was not a Masai to be seen anywhere about, but that he had discovered a spot where they had recently been encamped, and that from various indications he judged that they must have moved on an hour or so before; the man we saw having, no doubt, been left to report upon our movements.

Thereupon we landed; and, having posted a sentry, proceeded to cook and eat our evening meal. This done, we took the situation into our serious consideration. Of course, it was possible that the apparition of the Masai warrior had nothing to do with us, that he was merely one of a band bent upon some marauding and murdering expedition against another tribe. But when we recalled the threat of the caravan leader, and reflected on the ominous way in which the warrior had shaken his spear at us, this did not appear very probable. On the contrary, what did seem probable was that the party was after us and awaiting a favourable opportunity to attack us. This being so, there were two things that we could do – one of which was to go on, and the other to go back. The latter idea was, however, rejected at once, it being obvious that we should encounter as many dangers in retreat as in advance; and, besides, we had made up our minds to journey onwards at any price. Under these circumstances, however, we did not consider it safe to sleep ashore, so we got into our canoes, and, paddling out into the middle of the stream, which was not very wide here, managed to anchor them by means of big stones fastened to ropes made of coconut-fibre, of which there were several fathoms in each canoe.

Here the mosquitoes nearly ate us up alive, and this, combined with anxiety as to our position, effectually prevented me from sleeping as the others were doing, notwithstanding the attacks of the aforesaid Tana mosquitoes. And so I lay awake, smoking and reflecting on many things, but, being of a practical turn of mind, chiefly on how we were to give those Masai villains the slip. It was a beautiful moonlight night, and, notwithstanding the mosquitoes, and the great risk we were running from fever from sleeping in such a spot, and forgetting that I had the cramp very badly in my right leg from squatting in a constrained position in the canoe, and that the Wakwafi who was sleeping beside me smelt horribly, I really began to enjoy myself. The moonbeams played upon the surface of the running water that speeded unceasingly past us towards the sea, like men's lives towards the grave, till it glittered like a wide sheet of silver, that is in the open where the trees threw no shadows. Near the banks, however, it was very dark, and the night wind sighed sadly in the reeds. To our left, on the further side of the river, was a little sandy bay which was clear of trees, and here I could make out the forms of numerous antelopes advancing to the water, till suddenly there came an ominous roar, whereupon they all made off hurriedly. Then after a pause I caught sight of the massive form of His Majesty the Lion, coming down to drink his fill after meat. Presently he moved on, then came a crashing of the reeds about fifty yards above us, and a few minutes later a huge black mass rose out of the water, about twenty yards from me, and snorted. It was the head of a hippopotamus. Down it went without a sound, only to rise again within five yards of where I sat. This was decidedly too near to be comfortable, more especially as the hippopotamus was evidently animated by intense curiosity to know what on earth our canoes were. He opened his great mouth, to yawn, I suppose, and gave me an excellent view of his ivories; and I could not help reflecting how easily he could crunch up our frail canoe with a single bite. Indeed, I had half a mind to give him a ball from my eight-bore, but on reflection determined to let him alone unless he actually charged the boat. Presently he sank again as noiselessly as before, and I saw no more of him. Just then, on looking towards the bank on our right, I fancied that I caught sight of a dark figure flitting between the tree trunks. I have very keen sight, and I was almost sure that I saw something, but whether it was bird, beast, or man I could not say. At the moment, however, a dark cloud passed over the moon, and I saw no more of it. Just then, too, although all the other sounds of the forest had ceased, a species of horned owl with which I was well acquainted began to hoot with great persistency. After that, save for the rustling of trees and reeds when the wind caught them, there was complete silence.

But somehow, in the most unaccountable way, I had suddenly become nervous. There was no particular reason why I should be, beyond the ordinary reasons which surround the Central African traveller, and yet I undoubtedly was. If there is one thing more than another of which I have the most complete and entire scorn and disbelief, it is of presentiments, and yet here I was all of a sudden filled with and possessed by a most undoubted presentiment of approaching evil. I would not give way to it, however, although I felt the cold perspiration stand out upon my forehead.

I would not arouse the others. Worse and worse I grew, my pulse fluttered like a dying man's, my nerves thrilled with the horrible sense of impotent terror which anybody who is subject to nightmare will be familiar with, but still my will triumphed over my fears, and I lay quiet (for I was half sitting, half lying, in the bow of the canoe), only turning my face so as to command a view of Umslopogaas and the two Wakwafi who were sleeping alongside of and beyond me.

In the distance I heard a hippopotamus splash faintly, then the owl hooted again in a kind of unnatural screaming note,* and the wind began to moan plaintively through the trees, making a heart-chilling music. Above was the black bosom of the cloud, and beneath me swept the black flood of the water, and I felt as though I and Death were utterly alone between them. It was very desolate.

Suddenly my blood seemed to freeze in my veins, and my heart to stand still. Was it fancy, or were we moving? I turned my eyes to look for the other canoe which should be alongside of us. I could not see it, but instead I saw a lean and clutching black hand lifting itself above the gunwale of the little boat. Surely it was a nightmare! At the same instant a dim but devilish-looking face appeared to rise out of the water, and then came a lurch of the canoe, the quick flash of a knife, and an awful yell from the Wakwafi who was sleeping by my side (the same poor fellow whose odour had been annoying me), and something warm spurted into my face. In an instant the spell was broken; I knew that it was no nightmare, but that we were attacked by swimming Masai. Snatching at the first weapon that came to hand, which happened to be Umslopogaas' battleaxe, I struck with all my force in the direction in which I had seen the flash of the knife. The blow fell upon a man's arm, and, catching it against the thick wooden gunwale of the canoe, completely severed it from the body just above the wrist. As for its owner, he uttered no sound or cry. Like a ghost he came, and like a ghost he went, leaving behind

---

* No doubt this owl was a wingless bird. I afterwards learnt that the hooting of an owl is a favourite signal among the Masai tribes.   A.Q.

him a bloody hand still gripping a great knife, or rather a short sword, that was buried in the heart of our poor servant.

Instantly there arose a hubbub and confusion, and I fancied, rightly or wrongly, that I made out several dark heads gliding away towards the right-hand bank, whither we were rapidly drifting, for the rope by which we were moored had been severed with a knife. As soon as I had realised this fact, I also realised that the scheme had been to cut the boat loose so that it should drift on to the right bank (as it would have done with the natural swing of the current), where no doubt a party of Masai were waiting to dig their shovel-headed spears into us. Seizing one paddle myself, I told Umslopogaas to take another (for the remaining Askari was too frightened and bewildered to be of any use), and together we rowed vigorously out towards the middle of the stream; and not an instant too soon, for in another minute we should have been aground, and then there would have been an end of us.

As soon as we were well out, we set to work to paddle the canoe upstream again to where the other was moored; and very hard and dangerous work it was in the dark, and with nothing but the notes of Good's stentorian shouts, which he kept firing off at intervals like a fog-horn, to guide us. But at last we fetched up, and were thankful to find that they had not been molested at all. No doubt the owner of the same hand that severed our rope should have severed theirs also, but was led away from his purpose by an irresistible inclination to murder when he got the chance, which, while it cost us a man and him his hand, undoubtedly saved all the rest of us from massacre. Had it not been for that ghastly apparition over the side of the boat – an apparition that I shall never forget till my dying hour – the canoe would undoubtedly have drifted ashore before I realised what had happened, and this history would never have been written by me.

CHAPTER 3

The Mission Station

We made the remains of our rope fast to the other canoe, and sat waiting for the dawn and congratulating ourselves upon our merciful escape, which really seemed to result more from the special favour of Providence than from our own care or prowess. At last it came, and I have not often been more grateful to see the light, though so far as my canoe was concerned it revealed a ghastly sight. There in the bottom of the little boat lay the unfortunate Askari, the sime, or sword, in his bosom, and the severed hand gripping the handle. I could not bear the sight, so hauling up the stone which had served as an anchor to the other canoe, we made it fast to the murdered man and dropped him overboard, and down he went to the bottom, leaving nothing but a train of bubbles behind him. Alas! when our time comes, most of us like him leave nothing but bubbles behind, to show that we have been, and the bubbles soon burst. The hand of his murderer we threw into the stream, where it slowly sank. The sword, of which the handle was ivory, inlaid with gold (evidently Arab work), I kept and used as a hunting-knife, and very useful it proved.

Then, a man having been transferred to my canoe, we once more started on in very low spirits and not feeling at all comfortable as to the future, but fondly hoping to arrive at the 'Highlands' station by night. To make matters worse, within an hour of sunrise it came on to rain in torrents, wetting us to the skin, and even necessitating the occasional baling of the canoes, and as the rain beat down the wind we could not use the sails, and had to get along as best as we could with our paddles.

At eleven o'clock we halted on an open piece of ground on the left bank of the river, and, the rain abating a little, managed to make a fire and catch and broil some fish. We did not dare to wander about to search for game. At two o'clock we got off again, taking a supply of broiled fish with us, and shortly afterwards the rain came on harder than ever. Also the river began to get exceedingly difficult to navigate on account of the numerous rocks, reaches of shallow water, and the increased force of the current; so that it soon became clear to us that we should not reach the Revd Mackenzie's hospitable roof that night – a prospect that did not tend to enliven us. Toil as we would, we could not make more than an average of a mile an hour, and at five o'clock in the afternoon (by which time we were all utterly worn out) we reckoned that we were still quite ten miles below the station. This being so, we set to work to make the best arrangements we could for the night. After our recent experience, we simply did not dare to land, more especially as the banks of the Tana were clothed with dense bush that would have given cover to five thousand Masai, and at first I thought that we were going to have another night of it in the canoes. Fortunately, however, we espied a little rocky islet, not more than fifteen miles or so square, situated nearly in the middle of the river. For this we paddled, and, making fast the canoes, landed and made ourselves as comfortable as circumstances would permit, which was very uncomfortable indeed. As for the weather, it continued to be simply vile, the rain coming down in sheets till we were chilled to the marrow, and utterly preventing us from lighting a fire. There was, however, one consoling circumstance about this rain; our Askari declared that nothing would induce the Masai to make an attack in it, as they intensely disliked moving about in the wet, perhaps, as Good suggested, because they hate the idea of washing. We ate some insipid and sodden cold fish – that is, with the exception of Umslopogaas, who, like most Zulus, cannot bear fish – and took a pull of brandy, of which we fortunately had a few bottles left, and then began what, with one exception – when we same three white men nearly perished of cold on the snow of Sheba's Breast in the course of our journey to Kukuanaland – was, I think, the most trying night I ever experienced. It seemed absolutely endless, and once or twice I feared that two of the Askari would have died of the wet, cold, and exposure. Indeed, had it not been for timely doses of brandy I am sure that they would have died, for no African people can stand much exposure, which first paralyses and then kills them. I could see that even that iron old warrior Umslopogaas felt it keenly; though, in strange contrast to the Wakwafis, who groaned and bemoaned their fate unceasingly, he never uttered a single complaint. To make matters worse, about one in the morning we again heard the owl's ominous hooting, and had at once to prepare ourselves for another attack; though, if it had been attempted, I do not think that we could have offered a very effective resistance. But either the owl was a real one this time, or else the Masai were themselves too miserable to think of offensive operations, which, indeed, they rarely, if ever, undertake in bush veldt. At any rate, we saw nothing of them.

At last the dawn came gliding across the water, wrapped in wreaths of ghostly mist, and, with the daylight, the rain ceased; and then, out came the glorious sun, sucking up the mists and warming the chill air. Benumbed, and utterly exhausted, we dragged ourselves to our feet, and went and stood in the bright rays, and were thankful for them. I can quite understand how it is that primitive people become sun worshippers, especially if their conditions of life render them liable to exposure.

In half an hour more we were once again making fair progress with the help of a good wind. Our spirits had returned with the sunshine, and we were ready to laugh at difficulties and dangers that had been almost crushing on the previous day.

And so we went on cheerily till about eleven o'clock. Just as we were thinking of halting as usual, to rest and try to shoot something to eat, a sudden bend in the river brought us in sight of a substantial-looking European house with a veranda round it, splendidly situated upon a hill, and surrounded by a high stone wall with a ditch on the outer side. Right against and overshadowing the house was an enormous pine, the top of which we had seen through a glass for the last two days, but of course without knowing that it marked the site of the mission station. I was the first to see the house, and could not restrain myself from giving a hearty cheer, in which the others, including the natives, joined lustily. There was no thought of halting now. On we laboured, for, unfortunately, though the house seemed quite near, it was still a long way off by river, until at last, by one o'clock, we found ourselves at the bottom of the slope on which the building stood. Running the canoes to the bank, we disembarked, and were just hauling them up on to the shore, when we perceived three figures, dressed in ordinary English-looking clothes, hurrying down through a grove of trees to meet us.

'A gentleman, a lady, and a little girl,' ejaculated Good, after surveying the trio through his eyeglass, 'walking in a civilised fashion, through a civilised garden, to meet us in this place. Hang me, if this isn't the most curious thing we have seen yet!'

Good was right: it certainly did seem odd and out of place – more like a scene out of a dream or an Italian opera than a real tangible fact; and the sense of unreality was not lessened when we heard ourselves addressed in good broad Scotch, which, however, I cannot reproduce.

'How do you do, sirs,' said Mr Mackenzie, a grey-haired, angular man, with a kindly face and red cheeks; 'I hope I see you very well. My natives told me an hour ago they spied two canoes with white men in them coming up the river; so we have just come down to meet you.'

'And it is very glad that we are to see a white face again, let me tell you,' put in the lady – a charming and refined-looking person.

We took off our hats in acknowledgment, and proceeded to introduce ourselves.

'And now,' said Mr Mackenzie, 'you must all be hungry and weary; so come on, gentlemen, come on, and right glad we are to see you. The last white who visited us was Alphonse – you will see Alphonse presently – and that was a year ago.'

Meanwhile we had been walking up the slope of the hill, the lower portion of which was fenced off, sometimes with quince fences and sometimes with rough stone walls, into Kaffir gardens, just now full of crops of mealies, pumpkins, potatoes, etc. In the corners of these gardens were groups of neat mushroom-shaped huts, occupied by Mr Mackenzie's mission natives, whose women and children came pouring out to meet us as we walked. Through the centre of the gardens ran the roadway up which we were walking. It was bordered on each side by a line of orange trees, which, although they had only been planted ten years, had in the lovely climate of the uplands below Mt Kenia, the base of which is about five thousand feet above the coastline level, already grown to imposing proportions, and were positively laden with golden fruit. After a stiffish climb of a quarter of a mile or so – for the hillside was steep – we came to a splendid quince fence, also covered with fruit, which enclosed, Mr Mackenzie told us, a space of about four acres of ground that contained his private garden, house, church, and outbuildings, and, indeed, the whole hilltop. And what a garden it was! I have always loved a good garden, and I could have thrown up my hands for joy when I saw Mr Mackenzie's. First there were rows upon rows of standard European fruit trees, all grafted; for on top of this hill the climate was so temperate that nearly all the English vegetables, trees, and flowers flourished luxuriantly, even including several varieties of the apple, which, generally, runs to wood in a warm climate and obstinately refuses to fruit. Then there were strawberries and tomatoes (such tomatoes!), and melons and cucumbers, and, indeed, every sort of vegetable and fruit.

'Well, you have something like a garden!' I said, overpowered with admiration not untouched by envy.

'Yes,' answered the missionary, 'it is a very good garden, and has well repaid my labour; but it is the climate that I have to thank. If you stick a peach-stone into the ground it will bear fruit the fourth year, and a rose-cutting will bloom in a year. It is a lovely clime.'

Just then we came to a ditch about ten feet wide, and full of water, on the other side of which was a loopholed stone wall eight feet high, and with sharp flints plentifully set in mortar on the coping.

'There,' said Mr Mackenzie, pointing to the ditch and wall, 'this is my *magnum opus*; at least, this and the church, which is the other side of the house. It took me and twenty natives two years to dig the ditch and build the wall, but I never felt safe till it was done; and now I can defy all the savages in Africa, for the spring that fills the ditch is inside the wall, and bubbles out at the top of the hill winter and summer alike, and I always keep a store of four months' provision in the house.'

Crossing over a plank and through a very narrow opening in the wall, we entered into what Mrs Mackenzie called *her* domain – namely, the flower garden, the beauty of which is really beyond my power to describe. I do not think I ever saw such roses, gardenias, or camellias (all reared from seeds or cuttings sent from England); and there was also a patch given up to a collection of bulbous roots mostly collected by Miss Flossie, Mr Mackenzie's little daughter, from the surrounding country, some of which were surpassingly beautiful. In the middle of this garden, and exactly opposite the veranda, a beautiful fountain of clear water bubbled up from the ground, and fell into a stonework basin which had been carefully built to receive it, whence the overflow found its way by means of a drain to the moat round the outer wall, this moat in its turn serving as a reservoir, whence an unfailing supply of water was available to irrigate all the gardens below. The house itself, a massively built single-storeyed building, was roofed with slabs of stone, and had a handsome veranda in front. It was built on three sides of a square, the fourth side being taken up by the kitchens, which stood separate from the house – a very good plan in a hot country. In the centre of this square thus formed was, perhaps, the most remarkable object that we had yet seen in this charming place, and that was a single tree of the conifer tribe, varieties of which grow freely on the highlands of this part of Africa. This splendid tree, which Mr Mackenzie informed us was a landmark for fifty miles round, and which we had ourselves seen for the last forty miles of our journey, must have been nearly three hundred feet in height, the trunk measuring about sixteen feet in diameter at a yard from the ground. For some seventy feet it rose a beautiful tapering brown pillar without a single branch, but at that height splendid dark green boughs, which, looked at from below, had the appearance of gigantic fern-leaves, sprang out horizontally from the trunk, projecting right over the house and flower-garden, to both of which they furnished a grateful proportion of shade, without – being so high up – offering any impediment to the passage of light and air.

'What a beautiful tree!' exclaimed Sir Henry.

'Yes, you are right; it is a beautiful tree. There is not another like it in all the country round, that I know of,' answered Mr Mackenzie. 'I call it my watch tower. As you see, I have a rope ladder fixed to the lowest bough; and if I want to see anything that is going on within fifteen miles or so, all I have to do is to run up it with a spyglass. But you must be hungry, and I am sure the dinner is cooked. Come in, my friends; it is but a rough place, but well enough for these savage parts; and I can tell you what, we have got – a French cook.' And he led the way on to the veranda.

As I was following him, and wondering what on earth he could mean by this, there suddenly appeared, through the door that opened on to the veranda from the house, a dapper little man, dressed in a neat blue cotton suit, with shoes made of tanned hide, and remarkable for a bustling air and most enormous black mustachios, shaped into an upward curve, and coming to a point for all the world like a pair of buffalo-horns.

'Madame bids me for to say that dinnar is sarved. Messieurs, my compliments;' then suddenly perceiving Umslopogaas, who was loitering along after us and playing with his battleaxe, he threw up his hands in astonishment. 'Ah, mais quel homme!' he ejaculated in French, 'quel sauvage affreux! Take but note of his huge choppare and the great pit in his head.'

'Ay,' said Mr Mackenzie; 'what are you talking about, Alphonse?'

'Talking about!' replied the little Frenchman, his eyes still fixed upon Umslopogaas, whose general appearance seemed to fascinate him; 'why I talk of him' – and he rudely pointed – 'of ce monsieur noir.'

At this everybody began to laugh, and Umslopogaas, perceiving that he was the object of remark, frowned ferociously, for he had a most lordly dislike of anything like a personal liberty.

'Parbleu!' said Alphonse, 'he is angered – he makes the grimace. I like not his air. I vanish.' And he did with considerable rapidity.

Mr Mackenzie joined heartily in the shout of laughter which we indulged in. 'He is a queer character – Alphonse,' he said. 'By and by I will tell you his history; in the meanwhile let us try his cooking.'

'Might I ask,' said Sir Henry, after we had eaten a most excellent dinner, 'how you came to have a French cook in these wilds?'

'Oh,' answered Mrs Mackenzie, 'he arrived here of his own accord about a year ago, and asked to be taken into our service. He had got into some trouble in France, and fled to Zanzibar, where he found an application had been made by the French Government for his extradition. Whereupon he rushed off upcountry, and fell in, when nearly starved, with our caravan of men, who were bringing us our annual supply of goods, and was brought on here. You should get him to tell you the story.'

When dinner was over we lit our pipes, and Sir Henry proceeded to give our host a description of our journey up here, over which he looked very grave.

'It is evident to me,' he said, 'that those rascally Masai are following you, and I am very thankful that you have reached this house in safety. I do not think that they will dare to attack you here. It is unfortunate, though, that nearly all my men have gone down to the coast with ivory and goods. There are two hundred of them in the caravan, and the consequence is that I have not more than twenty men available for defensive purposes in case they should attack us. But, still, I will just give a few orders;' and, calling a black man who was loitering about outside in the garden, he went to the window, and addressed him in a Swahili dialect. The man listened, and then saluted and departed.

'I am sure I devoutly hope that we shall bring no such calamity upon you,' said I, anxiously, when he had taken his seat again. 'Rather than bring those bloodthirsty villains about your ears, we will move on and take our chance.'

'You will do nothing of the sort. If the Masai come, they come, and there is an end on it; and I think we can give them a pretty warm greeting. I would not show any man the door for all the Masai in the world.'

'That reminds me,' I said, 'the Consul at Lamu told me that he had had a letter from you, in which you said that a man had arrived here who reported that he had come across a white people in the interior. Do you think that there was any truth in his story? I ask, because I have once or twice in my life heard rumours from natives who have come down from the far north of the existence of such a race.'

Mr Mackenzie, by way of answer, went out of the room and returned, bringing with him a most curious sword. It was long, and all the blade, which was very thick and heavy, was to within a quarter of an inch of the cutting edge worked into an ornamental pattern exactly as we work soft wood with a fret-saw, the steel, however, being invariably pierced in such a way as not to interfere with the strength of the sword. This in itself was sufficiently curious, but what was still more so was that all the edges of the hollow spaces cut through the substance of the blade were most beautifully inlaid with gold, which was in some way that I cannot understand welded on to the steel.*

'There,' said Mr Mackenzie, 'did you ever see a sword like that?'
We all examined it and shook our heads.

'Well, I have got it to show you, because this is what the man who said he had seen the white people brought with him, and because it does more or less give an air of truth to what I should otherwise have set down as a lie. Look here; I will tell you all that I know about the matter, which is not much. One afternoon, just before sunset, I was sitting on the veranda, when a poor, miserable, starved-looking man came limping up and squatted down before me. I asked him where he came from and what he wanted, and thereon he plunged into a long rambling narrative about how he belonged to a tribe far in the north, and how his tribe was destroyed by another tribe, and he with a few other survivors driven still further north past a lake named Laga. Thence, it appears, he made his way to another lake that lay up in the mountains, "a lake without a bottom" he called it, and here his wife and brother died of an infectious sickness – probably smallpox –

---

* Since I saw the above I have examined hundreds of these swords, but have never been able to discover how the gold plates were inlaid in the fretwork. The armourers who make them in Zu-vendis bind themselves by oath not to reveal the secret. A.Q.

whereon the people drove him out of their villages into the wilderness, where he wandered miserably over mountains for ten days, after which he got into dense thorn forest, and was one day found there by some *white men* who were hunting, and who took him to a place where all the people were white and lived in stone houses. Here he remained a week shut up in a house, till one night a man with a white beard, whom he understood to be a "medicine-man", came and inspected him, after which he was led off and taken through the thorn forest to the confines of the wilderness, and given food and this sword (at least so he said), and turned loose.'

'Well,' said Sir Henry, who had been listening with breathless interest, 'and what did he do then?'

'Oh! he seems, according to his account, to have gone through sufferings and hardships innumerable, and to have lived for weeks on roots and berries, and such things as he could catch and kill. But somehow he did live, and at last by slow degrees made his way south and reached this place. What the details of his journey were I never learnt, for I told him to return on the morrow, bidding one of my headmen look after him for the night. The headman took him away, but the poor man had the itch so badly that the headman's wife would not have him in the hut for fear of catching it, so he was given a blanket and told to sleep outside. As it happened, we had a lion hanging about here just then, and most unhappily he winded this unfortunate wanderer, and, springing on him, bit his head almost off without the people in the hut knowing anything about it, and there was an end of him and his story about the white people; and whether or no there is any truth in it is more than I can tell you. What do you think, Mr Quatermain?'

I shook my head, and answered, 'I don't know. There are so many queer things hidden away in the heart of this great continent that I should be sorry to assert that there was no truth in it. Anyhow, we mean to try and find out. We intend to journey to Lekakisera, and thence, if we live to get so far, to this Lake Laga; and, if there are any white people beyond, we will do our best to find them.'

'You are very venturesome people,' said Mr Mackenzie, with a smile, and the subject dropped.

CHAPTER 4

Alphonse and His Annette

After dinner we thoroughly inspected all the outbuildings and grounds of the station, which I consider the most successful as well as the most beautiful place of the sort that I have seen in Africa. We then returned to the veranda, where we found Umslopogaas taking advantage of this favourable opportunity to clean all the rifles thoroughly. This was the only *work* that he ever did or was asked to do, for as a Zulu chief it was beneath his dignity to work with his hands; but such as it was he did it very well. It was a curious sight to see the great Zulu sitting there upon the floor, his battleaxe resting against the wall behind him, whilst his long aristocratic-looking hands were busily employed, delicately and with the utmost care, cleaning the mechanism of the breech-loaders. He had a name for each gun. One – a double four-bore belonging to Sir Henry – was the Thunderer; another, my 500 Express, which had a peculiarly sharp report, was 'the little one who spoke like a whip'; the Winchester repeaters were 'the women, who talked so fast that you could not tell one word from another'; the six Martinis were 'the common people'; and so on with them all. It was very curious to hear him addressing each gun as he cleaned it, as though it were an individual, and in a vein of the quaintest humour. He did the same with his battleaxe, which he seemed to look upon as an intimate friend, and to which he would at times talk by the hour, going over all his old adventures with it – and dreadful enough some of them were. By a piece of grim humour, he had named this axe 'Inkosi-kaas', which is the Zulu word for chieftainess. For a long while I could not make out why he gave it such a name, and at last I asked him, when he informed me that the axe was very evidently feminine, because of her womanly habit of prying very deep into things, and that she was clearly a chieftainess because all men fell down before her, struck dumb at the sight of her beauty and power. In the same way he would consult 'Inkosi-kaas' if in any dilemma; and when I asked him why he did so, he informed me it was because she must needs be wise, having 'looked into so many people's brains'.

I took up the axe and closely examined this formidable weapon. It was, as I have said, of the nature of a pole-axe. The haft, made out of an enormous rhinoceros horn, was three feet three inches long, about an inch and a quarter thick, and with a knob at the end as large as a Maltese orange, left there to prevent the hand from slipping. This horn haft, though so massive, was as flexible as cane, and practically unbreakable; but, to make assurance doubly sure, it was whipped round at intervals of a few inches with copper wire – all the parts where the hands grip being thus treated. Just above where the haft entered the head were scored a number of little nicks, each nick representing a man killed in battle with the weapon. The axe itself was made of the most beautiful steel, and apparently of European manufacture, though Umslopogaas did not know where it came from, having taken it from the hand of a chief he had killed in battle many years before. It was not very heavy, the head weighing two and a half pounds, as nearly as I could judge. The cutting part was slightly concave in shape – not convex, as it generally the case with savage battleaxes – and sharp as a razor, measuring five and three-quarter inches across the widest part. From the back of the axe sprang a stout spike four inches long, for the last two of which it was hollow, and shaped like a leather punch, with an opening for anything forced into the hollow at the punch end to be pushed out above – in fact, in this respect it exactly resembled a butcher's pole-axe. It was with this punch end, as we afterwards discovered, that Umslopogaas usually struck when fighting, driving a neat round hole in his adversary's skull, and only using the broad cutting edge for a circular sweep, or sometimes in a mêlée. I think he considered the punch a neater and more sportsman-like tool, and it was from his habit of pecking at his enemy with it that he got his name of 'Woodpecker'. Certainly in his hands it was a terribly efficient one.

Such was Umslopogaas' axe, Inkosi-kaas, the most remarkable and fatal hand-to-hand weapon that I ever saw, and one which he cherished as much as his own life. It scarcely ever left his hand except when he was eating, and then he always sat with it under his leg.

Just as I returned his axe to Umslopogaas, Miss Flossie came up and took me off to see her collection of flowers, African liliums, and blooming shrubs, some of which are very beautiful, many of the varieties being quite unknown to me and also, I believe, to botanical science. I asked her if she had ever seen or heard of the 'Goya' lily, which Central African explorers have told me they have occasionally met with and whose wonderful loveliness has filled them with astonishment. This lily, which the natives say blooms only once in ten years, flourishes in the most arid soil. Compared to the size of the bloom, the bulb is small, generally weighing about four pounds. As for the flower itself (which I afterwards saw under circumstances likely to impress its appearance fixedly in my mind), I know not how to describe its beauty and splendour, or the indescribable sweetness of its perfume. The flower – for it has only one bloom – rises from the crown of the bulb on a thick fleshy and flat-sided stem, the specimen that I saw measured fourteen inches in diameter, and is somewhat trumpet-shaped like the bloom of an ordinary 'longiflorum' set vertically. First there is the green sheath, which in its early stage is not unlike that of a water-lily, but which as the bloom opens splits into four portions and curls back gracefully towards the stem. Then comes the bloom itself, a single dazzling arch of white enclosing another cup of richest velvety crimson, from the heart of which rises a golden-coloured pistil. I have never seen anything to equal this bloom in beauty or fragrance, and as I believe it is but little known, I take the liberty to describe it at length. Looking at it for the first time I well remember that I realised how even in a flower there dwells something of the majesty of its Maker. To my great delight Miss Flossie told me that she knew the flower well and had tried to grow it in her garden, but without success, adding, however, that as it should be in bloom at this time of the year she thought that she could procure me a specimen.

After that I fell to asking her if she was not lonely up here among all these savage people and without any companions of her own age.

'Lonely?' she said. 'Oh, indeed no! I am as happy as the day is long, and besides I have my own companions. Why, I should hate to be buried in a crowd of white girls all just like myself so that nobody could tell the difference! Here,' she said, giving her head a little toss, 'I am I; and every native for miles around knows the "Water-lily" – for that is what they call me – and is ready to do what I want, but in the books that I have read about little girls in England it is not like that. Everybody thinks them a trouble, and they have to do what their schoolmistress likes. Oh! it would break my heart to be put in a cage like that and not to be free – free as the air.'

'Would you not like to learn?' I asked.

'So I do learn. Father teaches me Latin and French and arithmetic.'

'And are you never afraid among all these wild men?'

'Afraid? Oh no! they never interfere with me. I think they believe that I am "Ngai" (of the Divinity) because I am so white and have fair hair. And look here,' and diving her little hand into the bodice of her dress she produced a double-barrelled nickel-plated Derringer, 'I always carry that loaded, and if anybody tried to touch me I should shoot him. Once I shot a leopard that jumped upon my donkey as I was riding along. It frightened me very much, but I shot it in the ear and it fell dead, and I have its skin upon my bed. Look there!' she went on in an altered voice, touching me on the arm and pointing to some far-away object, 'I said just now that I had companions; there is one of them.'

I looked, and for the first time there burst upon my sight the glory of Mount Kenia. Hitherto the mountain had always been hidden in mist, but now its radiant beauty was unveiled for many thousand feet, although the base was still wrapped in vapour so that the lofty peak or pillar, towering nearly twenty thousand feet into the sky, appeared to be a fairy vision, hanging between earth and heaven, and based upon the clouds. The solemn majesty and beauty of this white peak are together beyond the power of my poor pen to describe. There it rose straight and sheer – a glittering white glory, its crest piercing the very blue of heaven. As I gazed at it with that little girl I felt my whole heart lifted up with an indescribable emotion, and for a moment great and wonderful thoughts seemed to break upon my mind, even as the arrows of the setting sun were breaking upon Kenia's snows. Mr Mackenzie's natives call the mountain the 'Finger of God', and to me it did seem eloquent of immortal peace and of the pure high calm that surely lies above this fevered world. Somewhere I had heard a line of poetry,

A thing of beauty is a joy for ever,

and now it came into my mind, and for the first time I thoroughly understood what it meant. Base, indeed, would be the man who could look upon that mighty snow-wreathed pile – that white old tombstone of the years – and not feel his own utter insignificance, and, by whatever name he calls Him, worship God in his heart. Such sights are like visions of the spirit; they throw wide the windows of the chamber of our small selfishness and let in a breath of that air that rushes round the rolling spheres, and for a while illumine our darkness with a far-off gleam of the white light which beats upon the Throne.

Yes, such things of beauty are indeed a joy for ever, and I can well understand what little Flossie meant when she talked of Kenia as her companion. As Umslopogaas, savage old Zulu that he was, said when I pointed out to him the peak hanging in the glittering air: 'A man might look thereon for a thousand years and yet be hungry to see.' But he gave rather another colour to his poetical idea when he added in a sort of chant, and with a touch of that weird imagination for which the man was remarkable, that when he was dead he should like his spirit to sit upon that snow-clad peak for ever, and to rush down the steep white sides in the breath of the whirlwind, or on the flash of the lightning, and 'slay, and slay, and slay'.

'Slay what, you old bloodhound?' I asked.

This rather puzzled him, but at length he answered – 'The other shadows.'

'So thou wouldst continue thy murdering even after death?' I said.

'I murder not,' he answered hotly; 'I kill in fair fight. Man is born to kill. He who kills not when his blood is hot is a woman, and no man. The people who kill not are slaves. I say I kill in fair fight; and when I am "in the shadow", as you white men say, I hope to go on killing in fair fight. May my shadow be accursed and chilled to the bone for ever if it should fall to murdering like a bushman with his poisoned arrows!' And he stalked away with much dignity, and left me laughing.

Just then the spies whom our host had sent out in the morning to find out if there were any traces of our Masai friends about, returned, and reported that the country had been scoured for fifteen miles round without a single Elmoran being seen, and that they believed that those gentry had given up the pursuit and returned whence they came. Mr Mackenzie gave a sigh of relief when he heard this, and so indeed did we, for we had had quite enough of the Masai to last us for some time. Indeed, the general opinion was that, finding we had reached the mission station in safety, they had, knowing its strength, given up the pursuit of us as a bad job. How ill-judged that view was the sequel will show.

After the spies had gone, and Mrs Mackenzie and Flossie had retired for the night, Alphonse, the little Frenchman, came out, and Sir Henry, who is a very good French scholar, got him to tell us how he came to visit Central Africa, which he did in a most extraordinary lingo, that for the most part I shall not attempt to reproduce.

'My grandfather,' he began, 'was a soldier of the Guard, and served under Napoleon. He was in the retreat from Moscow, and lived for ten days on his own leggings and a pair he stole from a comrade. He used to get drunk – he died drunk, and I remember playing at drums on his coffin. My father – '

Here we suggested that he might skip his ancestry and come to the point.

'Bien, messieurs!' replied this comical little man, with a polite bow. 'I did only wish to demonstrate that the military principle is not hereditary. My grandfather was a splendid man, six feet two high, broad in proportion, a swallower of fire and gaiters. Also he was remarkable for his moustache. To me there remains the moustache and – nothing more.

'I am, messieurs, a cook, and I was born at Marseilles. In that dear town I spent my happy youth. For years and years I washed the dishes at the Hotel Continental. Ah, those were golden days!' and he sighed. 'I am a Frenchman. Need I say, messieurs, that I admire beauty? Nay, I adore the fair. Messieurs, we admire all the roses in a garden, but we pluck one. I plucked one, and alas, messieurs, it pricked my finger. She was a chambermaid, her name Annette, her figure ravishing, her face an angel's, her heart – alas, messieurs, that I should have to own it! – black and slippery as a patent leather boot. I loved to desperation, I adored her to despair. She transported me – in every sense; she inspired me. Never have I cooked as I cooked (for I had been promoted at the hotel) when Annette, my adored Annette, smiled on me. Never' – and here his manly voice broke into a sob – 'never shall I cook so well again.' Here he melted into tears.

'Come, cheer up!' said Sir Henry in French, smacking him smartly on the back. 'There's no knowing what may happen, you know. To judge from your dinner today, I should say you were in a fair way to recovery.'

Alphonse stopped weeping, and began to rub his back. 'Monsieur,' he said, 'doubtless means to console, but his hand is heavy. To continue: we loved, and were happy in each other's love. The birds in their little nest could not be happier than Alphonse and his Annette. Then came the blow – sapristi! – when I think of it. Messieurs will forgive me if I wipe away a tear. Mine was an evil number; I was drawn for the conscription. Fortune would be avenged on me for having won the heart of Annette.

'The evil moment came; I had to go. I tried to run away, but I was caught by brutal soldiers, and they banged me with the butt-end of muskets till my mustachios curled with pain. I had a cousin a linen-draper, well-to-do, but very ugly. He had drawn a good number, and sympathised when they thumped me. "To thee, my cousin," I said, "to thee, in whose veins flows the blue blood of our heroic grandparent, to thee I consign Annette. Watch over her whilst I hunt for glory in the bloody field."

' "Make your mind easy," said he; "I will." As the sequel shows, he did!

'I went. I lived in barracks on black soup. I am a refined man and a poet by nature, and I suffered tortures from the coarse horror of my surroundings. There was a drill sergeant, and he had a cane. Ah, that cane, how it curled! Alas, never can I forget it!

'One morning came the news; my battalion was ordered to Tonquin. The drill sergeant and the other coarse monsters rejoiced. I – I made enquiries about Tonquin. They were not satisfactory. In Tonquin are savage Chinese who rip you open. My artistic tastes – for I am also an artist – recoiled from the idea of being ripped open. The great man makes up his mind quickly. I made up my mind. I determined not to be ripped open. I deserted.

'I reached Marseilles disguised as an old man. I went to the house of my cousin – he in whom runs my grandfather's heroic blood – and there sat Annette. It was the season of cherries. They took a double stalk. At each end was a cherry. My cousin put one into his mouth, Annette put the other in hers. Then they drew the stalks in till their eyes met – and alas, alas that I should have to say it! – they kissed. The game was a pretty one, but it filled me with fury. The heroic blood of my grandfather boiled up in me. I rushed into the kitchen. I struck my cousin with the old man's crutch. He fell – I had slain him. Alas, I believe that I did slay him. Annette screamed. The gendarmes came. I fled. I reached the harbour. I hid aboard a vessel. The vessel put to sea. The captain found me and beat me. He took an opportunity. He posted a letter from a foreign port to the police. He did not put me ashore because I cooked so well. I cooked for him all the way to Zanzibar. When I asked for payment he kicked me. The blood of my heroic grandfather boiled within me, and I shook my fist in his face and vowed to have my revenge. He kicked me again. At Zanzibar there was a telegram. I cursed the man who invented telegraphs. Now I curse him again. I was to be arrested for desertion, for murder, and que sais-je? I escaped from the prison. I fled, I starved. I met the men of Monsieur le Curé. They brought me here. I am full of woe. But I return not to France. Better to risk my life in these horrible places than to know the Bagne.'

He paused, and we nearly choked with laughter, having to turn our faces away.

'Ah! you weep, messieurs,' he said. 'No wonder – it is a sad story.'

'Perhaps,' said Sir Henry, 'the heroic blood of your grandparent will triumph after all; perhaps you will still be great. At any rate we shall see. And now I vote we go to bed. I am dead tired, and we had not much sleep on that confounded rock last night.'

And so we did, and very strange the tidy rooms and clean white sheets seemed to us after our recent experiences.

CHAPTER 5

Umslopogaas Makes a Promise

Next morning at breakfast I missed Flossie and asked where she was.

'Well,' said her mother, 'when I got up this morning I found a note put outside my door in which – But here it is, you can read it for yourself,' and she gave me the slip of paper on which the following was written:

> DEAREST M— It is just dawn, and I am off to the hills to get Mr Q— a bloom of the lily he wants, so don't expect me till you see me. I have taken the white donkey; and nurse and a couple of boys are coming with me – also something to eat, as I may be away all day, for I am determined to get the lily if I have to go twenty miles for it.
>
> *Flossie*

'I hope she will be all right,' I said, a little anxiously; 'I never meant her to trouble after the flower.'

'Ah, Flossie can look after herself,' said her mother; 'she often goes off in this way like a true child of the wilderness.' But Mr Mackenzie, who came in just then and saw the note for the first time, looked rather grave, though he said nothing.

After breakfast was over I took him aside and asked him whether it would not be possible to send after the girl and get her back, having in view the possibility of there still being some Masai hanging about, at whose hands she might come to harm.

'I fear it would be of no use,' he answered. 'She may be fifteen miles off by now, and it is impossible to say what path she has taken. There are the hills;' and he pointed to a long range of rising ground stretching almost parallel with the course followed by the river Tana, but gradually sloping down to a dense bush-clad plain about five miles short of the house.

Here I suggested that we might get up the great tree over the house and search the country round with a spyglass; and this, after Mr Mackenzie had given some orders to his people to try and follow Flossie's spoor, we did.

The ascent of the mighty tree was rather an alarming performance, even with a sound rope-ladder fixed at both ends to climb up, at least to a landsman; but Good came up like a lamplighter.

On reaching the height at which the first fern-shaped boughs sprang from the bole, we stepped without any difficulty upon a platform made of boards, nailed from one bough to another, and large enough to accommodate a dozen people. As for the view, it was simply glorious. In every direction the bush rolled away in great billows for miles and miles, as far as the glass would show, only here and there broken by the brighter green of patches of cultivation, or by the glittering surface of lakes. To the northwest, Kenia reared his mighty head, and we could trace the Tana river curling like a silver snake almost from his feet, and far away beyond us towards the ocean. It is a glorious country, and only wants the hand of civilised man to make it a most productive one.

But look as we would, we could see no signs of Flossie and her donkey, so at last we had to come down disappointed. On reaching the veranda I found Umslopogaas sitting there, slowly and lightly sharpening his axe with a small whetstone he always carried with him.

'What doest thou, Umslopogaas?' I asked.

'I smell blood,' was the answer; and I could get no more out of him.

After dinner we again went up the tree and searched the surrounding country with a spyglass, but without result. When we came down Umslopogaas was still sharpening Inkosi-kaas, although she already had an edge like a razor. Standing in front of him, and regarding him with a mixture of fear and fascination, was Alphonse. And certainly he did seem an alarming object – sitting there, Zulu fashion, on his haunches, a wild look upon his intensely savage and yet intellectual face, sharpening, sharpening,

sharpening at the murderous-looking axe.

'Oh, the monster, the horrible man!' said the little French cook, lifting his hands in amazement. 'See but the hole in his head; the skin beats on it up and down like a baby's! Who would nurse such a baby?' and he burst out laughing at the idea.

For a moment Umslopogaas looked up from his sharpening, and a sort of evil light played in his dark eyes.

'What does the little "buffalo-heifer" [so named by Umslopogaas, on account of his mustachios and feminine characteristics] say? Let him be careful, or I will cut his horns. Beware, little man monkey, beware!'

Unfortunately Alphonse, who was getting over his fear of him, went on laughing at 'ce drôle d'un monsieur noir'. I was about to warn him to desist, when suddenly the huge Zulu bounded off the veranda on to the open space where Alphonse was standing, his features alive with a sort of malicious enthusiasm, and began swinging the axe round and round over the Frenchman's head.

'Stand still,' I shouted; 'do not move as you value your life – he will not hurt you;' but I doubt if Alphonse heard me, being, fortunately for himself, almost petrified with horror.

Then followed the most extraordinary display of sword, or rather of axemanship, that I ever saw. First of all the axe went flying round and round over the top of Alphonse's head, with an angry whirl and such extraordinary swiftness that it looked like a continuous band of steel, ever getting nearer and yet nearer to that unhappy individual's skull, till at last it grazed it as it flew. Then suddenly the motion was changed, and it seemed to literally flow up and down his body and limbs, never more than an eighth of an inch from them, and yet never striking them. It was a wonderful sight to see the little man fixed there, having apparently realised that to move would be to run the risk of sudden death, while his black tormentor towered over him, and wrapped him round with the quick flashes of the axe. For a minute or more this went on, till suddenly I saw the moving brightness travel down the side of Alphonse's face, and then outwards and stop. As it did so a tuft of something black fell to the ground; it was the tip of one of the little Frenchman's curling mustachios.

Umslopogaas leant upon the handle of Inkosi-kaas, and broke into a long, low laugh; and Alphonse, overcome with fear, sank into a sitting posture on the ground, while we stood astonished at this exhibition of almost superhuman skill and mastery of a weapon. 'Inkosi-kaas is sharp enough,' he shouted; 'the blow that clipped the "buffalo-heifer's" horn would have split a man from the crown to the chin. Few could have struck it but I; none could have struck it and not taken off the shoulder too. Look, thou little heifer! Am I a good man to laugh at, thinkest thou? For a space hast thou stood within a hair's-breadth of death. Laugh not again, lest the hair's-breadth be wanting. I have spoken.'

'What meanest thou by such mad tricks?' I asked of Umslopogaas, indignantly. 'Surely thou art mad. Twenty times didst thou go near to slaying the man.'

'And yet, Macumazahn, I slew not. Thrice as Inkosi-kaas flew the spirit entered into me to end him, and send her crashing through his skull; but I did not. Nay, it was but a jest; but tell the "heifer" that it is not well to mock at such as I. Now I go to make a shield, for I smell blood, Macumazahn – of a truth I smell blood. Before the battle hast thou not seen the vulture grow of a sudden in the sky? They smell the blood, Macumazahn, and my scent is more keen than theirs. There is a dry ox-hide down yonder; I go to make a shield.'

'That is an uncomfortable retainer of yours,' said Mr Mackenzie, who had witnessed this extraordinary scene. 'He has frightened Alphonse out of his wits; look!' and he pointed to the Frenchman, who, with a scared white face and trembling limbs, was making his way into the house. 'I don't think that he will ever laugh at "le monsieur noir" again.'

'Yes,' answered I, 'it is ill jesting with such as he. When he is roused he is like a fiend, and yet he has a kind heart in his own fierce way. I remember years ago seeing him nurse a sick child for a week. He is a strange character, but true as steel, and a strong stick to rest on in danger.'

'He says he smells blood,' said Mr Mackenzie. 'I only trust he is not right. I am getting very fearful about my little girl. She must have gone far, or she would be home by now. It is half-past three o'clock.'

I pointed out that she had taken food with her, and very likely would not in the ordinary course of events return till nightfall; but I myself felt very anxious, and fear that my anxiety betrayed itself.

Shortly after this, the people whom Mr Mackenzie had sent out to search for Flossie returned, stating that they had followed the spoor of the donkey for a couple of miles and had then lost it on some stony ground, nor could they discover it again. They had, however, scoured the country far and wide, but without success.

After this the afternoon wore drearily on, and towards evening, there still being no signs of Flossie, our anxiety grew very keen. As for the poor mother, she was quite prostrated by her fears, and no wonder, but the father kept his head wonderfully well. Everything that could be done was done: people were sent out in all directions, shots were fired, and a continuous outlook kept from the great tree, but without avail.

And then it grew dark, and still no sign of fair-haired little Flossie.

At eight o'clock we had supper. It was but a sorrowful meal, and Mrs Mackenzie did not appear at it. We three also were very silent, for in addition to our natural anxiety as to the fate of the child, we were weighed down by the sense that we had brought this trouble on the head of our kind host. When supper was nearly at an end I made an excuse to leave the table. I wanted to get outside and think the situation over. I went on to the veranda and, having lit my pipe, sat down on a seat about a dozen feet from the right-hand end of the structure, which was, as the reader may remember, exactly opposite one of the narrow doors of the protecting wall that enclosed the house and flower garden. I had been sitting there perhaps six or seven minutes when I thought I heard the door move. I looked in that direction and I listened, but, being unable to make out anything, concluded that I must have been mistaken. It was a darkish night, the moon not having yet risen.

Another minute passed, when suddenly something round fell with a soft but heavy thud upon the stone flooring of the veranda, and came bounding and rolling along past me. For a moment I did not rise, but sat wondering what it could be. Finally, I concluded it must have been an animal. Just then, however, another idea struck me, and I got up quick enough. The thing lay quite still a few feet beyond me. I put down my hand towards it and it did not move: clearly it was not an animal. My hand touched it. It was soft and warm and heavy. Hurriedly I lifted it and held it up against the faint starlight.

It was a newly severed human head!

I am an old hand and not easily upset, but I own that that ghastly sight made me feel sick. How had the thing come there? Whose was it? I put it down and ran to the little doorway. I could see nothing, hear nobody. I was about to go out into the darkness beyond, but remembering that to do so was to expose myself to the risk of being stabbed, I drew back, shut the door, and bolted it. Then I returned to the veranda, and in as careless a voice as I could command called Curtis. I fear, however, that my tones must have betrayed me, for not only Sir Henry but also Good and Mackenzie rose from the table and came hurrying out.

'What is it?' said the clergyman, anxiously.

Then I had to tell them.

Mr Mackenzie turned pale as death under his red skin. We were standing opposite the hall door, and there was a light in it so that I could see. He snatched the head up by the hair and held it against the light.

'It is the head of one of the men who accompanied Flossie,' he said with a gasp. 'Thank God it is not hers!'

We all stood and stared at each other aghast. What was to be done?

Just then there was a knocking at the door that I had bolted, and a voice cried, 'Open, my father, open!'

The door was unlocked, and in sped a terrified man. He was one of the spies who had been sent out.

'My father,' he cried, 'the Masai are on us! A great body of them have passed round the hill and are moving towards the old stone kraal down by the little stream. My father, make strong thy heart! In the midst of them I saw the white ass, and on it sat the Water-lily [Flossie]. An Elmoran [young warrior] led the ass, and by its side walked the nurse weeping. The men who went with her in the morning I saw not.'

'Was the child alive?' asked Mr Mackenzie, hoarsely.

'She was white as the snow, but well, my father. They passed quite close to me, and looking up from where I lay hid I saw her face against the sky.'

'God help her and us!' groaned the clergyman.

'How many are there of them?' I asked.

'More than two hundred – two hundred and half a hundred.'

Once more we looked one on the other. What was to be done? Just then there rose a loud insistent cry outside the wall.

'Open the door, white man; open the door! A herald – a herald to speak with thee.' Thus cried the voice.

Umslopogaas ran to the wall, and, reaching with his long arms to the coping, lifted his head above it and gazed over.

'I see but one man,' he said. 'He is armed, and carries a basket in his hand.'

'Open the door,' I said. 'Umslopogaas, take thine axe and stand thereby. Let one man pass. If another follows, slay.'

The door was unbarred. In the shadow of the wall stood Umslopogaas, his axe raised above his head to strike. Just then the moon came out. There was a moment's pause, and then in stalked a Masai Elmoran, clad in the full war panoply that I have already described, but bearing a large basket in his hand. The moonlight shone bright upon his great spear as he walked. He was physically a splendid man, apparently about thirty-five years of age. Indeed, none of the Masai that I saw were under six feet high, though mostly quite young. When he got opposite to us he halted, put down the basket, and stuck the spike of his spear into the ground, so that it stood upright.

'Let us talk,' he said. 'The first messenger we sent to you could not talk;' and he pointed to the head which lay upon the paving of the stoep – a ghastly sight in the moonlight; 'but I have words to speak if ye have ears to hear. Also I bring presents;' and he pointed to the basket and laughed with an air of swaggering insolence that is perfectly indescribable, and yet which one could not but admire, seeing that he was surrounded by enemies.

'Say on,' said Mr Mackenzie.

'I am the "Lygonani" [war captain] of a party of the Masai of the Guasa Amboni. I and my men followed these three white men,' and he pointed to Sir Henry, Good, and myself, 'but they were too clever for us, and escaped hither. We have a quarrel with them, and are going to kill them.'

'Are you, my friend?' said I to myself.

'In following these men we this morning caught two black men, one black woman, a white donkey, and a white girl. One of the black men we killed – there is his head upon the pavement; the other ran away. The black woman, the little white girl, and the white ass we took and brought with us. In proof thereof have I brought this basket that she carried. Is it not thy daughter's basket?'

Mr Mackenzie nodded, and the warrior went on.

'Good! With thee and thy daughter we have no quarrel, nor do we wish to harm thee, save as to thy cattle, which we have already gathered, two hundred and forty head – a beast for every man's father.'*

Here Mr Mackenzie gave a groan, as he greatly valued this herd of cattle, which he bred with much care and trouble.

'So, save for the cattle, thou mayst go free; more especially,' he added frankly, glancing at the wall, 'as this place would be a difficult one to take. But as to these men it is otherwise; we have followed them for nights and days, and must kill them. Were we to return to our kraal without having done so, all the girls would make a mock of us. So, however troublesome it may be, they must die.

'Now I have a proposition for thee. We would not harm the little girl; she is too fair to harm, and has besides a brave spirit. Give us one of these three men – a life for a life – and we will let her go, and throw in the black woman with her also. This is a fair

* The Masai Elmoran or young warriors can own no property, so all the booty they may win in battle belongs to their fathers alone.   A.Q.

offer, white man. We ask but for one, not for the three; we must take another opportunity to kill the other two. I do not even pick my man, though I should prefer the big one,' pointing to Sir Henry; 'he looks strong, and would die more slowly.'

'And if I say I will not yield the man?' said Mr Mackenzie.

'Nay, say not so, white man,' answered the Masai, 'for then thy daughter dies at dawn, and the woman with her says thou hast no other child. Were she older I would take her for a servant; but as she is so young I will slay her with my own hand – ay, with this very spear. Thou canst come and see, an' thou wilt. I give thee a safe conduct;' and the fiend laughed aloud as his brutal jest.

Meanwhile I had been thinking rapidly, as one does in emergencies, and had come to the conclusion that I would exchange myself against Flossie. I scarcely like to mention the matter for fear it should be misunderstood. Pray do not let anyone be misled into thinking that there was anything heroic about this, or any such nonsense. It was merely a matter of common sense and common justice. My life was an old and worthless one, hers was young and valuable. Her death would pretty well kill her father and mother also, whilst nobody would be much the worse for mine; indeed, several charitable institutions would have cause to rejoice thereat. It was indirectly through me that the dear little girl was in her present position. Lastly, a man was better fitted to meet death in such a peculiarly awful form than a sweet young girl. Not, however, that I meant to let these gentry torture me to death – I am far too much of a coward to allow that, being naturally a timid man; my plan was to see the girl safely exchanged and then to shoot myself, trusting that the Almighty would take the peculiar circumstances of the case into consideration and pardon the act. All this and more went through my mind in very few seconds.

'All right, Mackenzie,' I said, 'you can tell the man that I will exchange myself against Flossie, only I stipulate that she shall be safely in this house before they kill me.'

'Eh?' said Sir Henry and Good simultaneously. 'That you don't.'

'No, no,' said Mr Mackenzie. 'I will have no man's blood upon my hands. If it please God that my daughter should die this awful death, His will be done. You are a brave man (which I am not by any means) and a noble man, Quatermain, but you shall not go.'

'If nothing else turns up I shall go,' I said decidedly.

'This is an important matter,' said Mackenzie, addressing the Lygonani, 'and we must think it over. You shall have our answer at dawn.'

'Very well, white man,' answered the savage indifferently; 'only remember if thy answer is late thy little white bud will never grow into a flower, that is all, for I shall cut it with this,' and he touched the spear. 'I should have thought that thou wouldst play a trick and attack us at night, but I know from the woman with the girl that your men are down at the coast, and that thou hast but twenty men here. It is not wise, white man,' he added with a laugh, 'to keep so small a garrison for your "boma" [kraal]. Well, good-night, and good-night to you also, other white men, whose eyelids I shall soon close once and for all. At dawn thou wilt bring me word. If not, remember it shall be as I have said.' Then turning to Umslopogaas, who had all the while been standing behind him and shepherding him as it were, 'Open the door for me, fellow, quick now.'

This was too much for the old chief's patience. For the last ten minutes his lips had been, figuratively speaking, positively watering over the Masai Lygonani, and this he could not stand. Placing his long hand on the Elmoran's shoulder he gripped it and gave him such a twist as brought him face to face with himself. Then, thrusting his fierce countenance to within a few inches of the Masai's evil feather-framed features, he said in a low growling voice: 'Seest thou me?'

'Ay, fellow, I see thee.'

'And seest thou this?' and he held Inkosi-kaas before his eyes.

'Ay, fellow, I see the toy; what of it?'

'Thou Masai dog, thou boasting windbag, thou capturer of little girls, with this "toy" will I hew thee limb from limb. Well for thee that thou art a herald, or even now would I strew thy members about the grass.'

The Masai shook his great spear and laughed loud and long as he answered, 'I would that thou stoodst against me man to man, and we would see,' and again he turned to go still laughing.

'Thou shalt stand against me man to man, be not afraid,' replied Umslopogaas, still in the same ominous voice. 'Thou shalt stand face to face with Umslopogaas, of the blood of Chaka, of the people of the Amazulu, a captain in the regiment of the Nkoma-bakosi, as many have done before, and bow thyself to Inkosi-kaas, as many have done before. Ay, laugh on, laugh on! tomorrow night shall the jackals laugh as they crunch thy ribs.'

When the Lygonani had gone, one of us thought of opening the basket he had brought as a proof that Flossie was really their prisoner. On lifting the lid it was found to contain a most lovely specimen of both bulb and flower of the Goya lily, which I have already described, in full bloom and quite uninjured, and what was more a note in Flossie's childish hand written in pencil upon a greasy piece of paper that had been used to wrap up some food in:

DEAREST FATHER AND MOTHER, [ran the note] The Masai caught us when we were coming home with the lily. I tried to escape but could not. They killed Tom: the other man ran away. They have not hurt nurse and me, but say that they mean to exchange us against one of Mr Quatermain's party. *I will have nothing of the sort*. Do not let anybody give his life for me. Try and attack them at night; they are going to feast on three bullocks they have stolen and killed. I have my pistol, and if no help comes by dawn I will shoot myself. They shall not kill me. If so, remember me always, dearest father and mother. I am very frightened, but I trust in God. I dare not write any more as they are beginning to notice. Goodbye.

Flossie

Scrawled across the outside of this was 'Love to Mr Quatermain. They are going to take up the basket, so he will get the lily.'

When I read those words, written by that brave little girl in an hour of danger sufficiently near and horrible to have turned the brain of a strong man, I own I wept, and once more in my heart I vowed that she should not die while my life could be given to save her.

Then eagerly, quickly, almost fiercely, we fell to discussing the situation. Again I said that I would go, and again Mackenzie negatived it, and Curtis and Good, like the true men that they are, vowed that, if I did, they would go with me, and die back to back with me.

'It is,' I said at last, 'absolutely necessary that an effort of some sort should be made before the morning.'

'Then let us attack them with what force we can muster, and take our chance,' said Sir Henry.

'Ay, ay,' growled Umslopogaas, in Zulu; 'spoken like a man, Incubu. What is there to be afraid of? Two hundred and fifty Masai, forsooth! How many are we? The chief there [Mr Mackenzie] has twenty men, and thou, Macumazahn, hast five men, and there are also five white men – that is, thirty men in all – enough, enough. Listen now, Macumazahn, thou who art very clever and old in war. What says the maid? These men eat and make merry; let it be their funeral feast. What said the dog whom I hope to hew down at daybreak? That he feared no attack because we were so few. Knowest thou the old kraal where the men have camped? I saw it this morning; it is thus:' and he drew an oval on the floor; 'here is the big entrance, filled up with thorn bushes, and opening on to a steep rise. Why, Incubu, thou and I with axes will hold it against an hundred men striving to break out! Look, now; thus shall the battle go. Just as the light begins to glint upon the oxen's horns – not before, or it will be too dark, and not later, or they will be awakening and perceive us – let Bougwan creep round with ten men to the top end of the kraal, where the narrow entrance is. Let them silently slay the sentry there so that he makes no sound, and stand ready. Then, Incubu, let thee and me and one of the Askari – the one with the broad chest – he is a brave man – creep to the wide entrance that is filled with thorn bushes, and there also slay the sentry, and armed with battleaxes take our stand also one on each side of the pathway, and one a few paces beyond to deal with such as pass the twain at the gate. It is there that the rush will come. That will leave sixteen men. Let these men be divided into two parties, with one of which shalt thou go, Macumazahn, and with one the "praying man" [Mr Mackenzie], and, all armed with rifles, let them make their way one to the right side of the kraal and one to the left; and when thou, Macumazahn, lowest like an ox, all shall open fire with the guns upon the sleeping men, being very careful not to hit the little maid. Then shall Bougwan at the far end and his ten men raise the war-cry, and, springing over the wall, put the Masai there to the sword. And it shall happen that, being yet heavy with food and sleep, and bewildered by the firing of the guns, the falling of men, and the spears of Bougwan, the soldiers shall rise and rush like wild game towards the thorn-stopped entrance, and there the bullets from either side shall plough through them, and there shall Incubu and the Askari and I wait for those who break across. Such is my plan, Macumazahn; if thou hast a better, name it.'

When he had done, I explained to the others such portions of his scheme as they had failed to understand, and they all joined with me in expressing the greatest admiration of the acute and skilful programme devised by the old Zulu, who was indeed, in his own savage fashion, the finest general I ever knew. After some discussion we determined to accept the scheme, as it stood, it being the only one possible under the circumstances, and giving the best chance of success that such a forlorn hope would admit of – which, however, considering the enormous odds and the character of our foe, was not very great.

'Ah, old lion!' I said to Umslopogaas, 'thou knowest how to lie in wait as well as how to bite, where to seize as well as where to hang on.'

'Ay, ay, Macumazahn,' he answered. 'For thirty years have I been a warrior, and have seen many things. It will be a good fight. I smell blood – I tell thee, I smell blood.'

CHAPTER 6

The Night Wears On

As may be imagined, at the very first sign of a Masai the entire population of the Mission Station had sought refuge inside the stout stone wall, and were now to be seen – men, women, and countless children – huddled up together in little groups, and all talking at once in awed tones of the awfulness of Masai manners and customs, and of the fate that they had to expect if those bloodthirsty savages succeeded in getting over the stone wall.

Immediately after we had settled upon the outline of our plan of action as suggested by Umslopogaas, Mr Mackenzie sent for four sharp boys of from twelve to fifteen years of age, and despatched them to various points where they could keep an outlook upon the Masai camp, with others to report from time to time what was going on. Other lads and even women were stationed at intervals along the wall in order to guard against the possibility of surprise.

After this the twenty men who formed his whole available fighting force were summoned by our host into the square formed by the house, and there, standing by the bole of the great conifer, he earnestly addressed them and our four Askari. Indeed, it formed a very impressive scene – one not likely to be forgotten by anybody who witnessed it. Immediately by the tree stood the angular form of Mr Mackenzie, one arm outstretched as he talked, and the other resting against the giant bole, his hat off, and his plain but kindly face clearly betraying the anguish of his mind. Next to him was his poor wife, who, seated on a chair, had her face hidden in her hand. On the other side of her was Alphonse, looking exceedingly uncomfortable, and behind him stood the three of us, with Umslopogaas' grim and towering form in the background, resting, as usual, on his axe. In front stood and squatted the group of armed men – some with rifles in their hands, and others with spears and shields – following with eager attention every word that fell from the speaker's lips. The white light of the moon peering in beneath the lofty boughs threw a strange wild glamour over the scene, whilst the melancholy soughing of the night wind passing through the millions of pine needles overhead added a sadness of its own to what was already a sufficiently tragic occasion.

'Men,' said Mr Mackenzie, after he had put all the circumstances of the case fully and clearly before them, and explained to them the proposed plan of our forlorn hope – 'men, for years I have been a good friend to you, protecting you, teaching you, guarding you and yours from harm, and ye have prospered with me. Ye have seen my child – the Water-lily, as ye call her – grow year by year, from tenderest infancy to tender childhood, and from childhood on towards maidenhood. She has been your children's playmate, she has helped to tend you when sick, and ye have loved her.'

'We have,' said a deep voice, 'and we will die to save her.'

'I thank you from my heart – I thank you. Sure am I that now, in this hour of darkest trouble; now that her young life is like to be cut off by cruel and savage men – who of a truth "know not what they do" – ye will strive your best to save her, and to save me and her mother from broken hearts. Think, too, of your own wives and children. If she dies, her death will be followed by an attack upon us here, and at the best, even if we hold our own, your houses and gardens will be destroyed, and your goods and cattle swept away. I am, as ye well know, a man of peace. Never in all these years have I lifted my hand to shed man's blood; but now I say strike, strike, in the name of God, Who bade us protect our lives and homes. Swear to me,' he went on with added fervour – 'swear to me that whilst a man of you remains alive ye will strive your uttermost with me and with these brave white men to save the child from a bloody and cruel death.'

'Say no more, my father,' said the same deep voice, that belonged to a stalwart elder of the Mission; 'we swear it. May we and ours die the death of dogs, and our bones be thrown to the jackals and the kites, if we break the oath! It is a fearful thing to do, my father, so few to strike at so many, yet will we do it or die in the doing. We swear!'

'Ay, thus say we all,' chimed in the others.

'Thus say we all,' said I.

'It is well,' went on Mr Mackenzie. 'Ye are true men and not broken reeds to lean on. And now, friends – white and black together – let us kneel and offer up our humble supplication to the Throne of Power, praying that He in the hollow of Whose hand lie all our lives, Who giveth life and giveth death, may be pleased to make strong our arms that we may prevail in what awaits us at the morning's light.'

And he knelt down, an example that we all followed except Umslopogaas, who still stood in the background, grimly leaning on Inkosi-kaas. The fierce old Zulu had no gods and worshipped nought, unless it were his battleaxe.

'Oh God of gods!' began the clergyman, his deep voice, tremulous with emotion, echoing up in the silence even to the leafy roof; 'Protector of the oppressed, Refuge of those in danger, Guardian of the helpless, hear Thou our prayer! Almighty Father, to Thee we come in supplication. Hear Thou our prayer! Behold, one child hast Thou given us – an innocent child, nurtured in Thy knowledge – and now she lies beneath the shadow of the sword, in danger of a fearful death at the hands of savage men. Be with her now, oh God, and comfort her! Save her, oh Heavenly Father! Oh God of battle, Who teacheth our hands to war and our fingers to fight, in Whose strength are hid the destinies of men, be Thou with us in the hour of strife. When we go forth into the shadow of death, make Thou us strong to conquer. Breathe Thou upon our foes and scatter them; turn Thou their strength to water, and bring their high-blown pride to nought; compass us about with Thy protection; throw over us the shield of Thy power; forget us not now in the hour of our sore distress; help us now that the cruel man would dash our little ones against the stones! Hear Thou our prayer! And for those of us who, kneeling now on earth in health before Thee, shall at the sunrise adore Thy Presence on the Throne, hear our prayer! Make them clean, oh God; wash away their offences in the blood of the Lamb; and when their spirits pass, oh receive Thou them into the haven of the just. Go forth, oh Father, go forth with us into the battle, as with the Israelites of old. Oh God of battle, hear Thou our prayer!'

He ceased, and after a moment's silence we all rose, and then began our preparations in good earnest. As Umslopogaas said, it was time to stop 'talking' and get to business. The men who were to form each little party were carefully selected, and still more carefully and minutely instructed as to what was to be done. After much consideration it was agreed that the ten men led by Good, whose duty it was to stampede the camp, were not to carry firearms; that is, with the exception of Good himself, who had a revolver as well as a short sword – the Masai 'sime' which I had taken from the body of our poor servant who was murdered in the canoe. We feared that if they had firearms the result of three cross-fires carried on at once would be that some of our own people would be shot; besides, it appeared to all of us that the work they had to do would best be carried out with cold steel – especially to Umslopogaas, who was, indeed, a great advocate of cold steel. We had with us four Winchester repeating rifles, besides half a dozen Martinis. I armed myself with one of the repeaters – my own; an excellent weapon for this kind of work, where great rapidity of fire is desirable, and fitted with ordinary flap-sights instead of the cumbersome sliding mechanism which they generally have. Mr Mackenzie took another, and the two remaining ones were given to two of his men who understood the use of them and were noted shots. The Martinis and some rifles of Mr Mackenzie's were served out, together with a plentiful supply of ammunition, to the other natives who were to form the two parties whose duty it was to be to open fire from separate sides of the kraal on the sleeping Masai, and who were fortunately all more or less accustomed to the use of a gun.

As for Umslopogaas, we know how he was armed – with an axe. It may be remembered that he, Sir Henry, and the strongest of the Askari were to hold the thorn-stopped entrance to the kraal against the anticipated rush of men striving to escape. Of course, for such a purpose as this guns were useless. Therefore Sir Henry and the Askari proceeded to arm themselves in like fashion. It so happened that Mr Mackenzie had in his little store a selection of the very best and English-made hammer-backed axe-heads. Sir Henry selected one of these weighing about two and a half pounds and very broad in the blade, and the Askari took another a size smaller. After Umslopogaas had put an extra edge on these two axe-heads, we fixed them to three feet six helves, of which Mr Mackenzie fortunately had some in stock, made of a light but exceedingly tough native wood, something like English ash, only more springy. When two suitable helves had been selected with great care and the ends of the hafts notched to prevent the hand from slipping, the axe-heads were fixed on them as firmly as possible, and the weapons immersed in a bucket of water for half an hour. The result of this was to swell the wood in the socket in such a fashion that nothing short of burning would get it out again. When this important matter had been attended to by Umslopogaas, I went into my room and proceeded to open a little tin-lined deal case, which contained – what do you think? – nothing more or less than four mail shirts.

It had happened to us three on a previous journey that we had made in another part of Africa to owe our lives to iron shirts of native make, and remembering this, I had suggested before we started on our present hazardous expedition that we should have some made to fit us. There was a little difficulty about this, as armour-making is pretty well an extinct art, but they can do most things in the way of steel work in Birmingham if they are put to it and you will pay the price, and the end of it was that they turned us out the loveliest steel shirts it is possible to see. The workmanship was exceedingly fine, the web being composed of thousands upon thousands of stout but tiny rings of the best steel made. These shirts, or rather steel-sleeved and high-necked jerseys, were lined with ventilated wash leather, were not bright, but browned like the barrel of a gun; and mine weighed exactly seven pounds and fitted me so well that I found I could wear it for days next to my skin without being chafed. Sir Henry had two, one of the ordinary make, viz. a jersey with little dependent flaps meant to afford some protection to the upper part of the thighs, and another of his own design fashioned on the pattern of the garments advertised as 'combinations' and weighing twelve pounds. This combination shirt, of which the seat was made of wash-leather, protected the whole body down to the knees, but was rather more cumbersome, inasmuch as it had to be laced up at the back and, of course, involved some extra weight. With these shirts were what looked like four brown cloth travelling caps with ear pieces. Each of these caps was, however, quilted with steel links so as to afford a most valuable protection for the head.

It seems almost laughable to talk of steel shirts in these days of bullets, against which they are of course quite useless; but where one has to do with savages, armed with cutting weapons such as assegais or battleaxes, they afford the most valuable protection, being, if well made, quite invulnerable to them. I have often thought that if only the English Government had in our savage wars, and more especially in the Zulu war, thought fit to serve out light steel shirts, there would be many a man alive today who, as it is, is dead and forgotten.

To return: on the present occasion we blessed our foresight in bringing these shirts, and also our good luck, in that they had not been stolen by our rascally bearers when they ran away with our goods. As Curtis had two, and after considerable deliberation, had made up his mind to wear his combination one himself – the extra three or four pounds' weight being a matter of no account to so strong a man, and the protection afforded to the thighs being a very important matter to a fighting man not armed with a shield of any kind – I suggested that he should lend the other to Umslopogaas, who was to share the danger and the glory of his post. He readily consented, and called the Zulu, who came bearing Sir Henry's axe, which he had now fixed up to his satisfaction, with him. When we showed him the steel shirt, and explained to him that we wanted him to wear it, he at first declined, saying that he had fought in his own skin for thirty years, and that he was not going to begin now to fight in an iron one. Thereupon I took a heavy spear, and, spreading the shirt upon the floor, drove the spear down upon it with all my strength, the weapon rebounding without leaving a mark upon the tempered steel. This exhibition half converted him; and when I pointed out to him how necessary it was that he should not let any old-fashioned prejudices he might possess stand in the way of a precaution which might preserve a valuable life at a time when men were scarce, and also that if he wore this shirt he might dispense with a shield, and so have both hands free, he yielded at once, and proceeded to invest his frame with the 'iron skin'. And indeed, although made for Sir Henry, it fitted the great Zulu like a skin. The two men were almost of a height; and, though Curtis looked the bigger man, I am inclined to think that the difference was more imaginary than real, the fact being that, although he was plumper and rounder, he was not really bigger, except in the arm. Umslopogaas had, comparatively speaking, thin arms, but they were as strong as wire ropes. At any rate, when they both stood, axe in hand, invested in the brown mail, which clung to their mighty forms like a web garment, showing the swell of every muscle and the curve of every line, they formed a pair that any ten men might shrink from meeting.

It was now nearly one o'clock in the morning, and the spies reported that, after having drunk the blood of the oxen and eaten enormous quantities of meat, the Masai were going to sleep round their watchfires; but that sentries had been posted at each opening of the kraal. Flossie, they added, was sitting not far from the wall in the centre of the western side of the kraal, and by her were the nurse and the white donkey, which was tethered to a peg. Her feet were bound with a rope, and warriors were lying about all round her.

As there was absolutely nothing further that could be done then we all took some supper, and went to lie down for a couple of hours. I could not help admiring the way in which old Umslopogaas flung himself upon the floor, and, unmindful of what was hanging over him, instantly sank into a deep sleep. I do not know how it was with the others, but I could not do as much. Indeed, as is usual with me on these occasions, I am sorry to say that I felt rather frightened; and, now that some of the enthusiasm had gone out of me, and I began to calmly contemplate what we had undertaken to do, truth compels me to add that I did not like it.

We were but thirty men all told, a good many of whom were no doubt quite unused to fighting, and we were going to engage two hundred and fifty of the fiercest, bravest, and most formidable savages in Africa, who, to make matters worse, were protected by a stone wall. It was, indeed, a mad undertaking, and what made it even madder was the exceeding improbability of our being able to take up our positions without attracting the notice of the sentries. Of course if we once did that – and any slight accident, such as the chance discharge of a gun, might do it – we were done for, for the whole camp would be up in a second, and our only hope lay in surprise.

The bed whereon I lay indulging in these uncomfortable reflections was near an open window that looked on to the veranda, through which came an extraordinary sound of groaning and weeping. For a time I could not make out what it was, but at last I got up and, putting my head out of the window, stared about. Presently I saw a dim figure kneeling on the end of the veranda and beating his breast – in which I recognised Alphonse. Not being able to understand his French talk or what on earth he was at, I called to him and asked him what he was doing.

'Ah, monsieur,' he sighed, 'I do make prayer for the souls of those whom I shall slay tonight.'

'Indeed,' I said, 'then I wish that you would do it a little more quietly.'

Alphonse retreated, and I heard no more of his groans. And so the time passed, till at length Mr Mackenzie called me in a whisper through the window, for of course everything had now to be done in the most absolute silence. 'Three o'clock,' he said: 'we must begin to move at half-past.'

I told him to come in, and presently he entered, and I am bound to say that if it had not been that just then I had not got a laugh anywhere about me, I should have exploded at the sight he presented armed for battle. To begin with, he had on a clergyman's black swallow-tail and a kind of broad-rimmed black felt hat, both of which he had donned on account, he said, of their dark colour. In his hand was the Winchester repeating rifle we had lent him; and stuck in an elastic cricketing belt, like those worn by English boys, were, first, a huge buckhorn-handled carving knife with a guard to it, and next a long-barrelled Colt's revolver.

'Ah, my friend,' he said, seeing me staring at his belt, 'you are looking at my "carver". I thought it might come in handy if we came to close quarters; it is excellent steel, and many is the pig I have killed with it.'

By this time everybody was up and dressing. I put on a light Norfolk jacket over my mail shirt in order to have a pocket handy to hold my cartridges, and buckled on my revolver. Good did the same, but Sir Henry put on nothing except his mail shirt, steel-lined cap, and a pair of 'veldt-schoons' or soft hide shoes, his legs being bare from the knees down. His revolver he strapped on round his middle outside the armoured shirt.

Meanwhile Umslopogaas was mustering the men in the square under the big tree and going the rounds to see that each was properly armed, etc. At the last moment we made one change. Finding that two of the men who were to have gone with the firing parties knew little or nothing of guns, but were good spearsmen, we took away their rifles, supplied them with shields and long spears of the Masai pattern, and took them off to join Curtis, Umslopogaas, and the Askari in holding the wide opening; it having become clear to us that three men, however brave and strong, were too few for the work.

CHAPTER 7

A Slaughter Grim and Great

Then there was a pause, and we stood there in the chilly silent darkness waiting till the moment came to start. It was, perhaps, the most trying time of all – that slow, slow quarter of an hour. The minutes seemed to drag along with leaden feet, and the quiet, the solemn hush, that brooded over all – big, as it were, with a coming fate, was most oppressive to the spirits. I once remember having to get up before dawn to see a man hanged, and I then went through a very similar set of sensations, only in the present instance my feelings were animated by that more vivid and personal element which naturally appertains rather to the person to be operated on than to the most sympathetic spectator. The solemn faces of the men, well aware that the short passage of an hour would mean for some, and perhaps all of them, the last great passage to the unknown or oblivion; the bated whispers in which they spoke; even Sir Henry's continuous and thoughtful examination of his woodcutter's axe and the fidgety way in which Good kept polishing his eyeglass, all told the same tale of nerves stretched pretty nigh to breaking-point. Only Umslopogaas, leaning as usual upon Inkosi-kaas and taking an occasional pinch of snuff, was to all appearance perfectly and completely unmoved. Nothing could touch his iron nerves.

The moon went down. For a long while she had been getting nearer and nearer to the horizon. Now she finally sank and left the world in darkness save for a faint grey tinge in the eastern sky that palely heralded the dawn.

Mr Mackenzie stood, watch in hand, his wife clinging to his arm and striving to stifle her sobs.

'Twenty minutes to four,' he said, 'it ought to be light enough to attack at twenty minutes past four. Captain Good had better be moving, he will want three or four minutes' start.'

Good gave one final polish to his eyeglass, nodded to us in a jocular sort of way – which I could not help feeling it must have cost him something to muster up – and, ever polite, took off his steel-lined cap to Mrs Mackenzie and started for his position at the head of the kraal, to reach which he had to make a detour by some paths known to the natives.

Just then one of the boys came in and reported that everybody in the Masai camp, with the exception of the two sentries who were walking up and down in front of the respective entrances, appeared to be fast asleep. Then the rest of us took the road. First came the guide, then Sir Henry, Umslopogaas, the Wakwafi Askari, and Mr Mackenzie's two mission natives armed with long spears and shields. I followed immediately after with Alphonse and five natives all armed with guns, and Mr Mackenzie brought up the rear with the six remaining natives.

The cattle kraal where the Masai were camped lay at the foot of the hill on which the house stood, or, roughly speaking, about eight hundred yards from the Mission buildings. The first five hundred yards of this distance we traversed quietly indeed, but at a good pace; after that we crept forward as silently as a leopard on his prey, gliding like ghosts from bush to bush and stone to stone. When I had gone a little way I chanced to look behind me, and saw the redoubtable Alphonse staggering along with white face and trembling knees, and his rifle, which was at full cock, pointed directly at the small of my back. Having halted and carefully put the rifle at 'safety', we started again, and all went well till we were within one hundred yards or so of the kraal, when his teeth began to chatter in the most aggressive way.

'If you don't stop that I will kill you,' I whispered savagely; for the idea of having all our lives sacrificed to a tooth-chattering cook was too much for me. I began to fear that he would betray us, and heartily wished we had left him behind.

'But, monsieur, I cannot help it,' he answered, 'it is the cold.'

Here was a dilemma, but fortunately I devised a plan. In the pocket of the coat I had on was a small piece of dirty rag that I had used sometime before to clean a gun with. 'Put this in your mouth,' I whispered again, giving him the rag; 'and if I hear another sound you are a dead man.' I knew that that would stifle the clatter of his teeth. I must have looked as if I meant what I said, for he instantly obeyed me, and continued his journey in silence.

Then we crept on again.

At last we were within fifty yards of the kraal. Between us and it was an open space of sloping grass with only one mimosa bush and a couple of tussocks of a sort of thistle for cover. We were still hidden in fairly thick bush. It was beginning to grow light. The stars had paled and a sickly gleam played about the east and was reflected on the earth. We could see the outline of the kraal clearly enough, and could also make out the faint glimmer of the dying embers of the Masai campfires. We halted and watched, for the sentry we knew was posted at the opening. Presently he appeared, a fine tall fellow, walking idly up and down within five paces of the thorn-stopped entrance. We had hoped to catch him napping, but it was not to be. He seemed particularly wide awake. If we could not kill that man, and kill him silently, we were lost. There we crouched and watched him. Presently Umslopogaas, who was a few paces ahead of me, turned and made a sign, and next second I saw him go down on his stomach like a snake, and, taking an opportunity when the sentry's head was turned, begin to work his way through the grass without a sound.

The unconscious sentry commenced to hum a little tune, and Umslopogaas crept on. He reached the shelter of the mimosa bush unperceived and there waited. Still the sentry walked up and down. Presently he turned and looked over the wall into the camp. Instantly the human snake who was stalking him glided on ten yards and got behind one of the tussocks of the thistle-like plant, reaching it as the Elmoran turned again. As he did so his eye fell upon this patch of thistles, and it seemed to strike him that it did not look quite right. He advanced a pace towards it – halted, yawned, stooped down, picked up a little pebble and threw it at it. It hit Umslopogaas upon the head, luckily not upon the armour shirt. Had it done so the clink would have betrayed us. Luckily, too, the shirt was browned and not bright steel, which would certainly have been detected. Apparently satisfied that there was nothing wrong, he then gave over his investigations and contented himself with leaning on his spear and standing gazing idly at the tuft. For at least three minutes did he stand thus, plunged apparently in a gentle reverie, and there we lay in the last extremity of anxiety, expecting every moment that we should be discovered or that some untoward accident would happen. I could hear Alphonse's teeth going like anything on the oiled rag, and turning my head round made an awful face at him. But I am bound to state that my own heart was at much the same game as the Frenchman's castanets, while the perspiration was pouring from my body, causing the wash-leather-lined shirt to stick to me unpleasantly, and altogether I was in the pitiable state known by schoolboys as a 'blue fright'.

At last the ordeal came to an end. The sentry glanced at the east, and appeared to note with satisfaction that his period of duty was coming to an end – as indeed it was, once and for all – for he rubbed his hands and began to walk again briskly to warm himself.

The moment his back was turned the long black snake glided on again, and reached the other thistle tuft, which was within a couple of paces of his return beat.

Back came the sentry and strolled right past the tuft, utterly unconscious of the presence that was crouching behind it. Had he looked down he could scarcely have failed to see, but he did not do so.

He passed, and then his hidden enemy erected himself, and with outstretched hand followed in his tracks.

A moment more, and, just as the Elmoran was about to turn, the great Zulu made a spring, and in the growing light we could see his long lean hands close round the Masai's throat. Then followed a convulsive twining of the two dark bodies, and in another second I saw the Masai's head bent back, and heard a sharp crack, something like that of a dry twig snapping, and he fell down upon the ground, his limbs moving spasmodically.

Umslopogaas had put out all his iron strength and broken the warrior's neck.

For a moment he knelt upon his victim, still gripping his throat till he was sure that there was nothing more to fear from him, and then he rose and beckoned to us to advance, which we did on all fours, like a colony of huge apes. On reaching the kraal we saw that the Masai had still further choked this entrance, which was about ten feet wide – no doubt in order to guard against attack – by dragging four or five tops of mimosa trees up to it. So much the better for us, I reflected; the more obstruction there was the slower would they be able to come through. Here we separated; Mackenzie and his party creeping up under the shadow of the wall to the left, while Sir Henry and Umslopogaas took their stations one on each side of the thorn fence, the two spearmen and the Askari lying down in front of it. I and my men crept on up the right side of the kraal, which was about fifty paces long.

When I was two-thirds up I halted, and placed my men at distances of four paces from one another, keeping Alphonse close to me, however. Then I peeped for the first time over the wall. It was getting fairly light now, and the first thing I saw was the white donkey, exactly opposite to me, and close by it I could make out the pale face of little Flossie, who was sitting as the lad had described, some ten paces from the wall. Round her lay many warriors, sleeping. At distances all over the surface of the kraal were the remains of fires, round each of which slept some five-and-twenty Masai, for the most part gorged with food. Now and then a man would raise himself, yawn, and look at the east, which was turning primrose; but none got up. I determined to wait another five minutes, both to allow the light to increase, so that we could make better shooting, and to give Good and his party – of whom we could see or hear nothing – every opportunity to make ready.

The quiet dawn began to throw her ever-widening mantle over plain and forest and river – mighty Kenia, wrapped in the silence of eternal snows, looked out across the earth – till presently a beam from the unrisen sun lit upon his heaven-kissing crest and purpled it with blood; the sky above grew blue, and tender as a mother's smile; a bird began to pipe his morning song, and a little breeze passing through the bush shook down the dewdrops in millions to refresh the waking world. Everywhere was peace and the happiness of arising strength, everywhere save in the heart of cruel man!

Suddenly, just as I was nerving myself for the signal, having already selected my man on whom I meant to open fire – a great fellow sprawling on the ground within three feet of little Flossie – Alphonse's teeth began to chatter again like the hoofs of a galloping giraffe, making a great noise in the silence. The rag had dropped out in the agitation of his mind. Instantly a Masai within three paces of us woke, and, sitting up, gazed about him, looking for the cause of the sound. Moved beyond myself, I brought the butt-end of my rifle down on to the pit of the Frenchman's stomach. This stopped his chattering; but, as he doubled up, he managed to let off his gun in such a manner that the bullet passed within an inch of my head.

There was no need for a signal now. From both sides of the kraal broke out a waving line of fire, in which I myself joined, managing with a snap shot to knock over my Masai by Flossie, just as he was jumping up. Then from the top end of the kraal there rang an awful yell, in which I rejoiced to recognise Good's piercing notes rising clear and shrill above the din, and in another second followed such a scene as I have never seen before nor shall again. With an universal howl of terror and fury the brawny crowd of savages within the kraal sprang to their feet, many of them to fall again beneath our well-directed hail of lead before they had moved a yard. For a moment they stood undecided, and then hearing the cries and curses that rose unceasingly from the top end of the kraal, and bewildered by the storm of bullets, they as by one impulse rushed down towards the thorn-stopped entrance. As they went we kept pouring our fire with terrible effect into the thickening mob as fast as we could load. I had emptied my repeater of the ten shots it contained and was just beginning to slip in some more when I bethought me of little Flossie. Looking up, I saw that the white donkey was lying kicking, having been knocked over either by one of our bullets or a Masai spear-thrust. There were no living Masai near, but the black nurse was on her feet and with a spear cutting the rope that bound Flossie's feet. Next second she ran to the wall of the kraal and began to climb over it, an example which the little girl followed. But Flossie was evidently very stiff and cramped, and could only go slowly, and as she went two Masai

Path from the Mission Station

Bush

Thistles

Curtis and four men

Where the sentry was killed

Watch-fires and sleeping Masai

Wide entrance to the kraal

Flossie

Quatermain and six men

Mr Mackenzie and six men

Banyan tree

Small entrance to the kraal

Good and ten men

flying down the kraal caught sight of her and rushed towards her to kill her. The first fellow came up just as the poor little girl, after a desperate effort to climb the wall, fell back into the kraal. Up flashed the great spear, and as it did so a bullet from my rifle found its home in the holder's ribs, and over he went like a shot rabbit. But behind him was the other man, and, alas, I had only that one cartridge in the magazine! Flossie had scrambled to her feet and was facing the second man, who was advancing with raised spear. I turned my head aside and felt sick as death. I could not bear to see him stab her. Glancing up again, to my surprise I saw the Masai's spear lying on the ground, while the man himself was staggering about with both hands to his head. Suddenly I saw a puff of smoke proceeding apparently from Flossie, and the man fell down headlong. Then I remembered the Derringer pistol she carried, and saw that she had fired both barrels of it at him, thereby saving her life. In another instant she had made an effort, and assisted by the nurse, who was lying on the top, had scrambled over the wall, and I knew that she was, comparatively speaking, safe.

All this takes time to tell, but I do not suppose that it took more than fifteen seconds to enact. I soon got the magazine of the repeater filled again with cartridges, and once more opened fire, not on the seething black mass which was gathering at the end of the kraal, but on fugitives who bethought them to climb the wall. I picked off several of these men, moving down towards the end of the kraal as I did so, and arriving at the corner, or rather the bend of the oval, in time to see, and by means of my rifle to assist in, the mighty struggle that took place there.

By this time some two hundred Masai – allowing that we had up to the present accounted for fifty – had gathered together in front of the thorn-stopped entrance, driven thither by the spears of Good's men, whom they doubtless supposed were a large force instead of being but ten strong. For some reason it never occurred to them to try and rush the wall, which they could have scrambled over with comparative ease; they all made for the fence, which was really a strongly interwoven fortification. With a bound the first warrior went at it, and even before he touched the ground on the other side I saw Sir Henry's great axe swing up and fall with awful force upon his feather head-piece, and he sank into the middle of the thorns. Then with a yell and a crash they began to break through as they might, and ever as they came the great axe swung and Inkosi-kaas flashed and they fell dead one by one, each man thus helping to build up a barrier against his fellows. Those who escaped the axes of the pair fell at the hands of the Askari and the two Mission Kaffirs, and those who passed scatheless from them were brought low by my own and Mackenzie's fire.

Faster and more furious grew the fighting. Single Masai would spring upon the dead bodies of their comrades, and engage one or other of the axemen with their long spears; but, thanks chiefly to the mail shirts, the result was always the same. Presently there was a great swing of the axe, a crashing sound, and another dead Masai. That is, if the man was engaged with Sir Henry. If it was Umslopogaas that he fought with the result indeed would be the

same, but it would be differently attained. It was but rarely that
the Zulu used the crashing double-handed stroke; on the contrary, he did little more than tap continually at his adversary's
head, pecking at it with the pole-axe end of the axe as a
woodpecker* pecks at rotten wood. Presently a peck would go
home, and his enemy would drop down with a neat little circular
hole in his forehead or skull, exactly similar to that which a
cheese-scoop makes in a cheese. He never used the broad blade of
the axe except when hard pressed, or when striking at a shield. He
told me afterwards that he did not consider it sportsman-like.

Good and his men were quite close by now, and our people had
to cease firing into the mass for fear of killing some of them (as it
was, one of them was slain in this way). Mad and desperate with
fear, the Masai by a frantic effort burst through the thorn fence
and piled-up dead, and, sweeping Curtis, Umslopogaas, and the
other three before them, into the open. And now it was that we
began to lose men fast. Down went our poor Askari who was
armed with the axe, a great spear standing out a foot behind his
back; and before long the two spearsmen who had stood with him
went down too, dying fighting like tigers; and others of our party
shared their fate. For a moment I feared the fight was lost –
certainly it trembled in the balance. I shouted to my men to cast
down their rifles, and to take spears and throw themselves into the
mêlée. They obeyed, their blood being now thoroughly up, and
Mr Mackenzie's people followed their example.

This move had a momentary good result, but still the fight hung
in the balance.

Our people fought magnificently, hurling themselves upon the
dark mass of Elmoran, hewing, thrusting, slaying, and being slain.
And ever above the din rose Good's awful yell of encouragement
as he plunged to wherever the fight was thickest; and ever, with an
almost machine-like regularity, the two axes rose and fell, carrying
death and disablement at every stroke. But I could see that the

---

* As I think I have already said, one of Umslopogaas's Zulu names was the
'Woodpecker'. I could never make out why he was called so until I saw him
in action with Inkosi-kaas, when I at once recognised the resemblance. A.Q.

strain was beginning to tell upon Sir Henry, who was bleeding from several flesh wounds: his breath was coming in gasps, and the veins stood out on his forehead like blue and knotted cords. Even Umslopogaas, man of iron that he was, was hard pressed. I noticed that he had given up 'woodpecking', and was now using the broad blade of Inkosi-kaas, 'browning' his enemy wherever he could hit him, instead of drilling scientific holes in his head. I myself did not go into the mêlée, but hovered outside like the swift 'back' in a football scrimmage, putting a bullet through a Masai whenever I got a chance. I was more use so. I fired forty-nine cartridges that morning, and I did not miss many shots.

Presently, do as we would, the beam of the balance began to rise against us. We had not more than fifteen or sixteen effectives left now, and the Masai had at least fifty. Of course if they had kept their heads, and shaken themselves together, they could soon have made an end of the matter; but that is just what they did not do, not having yet recovered from their start, and some of them having actually fled from their sleeping-places without their weapons. Still by now many individuals were fighting with their normal courage and discretion, and this alone was sufficient to defeat us. To make matters worse just then, when Mackenzie's rifle was empty, a brawny savage armed with a 'sime', or sword, made a rush for him. The clergyman flung down his gun, and drawing his huge carver from his elastic belt (his revolver had dropped out in the fight), they closed in desperate struggle. Presently, locked in a close embrace, missionary and Masai rolled on the ground behind the wall, and for some time I, being amply occupied with my own affairs, and in keeping my skin from being pricked, remained in ignorance of his fate or how the duel had ended.

To and fro surged the fight, slowly turning round like the vortex of a human whirlpool, and the matter began to look very bad for us. Just then, however, a fortunate thing happened. Umslopogaas, either by accident or design, broke out of the ring and engaged a warrior at some few paces from it. As he did so, another man ran up and struck him with all his force between his shoulders with his great spear, which, falling on the tough steel shirt, failed to pierce it and rebounded. For a moment the man stared aghast – protective armour being unknown among these tribes – and then he yelled out at the top of his voice – '*They are devils – bewitched, bewitched!*' And seized by a sudden panic, he threw down his spear, and began to fly. I cut short his career with a bullet, and Umslopogaas brained his man, and then the panic spread to the others.

'*Bewitched, bewitched!*' they cried, and tried to escape in every direction, utterly demoralised and broken-spirited, for the most part even throwing down their shields and spears.

On the last scene of that dreadful fight I need not dwell. It was a slaughter great and grim, in which no quarter was asked or given. One incident, however, is worth detailing. Just as I was hoping that it was all done with, suddenly from under a heap of slain where he had been hiding, an unwounded warrior sprang up, and, clearing the piles of dying dead like an antelope, sped like the wind up the kraal towards the spot where I was standing at the moment. But he was not alone, for Umslopogaas came gliding on his tracks with the peculiar swallow-like motion for which he was noted, and as they neared me I recognised in the Masai the herald of the previous night. Finding that, run as he would, his pursuer was gaining on him, the man halted and turned round to give battle. Umslopogaas also pulled up.

'Ah, ah,' he cried, in mockery, to the Elmoran, 'it is thou whom I talked with last night – the Lygonani! the Herald! the capturer of little girls – he who would kill a little girl! And thou didst hope to stand man to man and face to face with Umslopogaas, an Induna of the tribe of the Maquilisini, of the people of the Amazulu? Behold, thy prayer is granted! And I didst swear to hew thee limb from limb, thou insolent dog. Behold, I will do it even now!'

The Masai ground his teeth with fury, and charged at the Zulu with his spear. As he came, Umslopogaas deftly stepped aside, and swinging Inkosi-kaas high above his head with both hands, brought the broad blade down with such fearful force from behind upon the Masai's shoulder just where the neck is set into the frame, that its razor edge shore right through bone and flesh and muscle, almost severing the head and one arm from the body.

'*Ou!*' ejaculated Umslopogaas, contemplating the corpse of his foe; 'I have kept my word. It was a good stroke.'

CHAPTER 8

Alphonse Explains

And so the fight was ended. On returning from the shocking scene it suddenly struck me that I had seen nothing of Alphonse since the moment, some twenty minutes before – for though this fight has taken a long while to describe, it did not take long in reality – when I had been forced to hit him in the wind with the result of nearly getting myself shot. Fearing that the poor little man had perished in the battle, I began to hunt among the dead for his body, but, not being able either to see or hear anything of it, I concluded that he must have survived, and walked down the side of the kraal where we had first taken our stand, calling him by name. Now some fifteen paces back from the kraal wall stood a very ancient tree of the banyan species. So ancient was it that all the inside had in the course of ages decayed away, leaving nothing but a shell of bark.

'Alphonse,' I called, as I walked down the wall. 'Alphonse!'

'Oui, monsieur,' answered a voice. 'Here am I.'

I looked round but could see nobody. 'Where?' I cried.

'Here am I, monsieur, in the tree.'

I looked, and there, peering out of a hole in the trunk of the banyan about five feet from the ground, I saw a pale face and a pair of large mustachios, one clipped short and the other as lamentably out of curl as the tail of a newly whipped pug. Then, for the first time, I realised what I had suspected before – namely, that Alphonse was an arrant coward. I walked up to him. 'Come out of that hole,' I said.

'Is it finished, monsieur?' he asked anxiously; 'quite finished? Ah, the horrors I have undergone, and the prayers I have uttered!'

'Come out, you little wretch,' I said, for I did not feel amiable; 'it is all over.'

'So, monsieur, then my prayers have prevailed? I emerge,' and he did.

As we were walking down together to join the others, who were gathered in a group by the wide entrance to the kraal, which now resembled a veritable charnel-house, a Masai, who had escaped so far and been hiding under a bush, suddenly sprang up and charged furiously at us. Off went Alphonse with a howl of terror, and after him flew the Masai, bent upon doing some execution before he died. He soon overtook the poor little Frenchman, and would have finished him then and there had I not, just as Alphonse made a last agonised double in the vain hope of avoiding the yard of steel that was flashing in his immediate rear, managed to plant a bullet between the Elmoran's broad shoulders, which brought matters to a satisfactory conclusion so far as the Frenchman was concerned. But just then he tripped and fell flat, and the body of the Masai fell right on the top of him, moving convulsively in the death struggle. Thereupon there arose such a series of piercing howls that I concluded that before he died the savage must have managed to stab poor Alphonse. I ran up in a hurry and pulled the Masai off, and there beneath him lay Alphonse covered with blood and jerking himself about like a galvanised frog. Poor fellow! thought I, he is done for, and kneeling down by him I began to search for his wound as well as his struggles would allow.

'Oh, the hole in my back!' he yelled. 'I am murdered. I am dead. Oh, Annette!'

I searched again, but could see no wound. Then the truth dawned on me – the man was frightened, not hurt.

'Get up!' I shouted, 'Get up. Aren't you ashamed of yourself? You are not touched.'

Thereupon he rose, not a penny the worse. 'But, monsieur, I thought I was,' he said apologetically; 'I did not know that I had conquered.' Then, giving the body of the Masai a kick, he ejaculated triumphantly, 'Ah, dog of a black savage, thou art dead; what victory!'

Thoroughly disgusted, I left Alphonse to look after himself, which he did by following me like a shadow, and proceeded to join the others by the large entrance. The first thing that I saw was

Mackenzie, seated on a stone with a handkerchief twisted round his thigh, from which he was bleeding freely, having, indeed, received a spear-thrust that passed right through it, and still holding in his hand his favourite carving knife now bent nearly double, from which I gathered that he had been successful in his rough and tumble with the Elmoran.

'Ah, Quatermain!' he sang out in a trembling, excited voice, 'so we have conquered; but it is a sorry sight, a sorry sight;' and then breaking into broad Scotch and glancing at the bent knife in his hand, 'It fashes me sair to have bent my best carver on the breastbone of a savage,' and he laughed hysterically. Poor fellow, what between his wound and the killing excitement he had undergone his nerves were much shaken, and no wonder! It is hard upon a man of peace and kindly heart to be called upon to join in such a gruesome business. But there, fate puts us sometimes into very comical positions!

At the kraal entrance the scene was a strange one. The slaughter was over by now, and the wounded men had been put out of their pain, for no quarter had been given. The bush-closed entrance was trampled flat, and in place of bushes it was filled with the bodies of dead men. Dead men, everywhere dead men – they lay about in knots, they were flung by ones and twos in every position upon the open spaces, for all the world like the people on the grass in one of the London parks on a particularly hot Sunday in August. In front of this entrance, on a space which had been cleared of dead and of the shields and spears which were scattered in all directions as they had fallen or been thrown from the hands of their owners, stood and lay the survivors of the awful struggle, and at their feet were four wounded men. We had gone into the fight thirty strong, and of the thirty but fifteen remained alive, and five of them (including Mr Mackenzie) were wounded, two mortally. Of those who held the entrance, Curtis and the Zulu alone remained. Good had lost five men killed, I had lost two killed, and Mackenzie no less than five out of the six with him. As for the survivors they were, with the exception of myself who had never come to close quarters, red from head to foot – Sir Henry's armour might have been painted that colour – and utterly exhausted, except Umslopogaas, who, as he grimly stood on a little mound above a heap of dead, leaning as usual upon his axe, did not seem particularly distressed, although the skin over the hole in his head palpitated violently.

'Ah, Macumazahn!' he said to me as I limped up, feeling very sick, 'I told thee that it would be a good fight, and it has. Never have I seen a better, or one more bravely fought. As for this iron shirt, surely it is "tagati" [bewitched]; nothing could pierce it. Had it not been for the garment I should have been *there*,' and he nodded towards the great pile of dead men beneath him.

'I give it thee; thou art a brave man,' said Sir Henry, briefly.

'Koos!' answered the Zulu, deeply pleased both at the gift and the compliment. 'Thou, too, Incubu, didst bear thyself as a man, but I must give thee some lessons with the axe; thou dost waste thy strength.'

Just then Mackenzie asked about Flossie, and we were all greatly relieved when one of the men said he had seen her flying towards the house with the nurse. Then bearing such of the wounded as could be moved at the moment with us, we slowly made our way towards the Mission-house, spent with toil and bloodshed, but with the glorious sense of victory against over-whelming odds glowing in our hearts. We had saved the life of the little maid, and taught the Masai of those parts a lesson that they will not forget for ten years – but at what a cost!

Painfully we made our way up the hill which, just a little more than an hour before, we had descended under such different circumstances. At the gate of the wall stood Mrs Mackenzie waiting for us. When her eyes fell upon us, however, she shrieked out, and covered her face with her hands, crying, 'Horrible, horrible!' Nor were her fears allayed when she discovered her worthy husband being borne upon an improvised stretcher; but her doubts as to the nature of his injury were soon set at rest. Then when in a few brief words I had told her the upshot of the struggle (of which Flossie, who had arrived in safety, had been able to explain something) she came up to me and solemnly kissed me on the forehead.

'God bless you all, Mr Quatermain; you have saved my child's life,' she said simply.

Then we went in and got our clothes off and doctored our wounds; I am glad to say I had none, and Sir Henry's and Good's were, thanks to those invaluable chain shirts, of a comparatively harmless nature, and to be dealt with by means of a few stitches and sticking-plaster. Mackenzie's, however, were serious, though fortunately the spear had not severed any large artery. After that we had a bath, and what a luxury it was! And having clad ourselves in ordinary clothes, proceeded to the dining-room, where breakfast was set as usual. It was curious sitting down there, drinking tea and eating toast in an ordinary nineteenth-century sort of way just as though we had not employed the early hours in a regular primitive hand-to-hand Middle-Ages kind of struggle. As Good said, the whole thing seemed more as though one had had a bad nightmare just before being called, than as a deed done. When we were finishing our breakfast the door opened, and in came little Flossie, very pale and tottery, but quite unhurt. She kissed us all and thanked us. I congratulated her on the presence of mind she had shown in shooting the Masai with her Derringer pistol, and thereby saving her own life.

'Oh, don't talk of it!' she said, beginning to cry hysterically; 'I shall never forget his face as he went turning round and round, never – I can see it now.'

I advised her to go to bed and get some sleep, which she did, and awoke in the evening quite recovered, so far as her strength was concerned. It struck me as an odd thing that a girl who could find the nerve to shoot a huge black ruffian rushing to kill her with a spear should have been so affected at the thought of it afterwards; but it is, after all, characteristic of the sex. Poor Flossie! I fear that her nerves will not get over that night in the Masai camp for many a long year. She told me afterwards that it was the suspense that was so awful, having to sit there hour after hour through the livelong night utterly ignorant as to whether or not any attempt was to be made to rescue her. She said that on the whole she did not expect it, knowing how few of us, and how many of the Masai – who, by the way, came continually to stare at her, most of them never having seen a white person before, and handled her arms and hair with their filthy paws. She said also that she had made up her mind that if she saw no signs of succour by the time the first rays of the rising sun reached the kraal she would kill herself with the pistol, for the nurse had heard the Lygonani say that they were to be tortured to death as soon as the sun was up if one of the white men did not come in their place. It was an awful resolution to have to take, but she meant to act on it, and I have little doubt but what she would have done so. Although she was at an age when in England girls are in the schoolroom and come down to dessert, this 'child of the wilderness' had more courage, discretion, and power of mind than many a woman of mature age nurtured in idleness and luxury, with minds carefully drilled and educated out of any originality or self-resource that nature may have endowed them with.

When breakfast was over we all turned in and had a good sleep, only getting up in time for dinner; after which meal we once more adjourned, together with all the available population – men, women, youths, and girls – to the scene of the morning's slaughter, our object being to bury our own dead and get rid of the Masai by flinging them into the Tana River, which ran within fifty yards of the kraal. On reaching the spot we disturbed thousands upon thousands of vultures and a sort of brown bush eagle, which had been flocking to the feast from miles and miles away. Often have I watched these great and repulsive birds, and marvelled at the extraordinary speed with which they arrive on a scene of slaughter. A buck falls to your rifle, and within a minute high in the blue ether appears a speck that gradually grows into a vulture, then another, and another. I have heard many theories advanced to account for the wonderful power of perception nature has given these birds. My own, founded on a good deal of observation, is that the vultures, gifted as they are with powers of sight greater than those given by the most powerful glass, quarter out the heavens among themselves, and hanging in mid-air at a vast height – probably from two to three miles above the earth – keep watch, each of them, over an enormous stretch of country. Presently one of them spies food, and instantly begins to sink towards it. Thereon his next neighbour in the airy heights sailing leisurely through the blue gulf, at a distance perhaps of some miles, follows his example, knowing that food has been sighted. Down he goes, and all the vultures within sight of him follow after, and so do all those in sight of them. In this way the vultures for twenty miles round can be summoned to the feast in a few minutes.

We buried our dead in solemn silence, Good being selected to read the Burial Service over them (in the absence of Mr Mackenzie, confined to bed), as he was generally allowed to possess the best voice and most impressive manner. It was melancholy in the extreme, but, as Good said, it might have been worse, for we might have had 'to bury ourselves'. I pointed out that this would have been a difficult feat, but I knew what he meant.

Next we set to work to load an ox-wagon which had been brought round from the Mission with the dead bodies of the Masai, having first collected the spears, shields, and other arms. We loaded the wagon five times, about fifty bodies to the load, and emptied it into the Tana. From this it was evident that very few of the Masai could have escaped. The crocodiles must have been well fed that night. One of the last bodies we picked up was that of the sentry at the upper end. I asked Good how he managed to kill him, and he told me that he had crept up much as Umslopogaas had done, and stabbed him with his sword. He groaned a good deal, but fortunately nobody heard him. As Good said, it was a horrible thing to have to do, and most unpleasantly like cold-blooded murder.

And so with the last body that floated away down the current of the Tana ended the incident of our attack on the Masai camp. The spears and shields and other arms we took up to the Mission, where they filled an outhouse. One incident, however, I must not forget to mention. As we were returning from performing the obsequies of our Masai friends we passed the hollow tree where Alphonse had secreted himself in the morning. It so happened that the little man himself was with us assisting in our unpleasant task with a far better will than he had shown where live Masai were concerned. Indeed, for each body that he handled he found an appropriate sarcasm. Alphonse throwing Masai into the Tana was a very different creature from Alphonse flying for dear life from the spear of a live Masai. He was quite merry and gay, he clapped his hands and warbled snatches of French songs as the grim dead warriors went 'splash' into the running waters to carry a message of death and defiance to their kindred a hundred miles below. In short, thinking that he wanted taking down a peg, I suggested holding a court-martial on him for his conduct in the morning.

Accordingly we brought him to the tree where he had hidden, and proceeded to sit in judgement on him, Sir Henry explaining to him in the very best French the unheard-of cowardice and enormity of his conduct, more especially in letting the oiled rag out of his mouth, whereby he nearly aroused the Masai camp with teeth-chattering and brought about the failure of our plans: ending up with a request for an explanation.

But if we expected to find Alphonse at a loss and put him to open shame we were destined to be disappointed. He bowed and scraped and smiled, and acknowledged that his conduct might at first blush appear strange, but really it was not, inasmuch as his teeth were not chattering from fear – oh, dear no! oh, certainly not! he marvelled how the 'messieurs' could think of such a thing – but from the chill air of the morning. As for the rag, if monsieur could have but tasted its evil flavour, being compounded indeed of a mixture of stale paraffin oil, grease, and gunpowder, monsieur himself would have spat it out. But he did nothing of the sort; he determined to keep it there till, alas! his stomach 'revolted', and the rag was ejected in an access of involuntary sickness.

'And what have you to say about getting into the hollow tree?' asked Sir Henry, keeping his countenance with difficulty.

'But, monsieur, the explanation is easy; oh, most easy! it was thus: I stood there by the kraal wall, and the little grey monsieur hit me in the stomach so that my rifle exploded, and the battle began. I watched whilst recovering myself from monsieur's cruel blow; then, messieurs, I felt the heroic blood of my grandfather boil up in my veins. The sight made me mad. I ground my teeth! Fire flashed from my eyes! I shouted "En avant!" and longed to slay. Before my eyes there rose a vision of my heroic grandfather!

In short, I was mad! I was a warrior indeed! But then in my heart I heard a small voice: "Alphonse," said the voice, "restrain thyself, Alphonse! Give not way to this evil passion! These men, though black, are brothers! And thou wouldst slay them? Cruel Alphonse!" The voice was right. I knew it; I was about to perpetrate the most horrible cruelties: to wound! to massacre! to tear limb from limb! And how restrain myself? I looked round; I saw the tree, I perceived the hole. "Entomb thyself," said the voice, "and hold on tight! Thou wilt thus overcome temptation by main force!" It was bitter, just when the blood of my heroic grandfather boiled most fiercely; but I obeyed! I dragged my unwilling feet along; I entombed myself! Through the hole I watched the battle! I shouted curses and defiance on the foe! I noted them fall with satisfaction! Why not? I had not robbed them of their lives. Their gore was not upon my head. The blood of my heroic – '

'Oh, get along with you, you little cur!' broke out Sir Henry, with a shout of laughter, and giving Alphonse a good kick which sent him flying off with a rueful face.

In the evening I had an interview with Mr Mackenzie, who was suffering a good deal from his wounds, which Good, who was a skilful though unqualified doctor, was treating him for. He told me that this occurrence had taught him a lesson, and that, if he recovered safely, he meant to hand over the Mission to a younger man, who was already on his road to join him in his work, and return to England.

'You see, Quatermain,' he said, 'I made up my mind to it, this very morning, when we were creeping down those benighted savages. "If we live through this and rescue Flossie alive," I said to myself, "I will go home to England; I have had enough of savages." Well, I did not think that we should live through it at the time; but thanks be to God and you four, we have lived through it, and I mean to stick to my resolution, lest a worse thing befall us. Another such time would kill my poor wife. And besides, Quatermain, between you and me, I am well off; it is thirty thousand pounds I am worth today, and every farthing of it made by honest trade and savings in the bank at Zanzibar, for living here costs me next to nothing. So though it will be hard to leave this place, which I have made to blossom like a rose in the wilderness, and harder still to leave the people I have taught, I shall go.'

'I congratulate you on your decision,' answered I, 'for two reasons. The first is, that you owe a duty to your wife and daughter, and more especially to the latter, who should receive some education and mix with girls of her own race, otherwise she will grow up wild, shunning her kind. The other is, that as sure as I am standing here, sooner or later the Masai will try to avenge the slaughter inflicted on them today. Two or three men are sure to have escaped the confusion who will carry the story back to their people, and the result will be that a great expedition will one day be sent against you. It might be delayed for a year, but sooner or later it will come. Therefore, if only for that reason, I should go. When once they have learnt that you are no longer here they may perhaps leave the place alone.'*

'You are quite right,' answered the clergyman. 'I will turn my back upon this place in a month. But it will be a wrench, it will be a wrench.'

* By a sad coincidence, since the above was written by Mr Quatermain, the Masai have, in April 1886, massacred a missionary and his wife – Mr and Mrs Houghton – on this very Tana River, and at the spot described. These are, I believe, the first white people who are known to have fallen victims to this cruel tribe. ED.

CHAPTER 9

Into the Unknown

A week had passed, and we all sat at supper one night in the Mission dining-room, feeling very much depressed in spirits, for the reason that we were going to say goodbye to our kind friends, the Mackenzies, and depart upon our way at dawn on the morrow. Nothing more had been seen or heard of the Masai, and save for a spear or two which had been overlooked and was rusting in the grass, and a few empty cartridges where we had stood outside the wall, it would have been difficult to tell that the old cattle kraal at the foot of the slope had been the scene of so desperate a struggle. Mackenzie was, thanks chiefly to his being so temperate a man, rapidly recovering from his wound, and could get about on a pair of crutches; and as for the other wounded men, one had died of gangrene, and the rest were in a fair way to recovery. Mr Mackenzie's caravan of men had also returned from the coast, so that the station was now amply garrisoned.

Under these circumstances we concluded, warm and pressing as were the invitations for us to stay, that it was time to move on, first to Mount Kenia, and thence into the unknown in search of the mysterious white race which we had set our hearts on discovering. This time we were going to progress by means of the humble but useful donkey, of which we had collected no less than a dozen, to carry our goods and chattels, and, if necessary, ourselves. We had now but two Wakwafis left for servants, and found it quite impossible to get other natives to venture with us into the unknown parts we proposed to explore – and small blame to them. After all, as Mr Mackenzie said, it was odd that three men, each of whom possessed many of those things that are supposed to make life worth living – health, sufficient means, and position, etc. –

should from their own pleasure start out upon a wild-goose chase, from which the chances were they never would return. But then that is what Englishmen are, adventurers to the backbone; and all our magnificent muster-roll of colonies, each of which will in time become a great nation, testify to the extraordinary value of the spirit of adventure which at first sight looks like a mild form of lunacy. 'Adventurer' – he that goes out to meet whatever may come. Well, that is what we all do in the world one way or another, and, speaking for myself, I am proud of the title, because it implies a brave heart and a trust in Providence. Besides, when many and many a noted Croesus, at whose feet the people worship, and many and many a time-serving and word-coining politician are forgotten, the names of those grand-hearted old adventurers who have made England what she is, will be remembered and taught with love and pride to little children whose unshaped spirits yet slumber in the womb of centuries to be. Not that we three can expect to be numbered with such as these, yet have we done something – enough, perhaps, to throw a garment over the nakedness of our folly.

That evening, whilst we were sitting on the veranda, smoking a pipe before turning in, who should come up to us but Alphonse, and, with a magnificent bow, announce his wish for an interview. Being requested to 'fire away', he explained at some length that he was anxious to attach himself to our party – a statement that astonished me not a little, knowing what a coward the little man was. The reason, however, soon appeared. Mr Mackenzie was going down to the coast, and thence on to England. Now, if he went down country, Alphonse was persuaded that he would be seized, extradited, sent to France, and to penal servitude. This was the idea that haunted him, as King Charles's head haunted Mr Dick, and he brooded over it till his imagination exaggerated the danger ten times. As a matter of fact, the probability is that his offence against the laws of his country had long ago been forgotten, and that he would have been allowed to pass unmolested anywhere except in France; but he could not be got to see this. Constitutional coward as the little man was, he infinitely preferred to face the certain hardships and great risks and dangers of such an expedition as ours, than to expose himself, notwith-standing his intense longing for his native land, to the possible scrutiny of a police officer – which is after all only another exemplification of the truth that, to the majority of men, a far-off foreseen danger, however shadowy, is much more terrible than the most serious present emergency. After listening to what he had to say, we consulted among ourselves, and finally agreed, with Mr Mackenzie's knowledge and consent, to accept his offer. To begin with, we were very short-handed, and Alphonse was a quick, active fellow, who could turn his hand to anything, and cook – ah, he *could* cook! I believe that he would have made a palatable dish of those gaiters of his heroic grandfather which he was so fond of talking about. Then he was a good-tempered little man, and merry as a monkey, whilst his pompous, vainglorious talk was a source of infinite amusement to us; and what is more, he never bore malice. Of course, his being so pronounced a coward was a great drawback to him, but now that we knew his weakness we could more or less guard against it. So, after warning him of the undoubted risks he was exposing himself to, we told him that we would accept his offer on condition that he would promise implicit obedience to our orders. We also promised to give him wages at the rate of ten pounds a month should he ever return to a civilised country to receive them. To all of this he agreed with alacrity, and retired to write a letter to his Annette, which Mr Mackenzie promised to post when he got down country. He read it to us afterwards, Sir Henry translating, and a wonderful composition it was. I am sure the depth of his devotion and the narration of his sufferings in a barbarous country, 'far, far from thee, Annette, for whose adored sake I endure such sorrow,' ought to have touched the feelings of the stoniest-hearted chambermaid.

Well, the morrow came, and by seven o'clock the donkeys were all loaded, and the time of parting was at hand. It was a melancholy business, especially saying goodbye to dear little Flossie. She and I were great friends, and often used to have talks together – but her nerves had never got over the shock of that awful night when she lay in the power of those bloodthirsty Masai. 'Oh, Mr Quatermain,' she cried, throwing her arms round my neck and bursting into tears, 'I can't bear to say goodbye to you. I wonder when we shall meet again?'

'I don't know, my dear little girl,' I said, 'I am at one end of life and you are at the other. I have but a short time before me at best, and most things lie in the past, but I hope that for you there are many long and happy years, and everything lies in the future. By and by you will grow into a beautiful woman, Flossie, and all this wild life will be like a far-off dream to you; but I hope, even if we never do meet again, that you will think of your old friend and remember what I say to you now. Always try to be good, my dear, and to do what is right, rather than what happens to be pleasant, for in the end, whatever sneering people may say, what is good and what is happy are the same. Be unselfish, and whenever you can, give a helping hand to others – for the world is full of suffering, my dear, and to alleviate it is the noblest end that we can set before us. If you do that you will become a sweet and God-fearing woman, and make many people's lives a little brighter, and then you will not have lived, as so many of your sex do, in vain. And now I have given you a lot of old-fashioned advice, and so I am going to give you something to sweeten it with. You see this little piece of paper. It is what is called a cheque. When we are gone give it to your father with this note – not before, mind. You will marry one day, my dear little Flossie, and it is to buy you a wedding present which you are to wear, and your daughter after you, if you have one, in remembrance of Hunter Quatermain.'

Poor little Flossie cried very much, and gave me a lock of her bright hair in return, which I still have. The cheque I gave her was for a thousand pounds (which being now well off, and having no calls upon me except those of charity, I could well afford), and in the note I directed her father to invest it for her in Government security, and when she married or came of age to buy her the best diamond necklace he could get for the money and accumulated interest. I chose diamonds because I think that now that King Solomon's Mines are lost to the world, their price will never be much lower than it is at present, so that if in after-life she should ever be in pecuniary difficulties, she will be able to turn them into money.

Well, at last we got off, after much hand-shaking, hat-waving, and also farewell saluting from the natives, Alphonse weeping copiously (for he has a warm heart) at parting with his master and mistress; and I was not sorry for it at all, for I hate those goodbyes. Perhaps the most affecting thing of all was to witness Umslopogaas' distress at parting with Flossie, for whom the grim old warrior had conceived a strong affection. He used to say that she was as sweet to see as the only star on a dark night, and was never tired of loudly congratulating himself on having killed the Lygonani who had threatened to murder her. And that was the last we saw of the pleasant Mission-house – a true oasis in the desert – and of European civilisation. But I often think of the Mackenzies, and wonder how they got down country, and if they are now safe and well in England, and will ever see these words. Dear little Flossie! I wonder how she fares there where there are no black folk to do her imperious bidding, and no sky-piercing snow-clad Kenia for her to look at when she gets up in the morning. And so goodbye to Flossie.

After leaving the Mission-house we made our way, comparatively unmolested, past the base of Mount Kenia, which the Masai call 'Donyo Egere', or the 'speckled mountain', on account of the black patches of rock that appear upon its mighty spire, where the sides are too precipitous to allow of the snow lying on them; then on past the lonely lake Baringo, where one of our two remaining Askari, having unfortunately trodden on a puff-adder, died of snake-bite, in spite of all our efforts to save him. Thence we proceeded a distance of about a hundred and fifty miles to another magnificent snow-clad mountain called Lekakisera, which has never, to the best of my belief, been visited before by a European, but which I cannot now stop to describe. There we rested a fortnight, and then started out into the trackless and uninhabited forest of a vast district called Elgumi. In this forest alone there are more elephants than I ever met with or heard of before. The mighty mammals literally swarm there entirely unmolested by man, and only kept down by the natural law that prevents any animals increasing beyond the capacity of the country they inhabit to support them. Needless to say, however, we did not shoot many of them, first because we could not afford to waste ammunition, of which our stock was getting perilously low, a donkey loaded with it having been swept away in fording a flooded river; and secondly, because we could not carry away the ivory, and did not wish to kill for the mere sake of slaughter. So we let the great beasts be, only shooting one or two in self-protection. In this district, the elephants, being unacquainted with the hunter and his tender mercies, would allow one to walk up to within twenty yards of them in the open, while they stood, with their great ears cocked for all the world like puzzled and gigantic puppy-dogs, and stared at that new and extraordinary phenomenon – man. Occasionally, when the inspection did not prove satisfactory, the staring ended in a trumpet and a charge, but this did not often happen. When it did we had to use our rifles. Nor were elephants the only wild beasts in the great Elgumi forest. All sorts of large game abounded, including lions – confound them! I have always hated the sight of a lion since one bit my leg and lamed me for life. As a consequence, another thing that abounded was the dreadful tsetse fly, whose bite is death to domestic animals. Donkeys have, together with men, hitherto been supposed to enjoy a peculiar immunity from its attacks; but all I have to say, whether it was on account of their poor condition, or because the tsetse in those parts is more poisonous than usual, I do not know, but ours succumbed to its onslaught. Fortunately, however, that was not till two months or so after the bites had been inflicted, when suddenly, after a two days' cold rain, they all died, and on removing the skins of several of them I found the long yellow streaks upon the flesh which are characteristic of death from bites from the tsetse, marking the spot where the insect had inserted his proboscis. On emerging from the great Elgumi forest, we, still steering northwards, in accordance with the information Mr Mackenzie had collected from the unfortunate wanderer who reached him only to die so tragically, struck the base in due course of the large lake, called Laga by the natives, which is about fifty miles long by twenty broad, and of which, it may be remembered, he made mention. Thence we pushed on nearly a month's journey over great rolling uplands, something like those in the Transvaal, but diversified by patches of bush country.

All this time we were continually ascending at the rate of about one hundred feet every ten miles. Indeed the country was on a slope which appeared to terminate at a mass of snow-tipped mountains, for which we were steering, and where we learnt the second lake of which the wanderer had spoken as the lake without a bottom was situated. At length we arrived there, and, having ascertained that there *was* a large lake on top of the mountains, ascended three thousand feet more till we came to a precipitous cliff or edge, to find a great sheet of water some twenty miles square lying fifteen hundred feet below us, and evidently occupying an extinct volcanic crater or craters of vast extent. Perceiving villages on the border of this lake, we descended with great difficulty through forests of pine trees, which now clothed the precipitous sides of the crater, and were well received by the people, a simple, unwarlike folk, who had never seen or even heard of a white man before, and treated us with great reverence and kindness, supplying us with as much food and milk as we could eat and drink. This wonderful and beautiful lake lay, according to our aneroid, at a height of no less than 11,450 feet above sea-level, and its climate was quite cold, and not at all unlike that of England. Indeed, for the first three days of our stay there we saw little or nothing of the scenery on account of an unmistakable Scotch mist which prevailed. It was this rain that set the tsetse poison working in our remaining donkeys, so that they all died.

This disaster left us in a very awkward position, as we had now no means of transport whatever, though on the other hand we had not much to carry. Ammunition, too, was very short, amounting to but one hundred and fifty rounds of rifle cartridges and some fifty shotgun cartridges. How to get on we did not know; indeed it seemed to us that we had about reached the end of our tether. Even if we had been inclined to abandon the object of our search, which, shadow as it was, was by no means the case, it was ridiculous to think of forcing our way back some seven hundred miles to the coast in our present plight; so we came to the conclusion that the only thing to be done was to stop where we were – the natives being so well disposed and food plentiful – for the present, and abide events, and try to collect information as to the countries beyond.

Accordingly, having purchased a capital log canoe, large enough to hold us all and our baggage, from the headman of the village we were staying in, presenting him with three empty cold-drawn brass cartridges by way of payment, with which he was perfectly delighted, we set out to make a tour of the lake in order to find the most favourable place to make a camp. As we did not know if we should return to this village, we put all our gear into the canoe, and also a quarter of cooked water-buck, which when young is delicious eating, and off we set, natives having already gone before us in light canoes to warn the inhabitants of the other villages of our approach.

As we were puddling leisurely along Good remarked upon the extraordinary deep blue colour of the water, and said that he understood from the natives, who were great fishermen – fish, indeed, being their principal food – that the lake was supposed to be wonderfully deep, and to have a hole at the bottom through which the water escaped and put out some great fire that was raging below.

I pointed out to him that what he had heard was probably a legend arising from a tradition among the people which dated back to the time when one of the extinct parasitic volcanic cones was in activity. We saw several round the borders of the lake which had no doubt been working at a period long subsequent to the volcanic death of the central crater which now formed the bed of the lake itself. When it finally became extinct the people would imagine that the water from the lake had run down and put out the big fire below, more especially as, though it was constantly fed by streams running from the snow-tipped peaks about, there was no visible exit to it.

The farther shore of the lake we found, on approaching it, to consist of a vast perpendicular wall of rock, which held the water without any intermediate sloping bank, as elsewhere. Accordingly we paddled parallel with this precipice, at a distance of about a hundred paces from it, shaping our course for the end of the lake, where we knew that there was a large village.

As we went we began to pass a considerable accumulation of floating rushes, weed, boughs of trees, and other rubbish, brought, Good supposed, to this spot by some current, which he was much puzzled to account for. Whilst we were speculating about this, Sir Henry pointed out a flock of large white swans, which were feeding on the drift some little way ahead of us. Now I had already noticed swans flying about this lake, and, having never come across them before in Africa, was exceedingly anxious to obtain a specimen. I had questioned the natives about them, and learnt that they came from over the mountain, always arriving at certain periods of the year in the early morning, when it was very easy to catch them, on account of their exhausted condition. I also asked them what country they came from, when they shrugged their shoulders, and said that on the top of the great black precipice was stony inhospitable land, and beyond that were mountains with snow, and full of wild beasts, where no people lived, and beyond the mountains were hundreds of miles of dense thorn forest, so thick that even the elephants could not get through it, much less men. Next I asked them if they had ever heard of white people like ourselves living on the farther side of the mountains and the thorn forest, whereat they laughed. But afterwards a very old woman came and told me that when she was a little girl her grandfather had told her that in his youth *his* grandfather had crossed the desert and the mountains, and pierced the thorn forest, and seen a white people who lived in stone kraals beyond. Of course, as this took the tale back some two hundred and fifty years, the information was very indefinite; but still there it was again, and on thinking it over I grew firmly convinced that there was some truth in all these rumours, and equally firmly determined to solve the mystery. Little did I guess in what an almost miraculous way my desire was to be gratified.

Well, we set to work to stalk the swans, which kept drawing, as they fed, nearer and nearer to the precipice, and at last we pushed the canoe under shelter of a patch of drift within forty yards of them. Sir Henry had the shotgun, loaded with No. 1, and, waiting for a chance, got two in a line, and, firing at their necks, killed them both. Up rose the rest, thirty or more of them, with a mighty splashing; and, as they did so, he gave them the other barrel. Down came one fellow with a broken wing, and I saw the leg of another drop and a few feathers start out of his back; but he went on quite strong. Up went the swans, circling ever higher till at last they were mere specks level with the top of the frowning precipice, when I saw them form into a triangle and head off for the unknown north-east. Meanwhile we had picked up our two dead ones, and beautiful birds they were, weighing not less than about thirty pounds each, and were chasing the winged one, which had scrambled over a mass of driftweed into a pool of clear water beyond. Finding a difficulty in forcing the canoe through the rubbish, I told our only remaining Wakwafi servant, whom I knew to be an excellent swimmer, to jump over, dive under the drift, and catch him, knowing that as there were no crocodiles in this lake he could come to no harm. Entering into the fun of the thing, the man obeyed, and soon was dodging about after the winged swan in fine style, getting gradually nearer to the rock wall, against which the water washed as he did so.

Presently he gave up swimming after the swan, and began to cry out that he was being carried away; and, indeed, we saw that, though he was swimming with all his strength towards us, he was being drawn slowly to the precipice. With a few desperate strokes of our paddles we pushed the canoe through the crust of drift and rowed towards the man as hard as we could, but, fast as we went, he was drawn faster to the rock. Suddenly I saw that before us, just rising eighteen inches or so above the surface of the lake, was what looked like the top of the arch of a submerged cave or railway tunnel. Evidently, from the watermark on the rock several feet above it, it was generally entirely submerged; but there had been a dry season, and the cold had prevented the snow from melting as freely as usual; so the lake was low and the arch showed. Towards this arch our poor servant was being sucked with frightful rapidity. He was not more than ten fathoms from it, and we were about twenty when I saw it, and with little help from us the canoe flew along after him. He struggled bravely, and I thought that we should have saved him, when suddenly I perceived an expression of despair come upon his face, and there before our eyes he was sucked down into the cruel swirling blue depths, and vanished. At the same moment I felt our canoe seized as with a mighty hand, and propelled with resistless force towards the rock.

We realised our danger now and rowed, or rather paddled, furiously in our attempt to get out of the vortex. In vain; in another second we were flying straight for the arch like an arrow, and I thought that we were lost. Luckily I retained sufficient presence of mind to shout out, instantly setting the example by throwing myself into the bottom of the canoe, 'Down on your faces – down!' and the others had the sense to take the hint. In another instant there was a grinding noise, and the boat was pushed down till the water began to trickle over the sides, and I thought that we were gone. But no, suddenly the grinding ceased, and we could again feel the canoe flying along. I turned my head a little – I dared not lift it – and looked up. By the feeble light that yet reached the canoe, I could make out that a dense arch of rock hung just over our heads, and that was all. In another minute I could not even see as much as that, for the faint light had merged into shadow, and the shadows had been swallowed up in darkness, utter and complete.

For an hour or so we lay there, not daring to lift our heads for fear lest the brains should be dashed out of them, and scarcely able to speak even, on account of the noise of the rushing water which drowned our voices. Not, indeed, that we had much inclination to speak, seeing that we were overwhelmed by the awfulness of our position and the imminent fear of instant death, either by being dashed against the sides of the cavern, or on a rock, or being sucked down in the raging waters, or perhaps asphyxiated by want of air. All of these and many other modes of death presented themselves to my imagination as I lay at the bottom of the canoe, listening to the swirl of the hurrying waters which ran whither we knew not. One only other sound could I hear, and that was Alphonse's intermittent howl of terror coming from the centre of the canoe, and even that seemed faint and unnatural. Indeed, the whole thing overpowered my brain, and I began to believe that I was the victim of some ghastly spirit-shaking nightmare.

CHAPTER 10

The Rose of Fire

On we flew, drawn by the mighty current, till at last I noticed that the sound of the water was not half so deafening as it had been, and concluded that this must be because there was more room for the echoes to disperse in. I could now hear Alphonse's howls much more distinctly; they were made up of the oddest mixture of invocations to the Supreme Power and the name of his beloved Annette that it is possible to conceive; and, in short, though their evident earnestness saved them from profanity, were, to say the least, very remarkable. Taking up a paddle I managed to drive it into his ribs, whereon he, thinking that the end had come, howled louder than ever. Then I slowly and cautiously raised myself on my knees and stretched my hand upwards, but could touch no roof. Next I took the paddle and lifted it above my head as high as I could, but with the same result. I also thrust it out laterally to the right and left, but could touch nothing except water. Then I bethought me that there was in the boat, amongst our other remaining possessions, a bull's-eye lantern and a tin of oil. I groped about and found it, and having a match on me carefully lit it, and as soon as the flame had got a hold of the wick I turned it on down the boat. As it happened, the first thing the light lit on was the white and scared face of Alphonse, who, thinking that it was all over at last, and that he was witnessing a preliminary celestial phenomenon, gave a terrific yell and was with difficulty reassured with the paddle. As for the other three, Good was lying on the flat of his back, his eyeglass still fixed in his eye, and gazing blankly into the upper darkness. Sir Henry had his head resting on the thwarts of the canoe, and with his hand was trying to test the speed of the water. But when the beam of

light fell upon old Umslopogaas I could really have laughed. I
think I have said that we had put a roast quarter of water-buck
into the canoe. Well, it so happened that when we all prostrated
ourselves to avoid being swept out of the boat and into the water
by the rock roof, Umslopogaas's head had come down uncommonly near this roast buck, and so soon as he had recovered a
little from the first shock of our position it occurred to him that
he was hungry. Thereupon he coolly cut off a chop with Inkosi-
kaas, and was now employed in eating it with every appearance of
satisfaction. As he afterwards explained, he thought that he was
going 'on a long journey', and preferred to start on a full
stomach. It reminded me of the people who are going to be
hanged, and who are generally reported in the English daily
papers to have made 'an excellent breakfast'.

As soon as the others saw that I had managed to light the lamp,
we bundled Alphonse into the farther end of the canoe with a
threat which calmed him down wonderfully, that if he would
insist upon making the darkness hideous with his cries we would
put him out of suspense by sending him to join the Wakwafi and
wait for Annette in another sphere, and began to discuss the
situation as well as we could. First, however, at Good's suggestion, we bound two paddles mast-fashion in the bows so that
they might give us warning against any sudden lowering of the
roof of the cave or waterway. It was clear to us that we were in an
underground river or, as Alphonse defined it, 'main drain',
which carried off the superfluous waters of the lake. Such rivers
are well known to exist in many parts of the world, but it has not
often been the evil fortune of explorers to travel by them. That
the river was wide we could clearly see, for the light from the
bull's-eye lantern failed to reach from shore to shore, although
occasionally, when the current swept us either to one side or the
other, we could distinguish the rock wall of the tunnel, which, as
far as we could make out, appeared to arch about twenty-five feet
above our heads. As for the current itself, it ran, Good estimated,
at least eight knots, and, fortunately for us, was, as is usual,
fiercest in the middle of the stream. Still, our first act was to
arrange that one of us, with the lantern and a pole there was in

the canoe, should always be in the bows ready, if possible, to prevent us from being stove in against the side of the cave or any projecting rock. Umslopogaas, having already dined, took the first turn. This was absolutely, with one exception, all that we could do towards preserving our safety. The exception was that another of us took up a position in the stern with a paddle by means of which it was possible to steer the canoe more or less and to keep her from the sides of the cave. These matters attended to, we made a somewhat sparing meal off the cold buck's meat (for we did not know how long it might have to last us), and then feeling in rather better spirits I gave my opinion that, serious as it undoubtedly was, I did not consider our position altogether without hope, unless, indeed, the natives were right, and the river plunged straight down into the bowels of the earth. If not, it was clear that it must emerge somewhere, probably on the other side of the mountains, and in that case all we had to think of was to keep ourselves alive till we got there, wherever 'there' might be. But, of course, as Good lugubriously pointed out, on the other hand we might fall victims to a hundred unsuspected horrors – or the river might go on winding away inside the earth till it dried up, in which case our fate would indeed be an awful one.

'Well, let us hope for the best and prepare ourselves for the worst,' said Sir Henry, who is always cheerful and even spirited – a very tower of strength in the time of trouble. 'We have come out of so many queer scrapes together, that somehow I almost fancy we shall come out of this,' he added.

This was excellent advice, and we proceeded to take it each in our separate way – that is, except Alphonse, who had by now sunk into a sort of terrified stupor. Good was at the helm and Umslopogaas in the bows, so there was nothing left for Sir Henry and myself to do except to lie down in the canoe and think. It certainly was a curious, and indeed almost a weird, position to be placed in – rushing along, as we were, through the bowels of the earth, borne on the bosom of a Stygian river, something after the fashion of souls being ferried by Charon, as Curtis said. And how dark it was! The feeble ray from our little lamp did but serve to show the darkness. There in the bows sat old Umslopogaas, like Pleasure in the poem,* watchful and untiring, the pole ready to his hand, and behind in the shadow I could just make out the form of Good peering forward at the ray of light in order to make out how to steer with the paddle that he held and now and again dipped into the water.

'Well, well,' thought I, 'you have come in search of adventures, Allan my boy, and you have certainly got them. At your time of life, too! You ought to be ashamed of yourself; but somehow you are not, and, awful as it all is, perhaps you will pull through after all; and if you don't, why, you cannot help it, you see! And when all's said and done an underground river will make a very appropriate burying-place.'

At first, however, I am bound to say that the strain upon the nerves was very great. It is trying to the coolest and most experienced person not to know from one hour to another if he has five minutes more to live, but there is nothing in this world that one cannot get accustomed to, and in time we began to get accustomed even to that. And, after all, our anxiety, though no doubt natural, was, strictly speaking, illogical, seeing that we never know what is going to happen to us the next minute, even when we sit in a well-drained house with two policemen patrolling under the window – nor how long we have to live. It is all arranged for us, my sons, so what is the use of bothering?

It was nearly midday when we made our dive into darkness, and we had set our watch (Good and Umslopogaas) at two, having agreed that it should be of a duration of five hours. At seven o'clock, accordingly, Sir Henry and I went on, Sir Henry at the bow and I at the stern, and the other two lay down and went to sleep. For three hours all went well, Sir Henry only finding it necessary once to push us off from the side; and I that but little steering was required to keep us straight, as the violent current did all that was needed, though occasionally the canoe showed a tendency which had to be guarded against to veer and travel

* Mr Allan Quatermain misquotes – Pleasure sat at the helm.   ED.

broadside on. What struck me as the most curious thing about this wonderful river was: how did the air keep fresh? It was muggy and thick, no doubt, but still not sufficiently so to render it bad or even remarkably unpleasant. The only explanation that I can suggest is that the water of the lake had sufficient air in it to keep the atmosphere of the tunnel from absolute stagnation, this air being given out as it proceeded on its headlong way. Of course I only give the solution of the mystery for what it is worth, which perhaps is not much.

When I had been for three hours or so at the helm, I began to notice a decided change in the temperature, which was getting warmer. At first I took no notice of it, but when, at the expiration of another half-hour, I found that it was getting hotter and hotter, I called to Sir Henry and asked him if he noticed it, or if it was only my imagination. 'Noticed it!' he answered; 'I should think so. I am in a sort of Turkish bath.' Just about then the others woke up gasping, and were obliged to begin to discard their clothes. Here Umslopogaas had the advantage, for he did not wear any to speak of, except a moocha.

Hotter it grew, and hotter yet, till at last we could scarcely breathe, and the perspiration poured out of us. Half an hour more, and though we were all now stark naked, we could hardly bear it. The place was like an antechamber of the infernal regions proper. I dipped my hand into the water and drew it out almost with a cry; it was nearly boiling. We consulted a little thermometer we had – the mercury stood at 123 degrees. From the surface of the water rose a dense cloud of steam. Alphonse groaned out that we were already in purgatory, which indeed we were, though not in the sense that he meant it. Sir Henry suggested that we must be passing near the seat of some underground volcanic fire, and I am inclined to think, especially in the light of what subsequently occurred, that he was right. Our sufferings for some time after this really pass my powers of description. We no longer perspired, for all the perspiration had been sweated out of us. We simply lay in the bottom of the boat, which we were now physically incapable of directing, feeling like hot embers, and I fancy undergoing very much the same sensations that the poor fish do when they are dying on land – namely, that of slow suffocation. Our skins began to crack, and the blood to throb in our heads like the beating of a steam-engine.

This had been going on for some time, when suddenly the river turned a little, and I heard Sir Henry call out from the bows in a hoarse, startled voice, and, looking up, saw a most wonderful and awful thing. About half a mile ahead of us, and a little to the left of the centre of the stream – which we could now see was about ninety feet broad – a huge pillar-like jet of almost white flame rose from the surface of the water and sprang fifty feet into the air, when it struck the roof and spread out some forty feet in diameter, falling back in curved sheets of fire shaped like the petals of a full-blown rose. Indeed this awful gas jet resembled nothing so much as a great flaming flower rising out of the black water. Below was the straight stalk, a foot or more thick, and above the dreadful bloom. And as for the fearfulness of it and its fierce and awesome beauty, who can describe it? Certainly I cannot. Although we were now some five hundred yards away, it, notwithstanding the steam, lit up the whole cavern as clear as day, and we could see that the roof was here about forty feet above us, and washed perfectly smooth with water. The rock was black, and here and there I could make out long shining lines of ore running through it like great veins, but of what metal they were I know not.

On we rushed towards this pillar of fire, which gleamed fiercer than any furnace ever lit by man.

'Keep the boat to the right, Quatermain – to the right,' shouted Sir Henry, and a minute afterwards I saw him fall forward senseless. Alphonse had already gone. Good was the next to go. There they lay as though dead; only Umslopogaas and I kept our senses. We were within fifty yards of it now, and I saw the Zulu's head fall forward on his hands. He had gone too, and I was alone. I could not breathe; the fierce heat dried me up. For yards and yards round the great rose of fire the rock-roof was red-hot. The wood of the boat was almost burning. I saw the feathers on one of the dead swans begin to twist and shrivel up; but I would not give in. I knew that if I did we should pass within three or four yards of the gas jet and perish miserably. I set the paddle so as to turn the canoe as far from it as possible, and held on grimly.

My eyes seemed to be bursting from my head, and through my closed lids I could see the fierce light. We were nearly opposite now; it roared like all the fires of hell, and the water boiled furiously around it. Five seconds more. We were past; I heard the roar behind me.

Then I too fell senseless. The next thing that I recollect is feeling a breath of air upon my face. My eyes opened with great difficulty. I looked up. Far, far above me there was light, though around me was great gloom. Then I remembered and looked. The canoe still floated down the river, and in the bottom of it lay the naked forms of my companions. 'Were they dead?' I wondered. 'Was I left alone in this awful place?' I knew not. Next I became conscious of a burning thirst. I put my hand over the edge of the boat into the water and drew it up again with a cry. No wonder: nearly all the skin was burnt off the back of it. The water, however, was cold, or nearly so, and I drank pints and splashed myself all over. My body seemed to suck up the fluid as one may see a brick wall suck up rain after a drought; but where I was burnt the touch of it caused intense pain. Then I bethought myself of the others, and, dragging myself towards them with difficulty, I sprinkled them with water, and to my joy they began to recover – Umslopogaas first, then the others. Next they drank, absorbing water like so many sponges. Then, feeling chilly – a queer contrast to our recent sensations – we began as best we could to get into our clothes. As we did so Good pointed to the port side of the canoe: it was all blistered with heat, and in places actually charred. Had it been built like our civilised boats, Good said that the planks would certainly have warped and let in enough water to sink us; but fortunately it was dug out of the soft, willowy wood of a single great tree, and had sides nearly three inches and a bottom four inches thick. What that awful flame was we never discovered, but I suppose that there was at this spot a crack or hole in the bed of the river through which a vast volume of gas forced its way from its volcanic home in the bowels of the earth towards the upper air. How it first became ignited is, of course, impossible to say – probably, I should think, from some spontaneous explosion of mephitic gases.

As soon as we had got some things together and shaken ourselves together a little, we set to work to make out where we were now. I have said that there was light above, and on examination we found that it came from the sky. Our river that was, Sir Henry said, a literal realisation of the wild vision of the poet,* was no longer underground, but was running on its darksome way, not now through 'caverns measureless to man', but between two frightful cliffs which cannot have been less than two thousand feet high. So high were they, indeed, that though the sky was above us, where we were was dense gloom – not darkness indeed, but the gloom of a room closely shuttered in the daytime. Up on either side rose the great straight cliffs, grim and forbidding, till the eye grew dizzy with trying to measure their sheer height. The little space of sky that marked where they ended lay like a thread of blue upon their soaring blackness, which was unrelieved by any tree or creeper. Here and there, however, grew ghostly patches of a long grey lichen, hanging motionless to the rock as the white beard to the chin of a dead man. It seemed as though only the dregs or heavier part of the light had sunk to the bottom of this awful place. No bright-winged sunbeam could fall so low: they died far, far above our heads.

By the river's edge was a little shore formed of round fragments of rock washed into this shape by the constant action of water, and giving the place the appearance of being strewn with thousands of fossil cannon balls. Evidently when the water of the underground river is high there is no beach at all, or very little, between the border of the stream and the precipitous cliffs; but now there was a space of seven or eight yards. And here, on this beach, we determined to land, in order to rest ourselves a little after all that we had gone through and to stretch our limbs. It was a dreadful place, but it would give an hour's respite from the terrors of the river, and also allow of our repacking and arranging the canoe.

---

* Where Alph the sacred river ran / Through caverns measureless to man / Down to a sunless sea.

Accordingly we selected what looked like a favourable spot, and with some little difficulty managed to beach the canoe and scramble out on to the round, inhospitable pebbles.

'My word,' called out Good, who was on shore the first, 'what an awful place! It's enough to give one a fit.' And he laughed.

Instantly a thundering voice took up his words, magnifying them a hundred times. '*Give one a fit – Ho! ho! ho!*' – '*A fit, Ho! ho! ho!*' answered another voice in wild accents from far up the cliff – *a fit! a fit! a fit!* chimed in voice after voice – each flinging the words to and fro with shouts of awful laughter to the invisible lips of the other till the whole place echoed with the words and with shrieks of fiendish merriment, which at last ceased as suddenly as they had begun.

'Oh, mon Dieu!' yelled Alphonse, startled quite out of such self-command as he possessed.

'*Mon Dieu! Mon Dieu! Mon Dieu!*' the Titanic echoes thundered, shrieked, and wailed in every conceivable tone.

'Ah,' said Umslopogaas calmly, 'I clearly perceive that devils live here. Well, the place looks like it.'

I tried to explain to him that the cause of all the hubbub was a very remarkable and interesting echo, but he would not believe it.

'Ah,' he said, 'I know an echo when I hear one. There was one lived opposite my kraal in Zululand, and the Intombis [maidens] used to talk with it. But if what we hear is a full-grown echo, mine at home can only have been a baby. No, no – they are devils up there. But I don't think much of them, though,' he added, taking a pinch of snuff. 'They can copy what one says, but they don't seem to be able to talk on their own account, and they dare not show their faces,' and he relapsed into silence, and apparently paid no further attention to such contemptible fiends.

After this we found it necessary to keep our conversation down to a whisper – for it was really unbearable to have every word one uttered tossed to and fro like a tennis-ball, as precipice called to precipice.

But even our whispers ran up the rocks in mysterious murmurs till at last they died away in long-drawn sighs of sound. Echoes are delightful and romantic things, but we had more than enough of them in that dreadful gulf.

As soon as we had settled ourselves a little on the round stones, we went on to wash and dress our burns as well as we could. As we had but a little oil for the lantern, we could not spare any for this purpose, so we skinned one of the swans, and used the fat off its breast, which proved an excellent substitute. Then we repacked the canoe, and finally began to take some food, of which I need scarcely say we were in need, for our insensibility had endured for many hours, and it was, as our watches showed, midday. Accordingly we seated ourselves in a circle, and were soon engaged in discussing our cold meat with such appetite as we could muster, which, in my case at any rate, was not much, as I felt sick and faint after my sufferings of the previous night, and had besides a racking headache. It was a curious meal. The gloom was so intense that we could scarcely see the way to cut our food and convey it to our mouths. Still we got on pretty well, till I happened to look behind me – my attention being attracted by a noise of something crawling over the stones, and perceived sitting upon a rock in my immediate rear a huge species of black freshwater crab, only it was five times the size of any crab I ever saw. This hideous and loathsome-looking animal had projecting eyes that seemed to glare at one, very long and flexible antennae or feelers, and gigantic claws. Nor was I especially favoured with its company. From every quarter dozens of these horrid brutes were creeping up, drawn, I suppose, by the smell of the food, from between the round stones and out of holes in the precipice. Some were already quite close to us. I stared quite fascinated by the unusual sight, and as I did so I saw one of the beasts stretch out its huge claw and give the unsuspecting Good such a nip behind that he jumped up with a howl, and set the 'wild echoes flying' in sober earnest. Just then, too, another, a very large one, got hold of Alphonse's leg, and declined to part with it, and, as may be imagined, a considerable scene ensued. Umslopogaas took his axe and cracked the shell of one with the flat of it, whereon it set up a horrid screaming which the echoes multiplied a thousandfold, and began to foam at the mouth, a proceeding that drew hundreds more of its friends out of unsuspected holes and corners. Those on the spot perceiving that the animal was hurt fell upon it like creditors on a bankrupt, and literally rent it limb from limb with their huge pincers and devoured it, using their claws to convey the fragments to their mouths. Seizing whatever weapons were handy, such as stones or paddles, we commenced a war upon the monsters – whose numbers were increasing by leaps and bounds, and whose stench was overpowering. So fast as we cracked their armour others seized the injured ones and devoured them, foaming at the mouth, and screaming as they did so. Nor did the brutes stop at that. When they could they nipped hold of us – and awful nips they were – or tried to steal the meat. One enormous fellow got hold of the swan we had skinned and began to drag it off. Instantly a score of others flung themselves upon the prey, and then began a ghastly and disgusting scene. How the monsters foamed and screamed, and rent the flesh, and each other! It was a sickening and unnatural sight, and one that will haunt all who saw it till their dying day – enacted as it was in the deep, oppressive gloom, and set to the unceasing music of the many-toned nerve-shaking echoes. Strange as it may seem to say so, there was something so shockingly human about these fiendish creatures – it was as though all the most evil passions and desires of man had got into the shell of a magnified crab and gone mad. They were so dreadfully courageous and intelligent, and they looked as if they *understood*. The whole scene might have furnished material for another canto of Dante's 'Inferno', as Curtis said.

'I say, you fellows, let's get out of this or we shall all go off our heads,' sung out Good; and we were not slow to take the hint. Pushing the canoe, around which the animals were now crawling by hundreds and making vain attempts to climb, off the rocks, we bundled into it and got out into midstream, leaving behind us the fragments of our meal and the screaming, foaming, stinking mass of monsters in full possession of the ground.

'Those are the devils of the place,' said Umslopogaas with the air of one who has solved a problem, and upon my word I felt almost inclined to agree with him.

Umslopogaas' remarks were like his axe – very much to the point.

'What's to be done next?' said Sir Henry blankly.

'Drift, I suppose,' I answered, and we drifted accordingly. All the afternoon and well into the evening we floated on in the gloom beneath the far-off line of blue sky, scarcely knowing when day ended and night began, for down in that vast gulf the difference was not marked, till at length Good pointed out a star hanging right above us, which, having nothing better to do, we observed with great interest. Suddenly it vanished, the darkness became intense, and a familiar murmuring sound filled the air. 'Underground again,' I said with a groan, holding up the lamp. Yes, there was no doubt about it. I could just make out the roof. The chasm had come to an end and the tunnel had recommenced. And then there began another long, long night of danger and horror. To describe all its incidents would be too wearisome, so I will simply say that about midnight we struck on a flat projecting rock in midstream and were as nearly as possible overturned and drowned. However, at last we got off, and went upon the uneven tenor of our way. And so the hours passed till it was nearly three o'clock. Sir Henry, Good, and Alphonse were asleep, utterly worn out; Umslopogaas was at the bow with the pole, and I was steering, when I perceived that the rate at which we were travelling had perceptibly increased. Then, suddenly, I heard Umslopogaas make an exclamation, and next second came a sound as of parting branches, and I became aware that the canoe was being forced through hanging bushes or creepers. Another minute, and the breath of sweet open air fanned my face, and I felt that we had emerged from the tunnel and were floating upon clear water. I say felt, for I could see nothing, the darkness being absolutely pitchy, as it often is just before the dawn. But even this could scarcely damp my joy. We were out of that dreadful river, and wherever we might have got to this at least was something to be thankful for. And so I sat down and inhaled the sweet night air and waited for the dawn with such patience as I could command.

CHAPTER II

The Frowning City

For an hour or more I sat waiting (Umslopogaas having mean-while gone to sleep also) till at length the east turned grey, and huge misty shapes moved over the surface of the water like ghosts of long-forgotten dawns. They were the vapours rising from their watery bed to greet the sun. Then the grey turned to primrose, and the primrose grew to red. Next, glorious bars of light sprang up across the eastern sky, and through them the radiant messen-gers of the dawn came speeding upon their arrowy way, scattering the ghostly vapours and awaking the mountains with a kiss, as they flew from range to range and longitude to longitude. Another moment, and the golden gates were open and the sun himself came forth as a bridegroom from his chamber, with pomp and glory and a flashing as of ten million spears, and embraced the night and covered her with brightness, and it was day.

But as yet I could see nothing save the beautiful blue sky above, for over the water was a thick layer of mist exactly as though the whole surface had been covered with billows of cotton wool. By degrees, however, the sun sucked up the mists, and then I saw that we were afloat upon a glorious sheet of blue water of which I could not make out the shore. Some eight or ten miles behind us, however, there stretched as far as the eye could reach a range of precipitous hills that formed a retaining wall of the lake, and I have no doubt but that it was through some entrance in these hills that the subterranean river found its way into the open water. Indeed, I afterwards ascertained this to be the fact, and it will be some indication of the extraordinary strength and directness of the current of the mysterious river that the canoe, even at this distance, was still answering to it. Presently, too, I, or rather Umslopogaas, who woke up just then, discovered another indication, and a very unpleasant one it was. Perceiving some whitish object upon the water, Umslopogaas called my attention to it, and with a few strokes of the paddle brought the canoe to the spot, whereupon we discovered that the object was the body of a man floating face downwards. This was bad enough, but imagine my horror when Umslopogaas having turned him on to his back with the paddle, we recognised in the sunken features the lineaments of – whom do you suppose? None other than our poor servant who had been sucked down two days before in the waters of the subterranean river. It quite frightened me. I thought that we had left him behind for ever, and behold! borne by the current, he had made the awful journey with us, and with us had reached the end. His appearance also was dreadful, for he bore traces of having touched the pillar of fire – one arm being completely shrivelled up and all his hair being burnt off. The features were, as I have said, sunken, and yet they preserved upon them that awful look of despair that I had seen upon his living face as the poor fellow was sucked down. Really the sight unnerved me, weary and shaken as I felt with all that we had gone through, and I was heartily glad when suddenly and without any warning the body began to sink just as though it had had a mission, which having been accomplished, it retired; the real reason no doubt being that turning it on its back allowed a free passage to the gas. Down it went to the transparent depths – fathom after fathom we could trace its course till at last a long line of bright air-bubbles, swiftly chasing each other to the surface, alone remained where it had passed. At length these, too, were gone, and that was an end of our poor servant. Umslopogaas thoughtfully watched the body vanish.

'What did he follow us for?' he asked. ''Tis an ill omen for thee and me, Macumazahn.' And he laughed.

I turned on him angrily, for I dislike these unpleasant suggestions. If people have such ideas, they ought in common decency to keep them to themselves. I detest individuals who make one the subject of their disagreeable presentiments, or who, when they dream that they saw one hanged as a common felon, or some such horror, will insist upon telling one all about it at breakfast, even if they have to get up early to do it.

Just then, however, the others woke up and began to rejoice exceedingly at finding that we were out of that dreadful river and once more beneath the blue sky. Then followed a babel of talk and suggestions as to what we were to do next, the upshot of all of which was that, as we were excessively hungry, and had nothing whatsoever left to eat except a few scraps of biltong (dried game-flesh), having abandoned all that remained of our provisions to those horrible freshwater crabs, we determined to make for the shore. But a new difficulty arose. We did not know where the shore was, and, with the exception of the cliffs through which the subterranean river made its entry, could see nothing but a wide expanse of sparkling blue water. Observing, however, that the long flights of aquatic birds kept flying from our left, we concluded that they were advancing from their feeding-grounds on shore to pass the day in the lake, and accordingly headed the boat towards the quarter whence they came, and began to paddle. Before long, however, a stiffish breeze sprang up, blowing directly in the direction we wanted, so we improvised a sail with a blanket and the pole, which took us along merrily. This done, we devoured the remnants of our biltong, washed down with the sweet lake water, and then lit our pipes and awaited whatever might turn up.

When we had been sailing for an hour, Good, who was searching the horizon with the spy-glass, suddenly announced joyfully that he saw land, and pointed out that, from the change in the colour of the water, he thought we must be approaching the mouth of a river. In another minute we perceived a great golden dome, not unlike that of St Paul's, piercing the morning mists, and while we were wondering what in the world it could be, Good reported another and still more important discovery, namely, that a small sailing-boat was advancing towards us. This bit of news, which we were very shortly able to verify with our own eyes, threw us into a considerable flutter. That the natives of this unknown lake should understand the art of sailing seemed to suggest that they possessed some degree of civilisation. In a few more minutes it became evident that the occupant or occupants of the advancing boat had made us out. For a moment or two she hung in the wind as though in doubt, and then came tacking towards us with great swiftness. In ten more minutes she was within a hundred yards, and we saw that she was a neat little boat – not a canoe 'dug out', but built more or less in the European fashion with planks, and carrying a singularly large sail for her size. But our attention was soon diverted from the boat to her crew, which consisted of a man and a woman, *nearly as white as ourselves*.

We stared at each other in amazement, thinking that we must be mistaken; but no, there was no doubt about it. They were not fair, but the two people in the boat were decidedly of a white as distinguished from a black race, as white, for instance, as Spaniards or Italians. It was a patent fact. So it was true, after all; and, mysteriously led by a Power beyond our own, we had discovered this wonderful people. I could have shouted for joy when I thought of the glory and the wonder of the thing; and as it was, we all shook hands and congratulated each other on the unexpected success of our wild search. All my life had I heard rumours of a white race that existed in the highlands of this vast continent, and longed to put them to the proof, and now here I saw it with my own eyes, and was dumbfounded. Truly, as Sir Henry said, the old Roman was right when he wrote 'Ex Africa semper aliquid novi', which he tells me means that out of Africa there always comes some new thing.

The man in the boat was of a good but not particularly fine physique, and possessed straight black hair, regular aquiline features, and an intelligent face. He was dressed in a brown cloth garment, something like a flannel shirt without the sleeves, and in an unmistakable kilt of the same material. The legs and feet were bare. Round the right arm and left leg he wore thick rings of yellow metal that I judged to be gold. The woman had a sweet face, wild and shy, with large eyes and curling brown hair. Her dress was made of the same material as the man's, and consisted, as we afterwards discovered, first of a linen undergarment that hung down to her knee, and then of a single long strip of cloth, about four feet wide by fifteen long, which was wound round the body in graceful folds and finally flung over the left shoulder so that the end, which was dyed blue or purple or some other colour, according to the social standing of the wearer, hung down in front, the right arm and breast being, however, left quite bare. A more becoming dress, especially when, as in the present case, the wearer was young and pretty, it is quite impossible to conceive. Good (who has an eye for such things) was greatly struck with it, and so indeed was I. It was so simple and yet so effective.

Meanwhile, if we had been astonished at the appearance of the man and woman, it was clear that they were far more astonished at us. As for the man, he appeared to be overcome with fear and wonder, and for a while hovered round our canoe, but would not approach. At last, however, he came within hailing distance, and called to us in a language that sounded soft and pleasing enough, but of which we could not understand one word. So we hailed back in English, French, Latin, Greek, German, Zulu, Dutch, Sisutu, Kukuana, and a few other native dialects that I am acquainted with, but our visitor did not understand any of these tongues; indeed, they appeared to bewilder him. As for the lady, she was busily employed in taking stock of us, and Good was returning the compliment by staring at her hard through his eyeglass, a proceeding that she seemed rather to enjoy than otherwise. At length, the man, being unable to make anything of us, suddenly turned his boat round and began to head off for the shore, his little boat skimming away before the wind like a swallow. As she passed across our bows the man turned to attend to the large sail, and Good promptly took the opportunity to kiss his hand to the young lady. I was horrified at this proceeding, both on general grounds and because I feared that she might take offence, but to my delight she did not, for, first glancing round and seeing that her husband, or brother, or whoever he was, was engaged, she promptly kissed hers back.

'Ah!' said I. 'It seems that we have at last found a language that the people of this country understand.'

'In which case,' said Sir Henry, 'Good will prove an invaluable interpreter.'

I frowned, for I do not approve of Good's frivolities, and he knows it, and I turned the conversation to more serious subjects. 'It is very clear to me,' I said, 'that the man will be back before long with a host of his fellows, so we had best make up our minds as to how we are going to receive them.'

'The question is how will they receive us?' said Sir Henry.

As for Good he made no remark, but began to extract a small square tin case that had accompanied us in all our wanderings from under a pile of baggage. Now we had often remonstrated with Good about this tin case, inasmuch as it had been an awkward thing to carry, and he had never given any very explicit account as to its contents; but he had insisted on keeping it, saying mysteriously that it might come in very useful one day.

'What on earth are you going to do, Good?' asked Sir Henry.

'Do – why dress, of course! You don't expect me to appear in a new country in these things, do you?' and he pointed to his soiled and worn garments, which were however, like all Good's things, very tidy, and with every tear neatly mended.

We said no more, but watched his proceedings with breathless interest. His first step was to get Alphonse, who was thoroughly competent in such matters, to trim his hair and beard in the most approved fashion. I think that if he had had some hot water and a cake of soap at hand he would have shaved off the latter; but he had not. This done, he suggested that we should lower the sail of the canoe and all take a bath, which we did, greatly to the horror and astonishment of Alphonse, who lifted his hands and ejaculated that these English were indeed a wonderful people. Umslopogaas, who, though he was, like most high-bred Zulus, scrupulously cleanly in his person, did not see the fun of swimming about in a lake, also regarded the proceeding with mild amusement. We got back into the canoe much refreshed by the cold water, and sat to dry in the sun, whilst Good undid his tin box, and produced first a beautiful clean white shirt, just as it had left a London steam laundry, and then some garments wrapped first in brown, then in white, and finally in silver paper. We watched this undoing with the tenderest interest and much speculation. One by one Good removed the dull husks that hid their splendours, carefully folding and replacing each piece of paper as he did so; and there at last lay, in all the majesty of its golden epaulettes, lace, and buttons, a Commander of the Royal Navy's full-dress uniform – dress sword, cocked hat, shiny patent leather boots and all. We literally gasped.

'*What!*' we said, '*what!* Are you going to put those things on?'

'Certainly,' he answered composedly; 'you see so much depends upon a first impression, especially,' he added, 'as I observe that there are ladies about. One at least of us ought to be decently dressed.'

We said no more; we were simply dumbfounded, especially when we considered the artful way in which Good had concealed the contents of that box for all these months. Only one suggestion did we make – namely, that he should wear his mail shirt next his skin. He replied that he feared it would spoil the set of his coat, now carefully spread in the sun to take the creases out, but finally consented to this precautionary measure. The most amusing part of the affair, however, was to see old Umslopogaas's astonishment and Alphonse's delight at Good's transformation. When at last he stood up in all his glory, even down to the medals on his breast, and contemplated himself in the still waters of the lake, after the fashion of the young gentleman in ancient history, whose name I cannot remember, but who fell in love with his own shadow, the old Zulu could no longer restrain his feelings.

'Oh, Bougwan!' he said. 'Oh, Bougwan! I always thought thee an ugly little man, and fat – fat as the cows at calving time; and now thou art like a blue jay when he spreads his tail out. Surely, Bougwan, it hurts my eyes to look at thee.'

Good did not much like this allusion to his fat, which, to tell the truth, was not very well deserved, for hard exercise had brought him down three inches; but on the whole he was pleased at Umslopogaas's admiration. As for Alphonse, he was quite delighted.

'Ah! but Monsieur has the beautiful air – the air of the warrior. It is the ladies who will say so when we come to get ashore. Monsieur is complete; he puts me in mind of my heroic grand – '

Here we stopped Alphonse.

As we gazed upon the beauties thus revealed by Good, a spirit of emulation filled our breasts, and we set to work to get ourselves up as well as we could. The most, however, that we were able to do was to array ourselves in our spare suits of shooting clothes, of which we each had several, all the fine clothes in the world could never make it otherwise than scrubby and insignificant; but Sir Henry looked what he is, a magnificent man in his nearly new tweed suit, gaiters, and boots. Alphonse also got himself up to kill, giving an extra turn to his enormous moustaches. Even old Umslopogaas, who was not in a general way given to the vain adorning of his body, took some oil out of the lantern and a bit of tow, and polished up his head-ring with it till it shone like Good's patent leather boots. Then he put on the mail shirt Sir Henry had given him and his 'moocha', and, having cleaned up Inkosi-kaas a little, stood forth complete.

All this while, having hoisted the sail again as soon as we had finished bathing, we had been progressing steadily for the land, or, rather, for the mouth of a great river. Presently – in all about an hour and a half after the little boat had left us – we saw emerging from the river or harbour a large number of boats, ranging up to ten or twelve tons burden. One of these was propelled by twenty-four oars, and most of the rest sailed. Looking through the glass we soon made out that the row-boat was an official vessel, her crew being all dressed in a sort of uniform, whilst on the half-deck forward stood an old man of venerable appearance, and with a flowing white beard, and a sword strapped to his side, who was evidently the commander of the craft. The other boats were apparently occupied by people brought out by curiosity, and were rowing or sailing towards us as quickly as they could.

'Now for it,' said I. 'What is the betting? Are they going to be friendly or to put an end to us?'

Nobody could answer this question, and, not liking the warlike appearance of the old gentleman and his sword, we felt a little anxious.

Just then Good spied a school of hippopotami on the water about two hundred yards off us, and suggested that it would not be a bad plan to impress the natives with a sense of our power by shooting some of them if possible. This, unluckily enough, struck us as a good idea, and accordingly we at once got out our eight-bore rifles, for which we still had a few cartridges left, and prepared for action. There were four of the animals, a big bull, a cow, and two young ones, one three parts grown. We got up to them without difficulty, the great animals contenting themselves with sinking down into the water and rising again a few yards farther on; indeed, their excessive tameness struck me as being peculiar. When the advancing boats were about five hundred yards away, Sir Henry opened the ball by firing at the three parts grown young one. The heavy bullet struck it fair between the eyes, and, crashing through the skull, killed it, and it sank, leaving a long train of blood behind it. At the same moment I fired at the cow, and Good at the old bull. My shot took effect, but not fatally, and down went the hippopotamus with a prodigious splashing, only to rise again presently blowing and grunting furiously, dyeing all the water round her crimson, when I killed her with the left barrel. Good, who is an execrable shot, missed the head of the bull altogether, the bullet merely cutting the side of his face as it passed. On glancing up, after I had fired my second shot, I perceived that the people we had fallen among were evidently ignorant of the nature of firearms, for the consternation caused by our shots and their effect upon the animals was prodigious. Some of the parties in the boats began to cry out in fear; others turned and made off as hard as they could; and even the old gentleman with the sword looked greatly puzzled and alarmed, and halted his big row-boat. We had, however, but little time for observation, for just then the old bull, rendered furious by the wound he had received, rose fair within forty yards of us, glaring savagely. We all fired, and hit him in various places, and down he went, badly wounded. Curiosity now began to overcome the fear of the onlookers, and some of them sailed on up close to us, amongst these being the man and woman whom we had first seen a couple of hours or so before, who drew up almost alongside. Just then the great brute rose again within ten yards of their base, and instantly with a roar of fury made at it open-mouthed. The woman shrieked, and the man tried to give the boat way, but without success. In another second I saw the huge red jaws and gleaming ivories close with a crunch on the frail craft, taking an enormous mouthful out of its side and capsizing it. Down went the boat, leaving its occupants struggling in the water. Next moment, before we could do anything towards saving them, the huge and furious creature was up again and making open-mouthed at the poor girl, who was struggling in the water. Lifting my rifle just as the grinding jaws were about to close on her, I fired over her head right down the hippopotamus's throat. Over he went, and commenced turning round and round, snorting, and blowing red streams of blood through his nostrils. Before he could recover himself, however, I let him have the other barrel in the side of the throat, and that finished him. He never moved or struggled again, but instantly sank. Our next effort was directed towards saving the girl, the man having swum off towards another boat; and in this we were fortunately successful, pulling her into the canoe (amidst the shouts of the spectators) considerably exhausted and frightened, but otherwise unhurt.

Meanwhile the boats had gathered together at a distance, and we could see that the occupants, who were evidently much frightened, were consulting what to do. Without giving them time for further consideration, which we thought might result unfavourably to ourselves, we instantly took our paddles and advanced towards them, Good standing in the bow and taking off his cocked hat politely in every direction, his amiable features suffused by a bland but intelligent smile. Most of the craft retreated as we advanced, but a few held their ground, while the big row-boat came on to meet us. Presently we were alongside, and I could see that our appearance – and especially Good's and Umslopogaas's – filled the venerable-looking commander with astonishment, not unmixed with awe. He was dressed after the same fashion as the man we first met, except that his shirt was not made of brown cloth, but of pure white linen hemmed with purple. The kilt, however, was identical, and so were the thick rings of gold around the arm and beneath the left knee. The rowers wore only a kilt, their bodies being naked to the waist.

Good took off his hat to the old gentleman with an extra flourish, and enquired after his health in the purest English, to which he replied by laying the first two fingers of his right hand horizontally across his lips and holding them there for a moment, which we took as his method of salutation. Then he also addressed some remarks to us in the same soft accents that had distinguished our first interviewer, which we were forced to indicate we did not understand by shaking our heads and shrugging our shoulders. This last Alphonse, being to the manner born, did to perfection, and in so polite a way that nobody could take any offence. Then we came a standstill, till I, being exceedingly hungry, thought I might as well call attention to the fact, and did so first by opening my mouth and pointing down it, and then rubbing my stomach. These signals the old gentleman clearly understood, for he nodded his head vigorously, and pointed towards the harbour; and at the same time one of the men on his boat threw us a line and motioned to us to make it fast, which we did. The row-boat then took us in tow, and went with great rapidity towards the mouth of the river, accompanied by all the other boats. In about twenty minutes more we reached the entrance to the harbour, which was crowded with boats full of people who had come out to see us. We observed that all the occupants were more or less of the same type, though some were fairer than others. Indeed, we noticed certain ladies whose skin was of a most dazzling whiteness; and the darkest shade of colour which we saw was about that of a rather swarthy Spaniard. Presently the wide river gave a sweep, and when it did so an exclamation of astonishment and delight burst from our lips as we caught our first view of the place that we afterwards knew as Milosis, or the Frowning City (from mi, which means city, and losis, a frown).

At a distance of some five hundred yards from the river's bank rose a sheer precipice of granite, two hundred feet or so in height, which had no doubt once formed the bank itself – the intermediate space of land now utilised as docks and roadways having been gained by draining, and deepening and embanking the stream.

On the brow of this precipice stood a great building of the same granite that formed the cliff, built on three sides of a square, the fourth side being open, save for a kind of battlement pierced at its base by a little door. This imposing place we afterwards discovered was the palace of the queen, or rather of the queens. At the back of the palace the town sloped gently upwards to a flashing building of white marble, crowned by the golden dome which we had already observed. The city was, with the exception of this one building, entirely built of red granite, and laid out in regular blocks with splendid roadways between. So far as we could see also the houses were all one-storeyed and detached, with gardens round them, which gave some relief to the eye wearied with the vista of red granite. At the back of the palace a road of extraordinary width stretched away up the hill for a distance of a mile and a half or so, and appeared to terminate at an open space surrounding the gleaming building that crowned the hill. But right in front of us was the wonder and glory of Milosis – the great staircase of the palace, the magnificence of which took our breath away. Let the reader imagine, if he can, a splendid stairway, sixty-five feet from balustrade to balustrade, consisting of two vast flights, each of one hundred and twenty-five steps of eight inches in height by three feet broad, connected by a flat resting-place sixty feet in length, and running from the palace wall on the edge of the precipice down to meet a waterway or canal cut to its foot from the river. This marvellous staircase was supported upon a single enormous granite arch, of which the resting-place between the two flights formed the crown; that is, the connecting open space lay upon it. From this archway sprang a subsidiary flying arch, or rather something that resembled a flying arch in shape, such as none of us had seen in any other country, and of which the beauty and wonder surpassed all that we had ever imagined. Three hundred feet from point to point, and no less than five hundred and fifty round the curve, that half-arc soared touching the bridge it supported for a space of fifty feet only, one end resting on and built into the parent archway, and the other embedded in the solid granite of the side of the precipice.

This staircase with its supports was, indeed, a work of which any living man might have been proud, both on account of its magnitude and its surpassing beauty. Four times, as we afterwards learnt, did the work, which was commenced in remote antiquity, fail, and was then abandoned for three centuries when half-finished, till at last there rose a youthful engineer named Rademas, who said that he would complete it successfully, and staked his life upon it. If he failed he was to be hurled from the precipice he had undertaken to scale; if he succeeded, he was to be rewarded by the hand of the king's daughter. Five years was given to him to complete the work, and an unlimited supply of labour and material. Three times did his arch fall, till at last, seeing failure to be inevitable, he determined to commit suicide on the morrow of the third collapse. That night, however, a beautiful woman came to him in a dream and touched his forehead, and of a sudden he saw a vision of the completed work, and saw too through the masonry and how the difficulties connected with the flying arch that had hitherto baffled his genius were to be overcome. Then he awoke and once more commenced the work, but on a different plan, and behold! he achieved it, and on the last day of the five years he led the princess his bride up the stair and into the palace. And in due course he became king by right of his wife, and founded the present Zu-Vendi dynasty, which is to this day called the 'House of the Stairway', thus proving once more how energy and talent are the natural stepping-stones to grandeur. And to commemorate his triumph he fashioned a statue of himself dreaming, and of the fair woman who touched him on the forehead, and placed it in the great hall of the palace, and there it stands to this day.

Such was the great stair of Milosis, and such the city beyond. No wonder they named it the 'Frowning City', for certainly those mighty works in solid granite did seem to frown down upon our littleness in their sombre splendour. This was so even in the sunshine, but when the storm-clouds gathered on her imperial brow Milosis looked more like a supernatural dwelling-place, or some imagining of a poet's brain, than what she is – a mortal city, carved by the patient genius of generations out of the red silence of the mountainside.

CHAPTER 12

The Sister Queens

The big rowing-boat glided on up the cutting that ran almost to the foot of the vast stairway, and then halted at a flight of steps leading to the landing-place. Here the old gentleman disembarked, and invited us to do so likewise, which, having no alternative, and being nearly starved, we did without hesitation – taking our rifles with us, however. As each of us landed, our guide again laid his fingers on his lips and bowed deeply, at the same time ordering back the crowds which had assembled to gaze on us. The last to leave the canoe was the girl we had picked out of the water, for whom her companion was waiting. Before she went away she kissed my hand, I suppose as a token of gratitude for having saved her from the fury of the hippopotamus; and it seemed to me that she had by this time quite got over any fear she might have had of us, and was by no means anxious to return in such a hurry to her lawful owners. At any rate, she was going to kiss Good's hand as well as mine, when the young man interfered and led her off. As soon as we were on shore, a number of the men who had rowed the big boat took possession of our few goods and chattels, and started with them up the splendid staircase, our guide indicating to us by means of motions that the things were perfectly safe. This done, he turned to the right and led the way to a small house, which was, as I afterwards discovered, an inn. Entering into a good-sized room, we saw that a wooden table was already furnished with food, presumably in preparation for us. Here our guide motioned us to be seated on a bench that ran the length of the table. We did not require a second invitation, but at once fell to ravenously on the viands before us, which were served on wooden platters, and consisted of cold goat's-flesh, wrapped up in some kind of leaf that gave it a delicious flavour, green vegetables resembling lettuces, brown bread, and red wine poured from a skin into horn mugs. This wine was peculiarly soft and good, having something of the flavour of Burgundy. Twenty minutes after we sat down at that hospitable board we rose from it, feeling like new men. After all that we had gone through we needed two things, food and rest, and the food of itself was a great blessing to us. Two girls of the same charming cast of face as the first whom we had seen waited on us while we ate, and very nicely they did it. They were also dressed in the same fashion namely, in a white linen petticoat coming to the knee, and with the toga-like garment of brown cloth, leaving bare the right arm and breast. I afterwards found out that this was the national dress, and regulated by an iron custom, though of course subject to variations. Thus, if the petticoat was pure white, it signified that the wearer was unmarried; if white, with a straight purple stripe round the edge, that she was married and a first or legal wife; if with a black stripe, that she was a widow. In the same way the toga, or 'kaf', as they call it, was of different shades of colour, from pure white to the deepest brown, according to the rank of the wearer, and embroidered at the end in various ways. This also applies to the 'shirts' or tunics worn by the men, which varied in material and colour; but the kilts were always the same except as regards quality. One thing, however, every man and woman in the country wore as the national insignia, and that was the thick band of gold round the right arm above the elbow, and the left leg beneath the knee. People of high rank also wore a torque of gold round the neck, and I observed that our guide had one on.

So soon as we had finished our meal our venerable conductor, who had been standing all the while, regarding us with enquiring eyes, and our guns with something as like fear as his pride would allow him to show, bowed towards Good, whom he evidently took for the leader of the party on account of the splendour of his apparel, and once more led the way through the door and to the foot of the great staircase. Here we paused for a moment to admire two colossal lions, each hewn from a single block of pure black marble, and standing rampant on the terminations of the wide balustrades of the staircase. These lions are magnificently executed, and it is said were sculptured by Rademas, the great prince who designed the staircase, and who was without doubt, to judge from the many beautiful examples of his art that we saw afterwards, one of the finest sculptors who ever lived, either in this or any other country. Then we climbed almost with a feeling of awe up that splendid stair, a work executed for all time and that will, I do not doubt, be admired thousands of years hence by generations unborn unless an earthquake should throw it down. Even Umslopogaas, who as a general rule made it a point of honour not to show astonishment, which he considered undignified, was fairly startled out of himself, and asked if the 'bridge had been built by men or devils', which was his vague way of alluding to any supernatural power. But Alphonse did not care about it. Its solid grandeur jarred upon the frivolous little Frenchman, who said that it was all 'très magnifique, mais triste – ah, triste!' and went on to suggest that it would be improved if the balustrades were *gilt*.

On we went up the first flight of one hundred and twenty steps, across the broad platform joining it to the second flight, where we paused to admire the glorious view of one of the most beautiful stretches of country that the world can show, edged by the blue waters of the lake. Then we passed on up the stair till at last we reached the top, where we found a large standing space to which there were three entrances, all of small size. Two of these opened on to rather narrow galleries or roadways cut in the face of the precipice that ran round the palace walls and led to the principal thoroughfares of the city, and were used by the inhabitants passing up and down from the docks. These were defended by gates of bronze, and also, as we afterwards learnt, it was possible to let down a portion of the roadways themselves by withdrawing certain bolts, and thus render it quite impracticable for an enemy to pass. The third entrance consisted of a flight of ten curved black marble steps leading to a doorway cut in the palace wall. This wall was in itself a work of art, being built of huge blocks of granite to the height of forty feet, and so fashioned that its face was concave, whereby it was rendered practically impossible for it to be scaled. To this doorway our guide led us. The door, which was massive, and made of wood protected by an outer gate of bronze, was closed; but on our approach it was thrown wide, and we were met by the challenge of a sentry, who was armed with a heavy triangular-bladed spear, not unlike a bayonet in shape, and a cutting sword, and protected by breast and back plates of skilfully prepared hippopotamus hide, and a small round shield fashioned of the same tough material. The sword instantly attracted our attention; it was practically identical with the one in the possession of Mr Mackenzie which he had obtained from the ill-starred wanderer. There was no mistaking the gold-lined fretwork cut in the thickness of the blade. So the man had told the truth after all. Our guide instantly gave a password, which the soldier acknowledged by letting the iron shaft of his spear fall with a ringing sound upon the pavement, and we passed on through the massive wall into the courtyard of the palace. This was about forty yards square, and laid out in flower-beds full of lovely shrubs and plants, many of which were quite new to me. Through the centre of this garden ran a broad walk formed of powdered shells brought from the lake in the place of gravel. Following this we came to another doorway with a round heavy arch, which is hung with thick curtains, for there are no doors in the palace itself. Then came another short passage, and we were in the great hall of the palace, and once more stood astonished at the simple and yet overpowering grandeur of the place.

The hall is, as we afterwards learnt, one hundred and fifty feet long by eighty wide, and has a magnificent arched roof of carved wood. Down the entire length of the building there are on either side, and at a distance of twenty feet from the wall, slender shafts of black marble springing sheer to the roof, beautifully fluted, and with carved capitals. At one end of this great place which these pillars support is the group of which I have already spoken as executed by the King Rademas to commemorate his building of the staircase; and really, when we had time to admire it, its loveliness almost struck us dumb. The group, of which the figures are in white, and the rest is black marble, is about half as large again as life, and represents a young man of noble countenance and form sleeping heavily upon a couch. One arm is carelessly thrown over the side of this couch, and his head reposes upon the other, its curling locks partially hiding it. Bending over him, her hand resting on his forehead, is a draped female form of such white loveliness as to make the beholder's breath stand still. And as for the calm glory that shines upon her perfect face – well, I can never hope to describe it. But there it rests like the shadow of an angel's smile; and power, love, and divinity all have their part in it. Her eyes are fixed upon the sleeping youth, and perhaps the most extraordinary thing about this beautiful work is the success with which the artist has succeeded in depicting on the sleeper's worn and weary face the sudden rising of a new and spiritual thought as the spell begins to work within his mind. You can see that an inspiration is breaking in upon the darkness of the man's soul as the dawn breaks in upon the darkness of night. It is a glorious piece of statuary, and none but a genius could have conceived it. Between each of the black marble columns is some such group of figures, some allegorical, and some representing the persons and wives of deceased monarchs or great men; but none of them, in our opinion, comes up the one I have described, although several are from the hand of the sculptor and engineer, King Rademas.

In the exact centre of the hall was a solid mass of black marble about the size of a baby's armchair, which it rather resembled in appearance. This, as we afterwards learnt, was the sacred stone of this remarkable people, and on it their monarchs laid their hand after the ceremony of coronation, and swore by the sun to safeguard the interests of the empire, and to maintain its customs, traditions, and laws. This stone was evidently exceedingly ancient (as indeed all stones are), and was scored down its sides with long marks or lines, which Sir Henry said proved it to have been a fragment that at some remote period in its history had been ground in the iron jaws of glaciers. There was a curious prophecy about this block of marble, which was reported among the people to have fallen from the sun, to the effect that when it was shattered into fragments a king of alien race should rule over the land. As the stone, however, looked remarkably solid, the native princes seemed to have a fair chance of keeping their own for many a long year.

At the end of the hall is a dais spread with rich carpets, on which two thrones are set side by side. These thrones are shaped like great chairs, and made of solid gold. The seats are richly cushioned, but the backs are left bare, and on each is carved the emblem of the sun, shooting out his fiery rays in all directions. The footstools are golden lions couchant, with yellow topazes set in them for eyes. There are no other gems about them.

The place is lighted by numerous but narrow windows, placed high up, cut on the principle of the loopholes to be seen in ancient castles, but innocent of glass, which was evidently unknown here.

Such is a brief description of this splendid hall in which we now found ourselves, compiled of course from our subsequent knowledge of it. On this occasion we had but little time for observation, for when we entered we perceived that a large number of men were gathered together in front of the two thrones, which were unoccupied. The principal among them were seated on carved wooden chairs ranged to the right and the left of the thrones, but not in front of them, and were dressed in white tunics, with various embroideries and different coloured edgings, and armed with the usual pierced and gold-inlaid swords. To judge from the dignity of their appearance, they seemed one and all to be individuals of very great importance. Behind each of these great men stood a small knot of followers and attendants.

Seated by themselves, in a little group to the left of the throne, were six men of a different stamp. Instead of wearing the ordinary kilt, they were clothed in long robes of pure white linen, with the same symbol of the sun that is to be seen on the back of the chairs, emblazoned in gold thread upon the breast. This garment was girt up at the waist with a simple golden curb-like chain, from which hung long elliptic plates of the same metal, fashioned in shiny scales like those of a fish, that, as their wearers moved, jingled and reflected the light. They were all men of mature age and of a severe and impressive cast of features, which was rendered still more imposing by the long beards they wore.

The personality of one individual among them, however, impressed us at once. He seemed to stand out among his fellows and refuse to be overlooked. He was very old – eighty at least – and extremely tall, with a long snow-white beard that hung nearly to his waist. His features were aquiline and deeply cut, and his eyes were grey and cold-looking. The heads of the others were bare, but this man wore a round cap entirely covered with gold embroidery, from which we judged that he was a person of great importance; and indeed we afterwards discovered that he was Agon, the High Priest of the country. As we approached, all these men, including the priests, rose and bowed to us with the greatest courtesy, at the same time placing the two fingers across the lips in salutation. Then soft-footed attendants advanced from be-tween the pillars, bearing seats, which were placed in a line in front of the thrones. We three sat down, Alphonse and Umslo-pogaas standing behind us. Scarcely had we done so when there came a blare of trumpets from some passage to the right, and a similar blare from the left. Next a man with a long white wand of ivory appeared just in front of the right-hand throne, and cried out something in a loud voice, ending with the word *Nyleptha*, repeated three times; and another man, similarly attired, called out a similar sentence before the other throne, but ending with the word *Sorais*, also repeated thrice. Then came the tramp of armed men from each side entrance, and in filed about a score of picked and magnificently accoutred guards, who formed up on each side of the thrones, and let their heavy iron-handled spears fall simultaneously with a clash upon the black marble flooring. Another double blare of trumpets, and in from either side, each attended by six maidens, swept the two Queens of Zu-Vendis, everybody in the hall rising to greet them as they came.

I have seen beautiful women in my day, and am no longer thrown into transports at the sight of a pretty face; but language fails me when I try to give some idea of the blaze of loveliness that then broke upon us in the persons of these sister Queens. Both were young – perhaps five-and-twenty years of age – both were tall and exquisitely formed; but there the likeness stopped. One, Nyleptha, was a woman of dazzling fairness; her right arm and breast bare, after the custom of her people, showed like snow even against her white and gold-embroidered 'kaf', or toga. And as for her sweet face, all I can say is, that it was one that few men could look on and forget. Her hair, a veritable crown of gold, clustered in short ringlets over her shapely head, half hiding the ivory brow, beneath which eyes of deep and glorious grey flashed out in tender majesty. I cannot attempt to describe her other features, only the mouth was most sweet, and curved like Cupid's bow, and over the whole countenance there shone an indescribable look of loving-kindness, lit up by a shadow of delicate humour that lay upon her face like a touch of silver on a rosy cloud.

She wore no jewels, but on her neck, arm, and knee were the usual torques of gold, in this instance fashioned like a snake; and her dress was of pure white linen of excessive fineness, plentifully embroidered with gold and with the familiar symbols of the sun.

Her twin sister, Sorais, was of a different and darker type of beauty. Her hair was wavy like Nyleptha's but coal-black, and fell in masses on her shoulders; her complexion was olive, her eyes large, dark, and lustrous; the lips were full, and I thought rather cruel. Somehow her face, quiet and even cold as it is, gave an idea of passion in repose, and caused one to wonder involuntarily what its aspect would be if anything occurred to break the calm. It reminded me of the deep sea, that even on the bluest days never loses its visible stamp of power, and in its murmuring sleep is yet instinct with the spirit of the storm. Her figure, like her sister's, was almost perfect in its curves and outlines, but a trifle more rounded, and her dress was absolutely the same.

As this lovely pair swept onwards to their respective thrones, amid the deep attentive silence of the Court, I was bound to confess to myself that they did indeed fulfil my idea of royalty. Royal they were in every way – in form, in grace, and queenly dignity, and in the barbaric splendour of their attendant pomp. But methought that they needed no guards or gold to proclaim their power and bind the loyalty of wayward men. A glance from those bright eyes or a smile from those sweet lips, and while the red blood runs in the veins of youth women such as these will never lack subjects ready to do their biddings to the death.

But after all they were women first and queens afterwards, and therefore not devoid of curiosity. As they passed to their seats I saw both of them glance swiftly in our direction. I saw, too, that their eyes passed by me, seeing nothing to charm them in the person of an insignificant and grizzled old man. Then they looked with evident astonishment on the grim form of old Umslopogaas, who raised his axe in salutation. Attracted next by the splendour of Good's apparel, for a second their glance rested on him like a humming moth upon a flower, then off it darted to where Sir Henry Curtis stood, the sunlight from a window playing upon his yellow hair and peaked beard, and marking the outlines of his massive frame against the twilight of the somewhat gloomy hall. He raised his eyes, and they met the fair Nyleptha's full, and thus for the first time the goodliest man and woman that it has ever been my lot to see looked one upon another. And why it was I know not, but I saw the swift blood run up Nyleptha's skin as the pink lights run up the morning sky. Red grew her fair bosom and shapely arm, red the swanlike neck; the rounded cheeks blushed red as the petals of a rose, and then the crimson flood sank back to whence it came and left her pale and trembling.

I glanced at Sir Henry. He, too, had coloured up to the eyes.

'Oh, my word!' thought I to myself, 'the ladies have come on the stage, and now we may look to the plot to develop itself.' And I sighed and shook my head, knowing that the beauty of a woman is like the beauty of the lightning – a destructive thing and a cause of desolation. By the time that I had finished my reflections both the Queens were on the thrones, for all this had happened in about six seconds. Once more the unseen trumpets blared out, and then the Court seated itself, and Queen Sorais motioned to us to do likewise.

Next from among the crowd whither he had withdrawn stepped forward our guide, the old gentleman who had towed us ashore, holding by the hand the girl whom we had seen first and afterwards rescued from the hippopotamus. Having made obeisance he proceeded to address the Queens, evidently describing to them the way and place where we had been found. It was most amusing to watch the astonishment, not unmixed with fear, reflected upon their faces as they listened to his tale. Clearly they could not understand how we had reached the lake and been found floating on it, and were inclined to attribute our presence to supernatural causes. Then the narrative proceeded, as I judged from the frequent appeals that our guide made to the girl, to the point where we had shot the hippopotami, and we at once perceived that there was something very wrong about those hippopotami, for the history was frequently interrupted by indignant exclamations from the little group of white-robed priests and even from the courtiers, while the two Queens listened with an amazed expression, especially when our guide pointed to the rifles in our hands as being the means of destruction. And here, to make matters clear, I may as well explain at once that the inhabitants of Zu-Vendis are sun-worshippers, and that for some reason or another the hippopotamus is sacred among them. Not that they do not kill it, because at a certain season of the year they slaughter thousands – which are specially preserved in large lakes up the country – and use their hides for armour for soldiers; but this does not prevent them from considering these animals as sacred to the sun.* Now, as ill luck would have it, the particular hippopotami we had shot were a family of tame animals that were kept in the mouth of the port and daily fed by priests whose special duty it was to attend to them. When we shot them I thought that the brutes were suspiciously tame, and this was, as we afterwards ascertained, the cause of it. Thus it came about that in attempting to show off we had committed sacrilege of a most aggravated nature.

When our guide had finished his tale, the old man with the long beard and round cap, whose appearance I have already described, and who was, as I have said, the High Priest of the country, and known by the name of Agon, rose and commenced an impassioned harangue. I did not like the look of his cold grey eye as he fixed it on us. I should have liked it still less had I known that in the name of the outraged majesty of his god he was demanding that the whole lot of us should be offered up as a sacrifice by means of being burnt alive.

After he had finished speaking the Queen Sorais addressed him in a soft and musical voice, and appeared, to judge from his gestures of dissent, to be putting the other side of the question before him. Then Nyleptha spoke in liquid accents. Little did we

---

* Mr Quatermain does not seem to have been aware that it is common for animal-worshipping people to annually sacrifice the beasts they adore. See Herodotus, ii, 42. ED.

know that she was pleading for our lives. Finally, she turned and addressed a tall, soldier-like man of middle age with a black beard and a long plain sword, whose name, as we afterwards learnt, was Nasta, and who was the greatest lord in the country; apparently appealing to him for support. Now when Sir Henry had caught her eye and she had blushed so rosy red, I had seen that the incident had not escaped this man's notice, and, what is more, that it was eminently disagreeable to him, for he bit his lip and his hand tightened on his sword-hilt. Afterwards we learnt that he was an aspirant for the hand of this Queen in marriage, which accounted for it. This being so, Nyleptha could not have appealed to a worse person, for, speaking in slow, heavy tones, he appeared to confirm all that the High Priest Agon had said. As he spoke, Sorais put her elbow on her knee, and, resting her chin on her hand, looked at him with a suppressed smile upon her lips, as though she saw through the man, and was determined to be his match; but Nyleptha grew very angry, her cheek flushed, her eyes flashed, and she did indeed look lovely. Finally she turned to Agon and seemed to give some sort of qualified assent, for he bowed at her words; and as she spoke she moved her hands as though to emphasise what she said; while all the time Sorais kept her chin on her hand and smiled. Then suddenly Nyleptha made a sign, the trumpets blew again, and everybody rose to leave the hall save ourselves and the guards, whom she motioned to stay.

When they were all gone she bent forward and, smiling sweetly, partially by signs and partially by exclamations made it clear to us that she was very anxious to know where we came from. The difficulty was how to explain, but at last an idea struck me. I had my large pocket-book in my pocket and a pencil. Taking it out, I made a little sketch of a lake, and then as best I could I drew the underground river and the lake at the other end. When I had done this I advanced to the steps of the throne and gave it to her. She understood it at once and clapped her hands with delight, and then descending from the throne took it to her sister Sorais, who also evidently understood. Next she took the pencil from me, and after examining it with curiosity proceeded to make a series of delightful little sketches, the first representing herself holding out both hands in welcome, and a man uncommonly like Sir Henry taking them. Next she drew a lovely little picture of a hippopotamus rolling about dying in the water, and of an individual, in whom we had no difficulty in recognising Agon the High Priest, holding up his hands in horror on the bank. Then followed a most alarming picture of a dreadful fiery furnace and of the same figure, Agon, poking us into it with a forked stick. This picture perfectly horrified me, but I was a little reassured when she nodded sweetly and proceeded to make a fourth drawing – a man again uncommonly like Sir Henry, and of two women, in whom I recognised Sorais and herself, each with one arm around him, and holding a sword in protection over him. To all of these Sorais, who I saw was employed in carefully taking us all in – especially Curtis – signified her approval by nodding.

At last Nyleptha drew a final sketch of a rising sun, indicating that she must go, and that we should meet on the following morning; whereat Sir Henry looked so disappointed that she saw it, and, I suppose by way of consolation, extended her hand to him to kiss, which he did with pious fervour. At the same time Sorais, off whom Good had never taken his eyeglass during the whole indaba [interview], rewarded him by giving him her hand to kiss, though, while she did so, her eyes were fixed upon Sir Henry. I am glad to say that I was not implicated in these proceedings; neither of them gave *me* her hand to kiss.

Then Nyleptha turned and addressed the man who appeared to be in command of the bodyguard, apparently from her manner and his frequent obeisances, giving him very stringent and careful orders; after which, with a somewhat coquettish nod and smile, she left the hall, followed by Sorais and most of the guards.

When the Queens had gone, the officer whom Nyleptha had addressed came forward and with many tokens of deep respect led us from the hall through various passages to a sumptuous set of apartments opening out of a large central room lighted with brazen swinging lamps (for it was now dusk) and richly carpeted and strewn with couches. On a table in the centre of the room was set a profusion of food and fruit, and, what is more, flowers. There was a delicious wine also in ancient-looking sealed earthenware flagons, and beautifully chased golden and ivory cups to drink it from. Servants, male and female, also were there to minister to us, and whilst we ate, from some recess outside the apartment

> 'The silver lute did speak between
> The trumpet's lordly blowing;'

and altogether we found ourselves in a sort of earthly paradise which was only disturbed by the vision of that disgusting High Priest who intended to commit us to the flames. But so very weary were we with our labours that we could scarcely keep ourselves awake through the sumptuous meal, and as soon as it was over we indicated that we desired to sleep. As a further precaution against surprise we left Umslopogaas with his axe to sleep in the main chamber near the curtained doorways leading to the apartments which we occupied respectively, Good and I in the one, and Sir Henry and Alphonse in the other. Then throwing off our clothes, with the exception of the mail shirts, which we considered it safer to keep on, we flung ourselves down upon the low and luxurious couches, and drew the silk-embroidered coverlids over us.

In two minutes I was just dropping off when I was aroused by Good's voice.

'I say, Quatermain,' he said, 'did you ever see such eyes?'

'Eyes!' I said, crossly; 'what eyes?'

'Why, the Queen's, of course! Sorais, I mean – at least I think that is her name.'

'Oh, I don't know,' I yawned; 'I didn't notice them much: I suppose they are good eyes,' and again I dropped off.

Five minutes or so elapsed, and I was once more awakened.

'I say, Quatermain,' said the voice.

'Well,' I answered testily, 'what is it now?'

'Did you notice her ankle? The shape – '

This was more than I could stand. By my bed stood the veldtschoons I had been wearing. Moved quite beyond myself, I took them up and threw them straight at Good's head – and hit it.

Afterwards I slept the sleep of the just, and a very heavy sleep it must be. As for Good, I don't know if he went to sleep or if he continued to pass Sorais' beauties in mental review, and, what is more, I don't care.

CHAPTER 13

About the Zu-Vendi People

And now the curtain is down for a few hours, and the actors in this novel drama are plunged in dewy sleep. Perhaps we should except Nyleptha, whom the reader may, if poetically inclined, imagine lying in her bed of state encompassed by her maidens, tiring women, guards, and all the other people and appurtenances that surround a throne, and yet not able to slumber for thinking of the strangers who had visited a country where no such strangers had ever come before, and wondering, as she lay awake, who they were and what their past has been, and if she was ugly compared to the women of their native place. I, however, not being poetically inclined, will take advantage of the lull to give some account of the people among whom we found ourselves, compiled, needless to state, from information which we subsequently collected.

The name of this country, to begin at the beginning, is Zu-Vendis, from Zu, 'yellow', and Vendis, 'place or country'. Why it is called the Yellow Country I have never been able to ascertain accurately, nor do the inhabitants themselves know. Three reasons are, however, given, each of which would suffice to account for it. The first is that the name owes its origin to the great quantity of gold that is found in the land. Indeed, in this respect Zu-Vendis is a veritable Eldorado, the precious metal being extraordinarily plentiful. At present it is collected from purely alluvial diggings, which we subsequently inspected, and which are situated within a day's journey from Milosis, being mostly found in pockets and in nuggets weighing from an ounce up to six or seven pounds in weight. But other diggings of a similar nature are known to exist, and I have besides seen great veins of gold-bearing quartz. In Zu-Vendis gold is a much commoner metal than silver, and thus it has curiously enough come to pass that silver is the legal tender of the country.

The second reason given is, that at certain times of the year the native grasses of the country, which are very sweet and good, turn as yellow as ripe corn; and the third arises from a tradition that the people were originally yellow skinned, but grew white after living for many generations upon these high lands. Zu-Vendis is a country about the size of France, is, roughly speaking, oval in shape; and on every side cut off from the surrounding territory by illimitable forests of impenetrable thorn, beyond which are said to be hundreds of miles of morasses, deserts, and great mountains. It is, in short, a huge, high tableland rising up in the centre of the dark continent, much as in southern Africa flat-topped mountains rise from the level of the surrounding veldt. Milosis itself lies, according to my aneroid, at a level of about nine thousand feet above the sea, but most of the land is even higher, the greatest elevation of the open country being, I believe, about eleven thousand feet. As a consequence the climate is, comparatively speaking, a cold one, being very similar to that of southern England, only brighter and not so rainy. The land is, however, exceedingly fertile, and grows all cereals and temperate fruits and timber to perfection; and in the lower-lying parts even produces a hardy variety of sugar-cane. Coal is found in great abundance, and in many places crops out from the surface; and so is pure marble, both black and white. The same may be said of almost every metal except silver, which is scarce, and only to be obtained from a range of mountains in the north.

Zu-Vendis comprises in her boundaries a great variety of scenery, including two ranges of snow-clad mountains, one on the western boundary beyond the impenetrable belt of thorn forest, and the other piercing the country from north to south, and passing at a distance of about eighty miles from Milosis, from which town its higher peaks are distinctly visible. This range forms the chief watershed of the land. There are also three large lakes – the biggest, namely that whereon we emerged, and which is named Milosis after the city, covering some two hundred square miles of country – and numerous small ones, some of them salt.

The population of this favoured land is, comparatively speaking, dense, numbering at a rough estimate from ten to twelve millions. It is almost purely agricultural in its habits, and divided into great classes as in civilised countries. There is a territorial nobility, a considerable middle class, formed principally of merchants, officers of the army, etc.; but the great bulk of the people are well-to-do peasants who live upon the lands of the lords, from whom they hold under a species of feudal tenure. The best bred people in the country are, as I think I have said, pure whites with a somewhat southern cast of countenance; but the common herd are much darker, though they do not show any Negro or other African characteristics. As to their descent I can give no certain information. Their written records, which extend back for about a thousand years, give no hint of it. One very ancient chronicler does indeed, in alluding to some old tradition that existed in his day, talk of it as having probably originally 'come down with the people from the coast', but that may mean little or nothing. In short, the origin of the Zu-Vendi is lost in the mists of time. Whence they came or of what race they are no man knows. Their architecture and some of their sculptures suggest an Egyptian or possibly an Assyrian origin; but it is well known that their present remarkable style of building has only sprung up within the last eight hundred years, and they certainly retain no traces of Egyptian theology or customs. Again, their appearance and some of their habits are rather Jewish; but here again it seems hardly conceivable that they should have utterly lost all traces of the Jewish religion. Still, for aught I know, they may be one of the lost ten tribes whom people are so fond of discovering all over the world, or they may not. I do not know, and so can only describe them as I find them, and leave wiser heads than mine to make what they can out of it, if indeed this account should ever be read at all, which is exceedingly doubtful.

And now after I have said all this, I am, after all, going to hazard a theory of my own, though it is only a very little one, as the young lady said in mitigation of her baby. This theory is founded on a legend which I have heard among the Arabs on the east coast, which is to the effect that 'more than two thousand years ago' there were troubles in the country which was known as Babylonia, and that thereon a vast horde of Persians came down to Bushire, where they took ship and were driven by the north-east monsoon to the east coast of Africa, where, according to the legend, 'the sun and fire worshippers' fell into conflict with the belt of Arab settlers who even then were settled on the east coast, and finally broke their way through them, and, vanishing into the interior, were no more seen. Now, I ask, is it not at least possible that the Zu-Vendi people are the descendants of these 'sun and fire worshippers' who broke through the Arabs and vanished? As a matter of fact, there is a good deal in their characters and customs that tallies with the somewhat vague ideas that I have of Persians. Of course we have no books of reference here, but Sir Henry says that if his memory does not fail him, there was a tremendous revolt in Babylon about 500 BC, whereon a vast multitude were expelled from the city. Anyhow, it is a well-established fact that there have been many separate emigrations of Persians from the Persian Gulf to the east coast of Africa up to as lately as seven hundred years ago. There are Persian tombs at Kilwa, on the east coast, still in good repair, which bear dates showing them to be just seven hundred years old.*

* There is another theory which might account for the origin of the Zu-Vendi which does not seem to have struck my friend Mr Quatermain and his companions, and that is, that they are descendants of the Phoenicians. The cradle of the Phoenician race is supposed to have been on the western shore of the Persian Gulf. Thence, as there is good evidence to show, they emigrated in two streams, one of which took possession of the shores of Palestine, while the other is supposed by savants to have immigrated down the coast of Eastern Africa where, near Mozambique, signs and remains of their occupation are not wanting. Indeed, it would have been very extraordinary if they did not, when leaving the Persian Gulf, make straight for the East Coast, seeing that the north-east monsoon blows for six months in the year dead in that direction, while for the other six months it blows back again. And, by the way of illustrating the probability, I may add that to this day a very extensive trade is carried on between the Persian Gulf and Lamu and other East African ports as far south as Madagascar, which is of course the ancient Ebony Isle of *The Arabian Nights*. ED.

In addition to being an agricultural people, the Zu-Vendi are, oddly enough, excessively warlike, and as they cannot from the exigencies of their position make war upon other nations, they fight among each other like the famed Kilkenny cats, with the happy result that the population never outgrows the power of the country to support it. This habit of theirs is largely fostered by the political condition of the country. The monarchy is nominally an absolute one, save in so far as it is tempered by the power of the priests and the informal council of the great lords; but, as in many other institutions, the king's writ does not run unquestioned throughout the length and breadth of the land. In short, the whole system is a purely feudal one (though absolute serfdom or slavery is unknown), all the great lords holding nominally from the throne, but a number of them being practically independent, having the power of life and death, waging war against and making peace with their neighbours as the whim or their interests lead them, and even on occasion rising in open rebellion against their royal master or mistress, and, safely shut up in their castles and fenced cities, far from the seat of government, successfully defying them for years.

Zu-Vendis has had its king-makers as well as England, a fact that will be well appreciated when I state that eight different dynasties have sat upon the throne in the last one thousand years, every one of which took its rise from some noble family that succeeded in grasping the purple after a sanguinary struggle. At the date of our arrival in the country things were a little better than they had been for some centuries, the last king, the father of Nyleptha and Sorais, having been an exceptionally able and vigorous ruler, and, as a consequence, he kept down the power of the priests and nobles. On his death, two years before we reached Zu-Vendis, the twin sisters, his children, were, following an ancient precedent, called to the throne, since an attempt to exclude either would instantly have provoked a sanguinary civil war; but it was generally felt in the country that this measure was a most unsatisfactory one, and could hardly be expected to be permanent. Indeed, as it was, the various intrigues that were set on foot by ambitious nobles to obtain the hand of one or other of the queens in marriage had disquieted the country, and the general opinion was that there would be bloodshed before long.

I will now pass on to the question of the Zu-Vendi religion, which is nothing more or less than sun-worship of a pronounced and highly developed character. Around this sun-worship is grouped the entire social system of the Zu-Vendi. It sends its roots through every institution and custom of the land. From the cradle to the grave the Zu-Vendi follows the sun in every sense of the saying. As an infant he is solemnly held up in its light and dedicated to 'the symbol of good, the expression of power, and the hope of Eternity', the ceremony answering to our baptism. Whilst still a tiny child, his parents point out the glorious orb as the presence of a visible and beneficent god, and he worships it at its up-rising and down-setting. Then when still quite small, he goes, holding fast to the pendent end of his mother's 'kaf' (toga), up to the temple of the Sun of the nearest city, and there, when at midday the bright beams strike down upon the golden central altar and beat back the fire that burns thereon, he hears the white-robed priests raise their solemn chant of praise and sees the people fall down to adore, and then, amidst the blowing of the golden trumpets, watches the sacrifice thrown into the fiery furnace beneath the altar. Here he comes again to be declared 'a man' by the priests, and consecrated to war and to good works; here before the solemn altar he leads his bride; and here too, if differences shall unhappily arise, he divorces her.

And so on, down life's long pathway till the last mile is travelled, and he comes again armed indeed, and with dignity, but no longer a man. Here they bear him dead and lay his bier upon the falling brazen doors before the eastern altar, and when the last ray from the setting sun falls upon his white face the bolts are drawn and he vanishes into the raging furnace beneath and is ended.

The priests of the Sun do not marry, but are recruited as young men specially devoted to the work by their parents and supported by the State. The nomination to the higher offices of the priesthood lies with the Crown, but once appointed the nominees cannot be dispossessed, and it is scarcely too much to say that they really rule the land. To begin with, they are a united body sworn to obedience and secrecy, so that an order issued by the High Priest at Milosis will be instantly and unhesitatingly acted upon by the resident priest of a little country town three or four hundred miles off. They are the judges of the land, criminal and civil, an appeal lying only to the lord paramount of the district, and from him to the king; and they have, of course, practically unlimited jurisdiction over religious and moral offences, together with a right of excommunication, which, as in the faiths of more highly civilised lands, is a very effective weapon. Indeed, their rights and powers are almost unlimited, but I may as well state here that the priests of the Sun are wise in their generation, and do not push things too far. It is but very seldom that they go to extremes against anybody, being more inclined to exercise the prerogative of mercy than run the risk of exasperating the powerful and vigorous-minded people on whose neck they have set their yoke, lest it should rise and break it off altogether.

Another source of the power of the priests is their practical monopoly of learning, and their very considerable astronomical knowledge, which enables them to keep a hold on the popular mind by predicting eclipses and even comets. In Zu-Vendis only a few of the upper classes can read and write, but nearly all the priests have this knowledge, and are therefore looked upon as learned men.

The law of the country is, on the whole, mild and just, but differs in several respects from our civilised law. For instance, the law of England is much more severe upon offences against property than against the person, as becomes a people whose ruling passion is money. A man may half kick his wife to death or inflict horrible sufferings upon his children at a much cheaper rate of punishment than he can compound for the theft of a pair of old boots. In Zu-Vendis this is not so, for there they rightly or wrongly look upon the person as of more consequence than goods and chattels, and not, as in England, as a sort of necessary appendage to the latter. For murder the punishment is death, for treason death, for defrauding the orphan and the widow, for sacrilege, and for attempting to quit the country (which is looked on as a sacrilege) death. In each case the method of execution is the same, and a rather awful one. The culprit is thrown alive into the fiery furnace beneath one of the altars to the Sun. For all other offences, including the offence of idleness, the punishment is forced labour upon the vast national buildings which are always going on in some part of the country, with or without periodical floggings, according to the crime.

The social system of the Zu-Vendi allows considerable liberty to the individual, provided he does not offend against the laws and customs of the country. They are polygamous in theory, though most of them have only one wife on account of the expense. By law a man is bound to provide a separate establishment for each wife. The first wife also is the legal wife, and her children are said to be 'of the house of the Father'. The children of the other wives are of the houses of their respective mothers. This does not, however, imply any slur upon either mother or children. Again, a first wife can, on entering into the married state, make a bargain that her husband shall marry no other wife. This, however, is very rarely done, as the women are the great upholders of polygamy, which not only provides for their surplus numbers but gives greater importance to the first wife, who is thus practically the head of several households. Marriage is looked upon as primarily a civil contract, and, subject to certain conditions and to a proper provision for children, is dissoluble at the will of both contracting parties, the divorce, or 'unloosing', being formally and ceremoniously accomplished by going through certain portions of the marriage ceremony backwards.

The Zu-Vendi are on the whole a very kindly, pleasant, and light-hearted people. They are not great traders and care little about money, only working to earn enough to support themselves in that class of life in which they were born. They are exceedingly conservative, and look with disfavour upon changes. Their legal tender is silver, cut into little squares of different weights; gold is the baser coin, and is about of the same value as our silver. It is, however, much prized for its beauty, and largely used for ornaments and decorative purposes. Most of the trade, however, is carried on by means of sale and barter, payment being made in kind. Agriculture is the great business of the country, and is really well understood and carried out, most of the available acreage being under cultivation. Great attention is also given to the breeding of cattle and horses, the latter being unsurpassed by any I have ever seen either in Europe or Africa.

The land belongs theoretically to the Crown, and under the Crown to the great lords, who again divide it among smaller lords, and so on down to the little peasant farmer who works his forty 'reestu' (acres) on a system of half-profits with his immediate lord. In fact the whole system is, as I have said, distinctly feudal, and it interested us much to meet with such an old friend far in the unknown heart of Africa.

The taxes are very heavy. The State takes a third of a man's total earnings, and the priesthood about five per cent on the remainder. But on the other hand, if a man through any cause falls into bona fide misfortune the State supports him in the position of life to which he belongs. If he is idle, however, he is sent to work on the Government undertakings, and the State looks after his wives and children. The State also makes all the roads and builds all town houses, about which great care is shown, letting them out to families at a small rent. It also keeps up a standing army of about twenty thousand men, and provides watchmen, etc. In return for their five per cent the priests attend to the service of the temples, carry out all religious ceremonies, and keep schools, where they teach whatever they think desirable, which is not very much. Some of the temples also possess private property, but priests as individuals cannot hold property.

And now comes a question which I find some difficulty in answering. Are the Zu-Vendi a civilised or barbarous people? Sometimes I think the one, sometimes the other. In some branches of art they have attained the very highest proficiency. Take for instance their buildings and their statuary. I do not think that the latter can be equalled either in beauty or imaginative power anywhere in the world, and as for the former it may have been rivalled in ancient Egypt, but I am sure that it has never been since. But, on the other hand, they are totally ignorant of many other arts. Till Sir Henry, who happened to know something about it, showed them how to do it by mixing silica and lime, they could not make a piece of glass, and their crockery is rather primitive. A water-clock is their nearest approach to a watch; indeed, ours delighted them exceedingly. They know nothing about steam, electricity, or gunpowder, and mercifully for themselves nothing about printing or the penny post. Thus they are spared many evils, for of a truth our age has learnt the wisdom of the old-world saying, 'He who increaseth knowledge, increaseth sorrow.'

As regards their religion, it is a natural one for imaginative people who know no better, and might therefore be expected to turn to the sun and worship him as the all-Father, but it cannot justly be called elevating or spiritual. It is true that they do sometimes speak of the sun as the 'garment of the Spirit', but it is a vague term, and what they really adore is the fiery orb himself. They also call him the 'hope of eternity', but here again the meaning is vague, and I doubt if the phrase conveys any very clear impression to their minds. Some of them do indeed believe in a future life for the good – I know Nyleptha does firmly – but it is a private faith arising from the promptings of the spirit, not an essential of their creed. So on the whole I cannot say that I consider this sun-worship as a religion indicative of a civilised people, however magnificent and imposing its ritual, or however moral and high-sounding the maxims of its priests, many of whom, I am sure, have their own opinions on the whole subject; though of course they have nothing but praise for a system which provides them with so many of the good things of this world.

There are now only two more matters to which I need allude – namely, the language and the system of calligraphy. As for the former, it is soft-sounding, and very rich and flexible. Sir Henry says that it sounds something like modern Greek, but of course it has no connection with it. It is easy to acquire, being simple in its construction, and a peculiar quality about it is its euphony, and the way in which the sound of the words adapts itself to the meaning to be expressed. Long before we mastered the language, we could frequently make out what was meant by the ring of the sentence. It is on this account that the language lends itself so well to poetical declamation, of which these remarkable people are very fond. The Zu-Vendi alphabet seems, Sir Henry says, to be derived, like every other known system of letters, from a Phoenician source, and therefore more remotely still from the ancient Egyptian hieratic writing. Whether this is a fact I cannot say, not being learned in such matters. All I know about it is that their alphabet consists of twenty-two characters, of which a few, notably B, E, and O, are not very unlike our own. The whole affair is, however, clumsy and puzzling.* But as the people of Zu-Vendi are not given to the writing of novels, or of anything except business documents and records of the briefest character, it answers their purpose well enough.

* There are twenty-two letters in the Phoenician alphabet (see Appendix, Maspero's *Histoire ancienne des peuples de l'Orient*, p. 746, etc.) Unfortunately Mr Quatermain gives us no specimen of the Zu-Vendi writing, but what he here states seems to go a long way towards substantiating the theory advanced in the note on p. 370.   ED.

CHAPTER 14

The Flower Temple

It was half-past eight by my watch when I woke on the morning following our arrival at Milosis, having slept almost exactly twelve hours, and I must say that I did indeed feel better. Ah, what a blessed thing is sleep! and what a difference twelve hours of it or so makes to us after days and nights of toil and danger. It is like going to bed one man and getting up another.

I sat up upon my silken couch – never had I slept upon such a bed before – and the first thing that I saw was Good's eyeglass fixed on me from the recesses of his silken couch. There was nothing else of him to be seen except his eyeglass, but I knew from the look of it that he was awake, and waiting till I woke up to begin.

'I say, Quatermain,' he commenced sure enough, 'did you observe her skin? It is as smooth as the back of an ivory hairbrush.'

'Now look here, Good,' I remonstrated, when there came a sound at the curtain, which, on being drawn, admitted a functionary, who signified by signs that he was there to lead us to the bath. We gladly consented, and were conducted to a delightful marble chamber, with a pool of running crystal water in the centre of it, into which we gaily plunged. When we had bathed, we returned to our apartment and dressed, and then went into the central room where we had supped on the previous evening, to find a morning meal already prepared for us, and a capital meal it was, though I should be puzzled to describe the dishes. After breakfast we lounged round and admired the tapestries and carpets and some pieces of statuary that were placed about, wondering the while what was going to happen next. Indeed, by this time our minds were in such a state of complete bewilderment that we were, as a matter of fact, ready for anything that might arrive. As for our sense of astonishment, it was pretty well obliterated. Whilst we were still thus engaged, our friend the captain of the guard presented himself, and with many obeisances signified that we were to follow him, which we did, not without doubts and heart-searchings – for we guessed that the time had come when we should have to settle the bill for those confounded hippo-potami with our cold-eyed friend Agon, the High Priest. How-ever, there was no help for it, and personally I took great comfort in the promise of the protection of the sister Queens, knowing that if ladies have a will they can generally find a way; so off we started as though we liked it. A minute's walk through a passage and an outer court brought us to the great double gates of the palace that open on to the wide highway which runs uphill through the heart of Milosis to the Temple of the Sun a mile away, and thence down the slope on the farther side of the temple to the outer wall of the city.

These gates are very large and massive, and an extraordinarily beautiful work in metal. Between them – for one set is placed at the entrance to an interior, and one at that of the exterior wall – is a fosse, forty-five feet in width. This fosse is filled with water and spanned by a drawbridge, which when lifted makes the palace nearly impregnable to anything except siege guns. As we came, one half of the wide gates were flung open, and we passed over the drawbridge and presently stood gazing up one of the most imposing, if not the most imposing, roadways in the world. It is a hundred feet from curb to curb, and on either side, not cramped and crowded together, as is our European fashion, but each standing in its own grounds, and built equidistant from and in similar style to the rest, are a series of splendid, single-storeyed mansions, all of red granite. These are the town houses of the nobles of the Court, and stretch away in unbroken lines for a mile or more till the eye is arrested by the glorious vision of the Temple of the Sun that crowns the hill and heads the roadway.

As we stood gazing at this splendid sight, of which more anon, there suddenly dashed up to the gateway four chariots, each drawn by two white horses. These chariots are two-wheeled, and made of wood. They are fitted with a stout pole, the weight of which is supported by leathern girths that form a portion of the harness. The wheels are made with four spokes only, are tired with iron, and quite innocent of springs. In the front of the chariot, and immediately over the pole, is a small seat for the driver, railed round to prevent him from being jolted off. Inside the machine itself are three low seats, one at each side, and one with the back to the horses, opposite to which is the door. The whole vehicle is lightly and yet strongly made, and, owing to the grace of the curves, though primitive, not half so ugly as might be expected.

But if the chariots left something to be desired, the horses did not. They were simply splendid, not very large but strongly built, and well ribbed up, with small heads, remarkably large and round hoofs, and a great look of speed and blood. I have often wondered whence this breed, which presents many distinct characteristics, came, but like that of its owners, it history is obscure. Like the people the horses have always been there. The first and last of these chariots were occupied by guards, but the centre two were empty, except for the driver, and to these we were conducted. Alphonse and I got into the first, and Sir Henry, Good, and Umslopogaas into the one behind, and then suddenly off we went. And we did go! Among the Zu-Vendi it is not usual to trot horses either riding or driving, especially when the journey to be made is a short one – they go at full gallop. As soon as we were seated the driver called out, the horses sprang forward, and we were whirled away at a speed sufficient to take one's breath, and which, till I got accustomed to it, kept me in momentary fear of an upset. As for the wretched Alphonse, he clung with a despairing face to the side of what he called this 'devil of a *fiacre*', thinking that every moment was his last. Presently it occurred to him to ask where we were going, and I told him that, as far as I could ascertain, we were going to be sacrificed by burning. You should have seen his face as he grasped the side of the vehicle and cried out in his terror.

But the wild-looking charioteer only leant forward over his flying steeds and shouted; and the air, as it went singing past, bore away the sound of Alphonse's lamentations.

And now before us, in all its marvellous splendour and dazzling loveliness, shone out the Temple of the Sun – the peculiar pride of the Zu-Vendi, to whom it was what Solomon's, or rather Herod's, Temple was to the Jews. The wealth, and skill, and labour of generations had been given to the building of this wonderful place, which had been only finally completed within the last fifty years. Nothing was spared that the country could produce, and the result was indeed worthy of the effort, not so much on account of its size – for there are larger fanes in the world – as because of its perfect proportions, the richness and beauty of its materials, and the wonderful workmanship. The building (that stands by itself on a space of some eight acres of garden ground on the hilltop, around which are the dwelling-places of the priests) is built in the shape of a sunflower, with a dome-covered central hall, from which radiate twelve petal-shaped courts, each dedicated to one of the twelve months, and serving as the repositories of statues reared in memory of the illustrious dead. The width of the circle beneath the dome is three hundred feet, the height of the dome is four hundred feet, and the length of the rays is one hundred and fifty feet, and the height of their roofs three hundred feet, so that they run into the central dome exactly as the petals of the sunflower run into the great raised heart. Thus the exact measurement from the centre of the central altar to the extreme point of any one of the rounded rays would be three hundred feet (the width of the circle itself), or a total of six hundred feet from the rounded extremity of one ray or petal to the extremity of the opposite one.*

The building itself is of pure and polished white marble, which shows out in marvellous contrast to the red granite of the frowning city, on whose brow it glistens indeed like an imperial diadem upon the forehead of a dusky queen. The outer surface of the dome and of the twelve petal courts is covered entirely with thin sheets of beaten gold; and from the extreme point of the roof of each of these petals a glorious golden form with a trumpet in its

---

* These are internal measurements. A.Q.

hand and widespread wings is figured in the very act of soaring into space. I really must leave whoever reads this to imagine the surpassing beauty of these golden roofs flashing when the sun strikes – flashing like a thousand fires aflame on a mountain of polished marble – so fiercely that the reflection can be clearly seen from the great peaks of the range a hundred miles away.

It is a marvellous sight – this golden flower upborne upon the cool white marble walls, and I doubt if the world can show such another. What makes the whole effect even more gorgeous is that a belt of a hundred and fifty feet around the marble wall of the temple is planted with an indigenous species of sunflower, which were at the time when we first saw them a sheet of golden bloom.

The main entrance to this wonderful place is between the two northernmost of the rays or petal courts, and is protected first by the usual bronze gates, and then by doors made of solid marble, beautifully carved with allegorical subjects and overlaid with gold. When these are passed there is only the thickness of the wall, which is, however, twenty-five feet (for the Zu-Vendi build for all time), and another slight wall also of white marble, introduced in order to avoid causing a visible gap in the inner skin of the wall, and you stand in the circular hall under the great dome. Advancing to the central altar you look upon as beautiful a sight as the imagination of man can conceive. You are in the middle of the holy place, and above you the great white marble dome (for the

GROUND PLAN OF THE
TEMPLE OF THE SUN

a　Petal courts
b　Central and side altars
c　Central court
x　Brazen flooring
•　Figures of golden angels

inner skin, like the outer, is of polished marble throughout) arches away in graceful curves something like that of St Paul's in London, only at a slighter angle, and from the funnel-like opening at the exact apex a bright beam of light pours down upon the golden altar. At the east and the west are other altars, and other beams of light stab the sacred twilight to the heart. In every direction, 'white, mystic, wonderful', open out the ray-like courts, each pierced through by a single arrow of light that serves to illumine its lofty silence and dimly to reveal the monuments of the dead.*

Overcome at so awe-inspiring a sight, the vast loveliness of which thrills the nerves like a glance from beauty's eyes, you turn to the central golden altar, in the midst of which, though you cannot see it now, there burns a pale but steady flame crowned with curls of faint blue smoke. It is of marble overlaid with pure gold, in shape round like the sun, four feet in height, and thirty-six in circumference. Here also, hinged to the foundations of the altar, are twelve petals of beaten gold. All night and, except at one hour, all day also, these petals are closed over the altar itself exactly as the petals of a water-lily close over the yellow crown in stormy weather; but when the sun at midday pierces through the funnel in the dome and lights upon the golden flower, the petals open and reveal the hidden mystery, only to close again when the ray has passed.

Nor is this all. Standing in semicircles at equal distances from each other on the north and south of the sacred place are ten golden angels, or female winged forms, exquisitely shaped and draped. These figures, which are slightly larger than life-size, stand with bent heads in an attitude of adoration, their faces shadowed by their wings, and are most imposing and of exceeding beauty.

There is but one thing further which calls for description in this altar, which is, that to the east the flooring in front of it is not of pure white marble, as elsewhere throughout the building, but of solid brass, and this is also the case in front of the other two altars.

---

* Light was also admitted by sliding shutters under the eaves of the dome and in the roof. A.Q.

The eastern and western altars, which are semicircular in shape, and placed against the wall of the building, are much less imposing, and are not enfolded in golden petals. They are, however, also of gold, the sacred fire burns on each, and a golden-winged figure stands on either side of them. Two great golden rays run up the wall behind them, but where the third or middle one should be is an opening in the wall, wide on the outside, but narrow within, like a loophole turned inwards. Through the eastern loophole stream the first beams of the rising sun, and strike right across the circle, touching the folded petals of the great gold flower as they pass till they impinge upon the western altar. In the same way at night the last rays of the sinking sun rest for a while on the eastern altar before they die away into darkness. It is the promise of the dawn to the evening and the evening to the dawn.

With the exception of those three altars and the winged figures about them, the whole space beneath the vast white dome is utterly empty and devoid of ornamentation – a circumstance that to my fancy adds greatly to its splendour.

Such is a brief description of this wonderful and lovely building, to the glories of which, to my mind so much enhanced by their complete simplicity, I only wish I had the power to do justice. But I cannot, so it is useless talking more about it. But when I compare this great work of genius to some of the tawdry buildings and tinsel ornamentation produced in these latter days by European ecclesiastical architects, I feel that even highly civilised art might learn something from the Zu-Vendi masterpieces. I can only say that the exclamation which sprang to my lips as soon as my eyes first became accustomed to the dim light of that glorious building, and its white and curving beauties, perfect and thrilling as those of a naked goddess, grew upon me one by one, was, 'Well! a dog would feel religious here.' It is vulgarly put, but perhaps it conveys my meaning more clearly than any polished utterance.

At the temple gates our party was received by a guard of soldiers, who appeared to be under the orders of a priest; and by them we were conducted into one of the ray or 'petal' courts, as the priests call them, and there left for at least half an hour. Here we conferred together, and realising that we stood in great danger of our lives, determined, if any attempt should be made upon us, to sell them as dearly as we could – Umslopogaas announcing his fixed intention of committing sacrilege on the person of Agon, the High Priest, by splitting his head with Inkosi-kaas. From where we stood we could perceive that an immense multitude were pouring into the temple, evidently in expectation of some unusual event, and I could not help fearing that we had to do with it. And here I may explain that every day, when the sunlight falls upon the central altar, and the trumpets sound, a burnt sacrifice is offered to the Sun, consisting generally of the carcase of a sheep or ox, or sometimes of fruit or corn. This event comes off about midday; of course, not always exactly at that hour, but as Zu-Vendis is situated not far from the Line, although – being so high above the sea it is very temperate – midday and the falling of the sunlight on the altar were generally simultaneous. Today the sacrifice was to take place at about eight minutes past twelve.

Just at twelve o'clock a priest appeared, and made a sign, and the officer of the guard signified to us that we were expected to advance, which we did with the best grace that we could muster, all except Alphonse, whose irrepressible teeth instantly began to chatter. In a few seconds we were out of the court and looking at a vast sea of human faces stretching away to the farthest limits of the great circle, all straining to catch a glimpse of the mysterious strangers who had committed sacrilege; the first strangers, mind you, who, to the knowledge of the multitude, had ever set foot in Zu-Vendis since such time that the memory of man runneth not to the contrary.

As we appeared there was a murmur through the vast crowd that went echoing away up the great dome, and we saw a visible blush of excitement grow on the thousands of faces, like a pink light on a stretch of pale cloud, and a very curious effect it was. On we passed down a lane cut through the heart of the human mass, till presently we stood upon the brazen patch of flooring to the east of the central altar, and immediately facing it. For some thirty feet around the golden-winged figures the space was roped off, and the multitudes stood outside the ropes. Within were a circle of white-robed gold-cinctured priests holding long golden trumpets in their hands, and immediately in front of us was our friend Agon, the High Priest, with his curious cap upon his head. His was the only covered head in that vast assemblage. We took our stand upon the brazen space, little knowing what was prepared for us beneath, but I noticed a curious hissing sound proceeding apparently from the floor for which I could not account. Then came a pause, and I looked around to see if there was any sign of the two Queens, Nyleptha and Sorais, but they were not there. To the right of us, however, was a bare space that I guessed was reserved for them.

We waited, and presently a far-off trumpet blew, apparently high up in the dome. Then came another murmur from the multitude, and up a long lane, leading to the open space to our right, we saw the two Queens walking side by side. Behind them were some nobles of the Court, among whom I recognised the great lord Nasta, and behind them again a body of about fifty guards. These last I was very glad to see. Presently they had all arrived and taken their stand, the two Queens in the front, the nobles to the right and left, and the guards in a double semicircle behind them.

Then came another silence, and Nyleptha looked up and caught my eye; it seemed to me that there was meaning in her glance, and I watched it narrowly. From my eye it travelled down to the brazen flooring, on the outer edge of which we stood. Then followed a slight and almost imperceptible sidelong movement of the head. I did not understand it, and it was repeated. Then I guessed that she meant us to move back off the brazen floor. One more glance and I was sure of it – there was danger in standing on the floor. Sir Henry was placed on one side of me, Umslopogaas on the other. Keeping my eyes fixed straight before me, I whispered to them, first in Zulu and then in English, to draw slowly back inch by inch till half their feet were resting on the marble flooring where the brass ceased. Sir Henry whispered on to Good and Alphonse, and slowly, very very slowly, we shifted backwards; so slowly that nobody, except Nyleptha and Sorais, who saw everything, seemed to notice the movement. Then I glanced again at Nyleptha, and saw that, by an almost imperceptible nod, she indicated approval. All the while Agon's eyes were fixed upon the altar before him apparently in an ecstasy of contemplation, and mine were fixed upon the small of his back in another sort of ecstasy. Suddenly he flung up his long arm, and in a solemn and resounding voice commenced a chant, of which for convenience' sake I append a rough, a *very* rough, translation here, though, of course, I did not then comprehend its meaning. It was an invocation to the Sun, and ran somewhat as follows:

There is silence upon the face of the Earth and the waters
    thereof!
Yea, the silence doth brood on the waters like a nesting bird;
The silence sleepeth also upon the bosom of the profound
    darkness,
Only high up in the great spaces star doth speak unto star.
The Earth is faint with longing and wet with the tears of her
    desire;
The star-girdled night doth embrace her, but she is not
    comforted.
She lies enshrouded in mists like a corpse in the
    grave-clothes,
And stretches her pale hands to the East.

Lo! away in the farthest East there is the shadow of a light;
The Earth seeth and lifts herself. She looks out from
    beneath the hollow of her hand.
Then thy great angels fly forth from the Holy Place, oh Sun,
They shoot their fiery swords into the darkness and
    shrivel it up.
They climb the heavens and cast down the pale stars from
    their thrones;
Yea, they hurl the changeful stars back into the womb of
    the night;
They cause the moon to become wan as the face of a
    dying man,
And behold! Thy glory comes, oh Sun!

Oh, Thou beautiful one, Thou drapest thyself in fire.
The wide heavens are thy pathway: thou rollest o'er them
    as a chariot.
The Earth is thy bride. Thou dost embrace her and she
    brings forth children;
Yea, Thou favourest her, and she yields her increase.
Thou art the All Father and the giver of life, oh Sun.
The young children stretch out their hands and grow in
    thy brightness;
The old men creep forth and seeing remember their
    strength.
Only the dead forget Thee, oh Sun!

When Thou art wroth then Thou dost hide Thy face;
Thou drawest around Thee a thick curtain of shadows.
Then the Earth grows cold and the Heavens are dismayed;
They tremble, and the sound thereof is the sound of
    thunder:
They weep, and their tears are outpoured in the rain;
They sigh, and the wild winds are the voice of their sighing.
The flowers die, the fruitful fields languish and turn pale;
The old men and the little children go unto their appointed
    place
When Thou withdrawest thy light, oh Sun!

Say, what art Thou, oh Thou matchless Splendour –
Who set Thee on high, oh Thou flaming Terror?
When didst Thou begin, and when is the day of Thy
    ending?
Thou art the raiment of the living Spirit.*
None did place Thee on high, for Thou was the Beginning.

---

* This line is interesting as being one of the few allusions to be found in the
Zu-Vendi ritual to a vague divine essence independent of the material splendour of the orb they worship. 'Taia', the word used here, has a very indeter-
minate meaning, and signifies essence, vital principle, spirit, or even God.

Thou shalt not be ended when thy children are forgotten;
Nay, Thou shalt never end, for thy hours are eternal.
Thou sittest on high within thy golden house and measurest
    out the centuries.
Oh Father of Life! oh dark-dispelling Sun!

He ceased this solemn chant, which, though it seems a poor enough thing after going through my mill, is really beautiful and impressive in the original; and then, after a moment's pause, he glanced up towards the funnel-sloped opening in the dome and added,

Oh Sun, descend upon thine Altar!

As he spoke a wonderful and a beautiful thing happened. Down from on high flashed a splendid living ray of light, cleaving the twilight like a sword of fire. Full upon the closed petals it fell and ran shimmering down their golden sides, and then the glorious flower opened as though beneath the bright influence. Slowly it opened, and as the great petals fell wide and revealed the golden altar on which the fire ever burns, the priests blew a blast upon the trumpets, and from all the people there rose a shout of praise that beat against the domed roof and came echoing down the marble walls. And now the flower altar was open, and the sunlight fell full upon the tongue of sacred flame and beat it down, so that it wavered, sank, and vanished into the hollow recesses whence it rose. As it vanished, the mellow notes of the trumpets rolled out once more. Again the old priest flung up his hands and called aloud,

We sacrifice to thee, oh Sun!

Once more I caught Nyleptha's eye; it was fixed upon the brazen flooring.

'Look out,' I said, aloud; and as I said it, I saw Agon bend forward and touch something on the altar. As he did so, the great white sea of faces around us turned red and then white again, and a deep breath went up like a universal sigh. Nyleptha leant forward, and with an involuntary movement covered her eyes with her hand. Sorais turned and whispered to the officer of the royal bodyguard, and then with a rending sound the whole of the brazen flooring slid from before our feet, and there in its place was suddenly revealed a smooth marble shaft terminating in a most awful raging furnace beneath the altar, big enough and hot enough to heat the iron stern-post of a man-of-war.

With a cry of terror we sprang backwards, all except the wretched Alphonse, who was paralysed with fear, and would have fallen into the fiery furnace which had been prepared for us, had not Sir Henry caught him in his strong hand as he was vanishing and dragged him back.

Instantly there arose the most fearful hubbub, and we four got back to back, Alphonse dodging frantically round our little circle in his attempts to take shelter under our legs. We all had our revolvers on – for though we had been politely disarmed of our guns on leaving the palace, of course these people did not know what a revolver was. Umslopogaas, too, had his axe, of which no effort had been made to deprive him, and now he whirled it round his head and sent his piercing Zulu war-shout echoing up the marble walls in fine defiant fashion. Next second, the priests, baffled of their prey, had drawn swords from beneath their white robes and were leaping on us like hounds upon a stag at bay. I saw that, dangerous as action might be, we must act or be lost, so as the first man came bounding along – and a great tall fellow he was – I sent a heavy revolver ball through him, and down he fell at the mouth of the shaft, and slid, shrieking frantically, into the fiery gulf that had been prepared for us.

Whether it was his cries, or the, to them, awful sound and effect of the pistol shot, or what, I know not, but the other priests halted, paralysed and dismayed, and before they could come on again Sorais had called out something, and we, together with the two Queens and most of the courtiers, were being surrounded with a wall of armed men. In a moment it was done, and still the priests hesitated, and the people hung in the balance like a herd of startled buck as it were, making no sign one way or the other.

The last yell of the burning priest had died away, the fire had finished him, and a great silence fell upon the place.

Then the High Priest Agon turned, and his face was as the face of a devil. 'Let the sacrifice be sacrificed,' he cried to the Queens. 'Has not sacrilege enough been done by these strangers, and would ye, as Queens, throw the cloak of your majesty over evildoers? Are not the creatures sacred to the Sun dead? And is not a priest of the Sun also dead, but now slain by the magic of these strangers, who come as the winds out of heaven, whence we know not, and who are what we know not? Beware, oh Queens, how ye tamper with the great majesty of the God, even before His high altar! There is a Power that is more than your power; there is a Justice that is higher than your justice. Beware how ye lift an impious hand against it! Let the sacrifice be sacrificed, oh Queens.'

Then Sorais made answer in her deep quiet tones, that always seemed to me to have a suspicion of mockery about them, however serious the theme: 'Oh, Agon, thou hast spoken according to thy desire, and thou hast spoken truth. But it is thou who wouldst lift an impious hand against the justice of thy God. Bethink thee the midday sacrifice is accomplished; the Sun hath claimed his priest as a sacrifice.'

This was a novel idea, and the people applauded it.

'Bethink thee what are these men? They are strangers found floating on the bosom of a lake. Who brought them here? How came they here? How know you that they also are not servants of the Sun? Is this the hospitality that ye would have our nation show to those whom chance brings to them, to throw them to the flames? Shame on you! Shame on you! What is hospitality? To receive the stranger and show him favour. To bind up his wounds, and find a pillow for his head, and food for him to eat. But thy pillow is the fiery furnace, and thy food the hot savour of the flame. Shame on thee, I say!'

She paused a little to watch the effect of her speech upon the multitude, and seeing that it was favourable, changed her tone from one of remonstrance to one of command.

'Ho! place there,' she cried; 'place, I say; make way for the Queens, and those whom the Queens cover with their "kaf" (mantle).'

'And if I refuse, oh Queen?' said Agon between his teeth.

'Then will I cut a path with my guards,' was the proud answer;

'ay, even in the presence of the sanctuary, and through the bodies of thy priests.'

Agon turned livid with baffled fury. He glanced at the people as though meditating an appeal to them, but saw clearly that their sympathies were all the other way. The Zu-Vendi are a very curious and sociable people, and great as was their sense of the enormity that we had committed in shooting the sacred hippo-potami, they did not like the idea of the only real live strangers they had seen or heard of being consigned to a fiery furnace, thereby putting an end for ever to their chance of extracting knowledge and information from, and gossiping about us. Agon saw this and hesitated, and then for the first time Nyleptha spoke in her soft sweet voice.

'Bethink thee, Agon,' she said, 'as my sister Queen has said, these men may also be servants of the Sun. For themselves they cannot speak, for their tongues are tied. Let the matter be adjourned till such time as they have learnt our language. Who can be condemned without a hearing? When these men can plead for themselves, then it will be time to put them to the proof.'

Here was a clever loophole of escape, and the vindictive old priest took it, little as he liked it.

'So be it, oh Queens,' he said. 'Let the men go in peace, and when they have learnt our tongue then let them speak. And I, even I, will make humble supplication at the altar lest pestilence fall on the land by cause of the sacrilege.'

These words were received with a murmur of applause, and in another minute we were marching out of the temple surrounded by the royal guards.

But it was not till long afterwards that we learnt the exact substance of what had passed, and how hardly our lives had been wrung out of the cruel grip of the Zu-Vendi priesthood, in the face of which even the Queens were practically powerless. Had it not been for their strenuous efforts to protect us we should have been slain even before we set foot in the Temple of the Sun. The attempt to drop us bodily into the fiery pit as an offering was a last artifice to attain this end when several others quite unsuspected by us had already failed.

CHAPTER 15

Sorais' Song

After our escape from Agon and his pious crew we returned to our quarters in the palace and had a very good time. The two Queens, the nobles and the people vied with each other in doing us honour and showering gifts upon us. As for that painful little incident of the hippopotami it sank into oblivion, where we were quite content to leave it. Every day deputations and individuals waited on us to examine our guns and clothing, our chain shirts, and our instruments, especially our watches, with which they were much delighted. In short, we became quite the rage, so much so that some of the fashionable young swells among the Zu-Vendi began to copy the cut of some of our clothes, notably Sir Henry's shooting jacket. One day, indeed, a deputation waited on us and, as usual, Good donned his full-dress uniform for the occasion. This deputation seemed somehow to be a different class to those who generally came to visit us. They were little insignificant men of an excessively polite, not to say servile, demeanour; and their attention appeared to be chiefly taken up with observing the details of Good's full-dress uniform, of which they took copious notes and measurements. Good was much flattered at the time, not suspecting that he had to deal with the six leading tailors of Milosis. A fortnight afterwards, however, when on attending court as usual he had the pleasure of seeing some seven or eight Zu-Vendi 'mashers' arrayed in all the glory of a very fair imitation of his full-dress uniform, he changed his mind. I shall never forget his face of astonishment and disgust. It was after this, chiefly to avoid remark, and also because our clothes were wearing out and had to be saved up, that we resolved to adopt the native dress; and a very comfortable one we found it, though I am bound to say that

I looked sufficiently ridiculous in it, and as for Alphonse! Only Umslopogaas would have none of these things; when his moocha was worn out the fierce old Zulu made him a new one, and went about unconcerned, as grim and naked as his own battleaxe.

Meanwhile we pursued our study of the language steadily and made very good progress. On the morning following our adventure in the temple, three grave and reverend signiors presented themselves armed with manuscript books, ink-horns and feather pens, and indicated that they had been sent to teach us. So, with the exception of Umslopogaas, we all buckled to with a will, doing four hours a day. As for Umslopogaas, he would have none of that either. He did not wish to learn that 'woman's talk', not he; and when one of the teachers advanced on him with a book and an ink-horn and waved them before him in a mild persuasive way, much as a churchwarden invitingly shakes the offertory bag under the nose of a rich but niggardly parishioner, he sprang up with a fierce oath and flashed Inkosi-kaas before the eyes of our learned friend, and there was an end of the attempt to teach *him* Zu-Vendi.

Thus we spent our mornings in useful occupation which grew more and more interesting as we proceeded, and the afternoons were given up to recreation. Sometimes we made trips, notably one to the gold mines and another to the marble quarries both of which I wish I had space and time to describe; and sometimes we went out hunting buck with dogs trained for that purpose, and a very exciting sport it is, as the country is full of agricultural enclosures and our horses were magnificent. This is not to be wondered at, seeing that the royal stables were at our command, in addition to which we had four splendid saddle horses given to us by Nyleptha.

Sometimes, again, we went hawking, a pastime that is in great favour among the Zu-Vendi, who generally fly their birds at a species of partridge which is remarkable for the swiftness and strength of its flight. When attacked by the hawk this bird appears to lose its head, and, instead of seeking cover, flies high into the sky, thus offering wonderful sport. I have seen one of these partridges soar up almost out of sight when followed by the hawk. Still better sport is offered by a variety of solitary snipe as big as a small woodcock, which is plentiful in this country, and which is flown at with a very small, agile, and highly-trained hawk with an almost red tail. The zigzagging of the great snipe and the lightning rapidity of the flight and movements of the red-tailed hawk make the pastime a delightful one. Another variety of the same amusement is the hunting of a very small species of antelope with trained eagles; and it certainly is a marvellous sight to see the great bird soar and soar till he is nothing but a black speck in the sunlight, and then suddenly come dashing down like a cannon-ball upon some cowering buck that is hidden in a patch of grass from everything but that piercing eye. Still finer is the spectacle when the eagle takes the buck running.

On other days we would pay visits to the country seats at some of the great lords' beautiful fortified places, and the villages clustering beneath their walls. Here we saw vineyards and cornfields and well-kept park-like grounds, with such timber in them as filled me with delight, for I do love a good tree. There it stands so strong and sturdy, and yet so beautiful, a very type of the best sort of man. How proudly it lifts its bare head to the winter storms, and with what a full heart it rejoices when the spring has come again! How grand its voice is, too, when it talks with the wind: a thousand aeolian harps cannot equal the beauty of the sighing of a great tree in leaf. All day it points to the sunshine and all night to the stars, and thus passionless, and yet full of life, it endures through the centuries, come storm, come shine, drawing its sustenance from the cool bosom of its mother earth, and as the slow years roll by, learning the great mysteries of growth and of decay. And so on and on through generations, outliving individuals, customs, dynasties – all save the landscape it adorns and human nature – till the appointed day when the wind wins the long battle and rejoices over a reclaimed space, or decay puts the last stroke to his fungus-fingered work.

Ah, one should always think twice before one cuts down a tree!

In the evenings it was customary for Sir Henry, Good, and myself to dine, or rather sup, with their Majesties – not every night, indeed, but about three or four times a week, whenever they had not much company, or the affairs of state would allow of it. And I am bound to say that those little suppers were quite the most charming things of their sort that I ever had to do with. How true is the saying that the very highest in rank are always the most simple and kindly. It is from your half-and-half sort of people that you get pomposity and vulgarity, the difference between the two being very much what one sees every day in England between the old, out-at-elbows, broken-down county family, and the over-bearing, purse-proud people who come and 'take the place'. I really think that Nyleptha's greatest charm is her sweet simplicity, and her kindly genuine interest even in little things. She is the simplest woman I ever knew, and where her passions are not involved, one of the sweetest; but she can look queenly enough when she likes, and be as fierce as any savage too.

For instance, never shall I forget that scene when I for the first time was sure that she was really in love with Curtis. It came about in this way – all through Good's weakness for ladies' society. When we had been employed for some three months in learning Zu-Vendi, it struck Master Good that he was getting rather tired of the old gentlemen who did us the honour to lead us in the way that we should go, so he proceeded, without saying a word to anybody else, to inform them that it was a peculiar fact, but that we could not make any real progress in the deeper intricacies of a foreign language unless we were taught by ladies – young ladies, he was careful to explain. In his own country, he pointed out, it was habitual to choose the very best-looking and most charming girls who could be found to instruct any strangers who happened to come that way, etc.

All of this the old gentlemen swallowed open-mouthed. There was, they admitted, reason in what he said, since the contemplation of the beautiful, as their philosophy taught, induced a certain porosity of mind similar to that produced upon the physical body by the healthful influences of sun and air. Consequently it was probable that we might absorb the Zu-Vendi tongue a little faster if suitable teachers could be found. Another thing was that, as the female sex was naturally loquacious, good practice would be gained in the viva voce department of our studies.

To all of this Good gravely assented, and the learned gentlemen departed, assuring him that their orders were to fall in with our wishes in every way, and that, if possible, our views should be met.

Imagine, therefore the surprise and disgust of myself, and I trust and believe Sir Henry, when, on entering the room where we were accustomed to carry on our studies the following morning, we found, instead of our usual venerable tutors, three of the best-looking young women whom Milosis could produce – and that is saying a good deal – who blushed and smiled and curtseyed, and gave us to understand that they were there to carry on our instruction. Then Good, as we gazed at one another in bewilderment, thought fit to explain, saying that it had slipped his memory before – but the old gentlemen had told him, on the previous evening, that it was absolutely necessary that our further education should be carried on by the other sex. I was overwhelmed, and appealed to Sir Henry for advice in such a crisis.

'Well,' he said, 'you see the ladies are here, ain't they? If we sent them away, don't you think it might hurt their feelings, eh? One doesn't like to be rough, you see; and they look regular *blues*, don't they, eh?'

By this time Good had already begun his lessons with the handsomest of the three, and so with a sigh I yielded. That day everything went very well: the young ladies were certainly very clever, and they only smiled when we blundered. I never saw Good so attentive to his books before, and even Sir Henry appeared to tackle Zu-Vendi with a renewed zest. 'Ah,' thought I, 'will it always be thus?'

Next day we were much more lively, our work was pleasingly interspersed with questions about our native country, what the ladies were like there, etc., all of which we answered as best as we could in Zu-Vendi, and I heard Good assuring his teacher that her loveliness was to the beauties of Europe as the sun to the moon, to which she replied with a little toss of the head, that she was a plain teaching woman and nothing else, and that it was not kind 'to deceive a poor girl so'. Then we had a little singing that was really charming, so natural and unaffected. The Zu-Vendi love-songs are most touching. On the third day we were all quite intimate. Good narrated some of his previous love affairs to his fair teacher, and so moved was she that her sighs mingled with his own. I discoursed with mine, a merry blue-eyed girl, upon Zu-Vendian art, and never saw that she was waiting for an opportunity to drop a specimen of the cockroach tribe down my back, whilst in the corner Sir Henry and his governess appeared, so far as I could judge, to be going through a lesson framed on the great educational principles laid down by Wackford Squeers Esq., though in a very modified or rather spiritualised form. The lady softly repeated the Zu-Vendi word for 'hand', and he took hers; 'eyes', and he gazed deep into her brown orbs; 'lips', and – but just at that moment *my* young lady dropped the cockroach down my back and ran away laughing. Now if there is one thing I loathe more than another it is cockroaches, and moved quite beyond myself, and yet laughing at her impudence, I took up the cushion she had been sitting on and threw it after her. Imagine then my shame – my horror, and my distress – when the door opened, and, attended by two guards only, in walked *Nyleptha*. The cushion could not be recalled (it missed the girl and hit one of the guards on the head), but I instantly and ineffectually tried to look as though I had not thrown it. Good ceased his sighing, and began to murder Zu-Vendi at the top of his voice, and Sir Henry whistled and looked silly. As for the poor girls, they were utterly dumbfounded.

And Nyleptha! she drew herself up till her frame seemed to tower even above that of the tall guards, and her face went first red, and then pale as death.

'Guards,' she said in a quiet choked voice, and pointing at the fair but unconscious disciple of Wackford Squeers, 'slay me that woman.'

The men hesitated, as well they might.

'Will ye do my bidding,' she said again in the same voice, 'or will ye not?'

Then they advanced upon the girl with uplifted spears. By this time Sir Henry had recovered himself, and saw that the comedy was likely to turn into a tragedy.

'Stand back,' he said in a voice of thunder, at the same time getting in front of the terrified girl. 'Shame on thee, Nyleptha – shame! Thou shalt not kill her.'

'Doubtless thou hast good reason to try to protect her. Thou couldst hardly do less in honour,' answered the infuriated Queen; 'but she shall die – she shall die,' and she stamped her little foot.

'It is well,' he answered; 'then will I die with her. I am thy servant, oh Queen; do with me even as thou wilt.' And he bowed towards her, and fixed his clear eyes contemptuously on her face.

'I could wish to slay thee too,' she answered; 'for thou dost make a mock of me;' and then feeling that she was mastered, and I suppose not knowing what else to do, she burst into such a storm of tears and looked so royally lovely in her passionate distress, that, old as I am, I must say I envied Curtis his task of supporting her. It was rather odd to see him holding her in his arms considering what had just passed – a thought that seemed to occur to herself, for presently she wrenched herself free and went, leaving us all much disturbed.

Presently, however, one of the guards returned with a message to the girls that they were, on pain of death, to leave the city and return to their homes in the country, and that no further harm would come to them; and accordingly they went, one of them remarking philosophically that it could not be helped, and that it was a satisfaction to know that they had taught us a little serviceable Zu-Vendi. Mine was an exceedingly nice girl, and, overlooking the cockroach, I made her a present of my favourite lucky sixpence with a hole in it when she went away. After that our former masters resumed their course of instruction, needless to say to my great relief.

That night, when in fear and trembling we attended the royal supper table, we found that Nyleptha was laid up with a bad headache. That headache lasted for three whole days; but on the fourth she was present at supper as usual, and with the most gracious and sweet smile gave Sir Henry her hand to lead her to the table. No allusion was made to the little affair described above beyond her saying, with a charming air of innocence, that when she came to see us at our studies the other day she had been seized with a giddiness from which she had only now recovered. She supposed, she added with a touch of the humour that was common to her, that it was the sight of people working so hard which had affected her.

In reply Sir Henry said, dryly, that he had thought she did not look quite herself on that day, whereat she flashed one of those quick glances of hers at him, which if he had the feelings of a man must have gone through him like a knife, and the subject dropped entirely. Indeed, after supper was over Nyleptha condescended to put us through an examination to see what we had learnt, and to express herself well satisfied with the results. Indeed, she proceeded to give us, especially Sir Henry, a lesson on her own account, and very interesting we found it.

And all the while that we talked, or rather tried to talk, and laughed, Sorais would sit there in her carven ivory chair, and look at us and read us all like a book, only from time to time saying a few words, and smiling that quick ominous smile of hers which was more like a flash of summer lightning on a dark cloud than anything else. And as near to her as he dared would sit Good, worshipping through his eyeglass, for he really was getting seriously devoted to this sombre beauty, of whom, speaking personally, I felt terribly afraid. I watched her keenly, and soon I found out that for all her apparent impassibility she was at heart bitterly jealous of Nyleptha. Another thing I found out, and the discovery filled me with dismay, and that was, that she *also* was growing devoted to Sir Henry Curtis. Of course I could not be sure; it is not easy to read so cold and haughty a woman; but I noticed one or two little things, and, as elephant hunters know, dried grass shows which way the wind has set.

And so another three months passed over us, by which time we had all attained to a very considerable mastery of the Zu-Vendi language, which is an easy one to learn. And as the time went on we became great favourites with the people, and even with the courtiers, gaining an enormous reputation for cleverness, because, as I think I have said, Sir Henry was able to show them how to make glass, which was a national want, and also, by the help of a twenty-year almanac that we had with us, to predict various heavenly combinations which were quite unsuspected by the native astronomers. We even succeeded in demonstrating the principle of the steam-engine to a gathering of the learned men, who were filled with amazement; and several other things of the same sort we did. And so it came about that the people made up their minds that we must on no account be allowed to go out of the country (which indeed was an apparent impossibility even if we had wished it), and we were advanced to great honour and made officers to the bodyguards of the sister Queens while permanent quarters were assigned to us in the palace, and our opinion was asked upon questions of national policy.

But blue as the sky seemed, there was a cloud, and a big one, on the horizon. We had indeed heard no more of those confounded hippopotami, but it is not on that account to be supposed that our sacrilege was forgotten, or the enmity of the great and powerful priesthood headed by Agon appeased. On the contrary, it was burning the more fiercely because it was necessarily suppressed, and what had perhaps begun in bigotry was ending in downright direct hatred born of jealousy. Hitherto, the priests had been the wise men of the land, and were on this account, as well as from superstitious causes, looked on with peculiar veneration. But our arrival, with our outlandish wisdom and our strange inventions and hints of unimagined things, dealt a serious blow to this state of affairs, and, among the educated Zu-Vendi, went far towards destroying the priestly prestige. A still worse affront to them, however, was the favour with which we were regarded, and the trust that was reposed in us. All these things tended to make us excessively obnoxious to the great sacerdotal clan, the most powerful because the most united faction in the kingdom.

Another source of imminent danger to us was the rising envy of some of the great lords headed by Nasta, whose antagonism to us had at best been but thinly veiled, and which now threatened to break out into open flame. Nasta had for some years been a candidate for Nyleptha's hand in marriage, and when we appeared on the scene I fancy, from all I could gather, that though there were still many obstacles in his path, success was by no means out of his reach. But now all this had changed; the coy Nyleptha smiled no more in his direction, and he was not slow to guess the cause. Infuriated and alarmed, he turned his attention to Sorais, only to find that he might as well try to woo a mountain side. With a bitter jest or two about his fickleness, that door was closed on him for ever. So Nasta bethought himself of the thirty thousand wild swordsmen who would pour down at his bidding through the northern mountain passes, and no doubt vowed to adorn the gates of Milosis with our heads.

But first he determined, as I learned, to make one more attempt and to demand the hand of Nyleptha in the open Court after the formal annual ceremony of the signing of the laws that had been proclaimed by the Queens during the year.

Of this astounding fact Nyleptha heard with simulated nonchalance, and with a little trembling of the voice herself informed us of it as we sat at supper on the night preceding the great ceremony of the law-giving.

Sir Henry bit his lip, and do what he could to prevent it plainly showed his agitation.

'And what answer will the Queen be pleased to give to the great Lord?' asked I, in a jesting manner.

'Answer, Macumazahn' (for we had elected to pass by our Zulu names in Zu-Vendis), she said, with a pretty shrug of her ivory shoulder. 'Nay, I know not; what is a poor woman to do, when the wooer has thirty thousand swords wherewith to urge his love?' And from under her long lashes she glanced at Curtis.

Just then we rose from the table to adjourn into another room. 'Quatermain, a word, quick,' said Sir Henry to me. 'Listen. I have never spoken about it, but surely you have guessed: I love Nyleptha. What am I to do?'

Fortunately, I had more or less already taken the question into consideration, and was therefore able to give such answer as seemed the wisest to me.

'You must speak to Nyleptha tonight,' I said. 'Now is your time, now or never. Listen. In the sitting-chamber get near to her, and whisper to her to meet you at midnight by the Rademas statue at the end of the great hall. I will keep watch for you there. Now or never, Curtis.'

We passed on into the other room. Nyleptha was sitting, her hands before her, and a sad anxious look upon her lovely face. A little way off was Sorais talking to Good in her slow measured tones.

The time went on; in another quarter of an hour I knew that, according to their habit, the Queens would retire. As yet, Sir Henry had had no chance of saying a word in private: indeed, though we saw much of the royal sisters, it was by no means easy to see them alone. I racked my brains, and at last an idea came to me.

'Will the Queen be pleased,' I said, bowing low before Sorais, 'to sing to her servants? Our hearts are heavy this night; sing to us, oh Lady of the Night' (Sorais' favourite name among the people).

'My songs, Macumazahn, are not such as to lighten the heavy heart, yet will I sing if it pleases thee,' she answered; and she rose and went a few paces to a table whereon lay an instrument not unlike a zither, and struck a few wandering chords.

Then suddenly, like the notes of some deep-throated bird, her rounded voice rang out in song so wildly sweet, and yet with so eerie and sad a refrain, that it made the very blood stand still. Up, up soared the golden notes, that seemed to melt far away, and then to grow again and travel on, laden with all the sorrow of the world and all the despair of the lost. It was a marvellous song, but I had not time to listen to it properly. However, I got the words of it afterwards, and here is a translation of its burden, so far as it admits of being translated at all.

SORAIS' SONG

As a desolate bird that through darkness its lost way is
    winging,
As a hand that is helplessly raised when Death's sickle is
    swinging,
So is life! ay, the life that lends passion and breath to my
    singing.

As the nightingale's song that is full of a sweetness
    unspoken,
As a spirit unbarring the gates of the skies for a token,
So is love! ay, the love that shall fall when his pinion is
    broken.

As the tramp of the legions when trumpets their challenge
    are sending,
As the shout of the Storm-god when lightnings the black sky
    are rending,
So is power! ay, the power that shall lie in the dust at its
    ending.

So short is our life; yet with space for all things to forsake us,
A bitter delusion, a dream from which nought can awake us,
Till Death's dogging footsteps at morn or at eve shall
    o'ertake us.

Refrain

Oh, the world is fair at the dawning – dawning – dawning,
But the red sun sinks in blood – the red sun sinks in blood.

I only wish that I could write down the music too.

'Now, Curtis, now,' I whispered, when she began the second verse, and turned my back.

'Nyleptha,' he said – for my nerves were so much on the stretch that I could hear every word, low as it was spoken, even through Sorais' divine notes – 'Nyleptha, I must speak with thee this night, upon my life I must. Say me not nay; oh, say me not nay!'

'How can I speak with thee?' she answered, looking fixedly before her; 'Queens are not like other people. I am surrounded and watched.'

'Listen, Nyleptha, thus. I will be before the statue of Rademas in the great hall at midnight. I have the countersign and can pass in. Macumazahn will be there to keep guard, and with him the Zulu. Oh come, my Queen, deny me not.'

'It is not seemly,' she murmured, 'and tomorrow – '

Just then the music began to die in the last wail of the refrain, and Sorais slowly turned her round.

'I will be there,' said Nyleptha, hurriedly; 'on thy life see that thou fail me not.'

CHAPTER 16

Before the Statue

It was night – dead night – and the silence lay on the Frowning City like a cloud.

Secretly, as evildoers, Sir Henry Curtis, Umslopogaas, and myself threaded our way through the passages towards a by-entrance to the great Throne Chamber. Once we were met by the fierce rattling challenge of the sentry. I gave the countersign, and the man grounded his spear and let us pass. Also we were officers of the Queens' bodyguard, and in that capacity had a right to come and go unquestioned.

We gained the hall in safety. So empty and so still was it, that even when we had passed the sound of our footsteps yet echoed up the lofty walls, vibrating faintly and still more faintly against the carven roof, like ghosts of the footsteps of dead men haunting the place that once they trod.

It was an eerie spot, and it oppressed me. The moon was full, and threw great pencils and patches of light through the high windowless openings in the walls, that lay pure and beautiful upon the blackness of the marble floor, like white flowers on a coffin. One of these silver arrows fell upon the statue of the sleeping Rademas, and of the angel form bent over him, illumining it, and a small circle round it, with a soft clear light, reminding me of that with which Catholics illumine the altars of their cathedrals.

Here by the statue we took our stand, and waited. Sir Henry and I close together, Umslopogaas some paces off in the darkness, so that I could only just make out his towering outline leaning on the outline of an axe.

So long did we wait that I almost fell asleep resting against the cold marble, but was suddenly aroused by hearing Curtis give a quick catching breath. Then from far away there came a little sound as though the statues that lined the walls were whispering to each other some message of the ages.

It was the faint sweep of a lady's dress. Nearer it grew, and nearer yet. We could see a figure steal from patch to patch of moonlight, and even hear the soft fall of sandalled feet. Another second and I saw the black silhouette of the old Zulu raise its arm in mute salute, and Nyleptha was before us.

Oh, how beautiful she looked as she paused a moment just within the circle of the moonlight! Her hand was pressed upon her heart, and her white bosom heaved beneath it. Round her head a broidered scarf was loosely thrown, partially shadowing the perfect face, and thus rendering it even more lovely; for beauty, dependent as it is to a certain extent upon the imagination, is never so beautiful as when it is half hid. There she stood radiant but half doubting, stately and yet so sweet. It was but a moment, but I then and there fell in love with her myself, and have remained so to this hour; for, indeed, she looked more like an angel out of heaven than a loving, passionate, mortal woman. Low we bowed before her, and then she spoke.

'I have come,' she whispered, 'but it was at great risk. Ye know not how I am watched. The priests watch me. Sorais watches me with those great eyes of hers. My very guards are spies upon me. Nasta watches me too. Oh, let him be careful!' and she stamped her foot. 'Let him be careful; I am a woman, and therefore hard to drive. Ay, and I am a Queen, too, and can still avenge. Let him be careful, I say, lest in place of giving him my hand I take his head,' and she ended the outburst with a little sob, and then smiled up at us bewitchingly and laughed.

'Thou didst bid me come hither, my Lord Incubu' (Curtis had taught her to call him so). 'Doubtless it is about business of the State, for I know that thou art ever full of great ideas and plans for my welfare and my people's. So even as a Queen should I have come, though I greatly fear the dark alone,' and again she laughed and gave him a glance from her grey eyes.

At this point I thought it wise to move a little, since secrets 'of the State' should not be made public property; but she would not let me go far, peremptorily stopping me within five yards or so, saying that she feared surprise. So it came to pass that, however unwillingly, I heard all that passed.

'Thou knowest, Nyleptha,' said Sir Henry, 'that it was for none of these things that I asked thee to meet me at this lonely place. Nyleptha, waste not the time in pleasantry, but listen to me, for – I love thee.'

As he said the words I saw her face break up, as it were, and change. The coquetry went out of it, and in its place there shone a great light of love which seemed to glorify it, and make it like that of the marble angel overhead. I could not help thinking that it must have been a touch of prophetic instinct which made the long dead Rademas limn, in the features of the angel of his inspiring vision, so strange a likeness of his own descendant. Sir Henry, also, must have observed and been struck by the likeness, for, catching the look upon Nyleptha's face, he glanced quickly from it to the moonlit statue, and then back again at his beloved.

'Thou sayest thou dost love me,' she said in a low voice, 'and thy voice rings true, but how am I to know that thou dost speak the truth?

'Though,' she went on with proud humility, and in the stately third person which is so largely used by the Zu-Vendi, 'I be as nothing in the eyes of my lord,' and she curtseyed towards him, 'who comes from among a wonderful people, to whom my people are but children, yet here am I a queen and a leader of men, and if I would go to battle a hundred thousand spears shall sparkle in my train like stars glimmering down the path of the bent moon. And although my beauty be a little thing in the eyes of my lord,' and she lifted her broidered skirt and curtseyed again, 'yet here among my own people am I held right fair, and ever since I was a woman the great lords of my kingdom have made quarrel concerning me, as though forsooth,' she added with a flash of passion, 'I were a deer to be pulled down by the hungriest wolf, or a horse to be sold to the highest bidder. Let my lord pardon me if I weary my lord, but it hath pleased my lord to say that he loves me, Nyleptha, a Queen of the Zu-Vendi, and therefore would I say that though my love and my hand be not much to my lord, yet to me are they all.

'Oh!' she cried, with a sudden and thrilling change of voice, and modifying her dignified mode of address. 'Oh, how can I know that thou lovest but me? How can I know that thou wilt not weary of me and seek thine own place again, leaving me desolate? Who is there to tell me but that thou lovest some other woman, some fair woman unknown to me, but who yet draws breath beneath this same moon that shines on me tonight? Tell me *how* am I to know?' And she clasped her hands and stretched them out towards him and looked appealingly into his face.

'Nyleptha,' answered Sir Henry, adopting the Zu-Vendi way of speech; 'I have told thee that I love thee; how am I to tell thee how much I love thee? Is there then a measure for love? Yet will I try. I say not that I have never looked upon another woman with favour, but this I say that I love thee with all my life and with all my strength; that I love thee now and shall love thee till I grow cold in death, ay, and as I believe beyond my death, and on and on for ever: I say that thy voice is music to my ear, and thy touch as water to a thirsty land, that when thou art there the world is beautiful, and when I see thee not it is as though the light was dead. Oh, Nyleptha, I will never leave thee; here and now for thy dear sake I will forget my people and my father's house, yea, I renounce them all. By thy side will I live, Nyleptha, and at thy side will I die.'

He paused and gazed at her earnestly, but she hung her head like a lily, and said never a word.

'Look!' he went on, pointing to the statue on which the moonlight played so brightly. 'Thou seest that angel woman who rests her hand upon the forehead of the sleeping man, and thou seest how at her touch his soul flames up and shines out through his flesh, even as a lamp at the touch of the fire, so is it with me and thee, Nyleptha. Thou hast awakened my soul and called it forth, and now, Nyleptha, it is not mine, not mine, but *thine* and thine only. There is no more for me to say; in thy hands is my life.' And he leaned back against the pedestal of the statue, looking very pale, and his eyes shining, but proud and handsome as a god.

Slowly, slowly she raised her head, and fixed her wonderful eyes, all alight with the greatness of her passion, full upon his face, as though to read his very soul. Then at last she spoke, low indeed, but clearly as a silver bell.

'Of a truth, weak woman that I am, I do believe thee. Ill will be the day for thee and for me also if it be my fate to learn that I have believed a lie. And now hearken to me, oh man, who hath wandered here from far to steal my heart and make me all thine own. I put my hand upon thy hand thus, and thus I, whose lips have never kissed before, do kiss thee on the brow; and now by my hand and by that first and holy kiss, ay, by my people's weal and by my throne that like enough I shall lose for thee – by the name of my high House, by the sacred Stone and by the eternal majesty of the Sun, I swear that for thee will I live and die. And I swear that I will love thee and thee only till death, ay, and beyond, if as thou sayest there be a beyond, and that thy will shall be my will, and thy ways my ways.

'Oh see, see, my lord! thou knowest not how humble is she who loves; I, who am a Queen, I kneel before thee, even at thy feet I do my homage;' and the lovely impassioned creature flung herself down on her knees on the cold marble before him. And after that I really do not know, for I could stand it no longer, and cleared off to refresh myself with a little of old Umslopogaas' society, leaving them to settle it their own way, and a very long time they were about it.

I found the old warrior leaning on Inkosi-kaas as usual, and surveying the scene in the patch of moonlight with a grim smile of amusement.

'Ah, Macumazahn,' he said, 'I suppose it is because I am getting old, but I don't think that I shall ever learn to understand the ways of you white people. Look there now, I pray thee, they are a pretty pair of doves, but what is all the fuss about, Macumazahn? He wants a wife, and she wants a husband, then why does he not pay his cows down* like a man and have done with it? It would save a deal of trouble, and we should have had our night's sleep. But there they go, talk, talk, talk, and kiss, kiss, kiss, like mad things. Eugh!'

---

* Alluding to the Zulu custom.   A.Q.

Some three-quarters of an hour afterwards the 'pair of doves' came strolling towards us, Curtis looking slightly silly, and Nyleptha remarking calmly that the moonlight made very pretty effects on the marble. Then, for she was in a most gracious mood, she took my hand and said that I was 'her lord's' dear friend, and therefore most dear to her – not a word for my own sake, you see. Next she lifted Umslopogaas' axe, and examined it curiously, saying significantly as she did so that he might soon have cause to use it in defence of her.

After that she nodded prettily to us all, and casting a tender glance at her lover, glided off into the darkness like a beautiful vision.

When we got back to our quarters, which we did without accident, Curtis asked me jocularly what I was thinking about.

'I am wondering,' I answered, 'on what principle it is arranged that some people should find beautiful queens to fall in love with them, while others find nobody at all, or worse than nobody; and I am also wondering how many brave men's lives this night's work will cost.' It was rather nasty of me, perhaps, but somehow all the feelings do not evaporate with age, and I could not help being a little jealous of my old friend's luck. Vanity, my sons; vanity of vanities!

On the following morning, Good was informed of the happy occurrence, and positively rippled with smiles that, originating somewhere about the mouth, slowly travelled up his face like the rings in a duckpond, till they flowed over the brim of his eyeglass and went where sweet smiles go. The fact of the matter, however, was that not only was Good rejoiced about the thing on its own merits but also for personal reasons. He adored Sorais quite as earnestly as Sir Henry adored Nyleptha, and his adoration had not altogether prospered. Indeed, it had seemed to him and to me also that the dark Cleopatra-like queen favoured Curtis in her own curious inscrutable way much more than Good. Therefore it was a relief to him to learn that his unconscious rival was permanently and satisfactorily attached in another direction. His face fell a little, however, when he was told that the whole thing was to be kept as secret as the dead, above all from Sorais for the present, inasmuch as the political convulsion which would follow such an announcement at the moment would be altogether too great to face and would very possibly, if prematurely made, shake Nyleptha from her throne.

That morning we again attended in the Throne Hall, and I could not help smiling to myself when I compared the visit to our last, and reflecting that, if walls could speak, they would have strange tales to tell.

What actresses women are! There, high upon her golden throne, draped in her blazoned 'kaf' or robe of state, sat the fair Nyleptha, and when Sir Henry came in a little late, dressed in the full uniform of an officer of her guard and humbly bent himself before her, she merely acknowledged his salute with a careless nod and turned her head coldly aside. It was a very large Court, for not only did the signing of the laws attract many outside of those whose duty it was to attend, but also the rumour that Nasta was going to publicly ask the hand of Nyleptha in marriage had gone abroad, with the result that the great hall was crowded to its utmost capacity. There were our friends the priests in force, headed by Agon, who regarded us with a vindictive eye; and a most imposing band they were, with their long white embroidered robes girt with a golden chain from which hung the fish-like scales. There, too, were a number of the lords, each with a band of brilliantly attired attendants, and prominent among them was Nasta, stroking his black beard meditatively and looking unusually pleasant. It was a splendid and impressive sight, especially when the officer after having read out each law handed them to the Queens to sign, whereon the trumpets blared out and the Queens' guard grounded their spears with a crash in salute. This reading and signing of the laws took a long time, but at length it came to an end, the last one reciting that 'whereas distinguished strangers, etc.', and proceeding to confer on the three of us the rank of 'lords', together with certain military commands and large estates bestowed by the Queen. When it was read the trumpets blared and the spears clashed down as usual, but I saw some of the lords turn and whisper to each other, while Nasta ground his teeth. They did not like the favour that was shown to us, which under all the circumstances was not perhaps unnatural.

Then there came a pause, and Nasta stepped forward and bowing humbly, though with no humility in his eye, craved a boon at the hands of the Queen Nyleptha.

Nyleptha turned a little pale, but bowed graciously, and prayed the 'well-beloved lord' to speak on, whereon in a few straightforward soldier-like words he asked her hand in marriage.

Then, before she could find words to answer, the High Priest Agon took up the tale, and in a speech of real eloquence and power pointed out the many advantages of the proposed alliance; how it would consolidate the kingdom, for Nasta's dominions, of which he was virtually king, were to Zu-Vendis much what Scotland used to be to England; how it would gratify the wild mountaineers and be popular among the soldiery, for Nasta was a famous general; how it would set her dynasty firmly on the throne, and would gain the blessing and approval of the 'Sun', i.e. of the office of the High Priest, and so on. Many of his arguments were undoubtedly valid, and there was, looking at it from a political point of view, everything to be said for the marriage. But unfortunately it is difficult to play the game of politics with the persons of young and lovely queens as though they were ivory effigies of themselves on a chessboard. Nyleptha's face, while Agon spouted away, was a perfect study; she smiled indeed, but beneath the smile it set like a stone, and her eyes began to flash ominously.

At last he stopped, and she prepared herself to answer. Before she did so, however, Sorais leant towards her and said in a voice sufficiently loud for me to catch what she said, 'Bethink thee well, my sister, ere thou dost speak, for methinks that our thrones may hang upon thy words.'

Nyleptha made no answer, and with a shrug and a smile Sorais leant back again and listened.

'Of a truth a great honour has been done to me,' she said, 'that my poor hand should not only have been asked in marriage, but that Agon here should be so swift to pronounce the blessing of the Sun upon my union. Methinks that in another minute he would have wed us fast ere the bride had said her say. Nasta, I thank thee, and I will bethink me of thy words, but now as yet I have no mind for marriage, that is a cup of which none know the taste until they begin to drink it. Again I thank thee, Nasta,' and she made as though she would rise.

The great lord's face turned almost as black as his beard with fury, for he knew that the words amounted to a final refusal of his suit.

'Thanks be to the Queen for her gracious words,' he said, restraining himself with difficulty and looking anything but grateful, 'my heart shall surely treasure them. And now I crave another boon, namely, the royal leave to withdraw myself to my own poor cities in the north till such time as the Queen shall say my suit nay or yea. Mayhap,' he added, with a sneer, 'the Queen will be pleased to visit me there, and to bring with her these stranger lords,' and he scowled darkly towards us. 'It is but a poor country and a rough, but we are a hardy race of mountaineers, and there shall be gathered thirty thousand swordsmen to shout a welcome to her.'

This speech, which was almost a declaration of rebellion, was received in complete silence, but Nyleptha flushed up and answered it with spirit.

'Oh, surely, Nasta, I will come, and the strange lords in my train, and for every man of thy mountaineers who calls thee Prince, will I bring two from the lowlands who call me Queen, and we will see which is the staunchest breed. Till then farewell.'

The trumpets blared out, the Queens rose, and the great assembly broke up in murmuring confusion, and for myself I went home with a heavy heart foreseeing civil war.

After this there was quiet for a few weeks. Curtis and the Queen did not often meet, and exercised the utmost caution not to allow the true relation in which they stood to each other to leak out; but do what they would, rumours as hard to trace as a buzzing fly in a dark room, and yet quite as audible, began to hum round and round, and at last to settle on her throne.

CHAPTER 17

The Storm Breaks

And now it was that the trouble which at first had been but a cloud as large as a man's hand began to loom very black and big upon our horizon, namely, Sorais' preference for Sir Henry. I saw the storm drawing nearer and nearer; and so, poor fellow, did he. The affection of so lovely and highly-placed a woman was not a thing that could in a general way be considered a calamity by any man, but, situated as Curtis was, it was a grievous burden to bear.

To begin with, Nyleptha, though altogether charming, was, it must be admitted, of a rather jealous disposition, and was sometimes apt to visit on her lover's head her indignation at the marks of what Alphonse would have called the 'distinguished consideration' with which her royal sister favoured him. Then the enforced secrecy of his relation to Nyleptha prevented Curtis from taking some opportunity of putting a stop, or trying to put a stop, to this false condition of affairs, by telling Sorais, in a casual but confidential way, that he was going to marry her sister. A third sting in Sir Henry's honey was that he knew that Good was honestly and sincerely attached to the ominous-looking but most attractive Lady of the Night. Indeed, poor Bougwan was wasting himself to a shadow of his fat and jolly self about her, his face getting so thin that his eyeglass would scarcely stick in it; while she, with a sort of careless coquetry, just gave him encouragement enough to keep him going, thinking, no doubt, that he might be useful as a stalking-horse. I tried to give him a hint, in as delicate a way as I could, but he flew into a huff and would not listen to me, so I was determined to let ill alone, for fear of making it worse. Poor Good, he really was very ludicrous in his distress, and went in for all sorts of absurdities, under the belief that he was advancing his suit. One of them was the writing – with the assistance of one of the grave and revered signiors who instructed us, and who, whatever may have been the measure of his erudition, did not understand how to scan a line – of a most interminable Zu-Vendi love-song, of which the continually recurring refrain was something about 'I will kiss thee; oh yes, I will kiss thee!' Now among the Zu-Vendi it is a common and most harmless thing for young men to serenade ladies at night, as I believe they do in the southern countries of Europe, and sing all sorts of nonsensical songs to them. The young men may or may not be serious; but no offence is meant and none is taken, even by ladies of the highest rank, who accept the whole thing as an English girl would a gracefully-turned compliment.

Availing himself of this custom, Good bethought him that would serenade Sorais, whose private apartments, together with those of her maidens, were exactly opposite our own, on the further side of a narrow courtyard which divided one section of the great palace from another. Accordingly, having armed himself with a native zither, on which, being an adept with the light guitar, he had easily learned to strum, he proceeded at midnight – the fashionable hour for this sort of caterwauling – to make night hideous with his amorous yells. I was fast asleep when they began, but they soon woke me up – for Good possesses a tremendous voice and has no notion of time – and I ran to my window-place to see what was the matter. And there, standing in the full moonlight in the courtyard, I perceived Good, adorned with an enormous ostrich feather head-dress and a flowing silken cloak, which it is the right thing to wear upon these occasions, and shouting out the abominable song which he and the old gentleman had evolved, to a jerky, jingling accompaniment. From the direction of the quarters of the maids of honour came a succession of faint sniggerings; but the apartments of Sorais herself – whom I devoutly pitied if she happened to be there – were silent as the grave. There was absolutely no end to that awful song, with its eternal 'I will kiss thee!' and at last neither I nor Sir Henry, whom I had summoned to enjoy the sight, could stand it any longer; so, remembering the dear old story, I put my head to the window opening, and shouted, 'For Heaven's sake, Good, don't go on talking about it, but *kiss* her and let's all go to sleep!' That choked him off, and we had no more serenading.

The whole thing formed a laughable incident in a tragic business. How deeply thankful we ought to be that even the most serious matters have generally a silver lining about them in the shape of a joke, if only people could see it. The sense of humour is a very valuable possession in life, and ought to be cultivated in the Board schools – especially in Scotland.

Well, the more Sir Henry held off the more Sorais came on, as is not uncommon in such cases, till at last things got very queer indeed. Evidently she was, by some strange perversity of mind, quite blinded to the true state of the case; and I, for one, greatly dreaded the moment of her awakening. Sorais was a dangerous woman to be mixed up with, either with or without one's consent. At last the evil moment came, as I saw it must come. One fine day, Good having gone out hawking, Sir Henry and I were sitting quietly talking over the situation, especially with reference to Sorais, when a Court messenger arrived with a written note, which we with some difficulty deciphered, and which was to the effect that 'the Queen Sorais commanded the attendance of the Lord Incubu in her private apartments, whither he would be conducted by the bearer'.

'Oh my word!' groaned Sir Henry. 'Can't you go instead, old fellow?'

'Not if I know it,' I said with vigour. 'I had rather face a wounded elephant with a shotgun. Take care of your own business, my boy. If you will be so fascinating you must take the consequences. I would not be in your place for an empire.'

'You remind me of when I was going to be flogged at school and the other boys came to console me,' he said gloomily. 'What right has this Queen to command my attendance, I should like to know? I won't go.'

'But you must; you are one of her officers and bound to obey her, and she knows it. And after all it will soon be over.'

'That's just what they used to say,' he said again. 'I only hope she won't put a knife into me. I believe that she is quite capable of it.' And off he started very faintheartedly, and no wonder.

I sat and waited, and at the end of about forty-five minutes he returned, looking a good deal worse than when he went.

'Give me something to drink,' he said hoarsely.

I got him a cup of wine, and asked what was the matter.

'What is the matter? Why if ever there was trouble there's trouble now. You know when I left you? Well, I was shown straight into Sorais' private chamber, and a wonderful place it is; and there she sat, quite alone, upon a silken couch at the end of the room, playing gently upon that zither of hers. I stood before her, and for a while she took no notice of me, but kept on playing and singing a little, and very sweet music it was. At last she looked up and smiled.

' "So thou art come," she said. "I thought perchance thou hadst gone about the Queen Nyleptha's business. Thou art ever on her business, and I doubt not a good servant and a true."

'To this I merely bowed, and said I was there to receive the Queen's word.

' "Ah yes, I would talk with thee, but be thou seated. It wearies me to look so high," and she made room for me beside her on the couch, placing herself with her back against the end, so as to have a view of my face.

' "It is not meet," I said, "that I should make myself equal with the Queen."

' "I said be seated," was her answer, so I sat down, and she began to look at me with those dark eyes of hers. There she sat like an incarnate spirit of beauty, hardly talking at all, and when she did, very low, but all the while looking at me. There was a white flower in her black hair, and I tried to keep my eyes on it and count the petals, but it was of no use. At last, whether it was her gaze, or the perfume in her hair, or what I do not know, but I almost felt as though I was being mesmerised. At last she roused herself.

' "Incubu," she said, "lovest thou power?"

'I replied that I supposed all men loved power of one sort or another.

' "Thou shalt have it," she said. "Lovest thou wealth?"

'I said I liked wealth for what it brought.

' "Thou shalt have it," she said. "And lovest thou beauty?"

'To this I replied that I was very fond of statuary and architecture, or something silly of that sort, at which she frowned, and there was a pause. By this time my nerves were on such a stretch that I was shaking like a leaf. I knew that something awful was going to happen, but she held me under a kind of spell, and I could not help myself.

' "Incubu," she said at length, "wouldst thou be a king? Listen, wouldst thou be a king? Behold, stranger, I am minded to make thee king of all Zu-Vendis, ay and husband of Sorais of the Night. Nay, peace and hear me. To no man among my people had I thus opened out my secret heart, but thou art an outlander and therefore I speak without shame, knowing all I have to offer and how hard it had been thee to ask. See, a crown lies at thy feet, my lord Incubu, and with that fortune a woman whom some have wished to woo. Now mayst thou answer, oh my chosen, and soft shall thy words fall upon mine ears."

' "Oh Sorais," I said, "I pray thee speak not thus" – you see I had not time to pick and choose my words – "for this thing cannot be. I am betrothed to thy sister Nyleptha, oh Sorais, and I love her and her alone."

'Next moment it struck me that I had said an awful thing, and I looked up to see the results. When I spoke, Sorais' face was hidden in her hands, and as my words reached her she slowly raised it, and I shrank back dismayed. It was ashy white, and her eyes were flaming. She rose to her feet and seemed to be choking, but the awful thing was that she was so quiet about it all. Once she looked at a side table, on which lay a dagger, and from it to me, as though she thought of killing me; but she did not take it up. At last she spoke one word, and one only – "*Go!*"

'And I went, and glad enough I was to get out of it, and here I am. Give me another cup of wine, there's a good fellow, and tell me, what is to be done?'

I shook my head, for the affair was indeed serious. As one of the poets says, 'Hell hath no fury like a woman scorned', more especially if the woman is a queen and a Sorais, and indeed I feared the very worst, including imminent danger to ourselves.

'Nyleptha had better be told of this at once,' I said, 'and perhaps I had better tell her; she might receive your account with suspicion.'

'Who is captain of her guard tonight?' I went on.

'Good.'

'Very well then, there will be no chance of her being got at. Don't look surprised. I don't think that her sister would stick at that. I suppose one must tell Good of what has happened.'

'Oh, I don't know,' said Sir Henry. 'It would hurt his feelings, poor fellow! You see, he takes a lively personal interest in Sorais.'

'That's true; and after all, perhaps there is no need to tell him. He will find out the truth soon enough. Now, you mark my words, Sorais will throw in her lot with Nasta, who is sulking up in the North there, and there will be such a war as has not been known in Zu-Vendis for centuries. Look there!' and I pointed to two Court messengers, who were speeding away from the door of Sorais' private apartments. 'Now follow me,' and I ran up a stairway into an outlook tower that rose from the roof of our quarters, taking the spyglass with me, and looked out over the palace wall. The first thing we saw was one of the messengers speeding towards the Temple, bearing, without any doubt, the Queen's word to the High Priest Agon, but for the other I searched in vain. Presently, however, I spied a horseman riding furiously through the northern gate of the city, and in him I recognised the other messenger.

'Ah!' I said, 'Sorais is a woman of spirit. She is acting at once, and will strike quick and hard. You have insulted her, my boy, and the blood will flow in rivers before the stain is washed away, and yours with it, if she can get hold of you. Well, I'm off to Nyleptha. Just you stop where you are, old fellow, and try to get your nerves straight again. You'll need them all, I can tell you, unless I have observed human nature in the rough for fifty years for nothing.' And off I went accordingly.

I gained audience of the Queen without trouble. She was expecting Curtis, and was not best pleased to see my mahogany-coloured face instead.

'Is there aught wrong with my Lord, Macumazahn, that he waits not upon me? Say, is he sick?'

I said that he was well enough, and then, without further ado, I plunged into my story and told it from beginning to end. Oh, what a rage she flew into! It was a sight to see her, she looked so lovely.

'How darest thou come to me with such a tale?' she cried. 'It is a lie to say that my lord was making love to Sorais, my sister.'

'Pardon me, oh Queen,' I answered, 'I said that Sorais was making love to thy lord.'

'Spin me no spiders' webs of words. Is not the thing the same thing? The one giveth, the other taketh; but the gift passes, and what matters it which is the most guilty? Sorais! oh, I hate her – Sorais is a queen and my sister. She had not stooped so low had he not shown the way. Oh, truly hath the poet said that man is like a snake, whom to touch is poison, and whom none can hold.'

'The remark, oh Queen, is excellent, but methinks thou hast misread the poet. Nyleptha,' I went on, 'thou knowest well that thy words are empty foolishness, and that this is no time for folly.'

'How darest thou?' she broke in, stamping her foot. 'Hast my false lord sent thee to me to insult me also? Who art thou, stranger, that thou shouldst speak to me, the Queen, after this sort? How darest thou?'

'Yea, I dare. Listen. The moments which thou dost waste in idle anger may well cost thee thy crown and all of us our lives. Already Sorais' horsemen go forth and call to arms. In three days' time Nasta will rouse himself in his fastnesses like a lion in the evening, and his growling will be heard throughout the North. The "Lady of the Night" (Sorais) hath a sweet voice, and she will not sing in vain. Her banner will be borne from range to range and valley to valley, and warriors will spring up in its track like dust beneath a whirlwind; half the army will echo her war-cry; and in every town and hamlet of this wide land the priests will call out against the foreigner and will preach her cause as holy. I have spoken, oh Queen!'

Nyleptha was quite calm now; her jealous anger had passed; and putting off the character of a lovely headstrong lady, with a rapidity and completeness that distinguished her, she put on that of a queen and a woman of business. The transformation was sudden but entire.

'Thy words are very wise, Macumazahn. Forgive me my folly. Ah, what a Queen I should be if only I had no heart! To be heartless – that is to conquer all. Passion is like the lightning, it is beautiful, and it links the earth to heaven, but alas it blinds!

'And thou thinkest that my sister Sorais would levy war upon me. So be it. She shall not prevail against me. I, too, have my friends and my retainers. There are many, I say, who will shout "Nyleptha!" when my pennon runs up on peak and pinnacle, and the light of my beacon fires leaps tonight from crag to crag, bearing the message of my war. I will break her strength and scatter her armies. Eternal night shall be the portion of Sorais of the Night. Give me that parchment and the ink. So. Now summon the officer in the ante-room. He is a trusty man.'

I did as I was bid! and the man, a veteran and quiet-looking gentleman of the guard, named Kara, entered, bowing low.

'Take this parchment,' said Nyleptha; 'it is thy warrant; and guard every place of in and outgoing in the apartments of my sister Sorais, the "Lady of the Night", and a Queen of the Zu-Vendi. Let none come in and none go out, or thy life shall pay the cost.'

The man looked startled, but he merely said, 'The Queen's word be done,' and departed. Then Nyleptha sent a messenger to Sir Henry, and presently he arrived looking uncommonly uncomfortable. I thought that another outburst was about to follow, but wonderful are the ways of woman; she said not a word about Sorais and his supposed inconstancy, greeting him with a friendly nod, and stating simply that she required his advice upon high matters. All the same there was a look in her eye, and a sort of suppressed energy in her manner towards him, that makes me think that she had not forgotten the affair, but was keeping it for a private occasion.

Just after Curtis arrived the officer returned, and reported that Sorais was *gone*. The bird had flown to the Temple, stating that she was going, as was sometimes the custom among Zu-Vendi ladies of rank, to spend the night in meditation before the altar. We looked at each other significantly. The blow had fallen very soon.

Then we set to work.

Generals who could be trusted were summoned from their quarters, and as much of the State affairs as was thought desirable was told to each, strict injunctions being given to them to get all their available force together. The same was done with such of the more powerful lords as Nyleptha knew she could rely on, several of whom left that very day for distant parts of the country to gather up their tribesmen and retainers. Sealed orders were dispatched to the rulers of far-off cities, and some twenty messengers were sent off before nightfall with instructions to ride early and late till they reached the distant chiefs to whom their letters were addressed: also many spies were set to work. All the afternoon and evening we laboured, assisted by some confidential scribes, Nyleptha showing an energy and resource of mind that astonished me, and it was eight o'clock before we got back to our quarters. Here we heard from Alphonse, who was deeply aggrieved because our non-return had spoilt his dinner (for he had turned cook again now), that Good had come back from his hawking and gone on duty. As instructions had already been given to the officer of the outer guard to double the sentries at the gate, and as we had no reason to fear any immediate danger, we did not think it worth while to hunt him up and tell him anything of what had passed, which at best was, under the peculiar circumstances of the case, one of those tasks that one prefers to postpone, so after swallowing our food we turned in to get some much-needed rest. Before we did so, however, it occurred to Curtis to tell old Umslopogaas to keep a look-out in the neighbourhood of Nyleptha's private apartments. Umslopogaas was now well known about the place, and by the Queen's order allowed to pass whither he would by the guards, a permission of which he often availed himself by roaming about the palace during the still hours in a nocturnal fashion that he favoured, and which is by no means uncommon amongst Africans generally. His presence in the corridors would not, therefore, be likely to excite remark. Without any comment the Zulu took up his axe and departed, and we also departed to bed.

I seemed to have been asleep but a few minutes when I was

awakened by a peculiar sensation of uneasiness. I felt that somebody was in the room and looking at me, and instantly sat up, to see to my surprise that it was already dawn, and that there, standing at the foot of my couch and looking peculiarly grim and gaunt in the grey light, was Umslopogaas himself.

'How long hast thou been there?' I asked testily, for it is not pleasant to be aroused in such a fashion.

'Mayhap the half of an hour, Macumazahn. I have a word for thee.'

'Speak on,' I said, now wide enough awake.

'As I was bid I went last night to the place of the White Queen and hid myself behind a pillar in the second anteroom, beyond which is the sleeping-place of the Queen. Bougwan (Good) was in the first anteroom alone, and outside the curtain of that room was a sentry, but I had a mind to see if I could pass in unseen, and I did, gliding behind them both. There I waited for many hours, when suddenly I perceived a dark figure coming secretly towards me. It was the figure of a woman, and in her hand she held a dagger. Behind that figure crept another unseen by the woman. It was Bougwan following in her tracks. His shoes were off, and for so fat a man he followed very well. The woman passed me, and the starlight shone upon her face.'

'Who was it?' I asked impatiently.

'The face was the face of the "Lady of the Night", and of a truth she is well named.

'I waited, and Bougwan passed me also. Then I followed. So we went slowly and without a sound up the long chamber. First the woman, then Bougwan, and then I; and the woman saw not Bougwan, and Bougwan saw not me. At last the "Lady of the Night" came to the curtains that shut off the sleeping place of the White Queen, and put out her left hand to part them. She passed through, and so did Bougwan, and so did I. At the far end of the room is the bed of the Queen, and on it she lay very fast asleep. I could hear her breathe, and see one white arm lying on the coverlid like a streak of snow on the dry grass. The "Lady of the Night" doubled herself *thus*, and with the long knife lifted crept towards the bed. So straight did she gaze thereat that she never thought to look behind her. When she was quite close Bougwan touched her on the arm, and she caught her breath and turned, and I saw the knife flash, and heard it strike. Well was it for Bougwan that he had the skin of iron on him, or he had been pierced. Then for the first time he saw who the woman was, and without a word he fell back astonished, and unable to speak. She, too, was astonished, and spoke not, but suddenly she laid her finger on her lip, thus, and walked towards and through the curtain, and with her went Bougwan. So close did she pass to me that her dress touched me, and I was nigh to slaying her as she went. In the first outer room she spoke to Bougwan in a whisper and, clasping her hands thus, she pleaded with him, but what she said I know not. And so they passed on to the second outer room, she pleading and he shaking his head, and saying, "Nay, nay, nay". And it seemed to me that he was about to call the guard, when she stopped talking and looked at him with great eyes, and I saw that he was bewitched by her beauty. Then she stretched out her hand and he kissed it, whereon I gathered myself together to advance and take her, seeing that now had Bougwan become a woman, and no longer knew the good from the evil, when behold! she was gone.'

'Gone!' I ejaculated.

'Ay, gone, and there stood Bougwan staring at the wall like one asleep, and presently he went too, and I waited a while and came away also.'

'Art thou sure, Umslopogaas,' said I, 'that thou hast not been a dreamer this night?'

In reply he opened his left hand, and produced about three inches of a blade of a dagger of the finest steel. 'If I be, Macumazahn, behold what the dream left with me. The knife broke upon Bougwan's bosom and as I passed I picked this up in the sleeping-place of the White Queen.'

CHAPTER 18

War! Red War!

Telling Umslopogaas to wait, I tumbled into my clothes and went off with him to Sir Henry's room, where the Zulu repeated his story word for word. It was a sight to watch Curtis' face as he heard it.

'Great Heavens!' he said: 'here have I been sleeping away while Nyleptha was nearly murdered – and all through me, too. What a fiend that Sorais must be! It would have served her well if Umslopogaas had cut her down in the act.'

'Ay,' said the Zulu. 'Fear not; I should have slain her ere she struck. I was but waiting the moment.'

I said nothing, but I could not help thinking that many a thousand doomed lives would have been saved if he had meted out to Sorais the fate she meant for her sister. And, as the issue proved, I was right.

After he had told his tale Umslopogaas went off unconcernedly to get his morning meal, and Sir Henry and I fell to talking.

At first he was very bitter against Good, who, he said, was no longer to be trusted, having designedly allowed Sorais to escape by some secret stair when it was his duty to have handed her over to justice. Indeed, he spoke in the most unmeasured terms on the matter. I let him run on awhile, reflecting to myself how easy we find it to be hard on the weaknesses of others, and how tender we are to our own.

'Really, my dear fellow,' I said at length, 'one would never think, to hear you talk, that you were the man who had an interview with this same lady yesterday, and found it rather difficult to resist her fascinations, notwithstanding your ties to one of the loveliest and most loving women in the world. Now suppose it was Nyleptha who had tried to murder Sorais, and *you* had caught her, and she had pleaded with you, would you have been so very eager to hand her over to an open shame, and to death by fire? Just look at the matter through Good's eyeglass for a minute before you denounce an old friend as a scoundrel.'

He listened to this jobation submissively, and then frankly acknowledged that he had spoken hardly. It is one of the best points in Sir Henry's character that he is always ready to admit it when he is in the wrong.

But, though I spoke up thus for Good, I was not blind to the fact that, however natural his behaviour might be, it was obvious that he was being involved in a very awkward and disgraceful complication. A foul and wicked murder had been attempted, and he had let the murderess escape, and thereby, among other things, allowed her to gain a complete ascendency over himself. In fact, he was in a fair way to become her tool – and no more dreadful fate can befall a man than to become the tool of an unscrupulous woman, or indeed of any woman. There is but one end to it: when he is broken, or has served her purpose, he is thrown away – turned out on the world to hunt for his lost self-respect. Whilst I was pondering thus, and wondering what was to be done – for the whole subject was a thorny one – I suddenly heard a great clamour in the courtyard outside, and distinguished the voice of Umslopogaas and Alphonse, the former cursing furiously, and the latter yelling in terror.

Hurrying out to see what was the matter, I was met by a ludicrous sight. The little Frenchman was running up the courtyard at an extraordinary speed, and after him sped Umslopogaas like a great greyhound. Just as I came out he caught him, and, lifting him right off his legs, carried him some paces to a beautiful but very dense flowering shrub which bore a flower not unlike the gardenia, but was covered with short thorns. Next, despite his howls and struggles, he with one mighty thrust plunged poor Alphonse head first into the bush, so that nothing but the calves of his legs and heels remained in evidence. Then, satisfied with what he had done, the Zulu folded his arms and stood grimly contemplating the Frenchman's kicks, and listening to his yells, which were awful.

'What art thou doing?' I said, running up. 'Wouldst thou kill the man? Pull him out of the bush!'

With a savage grunt he obeyed, seizing the wretched Alphonse by the ankle, and with a jerk that must have nearly dislocated it, tearing him out of the heart of the shrub. Never did I see such a sight as he presented, his clothes half torn off his back, and bleeding as he was in every direction from the sharp thorns. There he lay and yelled and rolled, and there was no getting anything out of him.

At last, however, he got up and, ensconcing himself behind me, cursed old Umslopogaas by every saint in the calendar, vowing by the blood of his heroic grandfather that he would poison him, and 'have his revenge'.

At last I got to the truth of the matter. It appeared that Alphonse habitually cooked Umslopogaas's porridge, which the latter ate for breakfast in the corner of the courtyard, just as he would have done at home in Zululand, from a gourd, and with a wooden spoon. Now Umslopogaas had, like many Zulus, a great horror of fish, which he considered a species of water-snake; so Alphonse, who was as fond of playing tricks as a monkey, and who was also a consummate cook, determined to make him eat some. Accordingly he grated up a quantity of white fish very finely, and mixed it with the Zulu's porridge, who swallowed it nearly all down in ignorance of what he was eating. But, unfortunately for Alphonse, he could not restrain his joy at this sight, and came capering and peering round, till at last Umslopogaas, who was very clever in his way, suspected something, and, after a careful examination of the remains of his porridge, discovered 'the buffalo heifer's trick', and, in revenge, served him as I have said. Indeed, the little man was fortunate not to get a broken neck for his pains; for, as one would have thought, he might have learnt from the episode of his display of axemanship that 'le Monsieur noir' was an ill person to play practical jokes upon.

This incident was unimportant enough in itself, but I narrate it because it led to serious consequences. As soon as he had stanched the bleeding from his scratches and washed himself, Alphonse went off still cursing, to recover his temper, a process which I knew from experience would take a very long time. When he had gone I gave Umslopogaas a jobation and told him that I was ashamed of his behaviour.

'Ah, well, Macumazahn,' he said, 'you must be gentle with me, for here is not my place. I am weary of it, weary to death of eating and drinking, of sleeping and giving in marriage. I love not this soft life in stone houses that takes the heart out of a man, and turns his strength to water and his flesh to fat. I love not the white robes and the delicate women, the blowing of trumpets and the flying of hawks. When we fought the Masai at the kraal yonder, ah, then life was worth the living, but here is never a blow struck in anger, and I begin to think I shall go the way of my fathers and lift Inkosi-kaas no more,' and he held up the axe and gazed at it in sorrow.

'Ah,' I said, 'that is thy complaint, is it? Thou hast the blood-sickness, hast thou? And the Woodpecker wants a tree. And at thy age, too. Shame on thee! Umslopogaas.'

'Ay, Macumazahn, mine is a red trade, yet is it better and more honest than some. Better is it to slay a man in fair fight than to suck out his heart's blood in buying and selling and usury after your white fashion. Many a man have I slain, yet is there never a one that I should fear to look in the face again, ay, many are there who once were friends, and whom I should be right glad to snuff with. But there! there! thou hast thy ways, and I mine: each to his own people and his own place. The high-veldt ox will die in the fat bush country, and so is it with me, Macumazahn. I am rough, I know it, and when my blood is warm I know not what to do, but yet wilt thou be sorry when the night swallows me and I am utterly lost in blackness, for in thy heart thou lovest me, my father, Macumazahn the fox, though I be nought but a broken-down Zulu war-dog – a chief for whom there is no room in his own kraal, an outcast and a wanderer in strange places: ay, I love thee, Macumazahn, for we have grown grey together, and there is that between us that cannot be seen, and yet is too strong for breaking;' and he took his snuff-box, which was made of an old brass cartridge, from the slit in his ear where he always carried it, and handed it to me for me to help myself.

I took the pinch of snuff with some emotion. It was quite true, I was much attached to the bloodthirsty old ruffian. I do not know what was the charm of his character, but it had a charm; perhaps it was its fierce honesty and directness; perhaps one admired his almost superhuman skill and strength, or it may have been simply that he was so absolutely unique. Frankly, with all my experience of savages, I never knew a man quite like him, he was so wise and yet such a child with it all; and though it seems laughable to say so, like the hero of the Yankee parody, he 'had a tender heart'. Anyway, I was very fond of him, though I should never have thought of telling him so.

'Ay, old wolf,' I said, 'thine is a strange love. Thou wouldst split me to the chin if I stood in thy path tomorrow.'

'Thou speakest truth, Macumazahn, that would I if it came in the way of duty, but I should love thee all the same when the blow had gone fairly home. Is there any chance of some fighting here, Macumazahn?' he went on in an insinuating voice. 'Methought that what I saw last night did show that the two great Queens were vexed one with another. Else had the "Lady of the Night" not brought that dagger with her.'

I agreed with him that it showed that more or less pique and irritation existed between the ladies, and told him how things stood, and that they were quarrelling over Incubu.

'Ah, is it so?' he exclaimed, springing up in delight; 'then will there be war as surely as the rivers rise in the rains – war to the end. Women love the last blow as well as the last word, and when they fight for love they are pitiless as a wounded buffalo. See thou, Macumazahn, a woman will swim through blood to her desire, and think nought of it. With these eyes have I seen it once, and twice also. Ah, Macumazahn, we shall see this fine place of houses burning yet, and hear the battle cries come ringing up the street. After all, I have not wandered for nothing. Can this folk fight, think ye?'

Just then Sir Henry joined us, and Good arrived, too, from another direction, looking very pale and hollow-eyed. The moment Umslopogaas saw the latter he stopped his bloodthirsty talk and greeted him.

'Ah, Bougwan,' he cried, 'greeting to thee, Inkoos! Thou art surely weary. Didst thou hunt too much yesterday?' Then, without waiting for an answer, he went on – 'Listen, Bougwan, and I will tell thee a story; it is about a woman, therefore wilt thou hear it, is it not so?

'There was a man and he had a brother, and there was a woman who loved the man's brother and was beloved of the man. But the man's brother had a favourite wife and loved not the woman, and he made a mock of her. Then the woman, being very cunning and fierce-hearted for revenge, took counsel with herself and said to the man, "I love thee, and if thou wilt make war upon thy brother I will marry thee." And he knew it was a lie, yet because of his great love of the woman, who was very fair, did he listen to her words and made war. And when many people had been killed his brother sent to him, saying, "Why slayest thou me? What hurt have I done unto thee? From my youth up have I not loved thee? When thou wast little did I not nurture thee, and have we not gone down to war together and divided the cattle, girl by girl, ox by ox, and cow by cow? Why slayest thou me, my brother, son of my own mother?"

'Then the man's heart was heavy, and he knew that his path was evil, and he put aside the tempting of the woman and ceased to make war on his brother, and lived at peace in the same kraal with him. And after a time the woman came to him and said, "I have lost the past, I will be thy wife." And in his heart he knew that it was a lie and that she thought the evil thing, yet because of his love did he take her to wife.

'And the very night that they were wed, when the man was plunged into a deep sleep, did the woman arise and take his axe from his hand and creep into the hut of his brother and slay him in his rest. Then did she slink back like a gorged lioness and place the thong of the red axe back upon his wrist and go her ways.

'And at the dawning the people came shouting, "Lousta is slain in the night," and they came unto the hut of the man, and there he lay asleep and by him was the red axe. Then did they remember the war and say, "Lo! he hath of a surety slain his brother," and they would have taken and killed him, but he rose and fled swiftly, and as he fleeted by he slew the woman.

'But death could not wipe out the evil she had done, and on him rested the weight of all her sin. Therefore is he an outcast and his name a scorn among his own people; for on him, and him only, resteth the burden of her who betrayed. And, therefore, does he wander afar, without a kraal and without an ox or a wife, and therefore will he die afar like a stricken buck and his name be accursed from generation to generation, in that the people say that he slew his brother, Lousta, by treachery in the night-time.'

The old Zulu paused, and I saw that he was deeply agitated by his own story. Presently he lifted his head, which he had bowed to his breast, and went on: 'I was the man, Bougwan. Ou! *I* was that man, and now hark thou! Even as I am so wilt thou be – a tool, a plaything, an ox of burden to carry the evil deeds of another. Listen! When thou didst creep after the "Lady of the Night" *I* was hard upon thy track. When she struck thee with the knife in the sleeping place of the White Queen *I* was there also; when thou didst let her slip away like a snake in the stones *I* saw thee, and I knew that she had bewitched thee and that a true man had abandoned the truth, and he who aforetime loved a straight path had taken a crooked way. Forgive me, my father, if my words are sharp, but out of a full heart are they spoken. See her no more, so shalt thou go down with honour to the grave. Else because of the beauty of a woman that weareth as a garment of fur shalt thou be even as I am, and perchance with more cause. I have said.'

Throughout this long and eloquent address Good had been perfectly silent, but when the tale began to shape itself so aptly to his own case, he coloured up, and when he learnt that what had passed between him and Sorais had been overseen he was evidently much distressed. And now, when at last he spoke, it was in a tone of humility quite foreign to him.

'I must say,' he said, with a bitter little laugh, 'that I scarcely thought that I should live to be taught my duty by a Zulu; but it just shows what we can come to. I wonder if you fellows can understand how humiliated I feel, and the bitterest part of it is that I deserve it all. Of course I should have handed Sorais over to the guard, but I could not, and that is a fact. I let her go and I promised to say nothing, more is the shame to me. She told me that if I would side with her she would marry me and make me king of this country, but thank goodness I did find the heart to say that even to marry her I could not desert my friends. And now you can do what you like, I deserve it all. All I have to say is that I hope that you may never love a woman with all your heart and then be so sorely tempted of her,' and he turned to go.

'Look here, old fellow,' said Sir Henry, 'just stop a minute. I have a little tale to tell you too.' And he went on to narrate what had taken place on the previous day between Sorais and himself.

This was a finishing stroke to poor Good. It is not pleasant to any man to learn that he has been made a tool of, but when the circumstances are as peculiarly atrocious as in the present case, it is about as bitter a pill as anybody can be called on to swallow.

'Do you know,' he said, 'I think that between you, you fellows have about worked a cure,' and he turned and walked away, and I for one felt very sorry for him. Ah, if the moths would always carefully avoid the candle, how few burnt wings there would be!

That day was a Court day, when the Queens sat in the great hall and received petitions, discussed laws, money grants, and so forth, and thither we adjourned shortly afterwards. On our way we were joined by Good, who was looking exceedingly depressed.

When we got into the hall Nyleptha was already on her throne and proceeding with business as usual, surrounded by councillors, courtiers, lawyers, priests, and an unusually strong guard. It was, however, easy to see from the air of excitement and expectation on the faces of everybody present that nobody was paying much attention to ordinary affairs, the fact being that the knowledge that civil war was imminent had now got abroad. We saluted Nyleptha and took our accustomed places, and for a little while things went on as usual, when suddenly the trumpets began to call outside the palace, and from the great crowd that was gathered there in anticipation of some unusual event there rose a roar of '*Sorais! Sorais!*'

Then came the roll of many chariot wheels, and presently the great curtains at the end of the hall were drawn wide and through them entered the 'Lady of the Night' herself. Nor did she come alone. Preceding her was Agon, the High Priest, arrayed in his most gorgeous vestments, and on either side were other priests. The reason for their presence was obvious – coming with them it would have been sacrilege to attempt to detain her. Behind her were a number of the great lords, and behind them a small body of picked guards. A glance at Sorais herself was enough to show that her mission was of no peaceful kind, for in place of her gold embroidered 'kaf' she wore a shining tunic formed of golden scales, and on her head a little golden helmet. In her hand, too, she bore a toy spear, beautifully made and fashioned of solid silver. Up the hall she came, looking like a lioness in her conscious pride and beauty, and as she came the spectators fell back bowing and made a path for her. By the sacred stone she halted, and laying her hand on it, she cried out with a loud voice to Nyleptha on the throne, 'Hail, oh Queen!'

'All hail, my royal sister!' answered Nyleptha. 'Draw thou near. Fear not, I give thee safe conduct.'

Sorais answered with a haughty look, and swept on up the hall till she stood right before the thrones.

'A boon, oh Queen!' she cried again.

'Speak on, my sister; what is there that I can give thee who hath half our kingdom?'

'Thou canst tell me a true word – me and the people of Zu-Vendis. Art thou, or art thou not, about to take this foreign wolf,' and she pointed to Sir Henry with her toy spear, 'to be a husband to thee, and share thy bed and throne?'

Curtis winced at this, and turning towards Sorais, said to her in a low voice, 'Methinks that yesterday thou hadst other names than wolf to call me by, oh Queen!' and I saw her bite her lips as, like a danger flag, the blood flamed red upon her face. As for Nyleptha, who is nothing if not original, she, seeing that the thing was out, and that there was nothing further to be gained by concealment, answered the question in a novel and effectual manner, inspired thereto, as I firmly believe, by coquetry and a desire to triumph over her rival.

Up she rose and, descending from the throne, swept in all the glory of her royal grace on to where her lover stood. There she stopped and untwined the golden snake that was wound around her arm. Then she bade him kneel, and he dropped on one knee on the marble before her, and next, taking the golden snake with both her hands, she bent the pure soft metal round his neck, and when it was fast, deliberately kissed him on the brow and called him her 'dear lord'.

'Thou seest,' she said, when the excited murmur of the spectators had died away, addressing her sister as Sir Henry rose to his feet, 'I have put my collar round the "wolf's" neck, and behold! he shall be my watchdog, and that is my answer to thee, Queen Sorais, my sister, and to those with thee. Fear not,' she went on, smiling sweetly on her lover, and pointing to the golden snake she had twined round his massive throat, 'if my yoke be heavy, yet is it of pure gold, and it shall not gall thee.'

Then, turning to the audience, she continued in a clear proud tone, 'Ay, Lady of the Night, Lords, Priests, and People here gathered together, by this sign do I take the foreigner to husband, even here in the face of you all. What, am I a Queen, and yet not free to choose the man whom I will love? Then should I be lower than the meanest girl in all my provinces. Nay, he hath won my heart, and with it goes my hand, and throne, and all I have – ay, had he been a beggar instead of a great lord fairer and stronger than any here, and having more wisdom and knowledge of strange things, I had given him all, how much more so being what he is!' And she took his hand and gazed proudly on him, and holding it, stood there boldly facing the people. And such was her sweetness and the power and dignity of her person, and so beautiful she looked standing hand in hand there at her lover's side, so sure of him and of herself, and so ready to risk all things and endure all things for him, that most of those who saw the sight, which I am sure no one of them will ever forget, caught the fire from her eyes and the happy colour from her blushing face, and cheered her like wild things. It was a bold stroke for her to make, and it appealed to the imagination; but human nature in Zu-Vendis, as elsewhere, loves that which is bold and not afraid to break a rule, and is moreover peculiarly susceptible to appeals to its poetical side.

And so the people cheered till the roof rang; but Sorais of the

Night stood there with downcast eyes, for she could not bear to see her sister's triumph, which robbed her of the man whom she had hoped to win, and in the awfulness of her jealous anger she trembled and turned white like an aspen in the wind. I think I have said somewhere of her that she reminded me of the sea on a calm day, having the same aspect of sleeping power about her. Well, it was all awake now, and like the face of the furious ocean it awed and yet fascinated me. A really handsome woman in a royal rage is always a beautiful sight, but such beauty and such a rage I never saw combined before, and I can only say that the effect produced was well worthy of the two.

She lifted her white face, the teeth set, and there were purple rings beneath her glowing eyes. Thrice she tried to speak and thrice she failed, but at last her voice came. Raising her silver spear, she shook it, and the light gleamed from it and from the golden scales of her cuirass.

'And thinkest thou, Nyleptha,' she said in notes which pealed through the great hall like a clarion, 'thinkest thou that I, Sorais, a Queen of the Zu-Vendi, will brook that this base outlander shall sit upon my father's throne and rear up half-breeds to fill the place of the great House of the Stairway? Never! never! while there is life in my bosom and a man to follow me and a spear to strike with. Who is on my side? Who?

'Now hand thou over this foreign wolf and those who came hither to prey with him to the doom of fire, for have they not committed the deadly sin against the sun? or, Nyleptha, I give thee War – red War! Ay, I say to thee that the path of thy passion shall be marked out by the blazing of thy towns and watered with the blood of those who cleave to thee. On thy head rest the burden of the deed, and in thy ears ring the groans of the dying and the cries of the widows and those who are left fatherless for ever and for ever.

'I tell thee I will tear thee, Nyleptha, the White Queen, from thy throne, and that thou shalt be hurled – ay, hurled even from the topmost stair of the great way to the foot thereof, in that thou hast covered the name of the House of him who built it with black shame. And I tell ye strangers – all save Bougwan, whom because thou didst do me a service I will save alive if thou wilt leave these men and follow me' (here poor Good shook his head vigorously and ejaculated 'Can't be done' in English) – 'that I will wrap you in sheets of gold and hang you yet alive in chains from the four golden trumpets of the four angels that fly east and west and north and south from the giddiest pinnacles of the Temple, so that ye may be a token and a warning to the land. And as for thee, Incubu, thou shalt die in yet another fashion that I will not tell thee now.'

She ceased, panting for breath, for her passion shook her like a storm, and a murmur, partly of horror and partly of admiration, ran through the hall. Then Nyleptha answered calmly and with dignity: 'Ill would it become my place and dignity, oh sister, so to speak as thou hast spoken and so to threat as thou hast threatened. Yet if thou wilt make war, then will I strive to bear up against thee, for if my hand seem soft, yet shalt thou find it of iron when it grips thine armies by the throat. Sorais, I fear thee not. I weep for that which thou wilt bring upon our people and on thyself, but for myself I say – I fear thee not. Yet thou, who but yesterday didst strive to win my lover and my lord from me, whom today thou dost call a "foreign wolf", to be *thy* lover and *thy* lord' (here there was an immense sensation in the hall), 'thou who but last night, as I have learnt but since thou didst enter here, didst creep like a snake into my sleeping-place – ay, even by a secret way, and wouldst have foully murdered me, thy sister, as I lay asleep – '

'It is false, it is false!' rang out Agon's and a score of other voices.

'It is *not* false,' said I, producing the broken point of the dagger and holding it up. 'Where is the haft from which this flew, oh Sorais?'

'It is not false,' cried Good, determined at last to act like a loyal man. 'I took the Lady of the Night by the White Queen's bed, and on my breast the dagger broke.'

'Who is on my side?' cried Sorais, shaking her silver spear, for she saw that public sympathy was turning against her. 'What, Bougwan, thou comest not?' she said, addressing Good, who was standing close to her, in a low, concentrated voice. 'Thou pale-souled fool, for a reward thou shalt eat out thy heart with love of me and not be satisfied, and thou mightest have been my husband and a king! At least I hold *thee* in chains that cannot be broken.

'*War! War! War!*' she cried. 'Here, with my hand upon the sacred stone that shall endure, so runs the prophecy, till the Zu-Vendi set their necks beneath an alien yoke, I declare war to the end. Who follows Sorais of the Night to victory and honour?'

Instantly the whole concourse began to break up in indescribable confusion. Many present hastened to throw in their lot with the 'Lady of the Night', but some came from her following to us. Amongst the former was an under officer of Nyleptha's own guard, who suddenly turned and made a run for the doorway through which Sorais' people were already passing. Umslopogaas, who was present and had taken the whole scene in, seeing with admirable presence of mind that if this soldier got away others would follow his example, seized the man, who drew his sword and struck at him. Thereon the Zulu sprang back with a wild shout, and, avoiding the sword cuts, began to peck at his foe with his terrible axe, till in a few seconds the man's fate overtook him and he fell with a clash heavily and quite dead upon the marble floor.

This was the first blood spilt in the war.

'Shut the gates,' I shouted, thinking that we might perhaps catch Sorais so, and not being troubled with the idea of committing sacrilege. But the order came too late, her guards were already passing through them, and in another minute the streets echoed with the furious galloping of horses and the rolling of her chariots.

So, drawing half the people after her, Sorais was soon passing like a whirlwind through the Frowning City on her road to her headquarters at M'Arstuna, a fortress situated a hundred and thirty miles to the north of Milosis.

And after that the city was alive with the endless tramp of regiments and preparations for the gathering war, and old Umslopogaas once more began to sit in the sunshine and go through a show of sharpening Inkosi-kaas's razor edge.

CHAPTER 19

A Strange Wedding

One person, however, did not succeed in getting out in time before the gates were shut, and that was the High Priest Agon, who, as we had every reason to believe, was Sorais' great ally, and the heart and soul of her party. This cunning and ferocious old man had not forgiven us for those hippopotami, or rather that was what he said. What he meant was that he would never brook the introduction of our wider ways of thought and foreign learning and influence while there was a possibility of stamping us out. Also he knew that we possessed a different system of religion, and no doubt was in daily terror of our attempting to introduce it into Zu-Vendis. One day he asked me if we had any religion in our country, and I told him that so far as I could remember we had ninety-five different ones. You might have knocked him down with a feather, and really it is difficult not to pity a high priest of a well-established cult who is haunted by the possible approach of one or all of ninety-five new religions.

When we knew that Agon was caught, Nyleptha, Sir Henry, and I discussed what was to be done with him. I was for closely incarcerating him, but Nyleptha shook her head, saying that it would produce a disastrous effect throughout the country. 'Ah!' she added, with a stamp of her foot, 'if I win and am once really Queen, I will break the power of those priests, with their rites and revels and dark secret ways.' I only wished that old Agon could have heard her, it would have frightened him.

'Well,' said Sir Henry, 'if we are not to imprison him, I suppose that we may as well let him go. He is of no use here.'

Nyleptha looked at him in a curious sort of way, and said in a dry little voice, 'Thinkest thou so, my lord?'

'Eh?' said Curtis. 'No, I do not see what is the use of keeping him.'

She said nothing, but continued looking at him in a way that was as shy as it was sweet.

Then at last he understood.

'Forgive me, Nyleptha,' he said, rather tremulously. 'Dost thou mean that thou wilt marry me, even now?'

'Nay, I know not; let my lord say,' was her rapid answer; 'but if my lord wills, the priest is there and the altar is there' – pointing to the entrance to a private chapel – 'and am I not ready to do the will of my lord? Listen, oh my lord! In eight days or less thou must leave me and go down to war, for thou shalt lead my armies, and in war – men sometimes fall, and so I would for a little space have had thee all my own, if only for memory's sake;' and the tears overflowed her lovely eyes and rolled down her face like heavy drops of dew down the red heart of a rose.

'Mayhap, too,' she went on, 'I shall lose my crown, and with my crown my life and thine also. Sorais is very strong and very bitter, and if she prevails she will not spare. Who can read the future? Happiness is the world's White Bird, that alights seldom, and flies fast and far till one day he is lost in the clouds. Therefore should we hold him fast if by any chance he rests for a little space upon our hand. It is not wise to neglect the present for the future, for who knows what the future will be, Incubu? Let us pluck our flowers while the dew is on them, for when the sun is up they wither and on the morrow will others bloom that we shall never see.' And she lifted her sweet face to him and smiled into his eyes, and once more I felt a curious pang of jealousy and turned and went away. They never took much notice of whether I was there or not, thinking, I suppose, that I was an old fool, and that it did not matter one way or the other, and really I believe that they were right.

So I went back to our quarters and ruminated over things in general, and watched old Umslopogaas whetting his axe outside the window as a vulture whets his beak beside a dying ox.

And in about an hour's time Sir Henry came tearing over, looking very radiant and wildly excited, and found Good and myself and even Umslopogaas, and asked us if we should like to assist at a real wedding. Of course we said yes, and off we went to the chapel, where we found Agon looking as sulky as any High Priest possibly could, and no wonder. It appeared that he and Nyleptha had a slight difference of opinion about the coming ceremony. He had flatly refused to celebrate it, or to allow any of his priests to do so, whereupon Nyleptha became very angry and told him that she, as Queen, was head of the Church, and meant to be obeyed. Indeed, she played the part of a Zu-Vendi Henry the Eighth to perfection, and insisted that, if she wanted to be married, she would be married, and that he should marry her.*

He still refused to go through the ceremony, so she clinched her argument thus – 'Well, I cannot execute a High Priest, because there is an absurd prejudice against it, and I cannot imprison him because all his subordinates would raise a crying that would bring the stars down on Zu-Vendis and crush it; but I *can* leave him to contemplate the altar of the Sun without anything to eat, because that is his natural vocation, and if thou wilt not marry me, O Agon! thou shalt be placed before the altar yonder with nought but a little water till such time as thou hast reconsidered the matter.'

Now, as it happened, Agon had been hurried away that morning without his breakfast, and was already exceedingly hungry, so he presently modified his views and consented to marry them, saying at the same time that he washed his hands of all responsibility in the matter.

So it chanced that presently, attended only by two of her favourite maidens, came the Queen Nyleptha, with happy blushing face and downcast eyes, dressed in pure white, without embroidery of any sort, as seems to be the fashion on these occasions in most countries of the world. She did not wear a single ornament, even her gold circlets were removed, and I thought that if possible she looked more lovely than ever without them, as really superbly beautiful women do.

---

* In Zu-Vendis members of the Royal House can only be married by the High Priest or a formally appointed deputy. A.Q.

She came, curtseyed low to Sir Henry, and then took his hand and led him up before the altar, and after a little pause, in a slow, clear voice uttered the following words, which are customary in Zu-Vendis if the bride desires and the man consents: 'Thou dost swear by the Sun that thou wilt take no other woman to wife unless I lay my hand upon her and bid her come?'

'I swear it,' answered Sir Henry; adding in English, 'One is quite enough for me.'

Then Agon, who had been sulking in a corner near the altar, came forward and gabbled off something into his beard at such a rate that I could not follow it, but it appeared to be an invocation to the Sun to bless the union and make it fruitful. I observed that Nyleptha listened very closely to every word, and afterwards discovered that she was afraid lest Agon should play her a trick, and by going through the invocations backwards divorce them instead of marry them. At the end of the invocations they were asked, as in our service, if they took each other for husband and wife, and on their assenting they kissed each other before the altar, and the service was over, so far as their rites were concerned. But it seemed to me that there was yet something wanting, and so I produced a Prayer Book, which has, together which the 'Ingoldsby Legends', that I often read when I lie awake at night, accompanied me in all my later wanderings. I gave it to my poor boy Harry years ago, and after his death I found it among his things and took it back again.

'Curtis,' I said, 'I am not a clergyman, and I do not know if what I am going to propose is allowable – I know it is not legal – but if you and the Queen have no objection I should like to read the English marriage service over you. It is a solemn step which you are taking, and I think that you ought, so far as circumstances will allow, to give it the sanction of your own religion.'

'I have thought of that,' he said, 'and I wish you would. I do not feel half married yet.'

Nyleptha raised no objection, fully understanding that her husband wished to celebrate the marriage according to the rites prevailing in his own country, and so I set to work and read the service, from 'Dearly beloved' to 'amazement', as well as I could;

and when I came to 'I, Henry, take thee, Nyleptha,' I translated, and also 'I, Nyleptha, take thee, Henry,' which she repeated after me very well. Then Sir Henry took a plain gold ring from his little finger and placed it on hers, and so on to the end. The ring had been Curtis' mother's wedding-ring, and I could not help thinking how astonished the dear old Yorkshire lady would have been if she could have foreseen that her wedding-ring was to serve a similar purpose for Nyleptha, a Queen of the Zu-Vendi.

As for Agon, he was with difficulty kept calm while this second ceremony was going on, for he at once understood that it was religious in its nature, and doubtless bethought him of the ninety-five new faiths which loomed so ominously in his eyes. Indeed, he at once set me down as a rival High Priest, and hated me accordingly. However, in the end off he went, positively bristling with indignation, and I knew that we might look out for danger from his direction.

And off went Good and I, and old Umslopogaas also, leaving the happy pair to themselves, and very low we all felt. Marriages are supposed to be cheerful things, but my experience is that they are very much the reverse to everybody, except perhaps the two people chiefly interested. They mean the breaking-up of so many old ties as well as the undertaking of so many new ones, and there is always something sad about the passing away of the old order. Now to take this case for instance: Sir Henry Curtis is the best and kindest fellow and friend in the world, but he has never been quite the same since that little scene in the chapel. It is always Nyleptha this and Nyleptha that – Nyleptha, in short, from morning till night in one way or another, either expressed or understood. And as for the old friends – well, of course they have taken the place that old friends ought to take, and which ladies are as a rule very careful to see they do take when a man marries, and that is, the second place. Yes, he would be angry if anybody said so, but it is a fact for all that. He is not quite the same, and Nyleptha is very sweet and very charming, but I think that she likes him to understand that she has married *him*, and not Quatermain, Good, and Co. But there! what is the use of grumbling? It is all very right and proper, as any married lady would have no difficulty in explaining, and I am a selfish, jealous old man, though I hope I never show it.

So Good and I went and ate in silence and then indulged in an extra fine flagon of old Zu-Vendian to keep our spirits up, and presently one of our attendants came and told a story that gave us something to think about.

It may, perhaps, be remembered that, after his quarrel with Umslopogaas, Alphonse had gone off in an exceedingly ill temper to sulk over his scratches. Well, it appears that he walked right past the Temple to the Sun, down the wide road on the further side of the slope it crowns, and thence on into the beautiful park, or pleasure gardens, which are laid out just beyond the outer wall. After wandering about there for a little he started to return, but was met near the outer gate by Sorais' train of chariots, which were galloping furiously along the great northern road. When she caught sight of Alphonse, Sorais halted her train and called to him. On approaching he was instantly seized and dragged into one of the chariots and carried off, 'crying out loudly', as our informant said, and as from my general knowledge of him I can well believe.

At first I was much puzzled to know what object Sorais could have had in carrying off the poor little Frenchman. She could hardly stoop so low as to try to wreak her fury on one whom she knew was only a servant. At last, however, an idea occurred to me. We three were, as I think I have said, much revered by the people of Zu-Vendis at large, both because we were the first strangers they had ever seen, and because we were supposed to be the possessors of almost supernatural wisdom. Indeed, though Sorais' cry against the 'foreign wolves' – or, to translate it more accurately, 'foreign hyenas' – was sure to go down very well with the nobles and the priests, it was not as we learnt, likely to be particularly effectual amongst the bulk of the population. The Zu-Vendi people, like the Athenians of old, are ever seeking for some new thing, and just because we were so new our presence was on the whole acceptable to them. Again, Sir Henry's magnificent personal appearance made a deep impression upon a race who possess a greater love of beauty than any other I have ever been acquainted with. Beauty may be prized in other countries, but in Zu-Vendis it is almost worshipped, as indeed the national love of statuary shows. The people said openly in the market-places that there was not a man in the country to touch Curtis in personal appearance, as with the exception of Sorais there was no woman who could compete with Nyleptha, and that therefore it was meet that they should marry; and that he had been sent by the Sun as a husband for their Queen. Now, from all this it will be seen that the outcry against us was to a considerable extent fictitious, and nobody knew it better than Sorais herself. Consequently it struck me that it might have occurred to her that down in the country and among the country people, it would be better to place the reason of her conflict with her sister upon other and more general grounds than Nyleptha's marriage with the stranger. It would be easy in a land where there had been so many civil wars to rake out some old cry that would stir up the recollection of buried feuds, and, indeed, she soon found an effectual one. This being so, it was of great importance to her to have one of the strangers with her whom she could show to the common people as a great Outlander, who had been so struck by the justice of her cause that he had elected to leave his companions and follow her standard.

This, no doubt, was the cause of her anxiety to get a hold of Good, whom she would have used till he ceased to be of service and then cast off. But Good having drawn back she grasped at the opportunity of securing Alphonse, who was not unlike him in personal appearance though smaller, no doubt with the object of showing him off in the cities and country as the great Bougwan himself. I told Good that I thought that that was her plan, and his face was a sight to see – he was so horrified at the idea.

'What,' he said, 'dress up that little wretch to represent me? Why, I shall have to get out of the country! My reputation will be ruined for ever.'

I consoled him as well as I could, but it is not pleasant to be personated all over a strange country by an arrant little coward, and I can quite sympathise with his vexation.

Well, that night Good and I messed as I have said in solitary

grandeur, feeling very much as though we had just returned from
burying a friend instead of marrying one, and next morning the
work began in good earnest. The messages and orders which had
been despatched by Nyleptha two days before now began to take
effect, and multitudes of armed men came pouring into the city.
We saw, as may be imagined, but very little of Nyleptha and not
too much of Curtis during those next few days, but Good and I sat
daily with the council of generals and loyal lords, drawing up
plans of action, arranging commissariat matters, the distribution
of commands, and a hundred and one other things. Men came in
freely, and all the day long the great roads leading to Milosis were
spotted with the banners of lords arriving from their distant
places to rally round Nyleptha.

After the first few days it became clear that we should be able to
take the field with about forty thousand infantry and twenty
thousand cavalry, a very respectable force considering how short
was the time we had to collect it, and that about half the regular
army had elected to follow Sorais.

But if our force was large, Sorais' was, according to the reports
brought in day by day by our spies, much larger. She had taken up
her headquarters at a very strong town called M'Arstuna, situated,
as I have said, to the north of Milosis, and all the countryside was
flocking to her standard. Nasta had poured down from his
highlands and was on his way to join her with no less than twenty-
five thousand of his mountaineers, the most terrible soldiers to
face in all Zu-Vendis. Another mighty lord, named Belusha, who
lived in the great horse-breeding district, had come in with twelve
thousand cavalry, and so on. Indeed, what between one thing and
another, it seemed certain that she would gather a fully armed
host of nearly one hundred thousand men.

And then came news that Sorais was proposing to break up her
camp and march on the Frowning City itself, desolating the
country as she came. Thereon arose the question whether it
would be best to meet her at Milosis or to go out and give her
battle. When our opinion was asked upon the subject, Good and I
unhesitatingly gave it in favour of an advance. If we were to shut
ourselves up in the city and wait to be attacked, it seemed to us

that our inaction would be set down to fear. It is so important, especially on an occasion of this sort, when a very little will suffice to turn men's opinions one way or the other, to be up and doing something. Ardour for a cause will soon evaporate if the cause does not move but sits down to conquer. Therefore we cast our vote for moving out and giving battle in the open, instead of waiting till we were drawn from our walls like a badger from a hole.

Sir Henry's opinion coincided with ours, and so, needless to say, did that of Nyleptha, who, like a flint, was always ready to flash out fire. A great map of the country was brought and spread out before her. About thirty miles this side of M'Arstuna, where Sorais lay, and ninety odd miles from Milosis, the road ran over a neck of land some two and a half miles in width, and flanked on either side by forest-clad hills which, without being lofty, would, if the road were blocked, be quite impracticable for a great baggage-laden army to cross. She looked earnestly at the map, and then, with a quickness of perception that in some women amounts almost to an instinct, she laid her finger upon this neck of rising ground, and turning to her husband, said, with a proud air of confidence and a toss of the golden head – 'Here shalt thou meet Sorais' armies. I know the spot, here shalt thou meet them, and drive them before thee like dust before the storm.'

But Curtis looked grave and said nothing.

CHAPTER 20

The Battle of the Pass

It was on the third morning after this incident of the map that Sir Henry and I started. With the exception of a small guard, all the great host had moved on the night before, leaving the Frowning City very silent and empty. Indeed, it was found impossible to leave any garrison with the exception of a personal guard for Nyleptha, and about a thousand men who from sickness or one cause or another were unable to proceed with the army; but as Milosis was practically impregnable, and as our enemy was in front of and not behind us, this did not so much matter.

Good and Umslopogaas had gone on with the army, but Nyleptha accompanied Sir Henry and myself to the city gates, riding a magnificent white horse called Daylight, which was supposed to be the fleetest and most enduring animal in Zu-Vendis. Her face bore traces of recent weeping, but there were no tears in her eyes now, indeed she was bearing up bravely against what must have been a bitter trial to her. At the gate she reined in her horse and bade us farewell. On the previous day she had reviewed and addressed the officers of the great army, speaking to them such high, eloquent words, and expressing so complete a confidence in their valour and in their ultimate victory, that she quite carried their hearts away, and as she rode from rank to rank they cheered her till the ground shook. And now today the same mood seemed to be on her.

'Fare thee well, Macumazahn!' she said. 'Remember, I trust to thy wits, which are as a needle to a spear-handle compared to those of my people, to save us from Sorais. I know that thou wilt do thy duty.'

I bowed and explained to her my horror of fighting, and my fear lest I should lose my head, at which she laughed gently and turned to Curtis.

'Fare thee well, my lord!' she said. 'Come back with victory, and as a king, or on thy soldiers' spears.'*

Sir Henry said nothing, but turned his horse to go; perhaps he had a bit of a lump in his throat. One gets over it afterwards, but these sort of partings are trying when one has only been married a week.

'Here,' added Nyleptha, 'will I greet thee when ye return in triumph. And now, my lords, once more, farewell!'

Then we rode on, but when we had gone a hundred and fifty yards or so, we turned and perceived her still sitting on her horse at the same spot, and looking out after us beneath her hand, and that was the last we saw of her. About a mile farther on, however, we heard galloping behind us, and looking round, saw a mounted soldier coming towards us, leading Nyleptha's matchless steed – Daylight.

'The Queen sends the white stallion as a farewell gift to her Lord Incubu, and bids me tell my lord that he is the fleetest and most enduring horse in all the land,' said the soldier, bending to his saddle-bow before us.

At first Sir Henry did not want to take the horse, saying that he was too good for such rough work, but I persuaded him to do so, thinking that Nyleptha would be hurt if he did not. Little did I guess at the time what service that noble horse would render in our sorest need. It is curious to look back and realise upon what trivial and apparently coincidental circumstances great events frequently turn as easily and naturally as a door on its hinges.

Well, we took the horse, and a beauty he was, it was a perfect pleasure to see him move, and Curtis having sent back his greetings and thanks, we proceeded on our journey.

By midday we overtook the rearguard of the great army of which Sir Henry then formally took over the command. It was a heavy responsibility, and it oppressed him very much, but the

---

* Alluding to the Zu-Vendi custom of carrying dead officers on a frame-work of spears.

Queen's injunctions on the point were such as did not admit of being trifled with. He was beginning to find out that greatness has its responsibilities as well as its glories.

Then we marched on without meeting with any opposition, almost indeed without seeing anybody, for the populations of the towns and villages along our route had for the most part fled, fearing lest they should be caught between the two rival armies and ground to powder like grain between the upper and the nether stones.

On the evening of the fourth day, for the progress of so great a multitude was necessarily slow, we camped two miles this side of the neck or ridge I have spoken of, and our outposts brought us word that Sorais with all her power was rolling down upon us, and had pitched her camp that night ten miles the farther side of the neck.

Accordingly before dawn we sent forward fifteen hundred cavalry to seize the position. Scarcely had they occupied it, however, before they were attacked by about as many of Sorais' horsemen, and a very smart little cavalry fight ensued, with a loss to us of about thirty men killed. On the advance of our supports, however, Sorais' force drew off, carrying their dead and wounded with them.

The main body of the army reached the neck about dinner-time, and I must say that Nyleptha's judgement had not failed her, it was an admirable place to give battle in, especially to a superior force.

The road ran down a mile or more, through ground too broken to admit of the handling of any considerable force, till it reached the crest of a great green wave of land, that rolled down a gentle slope to the banks of a little stream, and then rolled away again up a still gentler slope to the plain beyond, the distance from the crest of the land-wave down to the stream being a little over half a mile, and from the stream up to the plain beyond a trifle less. The length of this wave of land at its highest point, which corresponded exactly with the width of the neck of the land between the wooded hills, was about two miles and a quarter, and it was protected on either side by dense, rocky, bush-clad ground, that afforded a most valuable cover to the flanks of the army and rendered it almost impossible for them to be turned.

It was on the hither slope of this neck of land that Curtis encamped his army in the same formation that he had, after consultation with the various generals, Good, and myself, determined that they should occupy in the great pitched battle which now appeared to be imminent.

Our force of sixty thousand men was, roughly speaking, divided as follows. In the centre was a dense body of twenty thousand foot-soldiers, armed with spears, swords, and hippopotamus-hide shields, breast and back plates.* These formed the chest of the army, and were supported by five thousand foot, and three thousand horse in reserve. On either side of this chest were stationed seven thousand horse arranged in deep, majestic squadrons; and beyond and on either side but slightly in front of them again were two bodies, each numbering about seven thousand five hundred spearmen, forming the right and left wings of the army, and each supported by a contingent of some fifteen hundred cavalry. This makes in all sixty thousand men.

Curtis commanded in chief, I was in command of the seven thousand horse between the chest and right wing, which was commanded by Good, and the other battalions and squadrons were entrusted to Zu-Vendis generals.

Scarcely had we taken up our positions before Sorais' vast army began to swarm on the opposite slope about a mile in front of us, till the whole place seemed alive with the multitude of her spearpoints, and the ground shook with the tramp of her battalions. It was evident that the spies had not exaggerated; we were outnumbered by at least a third. At first we expected that Sorais was going to attack us at once, as the clouds of cavalry which hung upon her flanks executed some threatening demonstrations, but she thought better of it, and there was no fight that day. As for the formation of her great forces I cannot now describe it with accuracy, and it would only serve to bewilder if I did, but I may say, generally, that in its leading features it

* The Zu-Vendi people do not use bows.   A.Q.

resembled our own, only her reserve was much greater.

Opposite our right wing, and forming Sorais' left wing, was a great army of dark, wild-looking men, armed with sword and shield only, which, I was informed, was composed of Nasta's twenty-five thousand savage hillsmen.

'My word, Good,' said I, when I saw them, 'you will catch it tomorrow when those gentlemen charge!' whereat Good not unnaturally looked rather anxious.

All day we watched and waited, but nothing happened, and at last night fell, and a thousand watch-fires twinkled brightly on the slopes, to wane and die one by one like the stars they resembled. As the hours wore on, the silence gradually gathered more deeply over the opposing hosts.

It was a very wearying night, for in addition to the endless things that had to be attended to, there was our gnawing suspense to reckon with. The fray which tomorrow would witness would be so vast, and the slaughter so awful, that stout indeed must the heart have been that was not overwhelmed at the prospect. And when I thought of all that hung upon it, I own I felt ill, and it made me very sad to reflect that these mighty forces were gathered for destruction, simply to gratify the jealous anger of a woman. This was the hidden power which was to send those dense masses of cavalry, flashing like human thunderbolts across the plain, and to roll together the fierce battalions as clouds when hurricane meets hurricane. It was a dreadful thought, and set one wondering about the responsibilities of the great ones of the earth. Deep into the night we sat, with pale faces and heavy hearts, and took counsel, whilst the sentries tramped up and down, down and up, and the armed and plumed generals came and went, grim and shadow-like.

And so the time wore away, till everything was ready for the coming slaughter; and I lay down and thought, and tried to get a little rest, but could not sleep for fear of the morrow – for who could say what the morrow would bring forth? Misery and death, this was certain; beyond that we knew not, and I confess I was very much afraid. But as I realised then, it is useless to question that eternal Sphinx, the future. From day to day she reads aloud the riddles of the yesterday, of which the puzzled wordlings of all ages have not answered one, nor ever will, guess they never so wildly or cry they never so loud.

And so at length I gave up wondering, being forced humbly to leave the issue in the balancing hands of Providence and the morrow.

And at last up came the red sun, and the huge camps awoke with a clash, and a roar, and gathered themselves together for battle. It was a beautiful and awe-inspiring scene, and old Umslopogaas, leaning on his axe, contemplated it with grim delight.

'Never have I seen the like, Macumazahn, never,' he said. 'The battles of my people are as the play of children to what this will be. Thinkest thou that they will fight it out?'

'Ay,' I answered sadly, 'to the death. Content thyself, "Wood-pecker", for once shalt thou peck thy fill.'

Time went on, and still there was no sign of an attack. A force of cavalry crossed the brook, indeed, and rode slowly along our front, evidently taking stock of our position and numbers. With this we did not attempt to interfere, as our decision was to stand strictly on the defensive, and not to waste a single man. The men breakfasted and stood to their arms, and the hours wore on. About midday, when the men were eating their dinner, for we thought they would fight better on full stomachs, a shout of 'Sorais, Sorais' arose like thunder from the enemy's extreme right, and taking the glass, I was able to clearly distinguish the 'Lady of the Night' herself, surrounded by a glittering staff, and riding slowly down the lines of her battalions. And as she went, that mighty, thundering shout rolled along before her like the rolling of ten thousand chariots, or the roaring of the ocean when the gale turns suddenly and carries the noise of it to the listeners' ears, till the earth shook, and the air was full of the majesty of sound.

Guessing that this was a prelude to the beginning of the battle, we remained still and made ready.

We had not long to wait. Suddenly, like flame from a cannon's mouth, out shot two great tongue-like forces of cavalry, and came charging down the slope towards the little stream, slowly at first, but gathering speed as they came. Before they got to the stream, orders reached me from Sir Henry, who evidently feared that the shock of such a charge, if allowed to fall unbroken upon our infantry, would be too much for them, to send five thousand sabres to meet the force opposite to me, at the moment when it began to mount the stiffest of the rise about four hundred yards from our lines. This I did, remaining behind myself with the rest of my men.

Off went the five thousand horsemen, drawn up in a wedge-like form, and I must say that the general in command handled them very ably. Starting at a hand gallop, for the first three hundred yards he rode straight at the tip of the tongue-shaped mass of cavalry which, numbering, so far as I could judge, about eight thousand sabres, was advancing to charge us. Then he suddenly swerved to the right and put on the pace, and I saw the great wedge curl round, and before the foe could check himself and turn to meet it, strike him about halfway down his length, with a crashing rending sound, like that of the breaking-up of vast sheets of ice. In sank the great wedge, into his heart, and as it cut its way hundreds of horsemen were thrown up on either side of it, just as the earth is thrown up by a ploughshare, or more like still, as the foaming water curls over beneath the bows of a rushing ship. In, yet in, vainly does the tongue twist its ends round in agony, like an injured snake, and strive to protect its centre; still farther in, by Heaven! right through, and so, amid cheer after cheer from our watching thousands, back again upon the severed ends, beating them down, driving them as a gale drives spray, till at last, amidst the rushing of hundreds of riderless horses, the flashing of swords, and the victorious clamour of their pursuers, the great force crumples up like an empty glove, then turns and gallops pell-mell for safety back to its own lines.

I do not think it reached them more than two-thirds as strong as it went out ten minutes before. The lines which were now advancing to the attack, opened and swallowed them up, and my force returned, having only suffered a loss of about five hundred men – not much, I thought, considering the fierceness of the struggle. I could also see that the opposing bodies of cavalry on our left wing were drawing back, but how the fight went with them I do not quite know. It is as much as I can do to describe what took place immediately around me.

By this time the dense masses of the enemy's left, composed almost entirely of Nasta's swordsmen, were across the little stream, and with alternate yells of 'Nasta' and 'Sorais', with dancing banners and gleaming swords, were swarming up towards us like ants.

Again I received orders to try and check this movement, and also the main advance against the chest of our army, by means of cavalry charges, and this I did to the best of my ability, by continually sending squadrons of about a thousand sabres out against them. These squadrons did the enemy much damage, and it was a glorious sight to see them flash down the hillside, and bury themselves like a living knife in the heart of the foe. But, also, we lost many men, for after the experience of a couple of these charges, which had drawn a sort of bloody St Andrew's cross of dead and dying through the centre of Nasta's host, our foes no longer attempted to offer an unyielding front to their irresistible weight, but opened out to let the rush go through, throwing themselves on the ground and hamstringing hundreds of horses as they passed.

And so, notwithstanding all that we could do, the enemy drew nearer, till at last he hurled himself upon Good's force of seven thousand five hundred regulars, who were drawn up to receive them in three strong squares. About the same time, too, an awful and heart-shaking roar told me that the main battle had closed in on the centre and extreme left. I raised myself in my stirrups and looked down to my left; so far as the eye could see there was a long dazzling shimmer of steel as the sun glanced upon falling sword and thrusting spear.

To and fro swung the contending lines in that dread struggle, now giving way, now gaining a little in the mad yet ordered confusion of attack and defence. But it was as much as I could do to keep count of what was happening to our own wing; and, as for the moment the cavalry had fallen back under cover of Good's three squares, I had a fair view of this.

Nasta's wild swordsmen were now breaking in red waves against the sullen rock-like squares. Time after time did they yell out their war-cries, and hurl themselves furiously against the long triple ridges of spear points, only to be rolled back as billows are when they meet the cliff.

And so for four long hours the battle raged almost without a pause, and at the end of that time, if we had gained nothing we had lost nothing. Two attempts to turn our left flank by forcing a way through the wood by which it was protected had been defeated; and as yet Nasta's swordsmen had, notwithstanding their desperate efforts, entirely failed to break Good's three squares, though they had thinned their numbers by quite a third.

As for the chest of the army where Sir Henry was with his staff and Umslopogaas, it had suffered dreadfully, but it had held its own with honour, and the same may be said of our left battle.

At last the attacks slackened, and Sorais' army drew back, having, I began to think, had enough of it. On this point, however, I was soon undeceived, for splitting up her cavalry into comparatively small squadrons, she charged us furiously with them, all along the line, and then once more sullenly rolled her tens of thousands of sword and spearmen down upon our weakened squares and squadrons; Sorais herself directing the movement, as fearless as a lioness heading the main attack. On they came like an avalanche – I saw her golden helm gleaming in the van – our counter charges of cavalry entirely failing to check their forward sweep. Now they had struck us, and our centre bent in like a bow beneath the weight of their rush – it parted, and had not the ten thousand men in reserve charged down to its support it must have been utterly destroyed. As for Good's three squares, they were swept backwards like boats upon an incoming tide, and the foremost one was burst into and lost half its remaining men. But the effort was too fierce and terrible to last. Suddenly the battle came, as it were, to a turning-point, and for a minute or two stood still.

Then it began to move towards Sorais' camp. Just then, too, Nasta's fierce and almost invincible highlanders, either because they were disheartened by their losses or by way of a ruse, fell back, and the remains of Good's gallant squares, leaving the positions they had held for so many hours, cheered wildly, and rashly followed them down the slope, whereon the swarms of swordsmen turned to envelop them, and once more flung themselves upon them with a yell. Taken thus on every side, what remained of the first square was quickly destroyed, and I perceived that the second, in which I could see Good himself mounted on a large horse, was on the point of annihilation. A few more minutes and it was broken, its streaming colours sank, and I lost sight of Good in the confused and hideous slaughter that ensued.

Presently, however, a cream-coloured horse with a snow-white mane and tail burst from the ruins of the square and came rushing past me riderless and with wide streaming reins, and in it I recognised the charger that Good had been riding. Then I hesitated no longer, but taking with me half my effective cavalry force, which now amounted to between four and five thousand men, I commended myself to God, and, without waiting for orders, I charged straight down upon Nasta's swordsmen. Seeing me coming, and being warned by the thunder of my horses' hoofs, the majority of them faced round, and gave us a right warm welcome. Not an inch would they yield; in vain did we hack and trample them down as we ploughed a broad red furrow through their thousands; they seemed to re-arise by hundreds, driving their terrible sharp swords into our horses, or severing their hamstrings, and then hacking the troopers who came to the ground with them almost into pieces. My horse was speedily killed under me, but luckily I had a fresh one, my own favourite, a coal-black mare Nyleptha had given me, being held in reserve behind, and on this I afterwards mounted. Meanwhile I had to get along as best I could, for I was pretty well lost sight of by my men in the mad confusion of the moment. My voice, of course, could not be heard in the midst of the clanging of steel and the shrieks of rage and agony. Presently I found myself mixed up with the remnants of the square, which had formed round its leader Good, and was fighting desperately for existence. I stumbled against somebody, and glancing down, caught sight of Good's eyeglass. He had been beaten to his knee. Over him was a great fellow swinging a heavy sword. Somehow I managed to run the man through with the sime I had taken from the Masai whose hand I had cut off; but as I did so, he dealt me a frightful blow on the left side and breast with the sword, and though my chain shirt saved my life, I felt that I was badly hurt. For a minute I fell on to my hands and knees among the dead and dying, and turned sick and faint. When I came to again I saw that Nasta's spearmen, or rather those of them who remained, were retreating back across the stream, and that Good was there by me smiling sweetly.

'Near go that,' he shouted; 'but all's well that ends well.'

I assented, but I could not help feeling that it had not ended well for me. I was sorely hurt.

Just then we saw the smaller bodies of cavalry stationed on our extreme right and left, and which were now reinforced by the three thousand sabres which we had held in reserve, flash out like arrows from their posts and fall upon the disordered flanks of Sorais' forces, and that charge decided the issue of the battle. In another minute or two the enemy was in slow and sullen retreat across the little stream, where they once more re-formed. Then came another lull, during which I managed to get a second horse, and received my orders to advance from Sir Henry, and then with one fierce deep-throated roar, with a waving of banners and a wide flashing of steel, the remains of our army took the offensive and began to sweep down, slowly indeed, but irresistibly from the positions they had so gallantly held all day.

At last it was our turn to attack.

On we moved, over the piled-up masses of dead and dying, and were approaching the stream, when suddenly I perceived an extraordinary sight. Galloping wildly towards us, his arms tightly clasped around his horse's neck, against which his blanched cheek was tightly pressed, was a man arrayed in the full costume of a Zu-Vendi general, but in whom, as he came nearer, I recognised none other than our lost Alphonse. It was impossible even then to mistake those curling mustachios. In a minute he was tearing through our ranks and narrowly escaped being cut down, till at last somebody caught his horse's bridle, and he was brought to me just as a momentary halt occurred in our advance to allow what remained of our shattered squares to form into line.

'Ah, monsieur,' he gasped out in a voice that was nearly inarticulate with fright, 'grace to the sky, it is you! Ah, what I have endured! But you win, monsieur, you win; they fly, the *lâches*. But listen, monsieur – I forget, it is no good; the Queen is to be murdered tomorrow at the first light in the palace of Milosis; her guards will leave their posts, and the priests are going to kill her. Ah yes! they little thought it, but I was ensconced beneath a banner, and I heard it all.'

'What?' I said, horror-struck; 'what do you mean?'

'What I say, monsieur; that devil of a Nasta he went last night to settle the affair with the Archbishop [Agon]. The guard will leave open the little gate leading from the great stair and go away, and Nasta and Agon's priests will come in and kill her. Themselves they would not kill her.'

'Come with me,' I said, and, shouting to the staff-officer next to me to take over the command, I snatched his bridle and galloped as hard as I could for the spot, between a quarter and half a mile off, where I saw the royal pennon flying, and where I knew that I should find Curtis if he were still alive. On we tore, our horses clearing heaps of dead and dying men, and splashing through pools of blood, on past the long broken lines of spearmen to where, mounted on the white stallion Nyleptha had sent to him as a parting gift, I saw Sir Henry's form towering above the generals who surrounded him.

Just as we reached him the advance began again. A bloody cloth was bound around his head, but I saw that his eye was as bright and keen as ever. Beside him was old Umslopogaas, his axe red with blood, but looking quite fresh and uninjured.

'What's wrong, Quatermain?' he shouted.

'Everything. There is a plot to murder the Queen tomorrow at dawn. Alphonse here, who has just escaped from Sorais, has overheard it all,' and I rapidly repeated to him what the Frenchman had told me.

Curtis' face turned deadly pale and his jaw dropped.

'At dawn,' he gasped, 'and it is now sunset; it dawns before four and we are nearly a hundred miles off – nine hours at the outside. What is to be done?'

An idea entered into my head. 'Is that horse of yours fresh?' I said.

'Yes, I have only just got on to him – when my last was killed, and he has been fed.'

'So is mine. Get off him, and let Umslopogaas mount; he can ride well. We will be at Milosis before dawn, or if we are not – well, we cannot help it. No, no; it is impossible for you to leave now. You would be seen, and it would turn the fate of the battle. It is not half won yet. The soldiers would think you were making a bolt of it. Quick now.'

In a moment he was down, and at my bidding Umslopogaas sprang into the empty saddle.

'Now farewell,' I said. 'Send a thousand horsemen with remounts after us in an hour if possible. Stay, despatch a general to the left wing to take over the command and explain my absence.'

'You will do your best to save her, Quatermain?' he said in a broken voice.

'Ay, that I will. Go on; you are being left behind.'

He cast one glance at us, and accompanied by his staff galloped off to join the advance, which by this time was fording the little brook that now ran red with the blood of the fallen.

As for Umslopogaas and myself, we left that dreadful field as arrows leave a bow, and in a few minutes had passed right out of the sight of slaughter, the smell of blood, and the turmoil and shouting, which only came to our ears as a faint, far-off roaring like the sound of distant breakers.

Away! Away!

At the top of the rise we halted for a second to breathe our horses; and, turning, glanced at the battle beneath us, which, illumined as it was by the fierce rays of the sinking sun staining the whole scene red, looked from where we were more like some wild titanic picture than an actual hand-to-hand combat. The distinguishing scenic effect from that distance was the countless distinct flashes of light reflected from the swords and spears, otherwise the panorama was not so grand as might have been expected. The great green lap of sward in which the struggle was being fought out, the bold round outline of the hills behind, and the wide sweep of the plain beyond, seemed to dwarf it; and what was tremendous enough when one was in it, grew insignificant when viewed from the distance. But is it not thus with all the affairs and doings of our race about which we blow the loud trumpet and make such a fuss and worry? How utterly antlike, and morally and physically insignificant, must they seem to the calm eyes that watch them from the arching depths above!

'We win the day, Macumazahn,' said old Umslopogaas, taking in the whole situation with a glance of his practised eye. 'Look, the Lady of the Night's forces give on every side, there is no stiffness left in them, they bend like hot iron, they are fighting with but half a heart. But alas! the battle will in a manner be drawn, for the darkness gathers, and the regiments will not be able to follow and slay!' – and he shook his head sadly. 'But,' he added, 'I do not think that they will fight again. We have fed them with too strong a meat. Ah! it is well to have lived! At last I have seen a fight worth seeing.'

By this time we were on our way again, and as we went side by side I told him what our mission was, and how that, if it failed, all the lives that had been lost that day would have been lost in vain.

'Ah!' he said, 'nigh on a hundred miles and no horses but these, and to be there before the dawn! Well – away! away! man can but try, Macumazahn; and mayhap we shall be there in time to split that old "witch-finder's" [Agon's] skull for him. Once he wanted to burn us, the old "rain-maker", did he? And now he would set a snare for my mother [Nyleptha], would he? Good! So sure as my name is the name of the Woodpecker, so surely, be my mother alive or dead, will I split him to the beard. Ay, by T'Chaka's head I swear it!' and he shook Inkosi-kaas as he galloped. By now the darkness was closing in, but fortunately there would be a moon later, and the road was good.

On we sped through the twilight, the two splendid horses we bestrode had got their wind by this, and were sweeping along with a wide steady stride that neither failed nor varied for mile upon mile. Down the side of slopes we galloped, across wide vales that stretched to the foot of far-off hills. Nearer and nearer grew the blue hills; now we were travelling up their steeps, and now we were over and passing towards others that sprang up like visions in the far, faint distance beyond.

On, never pausing or drawing rein, through the perfect quiet of the night, that was set like a song to the falling music of our horses' hoofs; on, past deserted villages, where only some forgotten starving dog howled a melancholy welcome; on, past lonely moated dwellings; on, through the white patchy moonlight, that lay coldly upon the wide bosom of the earth, as though there was no warmth in it; on, knee to knee, for hour after hour!

We spake not, but bent us forward on the necks of those two glorious horses, and listened to their deep, long-drawn breaths as they filled their great lungs, and to the regular unfaltering ring of their round hoofs. Grim and black indeed did old Umslopogaas look beside me, mounted upon the great white horse, like Death in the Revelation of St John, as now and again lifting his fierce set face he gazed out along the road, and pointed with his axe towards some distant rise or house.

And so on, still on, without break or pause for hour after hour.

At last I felt that even the splendid animal that I rode was beginning to give out. I looked at my watch; it was nearly midnight, and we were considerably more than half way. On the top of a rise was a little spring, which I remembered because I had slept by it a few nights before, and here I motioned to Umslopogaas to pull up, having determined to give the horses and ourselves ten minutes to breathe in. He did so, and we dismounted – that is to say, Umslopogaas did, and then helped me off, for what with fatigue, stiffness, and the pain of my wound, I could not do so for myself; and then the gallant horses stood panting there, resting first one leg and then another, while the sweat fell drip, drip, from them, and the steam rose and hung in pale clouds in the still night air.

Leaving Umslopogaas to hold the horses, I hobbled to the spring and drank deep of its sweet waters. I had had nothing but a single mouthful of wine since midday, when the battle began, and I was parched up, though my fatigue was too great to allow me to feel hungry. Then, having laved my fevered head and hands, I returned, and the Zulu went and drank. Next we allowed the horses to take a couple of mouthfuls each – no more; and oh, what a struggle we had to get the poor beasts away from the water! There were yet two minutes, and I employed it in hobbling up and down to try and relieve my stiffness, and in inspecting the condition of the horses. My mare, gallant animal though she was, was evidently much distressed; she hung her head, and her eye looked sick and dull; but Daylight, Nyleptha's glorious horse – who, if he is served aright, should, like the steeds who saved great Rameses in his need, feed for the rest of his days out of a golden manger – was still comparatively speaking fresh, notwithstanding the fact that he had had by far the heavier weight to carry. He was 'tucked up', indeed, and his legs were weary, but his eye was bright and clear, and he held his shapely head up and gazed out into the darkness round him in a way that seemed to say that whoever failed *he* was good for those five-and-forty miles that yet lay between us and Milosis. Then Umslopogaas helped me into the saddle and – vigorous old savage that he was! – vaulted into his own without touching a stirrup, and we were off once more, slowly at first, till the horses got into their stride, and then more swiftly. So we passed over another ten miles, and then came a long, weary rise of some six or seven miles, and three times did my poor black mare nearly come to the ground with me. But on the top she seemed to gather herself together, and rattled down the slope with long, convulsive strides, breathing in gasps. We did that three or four miles more swiftly than any since we had started on our wild ride, but I felt it to be a last effort, and I was right. Suddenly my poor horse took the bit between her teeth and bolted furiously along a stretch of level ground for some three or four hundred yards, and then, with two or three jerky strides, pulled herself up and fell with a crash right on to her head, I rolling myself free as she did so. As I struggled to my feet the brave beast raised her head and looked at me with piteous bloodshot eyes, and then her head dropped with a groan and she was dead. Her heart was broken.

Umslopogaas pulled up beside the carcase, and I looked at him in dismay. There were still more than twenty miles to do by dawn, and how were we to do it with one horse? It seemed hopeless, but I had forgotten the old Zulu's extraordinary running powers.

Without a single word he sprang from the saddle and began to hoist me into it.

'What wilt thou do?' I asked.

'Run,' he answered, seizing my stirrup-leather.

Then off we went again, almost as fast as before; and oh, the relief it was to me to get that change of horses! Anybody who has ever ridden against time will know what it meant.

Daylight sped along at a long stretching hand-gallop, giving the gaunt Zulu a lift at every stride. It was a wonderful thing to see old Umslopogaas run mile after mile, his lips slightly parted and his nostrils agape like the horse's. Every five miles or so we stopped for a few minutes to let him get his breath, and then flew on again.

'Canst thou go farther,' I said at the third of these stoppages, 'or shall I leave thee to follow me?'

He pointed with his axe to a dim mass before us. It was the Temple of the Sun, now not more than five miles away.

'I reach it or I die,' he gasped.

Oh, that last five miles! The skin was rubbed from the inside of my legs, and every movement of my horse gave me anguish. Nor was that all. I was exhausted with toil, want of food and sleep, and also suffering very much from the blow I had received on my left side; it seemed as though a piece of bone or something was slowly piercing into my lung. Poor Daylight, too, was pretty nearly finished, and no wonder. But there was a smell of dawn in the air, and we might not stay; better that all three of us should die upon the road than that we should linger while there was life in us. The air was thick and heavy, as it sometimes is before the dawn breaks, and – another infallible sign in certain parts of Zu-Vendis that sunrise is at hand – hundreds of little spiders pendant on the end of long tough webs were floating about in it. These early-rising creatures, or rather their webs, caught upon the horse's and our own forms by scores, and, as we had neither the time nor the energy to brush them off, we rushed along covered with hundreds of long grey threads that streamed out a yard or more behind us – and a very strange appearance they must have given us. .

And now before us are the huge brazen gates of the outer wall of the Frowning City, and a new and horrible doubt strikes me: What if they will not let us in?

'*Open! open!*' I shout imperiously, at the same time giving the royal password. '*Open! open!* a messenger, a messenger with tidings of the war!'

'What news?' cried the guard. 'And who art thou that ridest so madly, and who is that whose tongue lolls out' – and it actually did – 'and who runs by thee like a dog by a chariot?'

'It is the Lord Macumazahn, and with him is his dog, his black dog. *Open! open!* I bring tidings.'

The great gates ran back on their rollers, and the drawbridge fell with a rattling crash, and we dashed on through the one and over the other.

'What news, my lord, what news?' cried the guard.

'Incubu rolls Sorais back, as the wind a cloud,' I answered, and was gone.

One more effort, gallant horse, and yet more gallant man!

So, fall not now, Daylight, and hold thy life in thee for fifteen short minutes more, old Zulu war-dog, and ye shall both live for ever in the annals of the land.

On, clattering through the sleeping streets. We are passing the Flower Temple now – one mile more, only one little mile – hold on, keep your life in thee, see the houses run past of themselves. Up, good horse, up, there – but fifty yards now. Ah! you see your stables and stagger on gallantly.

'Thank God, the palace at last!' and see, the first arrows of the dawn are striking on the Temple's golden dome.* But shall I get in here, or is the deed done and the way barred?

Once more I give the password and shout '*Open! open!*'

No answer, and my heart grows very faint.

Again I call, and this time a single voice replies, and to my joy I recognise it as belonging to Kara, a fellow-officer of Nyleptha's guards, a man I know to be as honest as the light – indeed, the same whom Nyleptha had sent to arrest Sorais on the day she fled to the temple.

'Is it thou, Kara?' I cry; 'I am Macumazahn. Bid the guard let down the bridge and throw wide the gate. Quick, quick!'

Then followed a space that seemed to me endless, but at length the bridge fell and one half of the gate opened and we got into the courtyard, where at last poor Daylight fell down beneath me, as I thought, dead. Except Kara, there was nobody to be seen, and his look was wild, and his garments were all torn. He had opened the gate and let down the bridge alone, and was now getting them up and shut again (as, owing to a very ingenious arrangement of cranks and levers, one man could easily do, and indeed generally did do).

'Where are the guard?' I gasped, fearing his answer as I never feared anything before.

'I know not,' he answered; 'two hours ago, as I slept, was I seized and bound by the watch under me, and but now, this very moment, have I freed myself with my teeth. I fear, I greatly fear, that we are betrayed.'

His words gave me fresh energy. Catching him by the arm, I

---

* Of course, the roof of the Temple, being so high, caught the light some time before the breaking of the dawn. A.Q.

staggered, followed by Umslopogaas, who reeled after us like a drunken man, through the courtyards, up the great hall, which was silent as the grave, towards the Queen's sleeping-place.

We reached the first ante-room – no guards; the second, still no guards. Oh, surely the thing was done! we were too late after all, too late! The silence and solitude of those great chambers was dreadful, and weighed me down like an evil dream. On, right into Nyleptha's chamber we rushed and staggered, sick at heart, fearing the very worst; we saw there was a light in it, ay, and a figure bearing the light. Oh, thank God, it is the White Queen herself, the Queen unharmed! There she stands in her night gear, roused, by the clatter of our coming, from her bed, the heaviness of sleep yet in her eyes, and a red blush of fear and shame mantling her lovely breast and cheek.

'Who is it?' she cries. 'What means this? Oh, Macumazahn, is it thou? Why lookest thou so wildly? Thou comest as one bearing evil tidings – and my lord – oh, tell me not my lord is dead – not dead!' she wailed, wringing her white hands.

'I left Incubu wounded, but leading the advance against Sorais last night at sundown; therefore let thy heart have rest. Sorais is beaten back all along her lines, and thy arms prevail.'

'I knew it,' she cried in triumph. 'I knew that he would win; and they called him Outlander, and shook their wise heads when I gave him the command! Last night at sundown, sayest thou, and it is not yet dawn? Surely – '

'Throw a cloak around thee, Nyleptha,' I broke in, 'and give us wine to drink; ay, and call thy maidens quick if thou wouldst save thyself alive. Nay, stay not.'

Thus adjured she ran and called through the curtains towards some room beyond, and then hastily put on her sandals and a thick cloak, by which time a dozen or so of half-dressed women were pouring into the room.

'Follow us and be silent,' I said to them as they gazed with wondering eyes, clinging one to another. So we went into the first ante-room.

'Now,' I said, 'give us wine to drink and food, if ye have it, for we are near to death.'

The room was used as a mess-room for the officers of the guards, and from a cupboard some flagons of wine and some cold flesh were brought forth, and Umslopogaas and I drank, and felt life flow back into our veins as the good red wine went down.

'Hark to me, Nyleptha,' I said, as I put down the empty tankard. 'Hast thou here among these thy waiting-ladies any two of discretion?'

'Ay,' she said, 'surely.'

'Then bid them go out by the side entrance to any citizens whom thou canst bethink thee of as men loyal to thee, and pray them come armed, with all honest folk that they can gather, to rescue thee from death. Nay, question not; do as I say, and quickly. Kara here will let out the maids.'

She turned, and selecting two of the crowd of damsels, repeated the words I had uttered, giving them besides a list of the names of the men to whom each should run.

'Go swiftly and secretly; go for your very lives,' I added.

In another moment they had left with Kara, whom I told to rejoin us at the door leading from the great courtyard on to the stairway as soon as he had made fast behind the girls. Thither, too, Umslopogaas and I made our way, followed by the Queen and her women. As we went we tore off mouthfuls of food, and between them I told her what I knew of the danger which encompassed her, and how we found Kara, and how all the guards and menservants were gone, and she was alone with her women in that great place; and she told me, too, that a rumour had spread through the town that our army had been utterly destroyed, and that Sorais was marching in triumph on Milosis, and how in consequence thereof all men had fallen away from her.

Though all this takes some time to tell, we had not been but six or seven minutes in the palace; and notwithstanding that the golden roof of the temple being very lofty was ablaze with the rays of the rising sun, it was not yet dawn, nor would be for another ten minutes. We were in the courtyard now, and here my wound pained me so that I had to take Nyleptha's arm, while Umslopogaas rolled along after us, eating as he went.

Now we were across it, and had reached the narrow doorway through the palace wall that opened on to the mighty stair.

I looked through and stood aghast, as well I might. The door was gone, and so were the outer gates of bronze – entirely gone. They had been taken from their hinges, and as we afterwards found, hurled from the stairway to the ground two hundred feet beneath. There in front of us was the semicircular standing-space, about twice the size of a large oval dining-table, and the ten curved black marble steps leading on to the main stair – and that was all.

CHAPTER 22

How Umslopogaas Held the Stair

We looked at one another.

'Thou seest,' I said, 'they have taken away the door. Is there aught with which we may fill the place? Speak quickly for they will be on us ere the daylight.' I spoke thus, because I knew that we must hold this place or none, as there were no inner doors in the palace, the rooms being separated one from another by curtains. I also knew that if we could by any means defend this doorway the murderers could get in nowhere else; for the palace is absolutely impregnable, that is, since the secret door by which Sorais had entered on that memorable night of attempted murder had, by Nyleptha's order, been closed up with masonry.

'I have it,' said Nyleptha, who, as usual with her, rose to the emergency in a wonderful way. 'On the farther side of the courtyard are blocks of cut marble – the workmen brought them there for the bed of the new statue of Incubu, my lord; let us block the door with them.'

I jumped at the idea; and having despatched one of the remaining maidens down the great stair to see if she could obtain assistance from the docks below, where her father, who was a great merchant employing many men, had his dwelling-place, and set another to watch through the doorway, we made our way back across the courtyard to where the hewn marble lay; and here we met Kara returning from despatching the first two messengers. There were the marble blocks, sure enough, broad, massive lumps, some six inches thick, and weighing about eighty pounds each, and there, too, were a couple of implements like small stretchers, that the workmen used to carry them on. Without delay we got some of the blocks on to the stretchers, and four of the girls carried them to the doorway.

'Listen, Macumazahn,' said Umslopogaas, 'if those low fellows come, it is I who will hold the stair against them till the door is built up. Nay, nay, it will be a man's death: gainsay me not, old friend. It has been a good day, let it now be good-night. See, I throw myself down to rest on the marble there; when their footsteps are nigh, wake thou me, not before, for I need my strength,' and without a word he went outside and flung himself down on the marble, and was instantly asleep.

At this time, I too was overcome, and was forced to sit down by the doorway, and content myself with directing operations. The girls brought the block, while Kara and Nyleptha built them up across the six-foot-wide doorway, a triple row of them, for less would be useless. But the marble had to be brought forty yards and then there were forty yards to run back, and though the girls laboured gloriously, even staggering along alone, each with a block in her arms, it was slow work, dreadfully slow.

The light was growing now, and presently, in the silence, we heard a commotion at the far-bottom of the stair, and the faint clinking of armed men. As yet the wall was only two feet high, and we had been eight minutes at the building of it. So they had come. Alphonse had heard aright.

The clanking sound came nearer, and in the ghostly grey of the dawning we could make out long files of men, some fifty or so in all, slowly creeping up the stair. They were now at the halfway standing place that rested on the great flying arch; and here, perceiving that something was going on above, they, to our great gain, halted for three or four minutes and consulted, then slowly and cautiously advanced again.

We had been nearly a quarter of an hour at the work now, and it was almost three feet high.

Then I woke Umslopogaas. The great man rose, stretched himself, and swung Inkosi-kaas round his head.

'It is well,' he said. 'I feel as a young man once more. My strength has come back to me, ay, even as a lamp flares up before it dies. Fear not, I shall fight a good fight; the wine and the sleep have put a new heart into me.

'Macumazahn, I have dreamed a dream. I dreamed that thou and I stood together on a star, and looked down on the world, and thou wast as a spirit, Macumazahn, for light flamed through thy flesh, but I could not see what was the fashion of mine own face. The hour has come for us, old hunter. So be it: we have had our time, but I would that in it I had seen some more such fights as yesterday's.

'Let them bury me after the fashion of my people, Macumazahn, and set my eyes towards Zululand;' and he took my hand and shook it, and then turned to face the advancing foe.

Just then, to my astonishment, the Zu-Vendi officer Kara clambered over our improvised wall in his quiet, determined sort of way, and took his stand by the Zulu, unsheathing his sword as he did so.

'What, comest thou too?' laughed out the old warrior. 'Welcome – a welcome to thee, brave heart! Ow! for the man who can die like a man; ow! for the death grip and the ringing of steel. Ow! we are ready. We wet our beaks like eagles, our spears flash in the sun; we shake our assegais, and are hungry to fight. Who comes to give greeting to the Chieftainess [Inkosi-kaas]? Who would taste her kiss, whereof the fruit is death? I, the Woodpecker, I, the Slaughterer, I the Swiftfooted! I, Umslopogaas, of the tribe of the Maquilisini, of the people of Amazulu, a captain of the regiment of the Nkomabakosi: I, Umslopogaas, the son of Indabazimbi, the son of Arpi the son of Mosilikaatze, I of the royal blood of T'Chaka, I of the King's House, I the Ringed Man, I the Induna, I call to them as a buck calls, I challenge them, I await them. Ow! it is thou, it is thou!'

As he spake, or rather chanted, his wild war-song, the armed men, among whom in the growing light I recognised both Nasta and Agon, came streaming up the stair with a rush, and one big fellow, armed with a heavy spear, dashed up the ten semicircular steps ahead of his comrades and struck at the great Zulu with the spear. Umslopogaas moved his body but not his legs, so that the blow missed him, and next instant Inkosi-kaas crashed through headpiece, hair and skull, and the man's corpse was rattling down the steps. As he dropped, his round hippopotamus-hide shield fell from his hand on to the marble, and the Zulu stooped down and seized it, still chanting as he did so.

In another second the sturdy Kara had also slain a man, and then began a scene the like of which has not been known to me.

Up rushed the assailants, one, two, three at a time, and as fast as they came, the axe crashed and the sword swung, and down they rolled again, dead or dying. And ever as the fight thickened, the old Zulu's eye seemed to get quicker and his arm stronger. He shouted out his war-cries and the names of chiefs whom he had slain, and the blows of his awful axe rained straight and true, shearing through everything they fell on. There was none of the scientific method he was so fond of about this last immortal fight of his; he had no time for it, but struck with his full strength, and at every stroke a man sank in his tracks, and went rattling down the marble steps.

They hacked and hewed at him with swords and spears, wounding him in a dozen places till he streamed red with blood; but the shield protected his head and the chain-shirt his vitals, and for minute after minute, aided by the gallant Zu-Vendi, he still held the stair.

At last Kara's sword broke, and he grappled with a foe, and they rolled down together, and he was cut to pieces, dying like the brave man that he was.

Umslopogaas was alone now, but he never blenched or turned. Shouting out some wild Zulu battle-cry, he beat down a foe, ay, and another, and another, till at last they drew back from the slippery blood-stained steps, and stared at him with amazement, thinking that he was no mortal man.

The wall of marble block was four feet six high now, and hope rose in my teeth as I leaned there against it a miserable helpless log, and ground my teeth, and watched that glorious struggle. I could do no more for I had lost my revolver in the battle.

And old Umslopogaas, he leaned too on his good axe, and, faint as he was with wounds, he mocked them, he called them 'women' – the grand old warrior, standing there one against so many! And for a breathing space none would come against him, notwith-standing Nasta's exhortations, till at last old Agon, who, to do him justice, was a brave man, mad with baffled rage, and seeing that the wall would soon be built and his plans defeated, shook the great spear he held, and rushed up the dripping steps.

'Ah, ah!' shouted the Zulu, as he recognised the priest's flowing white beard, 'it is thou, old "witch-finder"! Come on! I await thee, white "medicine man"; come on! come on! I have sworn to slay thee, and I ever keep my faith.'

On he came, taking him at his word, and drave the big spear with such force at Umslopogaas that it sunk right through the tough shield and pierced him in the neck. The Zulu cast down the transfixed shield, and that moment was Agon's last, for before he could free his spear and strike again, with a shout of 'There's for thee, Rain-maker!' Umslopogaas gripped Inkosi-kaas with both hands and whirled on high and drave her right on to his venerable head, so that Agon rolled down dead among the corpses of his fellow-murderers, and there was an end to him and his plots altogether. And even as he fell, a great cry rose from the foot of the stair, and looking out through the portion of the doorway that was yet unclosed, we saw armed men rushing up to the rescue, and called an answer to their shouts. Then the would-be murderers who yet remained on the stairway, and amongst whom I saw several priests, turned to fly, but, having nowhere to go, were butchered as they fled. Only one man stayed, and he was the great lord Nasta, Nyleptha's suitor, and the father of the plot. For a moment the black-bearded Nasta stood with bowed face leaning on his long sword as though in despair, and then, with a dreadful shout, he too rushed up at the Zulu, and, swinging the glittering sword around his head, dealt him such a mighty blow beneath his guard, that the keen steel of the heavy blade bit right through the chain armour and deep into Umslopogaas' side, for a moment paralysing him and causing him to drop his axe.

Raising the sword again, Nasta sprang forward to make an end of him, but little he knew his foe. With a shake and a yell of fury, the Zulu gathered himself together and sprang straight at Nasta's throat, as I have sometimes seen a wounded lion spring. He struck him full as his foot was on the topmost stair, and his long arms closing round him like iron bands, down they rolled together struggling furiously. Nasta was a strong man and a desperate, but he could not match the strongest man in Zululand, sore wounded though he was, whose strength was as the strength of a bull. In a minute the end came. I saw old Umslopogaas stagger to his feet – ay, and saw him by a single gigantic effort swing up the struggling Nasta and with a shout of triumph hurl him straight over the parapet of the bridge, to be crushed to powder on the rocks two hundred feet below.

The succour which had been summoned by the girl who had passed down the stair before the assassins passed up was at hand, and the loud shouts which reached us from the outer gates told us that the town was also aroused, and the men awakened by the women were calling to be admitted. Some of Nyleptha's brave ladies, who in their night-shifts and with their long hair streaming down their backs, just as they had been aroused from rest, went off to admit them at the side entrance, whilst others, assisted by the rescuing party outside, pushed and pulled down the marble blocks they had placed there with so much labour.

Soon the wall was down again, and through the doorway, followed by a crowd of rescuers, staggered old Umslopogaas, an awful and, in a way, a glorious figure. The man was a mass of wounds, and a glance at his wild eye told me that he was dying. The 'keshla' gum-ring upon his head was severed in two places by sword-cuts, one just over the curious hole in his skull, and the blood poured down his face from the gashes. Also on the right side of his neck was a stab from a spear, inflicted by Agon; there was a deep cut on his left arm just below where the mail shirt-sleeve stopped, and on the right side of his body the armour was severed by a gash six inches long, where Nasta's mighty sword had bitten through it and deep into its wearer's vitals.

On, axe in hand, he staggered, that dreadful-looking, splendid savage, and the ladies forgot to turn faint at the scene of blood, and cheered him, as well they might, but he never stayed or heeded. With outstretched arms and tottering gait he pursued his way, followed by us all along the broad shell-strewn walk that ran through the courtyard, past the spot where the blocks of marble lay, through the round arched doorway and the thick curtains that hung within it, down the short passage and into the great hall, which was now filling with hastily-armed men, who poured through the side entrance. Straight up the hall he went, leaving behind him a track of blood on the marble pavement, till at last he reached the sacred stone, which stood in the centre of it, and here his strength seemed to fail him, for he stopped and leaned upon his axe. Then suddenly he lifted up his voice and cried aloud – 'I die, I die – but it was a kingly fray. Where are they who came up the great stair? I see them not. Art thou there, Macumazahn, or art thou gone before to wait for me in the dark whither I go? The blood blinds me – the place turns round – I hear the voice of waters.'

Next, as though a new thought had struck him, he lifted the red axe and kissed the blade.

'Farewell, Inkosi-kaas,' he cried. 'Nay, nay, we will go together; we cannot part, thou and I. We have lived too long one with another, thou and I.

'One more stroke, only one! A good stroke! a straight stroke! a strong stroke!' and, drawing himself to his full height, with a wild heart-shaking shout, he with both hands began to whirl the axe round his head till it looked like a circle of flaming steel. Then, suddenly, with awful force he brought it down straight on to the crown of the mass of sacred stone. A shower of sparks flew up, and such was the almost superhuman strength of the blow, that the massive marble split with a rending sound into a score of pieces, whilst of Inkosi-kaas there remained but some fragments of steel and a fibrous rope of shattered horn that had been the handle. Down with a crash on to the pavement fell the fragments of the holy stone, and down with a crash on to them, still grasping the knob of Inkosi-kaas, fell the brave old Zulu – *dead*.

And thus the hero died.

A gasp of wonder and astonishment rose from all those who witnessed the extraordinary sight, and then somebody cried, '*The prophecy! the prophecy!* He has shattered the sacred stone!' and at once a murmuring arose.

'Ay,' said Nyleptha, with that quick wit which distinguishes her. 'Ay, my people, he has shattered the stone, and behold the prophecy is fulfilled, for a stranger king rules in Zu-Vendis. Incubu, my lord, hath beat Sorais back, and I fear her no more, and to him who hath saved the Crown it shall surely be. And this man,' she said, turning to me and laying her hand upon my shoulder, 'wot ye that, though wounded in the fight of yesterday, he rode with that old warrior who lies there, one hundred miles 'twixt sun set and rise to save me from the plots of cruel men. Ay, and he has saved me, by a very little, and therefore because of the deeds that they have done – deeds of glory such as our history cannot show the like – therefore I say that the name of Macumazahn and the name of dead Umslopogaas, ay, and the name of Kara, my servant, who aided him to hold the stair, shall be blazoned in letters of gold above my throne, and shall be glorious for ever while the land endures. I, the Queen, have said it.'

This spirited speech was met with loud cheering, and I said that after all we had only done our duty, as it is the fashion of both Englishmen and Zulus to do, and there was nothing to make an outcry about; at which they cheered still more, and then I was supported across the outer courtyard to my old quarters, in order that I might be put to bed. As I went, my eyes lit upon the brave horse Daylight that lay there, his white head outstretched on the pavement, exactly as he had fallen on entering the yard; and I bade those who supported me take me near him, that I might look on the good beast once more before he was dragged away. And as I looked, to my astonishment he opened his eyes and, lifting his head a little, whinnied faintly. I could have shouted for joy to find that he was not dead, only unfortunately I had not a shout left in me; but as it was, grooms were sent for and he was lifted up and wine poured down his throat, and in a fortnight he was as well and strong as ever, and is the pride and joy of all the people of Milosis, who, whenever they see him, point him out to the little children as the 'horse which saved the White Queen's life'.

Then I went on and got off to bed, and was washed and had my mail shirt removed. They hurt me a great deal in getting it off, and no wonder, for on my left breast and side was a black bruise the size of a saucer.

The next thing that I remember was the tramp of horsemen outside the palace wall, some ten hours later. I raised myself and asked what was the news, and they told me that a large body of cavalry sent by Curtis to assist the Queen had arrived from the scene of the battle, which they had left two hours after sundown. When they left, the wreck of Sorais' army was in full retreat upon M'Arstuna, followed by all our effective cavalry. Sir Henry was encamping the remains of his worn-out forces on the site (such is the fortune of war) that Sorais had occupied the night before, and proposed marching to M'Arstuna on the morrow. Having heard this, I felt that I could die with a light heart, and then everything became a blank.

When next I awoke the first thing I saw was the round disc of a sympathetic eyeglass, behind which was Good.

'How are you getting on, old chap?' said a voice from the neighbourhood of the eyeglass.

'What are you doing here?' I asked faintly. 'You ought to be at M'Arstuna – have you run away, or what?'

'M'Arstuna,' he replied cheerfully. 'Ah, M'Arstuna fell last week – you've been unconscious for a fortnight, you see – with all the honours of war, you know – trumpets blowing, flags flying, just as though they had had the best of it; but for all that, weren't they glad to go. Israel made for his tents, I can tell you – never saw such a sight in my life.'

'And Sorais?' I asked.

'Sorais – oh, Sorais is a prisoner; they gave her up, the scoundrels,' he added, with a change of tone – 'sacrificed the Queen to save their skins, you see. She is being brought up here, and I don't know what will happen to her, poor soul!' and he sighed.

'Where is Curtis?' I asked.

'He is with Nyleptha. She rode out to meet us today, and there was a grand to-do, I can tell you. He is coming to see you tomorrow; the doctors (for there is a medical "faculty" in Zu-Vendis as elsewhere) thought that he had better not come today.'

I said nothing, but somehow I thought to myself that notwith-standing the doctors he might have given me a look; but there, when a man is newly married and has just gained a great victory, he is apt to listen to the advice of doctors, and quite right too.

Just then I heard a familiar voice informing me that 'Monsieur must now couch himself,' and looking up perceived Alphonse's enormous black mustachios curling away in the distance.

'So you are here?' I said.

'Mais oui, Monsieur; the war is now finished, my military instincts are satisfied, and I return to nurse Monsieur.'

I laughed, or rather tried to; but whatever may have been Alphonse's failings as a warrior (and I fear that he did not come up to the level of his heroic grandfather in this particular, showing thereby how true is the saying that it is a bad thing to be overshadowed by some great ancestral name), a better or kinder nurse never lived. Poor Alphonse! I hope he will always think of me as kindly as I think of him.

On the morrow I saw Curtis and Nyleptha with him, and he told me the whole history of what had happened since Umslopogaas and I galloped wildly away from the battle to save the life of the Queen. It seemed to me that he had managed the thing exceedingly well, and showed great ability as a general. Of course, however, our loss had been dreadfully heavy – indeed, I am afraid to say how many perished in the desperate battle I have described, but I know that the slaughter has appreciably affected the male population of the country. He was very pleased to see me, dear fellow that he is, and thanked me with tears in his eyes for the little that I had been able to do. I saw him, however, start violently when his eyes fell upon my face.

As for Nyleptha, she was positively radiant now that 'her dear lord' had come back with no other injury than an ugly scar on his forehead. I do not believe that she allowed all the fearful slaughter that had taken place to weigh ever so little in the balance against this one fact, or even to greatly diminish her joy; and I cannot blame her for it, seeing that it is the nature of loving woman to look at all things through the spectacles of her love, and little does she reck of the misery of the many if the happiness of the *one* be assured. That is human nature, which the Positivists tell us is just perfection; so no doubt it is all right.

'And what art thou going to do with Sorais?' I asked her.

Instantly her bright brow darkened to a frown.

'Sorais,' she said, with a little stamp of the foot; 'ah, but Sorais!'

Sir Henry hastened to turn the subject.

'You will soon be about and all right again now, old fellow,' he said.

I shook my head and laughed.

'Don't deceive yourselves,' I said. 'I may be about for a little, but I shall never be all right again. I am a dying man, Curtis. I may die slow, but die I must. Do you know I have been spitting blood all the morning? I tell you there is something working away into my lung; I can feel it. There, don't look distressed; I have had my day, and am ready to go. Give me the mirror, will you? I want to look at myself.'

He made some excuse, but I saw through it and insisted, and at last he handed me one of the discs of polished silver set in a wooden frame like a hand-screen, which serve as looking-glasses in Zu-Vendis. I looked and put it down.

'Ah,' I said quietly, 'I thought so; and you talk of my getting all right!' I did not like to let them see how shocked I really was at my own appearance. My grizzled stubby hair was turned snow-white, and my yellow face was shrunk like an aged woman's and had two deep purple rings painted beneath the eyes.

Here Nyleptha began to cry, and Sir Henry again turned the subject, telling me that the artists had taken a cast of the dead body of old Umslopogaas, and that a great statue in black marble was to be erected of him in the act of splitting the sacred stone, which was to be matched by another statue in white marble of myself and the horse Daylight as he appeared when, at the termination of that wild ride, he sank beneath me in the courtyard of the palace. I have since seen these statues, which at the time of writing this, six months after the battle, are nearly finished; and very beautiful they are, especially that of Umslopogaas, which is exactly like him. As for that of myself, it is good, but they have idealised my ugly face a little, which is perhaps as well, seeing that thousands of people will probably look at it in the centuries to come, and it is not pleasant to look at ugly things.

Then they told me that Umslopogaas' last wish had been carried out, and that, instead of being cremated, as I shall be, after the usual custom here, he had been tied up, Zulu fashion, with his knees beneath his chin, and, having been wrapped in a thin sheet of beaten gold, entombed in a hole hollowed out of the masonry of the semicircular space at the top of the stair he defended so splendidly, which faces, as far as we can judge, almost exactly towards Zululand. There he sits, and will sit for ever, for they embalmed him with spices, and put him in an air-tight stone coffer, keeping his grim watch beneath the spot he held alone against a multitude; and the people say that at night his ghost rises and stands shaking the phantom of Inkosi-kaas at phantom foes. Certainly they fear during the dark hours to pass the place where the hero is buried.

Oddly enough, too, a new legend or prophecy has arisen in the land in that unaccountable way in which such things to arise among barbarous and semi-civilised people, blowing, like the wind, no man knows whence. According to this saying, so long as the old Zulu sits there, looking down the stairway he defended when alive, so long will the New House of the Stairway, springing from the union of the Englishman and Nyleptha, endure and flourish; but when he is taken from thence, or when, ages after, his bones at last crumble into dust, the House will fall, and the Stairway shall fall, and the Nation of the Zu-Vendi shall cease to be a Nation.

CHAPTER 23

I Have Spoken

It was a week after Nyleptha's visit, when I had begun to get about a little in the middle of the day, that a message came to me from Sir Henry to say that Sorais would be brought before them in the Queen's first antechamber at midday, and requesting my attendance if possible. Accordingly, greatly drawn by curiosity to see this unhappy woman once more, I made shift, with the help of that kind little fellow Alphonse, who is a perfect treasure to me, and that of another waiting-man, to reach the antechamber. I got there, indeed, before anybody else, except a few of the great Court officials who had been bidden to be present, but I had scarcely seated myself before Sorais was brought in by a party of guards, looking as beautiful and defiant as ever, but with a worn expression on her proud face. She was, as usual, dressed in her royal 'kaf', emblazoned with the emblem of the Sun, and in her right hand she still held the toy spear of silver. A pang of admiration and pity went through me as I looked at her, and struggling to my feet I bowed deeply, at the same time expressing my sorrow that I was not able, owing to my condition, to remain standing before her.

She coloured a little and then laughed bitterly. 'Thou dost forget, Macumazahn,' she said, 'I am no more a Queen, save in blood; I am an outcast and a prisoner, one whom all men should scorn, and none show deference to.'

'At least,' I replied, 'thou art still a lady, and therefore one to whom deference is due. Also, thou art in an evil case, and therefore it is doubly due.'

'Ah!' she answered, with a little laugh, 'thou dost forget that I would have wrapped thee in a sheet of gold and hung thee to the angel's trumpet at the topmost pinnacle of the Temple.'

'No,' I answered, 'I assure thee that I forgot it not; indeed, I often thought of it when it seemed to me that the battle of the Pass was turning against us; but the trumpet is there, and I am still here, though perchance not for long, so why talk of it now?'

'Ah!' she went on, 'the battle! the battle! Oh, would that I were once more a Queen, if only for one little hour, and I would take such a vengeance on those accursed jackals who deserted me in my need; that it should only be spoken of in whispers; those women, those pigeon-hearted half-breeds who suffered themselves to be overcome!' and she choked in her wrath.

'Ay, and that little coward beside thee,' she went on, pointing at Alphonse with the silver spear, whereat he looked very uncomfortable; 'he escaped and betrayed my plans. I tried to make a general of him, telling the soldiers it was Bougwan, and to scourge valour into him' (here Alphonse shivered at some unhappy recollection), 'but it was of no avail. He hid beneath a banner in my tent and thus overheard my plans. I would that I had slain him, but, alas! I held my hand.

'And thou, Macumazahn, I have heard of what thou didst; thou art brave, and hast a loyal heart. And the black one too, ah, he was a *man*. I would fain have seen him hurl Nasta from the stairway.'

'Thou art a strange woman, Sorais,' I said; 'I pray thee now plead with the Queen Nyleptha, that perchance she may show mercy unto thee.'

She laughed out loud. '*I* plead for mercy!' she said and at that moment the Queen entered, accompanied by Sir Henry and Good, and took her seat with an impassive face. As for poor Good, he looked intensely ill at ease.

'Greeting, Sorais!' said Nyleptha, after a short pause. 'Thou hast rent the kingdom like a rag, thou hast put thousands of my people to the sword, thou hast twice basely plotted to destroy my life by murder, thou hast sworn to slay my lord and his companions and to hurl me from the Stairway. What hast thou to say why thou shouldst not die? Speak, O Sorais!'

'Methinks my sister the Queen hath forgotten the chief count of the indictment,' answered Sorais in her slow musical tones. 'It runs thus: "Thou didst strive to win the love of my lord Incubu."

It is for this crime that my sister will slay me, not because I levied war. It is perchance happy for thee, Nyleptha, that I fixed my mind upon his love too late.

'Listen,' she went on, raising her voice. 'I have nought to say save that I would I had won instead of lost. Do thou with me even as thou wilt, O Queen, and let my lord the King there' (pointing to Sir Henry) – 'for now will he be King – carry out the sentence, as it is meet he should, for as he is the beginning of the evil, let him also be the end.' And she drew herself up and shot one angry glance at him from her deep fringed eyes, and then began to toy with her spear.

Sir Henry bent towards Nyleptha and whispered something that I could not catch, and then the Queen spoke.

'Sorais, ever have I been a good sister to thee. When our father died, and there was much talk in the land as to whether thou shouldst sit upon the throne with me, I being the elder, I gave my voice for thee and said, "Nay, let her sit. She is twin with me; we were born at a birth; wherefore should the one be preferred before the other?" And so has it ever been 'twixt thee and me, my sister. But now thou knowest in what sort thou hast repaid me, but I have prevailed, and thy life is forfeit, Sorais. And yet art thou my sister, born at a birth with me, and we played together when we were little and loved each other much, and at night we slept in the same cot with our arms each around the other's neck, and therefore even now does my heart go out to thee, Sorais.

'But not for that would I spare thy life, for thy offence has been too heavy; it doth drag down the wide wings of my mercy even to the ground. Also, while thou dost live the land will never be at peace.

'Yet shalt thou not die, Sorais, because my dear lord here hath begged thy life of me as a boon; therefore as a boon and as a marriage gift give I it to him, to do with even as he wills, knowing that, though thou dost love him, he loves thee not, Sorais, for all thy beauty. Nay, though thou art lovely as the night in all her stars, O Lady of the Night, yet it is me his wife whom he loves, and not thee, and therefore do I give thy life to him.'

Sorais flushed up to her eyes and said nothing, and I do not think that I ever saw a man look more miserable than did Sir Henry at that moment. Somehow, Nyleptha's way of putting the thing, though true and forcible enough, was not altogether pleasant.

'I understand,' stammered Curtis, looking at Good, 'I understood that you were attached – eh – attached to – to the Queen Sorais. I am – eh – not aware what the – in short, the state of your feelings may be just now; but if they happened to be that way inclined, it has struck me that – in short, it might put a satisfactory end to an unpleasant business. The lady also has ample private estates, where I am sure she would be at liberty to live unmolested as far as we are concerned, eh, Nyleptha? Of course, I only suggest.'

'So far as I am concerned,' said Good, colouring up, 'I am quite willing to forget the past; and if the Lady of the Night thinks me worth the taking I will marry her tomorrow, or when she likes, and try to make her a good husband.'

All eyes were now turned to Sorais, who stood with that same slow smile upon her beautiful face which I had noticed the first time that I ever saw her. She paused a little while, and cleared her throat, and then thrice she curtseyed low, once to Nyleptha, once to Curtis, and once to Good, and began to speak in measured tones.

'I thank thee, most gracious Queen and royal sister, for the loving-kindness thou hast shown me from my youth up, and especially in that thou hast been pleased to give my person and my fate as a gift to the Lord Incubu – the King that is to be. May prosperity, peace and plenty deck the life-path of one so merciful and so tender, even as flowers do. Long mayst thou reign, O great and glorious Queen, and hold thy husband's love in both thy hands, and many be the sons and daughters of thy beauty. And I thank thee, my Lord Incubu – the King that is to be – I thank thee a thousand times in that thou hast been pleased to accept that gracious gift, and to pass it on to thy comrade in arms and in adventure, the Lord Bougwan. Surely the act is worthy of thy greatness, my Lord Incubu. And now, lastly, I thank thee also, my Lord Bougwan, who in thy turn hast deigned to accept me and my poor beauty. I thank thee a thousand times, and I will add that thou art a good and honest man, and I put my hand upon my heart and swear that I would that I could say thee "yea". And now that I have rendered thanks to all in turn' – and again she smiled – 'I will add one short word.

'Little can you understand of me, Queen Nyleptha and my lords, if ye know not that for me there is no middle path; that I scorn your pity and hate you for it; that I cast off your forgiveness as though it were a serpent's sting; and that standing here, betrayed, deserted, insulted, and alone, I yet triumph over you, mock you, and defy you, one and all, and *thus* I answer you.' And then, of a sudden, before anybody guessed what she intended to do, she drove the little silver spear she carried in her hand into her side with such a strong and steady aim that the keen point projected through her back, and she fell prone upon the pavement.

Nyleptha shrieked, and poor Good almost fainted at the sight, while the rest of us rushed towards her. But Sorais of the Night lifted herself upon her hand, and for a moment fixed her glorious eyes intently on Curtis' face, as though there were some message in the glance, then dropped her head and sighed, and with a sob her dark but splendid spirit passed.

Well, they gave her a royal funeral, and there was an end of her.

*   *   *

It was a month after the last act of the Sorais tragedy that a great ceremony was held in the Flower Temple, and Curtis was formally declared King-Consort of Zu-Vendis. I was too ill to go myself; and indeed, I hate all that sort of thing, with the crowds and the trumpet-blowing and banner-waving; but Good, who was there (in his full-dress uniform), came back much impressed, and told me that Nyleptha had looked lovely, and Curtis had borne himself in a right royal fashion, and had been received with acclamations that left no doubt as to his popularity. Also he told me that when the horse Daylight was led along in the procession, the populace had shouted '*Macumazahn, Macuma-zahn!*' till they were hoarse, and would only be appeased when he, Good, rose in his chariot and told them that I was too ill to be present.

Afterwards, too, Sir Henry, or rather the King, came to see me, looking very tired, and vowing that he had never been so bored in his life; but I dare say that that was a slight exaggeration. It is not in human nature that a man should be altogether bored on such an extraordinary occasion; and, indeed, as I pointed out to him, it was a marvellous thing that a man, who but little more than one short year before had entered a great country as an unknown wanderer, should today be married to its beautiful and beloved Queen, and lifted, amidst public rejoicings, to its throne. I even went the length to exhort him in the future not to be carried away by the pride and pomp of absolute power, but always to strive to remember that he was first a Christian gentleman, and next a public servant, called by Providence to a great and almost unprecedented trust. These remarks, which he might fairly have resented, he was so good as to receive with patience, and even to thank me for making them.

It was immediately after this ceremony that I caused myself to be moved to the house where I am now writing. It is a very pleasant country seat, situated about two miles from the Frowning City, on to which it looks. That was five months ago, during the whole of which time I have, being confined to a kind of couch, employed my leisure in compiling this history of our wanderings from my journal and from our joint memories. It is probable that it will never be read, but it does not much matter whether it is or not; at any rate, it has served to while away many hours of suffering, for I have suffered a deal of pain lately. Thank God, however, there will not be much more of it.

*   *   *

It is a week since I wrote the above, and now I take up my pen for the last time, for I know that the end is at hand. My brain is still clear and I can manage to write, though with difficulty. The pain in my lung, which has been very bad during the last week, has suddenly quite left me, and been succeeded by a feeling of numbness of which I cannot mistake the meaning. And just as the pain has gone, so with it all fear of that end has departed, and I feel only as though I were going to sink into the arms of an unutterable rest. Happily, contentedly, and with the same sense of security with which an infant lays itself to sleep in its mother's arms, do I lay myself down in the arms of the Angel Death. All the tremors, all the heart-shaking fears which have haunted me through a life that seems long as I looked back upon it, have left me now; the storms have passed, and the Star of our Eternal Hope shines clear and steady on the horizon that seems so far from man, and yet is so very near to me tonight.

And so this is the end of it – a brief space of troubling, a few restless, fevered, anguished years, and then the arms of that great Angel Death. Many times have I been near to them, and now it is my turn at last, and it is well. Twenty-four hours more and the world will be gone from me, and with it all its hopes and all its fears. The air will close in over the space that my form filled and my place know me no more; for the dull breath of the world's forgetfulness will first dim the brightness of my memory, and then blot it out for ever, and of a truth I shall be dead. So is it with us all. How many millions have lain as I lie, and thought these thoughts and been forgotten! – thousands upon thousands of years ago they thought them, those dying men of the dim past; and thousands on thousands of years hence will their descendants think them and be in their turn forgotten. 'As the breath of the oxen in winter, as the quick star that runs along the sky, as a little shadow that loses itself at sunset,' as I once heard a Zulu called Ignosi put it, such is the order of our life, the order that passeth away.

Well, it is not a good world – nobody can say that it is, save those who wilfully blind themselves to facts. How can a world be good in which Money is the moving power, and Self-interest the guiding star? The wonder is not that it is so bad, but that there should be any good left in it.

Still, now that my life is over, I am glad to have lived, glad to have known the dear breath of woman's love, and that true friendship which can even surpass the love of woman, glad to have heard the laughter of little children, to have seen the sun and the moon and the stars, to have felt the kiss of the salt sea on my face, and watched the wild game trek down to the water in the moonlight. But I should not wish to live again!

Everything is changing to me. The darkness draws near, and the light departs. And yet it seems to me that through that darkness I can already see the shining welcome of many a long-lost face. Harry is there, and others; one above all, to my mind the sweetest and most perfect woman that ever gladdened this grey earth. But of her I have already written elsewhere, and at length, so why speak of her now? Why speak of her after this long silence, now that she is again so near to me, now that I go where she has gone?

The sinking sun is turning the golden roof of the great Temple to a fiery flame, and my fingers tire.

So to all who have known me, or known of me, to all who can think one kindly thought of the old hunter, I stretch out my hand from the far-off shore and bid a long farewell.

And now into the hands of Almighty God, who sent it, do I commit my spirit.

'*I have spoken*,' as the Zulus say.

CHAPTER 24

By Another Hand

A year has elapsed since our most dear friend Allan Quatermain wrote the words '*I have spoken*' at the end of his record of our adventures. Nor should I have ventured to make any additions to the record had it not happened that by a most strange accident a chance has arisen of its being conveyed to England. The chance is but a faint one, it is true; but, as it is not probable that another will arise in our lifetimes, Good and myself think that we may as well avail ourselves of it, such as it is. During the last six months several Frontier Commissions have been at work on the various boundaries of Zu-Vendis, with a view of discovering whether there exists any possible means of ingress or egress from the country, with the result that a channel of communication with the outer world hitherto overlooked has been discovered. This channel, apparently the only one (for I have discovered that it was by it that the native who ultimately reached Mr Mackenzie's mission station, and whose arrival in the country, together with the fact of his expulsion – for he *did* arrive about three years before ourselves – was for reasons of their own kept a dead secret by the priests to whom he was brought), is about to be effectually closed. But before this is done, a messenger is to be despatched bearing with him this manuscript, and also one or two letters from Good to his friends, and from myself to my brother George, whom it deeply grieves me to think I shall never see again, informing them, as our next heirs, that they are welcome to our effects in England, if the Court of Probate will allow them to take them,* inasmuch as we have made

* Of course the Court of Probate would allow nothing of the sort. ED.

up our minds never to return to Europe. Indeed, it would be impossible for us to leave Zu-Vendis even if we wished to do so.

The messenger who is to go – and I wish him joy of his journey – is Alphonse. For a long while he has been wearied to death of Zu-Vendis and its inhabitants. 'Oh, oui, c'est beau,' he says, with an expressive shrug; 'mais je m'ennuie; ce n'est pas chic.' Again, he complains dreadfully of the absence of cafés and theatres, and moans continually for his lost Annette, of whom he says he dreams three times a week. But I fancy his secret cause of disgust at the country, putting aside the homesickness to which every French-man is subject, is that the people here laugh at him so dreadfully about his conduct on the occasion of the great battle of the Pass about eighteen months ago, when he hid beneath a banner in Sorais's tent in order to avoid being sent forth to fight, which he says would have gone against his conscience. Even the little boys call out at him in the streets, thereby offending his pride and making his life unbearable. At any rate, he has determined to brave the horrors of a journey of almost unprecedented difficulty and danger, and also to run the risk of falling into the hands of the French police to answer for a certain little indiscretion of his own some years old (though I do not consider that a very serious matter), rather than remain in *ce triste pays*. Poor Alphonse! we shall be very sorry to part with him; but I sincerely trust, for his own sake and also for the sake of this history, which is, I think, worth giving to the world, that he may arrive in safety. If he does, and can carry the treasure we have provided him with in the shape of bars of solid gold, he will be, comparatively speaking, a rich man for life, and well able to marry his Annette, if she is still in the land of the living and willing to marry her Alphonse.

Anyhow, on the chance, I may as well add a word or two to dear old Quatermain's narrative.

He died at dawn on the day following that on which he wrote the last words of the last chapter. Nyleptha, Good and myself were present, and a most touching and yet in its way beautiful scene it was. An hour before the daybreak it became apparent to us that he was sinking, and our distress was very keen. Indeed, Good melted into tears at the idea – a fact that called forth a last gentle flicker of humour from our dying friend, for even at that hour he could be humorous. Good's emotion had, by loosening the muscles, naturally caused his eyeglass to fall from its accustomed place, and Quatermain, who always observed everything, observed this also.

'At last,' he gasped, with an attempt at a smile, 'I have seen Good without his eyeglass.'

After that he said no more till the day broke, when he asked to be lifted up to watch the rising of the sun for the last time.

'In a very few minutes,' he said, after gazing earnestly at it, 'I shall have passed through those golden gates.'

Ten minutes afterwards he raised himself and looked us fixedly in the face.

'I am going a stranger journey than any we have ever taken together. Think of me sometimes,' he murmured. 'God bless you all. I shall wait for you.' And with a sigh he fell back dead.

And so passed away a character that I consider went as near perfection as any it has ever been my lot to encounter.

Tender, constant, humorous, and possessing of many of the qualities that go to make a poet, he was yet almost unrivalled as a man of action and a citizen of the world. I never knew anyone so competent to form an accurate judgement of men and their motives. 'I have studied human nature all my life,' he would say, 'and I ought to know something about it,' and he certainly did. He had but two faults – one was his excessive modesty, and the other a slight tendency which he had to be jealous of anybody on whom he concentrated his affections. As regards the first of these points, anybody who reads what he has written will be able to form his own opinion; but I will add one last instance of it.

As the reader will doubtless remember, it is a favourite trick of his to talk of himself as a timid man, whereas really, though very cautious, he possessed a most intrepid spirit, and, what is more, never lost his head. Well, in the great battle of the Pass, where he got the wound that finally killed him, one would imagine from the account which he gives of the occurrence that it was a chance blow that fell on him in the scrimmage. As a matter of fact, however, he was wounded in a most gallant and successful attempt to save Good's life, at the risk and, as it ultimately turned out, at the cost of his own. Good was down on the ground, and one of Nasta's highlanders was about to dispatch him, when Quatermain threw himself on to his prostrate form and received the blow on his own body, and then, rising, killed the soldier.

As regards his jealousy, a single instance which I give in justice to myself and Nyleptha will suffice. The reader will, perhaps, recollect that in one or two places he speaks as though Nyleptha monopolised me, and he was left by both of us rather out in the cold. Now Nyleptha is not perfect, any more than any other woman is, and she may be a little *exigeante* at times, but as regards Quatermain the whole thing is pure imagination. Thus when he complains about my not coming to see him when he is ill, the fact was that, in spite of my entreaties, the doctors positively forbade it. Those little remarks of his pained me very much when I read them, for I loved Quatermain as dearly as though he were my own father, and should never have dreamed of allowing my marriage to interfere with that affection. But let it pass; it is, after all, but one little weakness, which makes no great show among so many and such lovable virtues.

Well, he died, and Good read the Burial Service over him in the presence of Nyleptha and myself; and then his remains were, in deference to the popular clamour, accorded a great public funeral, or rather cremation. I could not help thinking, however, as I marched in that long and splendid procession up to the Temple, how he would have hated the whole thing could he have been there to see it, for he had a horror of ostentation.

And so, a few minutes before sunset, on the third night after his death, they laid him on the brazen flooring before the altar, and waited for the last ray of the setting sun to fall upon his face. Presently it came, and struck him like a golden arrow, crowning the pale brows with glory, and then the trumpets blew, and the flooring revolved, and all that remained of our beloved friend fell into the furnace below.

We shall never see his like again if we live a hundred years. He was the ablest man, the truest gentleman, the firmest friend, the finest sportsman, and, I believe, the best shot in all Africa.

And so ended the very remarkable and adventurous life of Hunter Quatermain.

*   *   *

Since then things have gone very well with us. Good has been, and still is, busily employed in the construction of a navy on Lake Milosis and another of the large lakes, by means of which we hope to be able to increase trade and commerce, and also to overcome some very troublesome and warlike sections of the population who live upon their borders. Poor fellow! he is beginning to get over the sad death of that misguided but most attractive woman, Sorais, but it is a sad blow to him, for he was really deeply attached to her. I hope, however, that he will in time make a suitable marriage and get that unhappy business out of his head. Nyleptha has one or two young ladies in view, especially a daughter of Nasta's (who was a widower), a very fine imperial-looking girl, but with too much of her father's intriguing, and yet haughty, spirit to suit my taste.

As for myself, I should scarcely know where to begin if I set to work to describe my doings, so I had best leave them undescribed, and content myself with saying that, on the whole, I am getting on very well in my curious position of King-Consort – better, indeed, than I had any right to expect. But, of course, it is not all plain sailing, and I find the responsibilities very heavy. Still, I hope to be able to do some good in my time, and I intend to devote myself to two great ends – namely, to the consolidation of the various clans which together make up the Zu-Vendi people, under one strong central government, and to the sapping of the power of the priesthood. The first of these reforms will, if it can be carried out, put an end to the disastrous civil wars that have for centuries devastated this country; and the second, besides removing a source of political danger, will pave the road for the introduction of true religion in the place of this senseless Sun worship. I yet hope to see the shadow of the Cross of Christ lying on the golden dome of the Flower Temple; or, if I do not, that my successors may.

There is one more thing that I intend to devote myself to, and that is the total exclusion of all foreigners from Zu-Vendis. Not, indeed, that any more are ever likely to get here, but if they do, I warn them fairly that they will be shown the shortest way out of the country. I do not say this from any sense of inhospitality, but because I am convinced of the sacred duty that rests upon me of preserving to this, on the whole, upright and generous-hearted people the blessings of comparative barbarism. Where would all my brave army be if some enterprising rascal were to attack us with field-guns and Martini-Henrys? I cannot see that gunpowder, telegraphs, steam, daily newspapers, universal suffrage, etc., etc., have made mankind one whit the happier than they used to be, and I am certain that they have brought many evils in their train. I have no fancy for handing over this beautiful country to be torn and fought for by speculators, tourists, politicians and teachers, whose voice is as the voice of Babel, just as those horrible creatures in the valley of the underground river tore and fought for the body of the wild swan; nor will I endow it with the greed, drunkenness, new diseases, gunpowder, and general demoralisation which chiefly mark the progress of civilisation amongst unsophisticated peoples. If in due course it pleases Providence to throw Zu-Vendis open to the world, that is another matter; but of myself I will not take the responsibility, and I may add that Good entirely approves of my decision. Farewell.

Henry Curtis

December 15, 18—.

ps – I quite forgot to say that about nine months ago Nyleptha (who is very well and, in my eyes at any rate, more beautiful than ever) presented me with a son and heir. He is a regular curlyhaired, blue-eyed young Englishman in looks, and, though he is destined, if he lives, to inherit the throne of Zu-Vendis, I hope I may be able to bring him up to become what an English gentleman should be, and generally is – which is to my mind even a prouder and a finer thing than being born heir apparent to the great House of the Stairway, and, indeed, the highest rank that a man can reach upon this earth.

H. C.

NOTE BY GEORGE CURTIS ESQ.

The manuscript of this history, addressed to me in the handwriting of my dear brother Henry Curtis, whom we had given up for dead, and bearing the Aden postmark, reached me in safety on December 20, 18—, or a little more than two years after it left his hands in the far centre of Africa, and I hasten to give the astonishing story it contains to the world. Speaking for myself, I have read it with very mixed feelings; for though it is a great relief to know that he and Good are alive and strangely prosperous, I cannot but feel that for me and for all their friends they might as well be dead, since we can never hope to see them more.

They have cut themselves off from old England and from their homes and their relations for ever, and perhaps, under the circumstances, they were right and wise to do so.

How the MS came to be posted I have been quite unable to discover; but I presume, from the fact of its being posted at all, that the little Frenchman, Alphonse, accomplished his hazardous journey in safety. I have, however, advertised for him and caused various enquiries to be made in Marseilles and elsewhere with a view of discovering his whereabouts, but so far without the slightest success. Possibly he is dead, and the packet was posted by another hand; or possibly he is now happily wedded to his Annette, but still fears the vengeance of the law, and prefers to remain incognito. I cannot say, I have not yet abandoned my hopes of finding him, but I am bound to say that they grow fainter day by day, and one great obstacle to my search is that nowhere in the whole history does Mr Quatermain mention his surname. He is always spoken of as 'Alphonse', and there are so many Alphonses. The letters which my brother Henry says he is sending with the packet of manuscript have never arrived, so I presume that they are lost or destroyed.

GEORGE CURTIS

AUTHORITIES

A novelist is not usually asked, like a historian, for his 'Quellen'. As I have, however, judging from certain experiences in the past, some reason to anticipate such a demand, I wish to acknowledge my indebtedness to Mr Thomson's admirable history of travel *Through Masai Land* for much information as to the habits and customs of the tribes inhabiting that portion of the East Coast, and the country where they live; also to my brother, John G. Haggard, RN, HBM's consul at Madagascar, and formerly consul at Lamu, for many details furnished by him of the mode of life and war of those engaging people the Masai; also to my sister-in-law, Mrs John Haggard, who kindly put some difficult lines into rhyme for me; also to an extract in a review from some book of travel of which I cannot recollect the name, to which I owe the idea of the great crabs in the valley of the subterranean river.* But if I remember right, the crabs in the book when irritated projected their eyes quite out of their heads. I regret that I was not able to 'plagiarise' this effect, but I felt that, although crabs may, and doubtless do, behave thus in real life, in romance they 'will not do so'.

There is an underground river in *Peter Wilkins*, but at the time of writing the foregoing pages I had not read that quaint but entertaining work.

It has been pointed out to me that there exists a similarity between the scene of Umslopogaas frightening Alphonse with his axe and a scene in *Far from the Madding Crowd*. I regret this coincidence, and believe that the talented author of that work will not be inclined to accuse me of literary immorality on its account.

Finally, I may say that Mr Quatermain's little Frenchman appears to belong to the same class of beings as those English ladies whose long yellow teeth and feet of enormous size excite our hearty amusement in the pages of the illustrated Gallic press.

THE WRITER OF *Allan Quatermain*

---

* It is suggested to me that this book is *The Cruise of the Falcon*, with which work I am personally unacquainted.